GODINE DOUBLE DETECTIVES
Robin W. Winks, General Editor

THE MAN WHO LIKED TO LOOK AT HIMSELF

A FIX LIKE THIS

Two Mario Balzic Mysteries by

K. C. CONSTANTINE

Afterword by the Author

A GODINE DOUBLE DETECTIVE

David R. Godine · Boston

Published in 1983 by
DAVID R. GODINE, PUBLISHER, INC.
306 Dartmouth Street, Boston, Massachusetts 02116

Library of Congress Cataloging in Publication Data

Constantine, K. C.
    The man who liked to look at himself;
A fix like this.

    (A Godine double detective)
    "Two Mario Balzic mysteries."
    1. Detective and mystery stories, American.
I. Constantine, K. C.: A fix like this.   II. Title.
III. Series.
PS3553.0524A6   1983   813'.54   83-47507
ISBN 0-87923-468-7
                First edition

Printed in the United States of America

THE MAN WHO
LIKED TO LOOK AT HIMSELF

THEY WERE ON the Addleman farm, one of the dozen or so farms leased by the Rocksburg Police Rod and Gun Club for the small-game season. Mario Balzic, Rocksburg chief of police, had prepared himself for more than a week for the pleasures of hunting pheasant with a dog. What he had not prepared himself for was hunting with this dog of Lieutenant Harry Minyon's, this overweight, badly conditioned, ill-tempered Weimaraner.

When Balzic thought about it, he wondered how he had let himself be fooled for a minute that the dog would be different from her master. From the first, Minyon had very clumsily masked the arrogance behind his great, florid face with a flurry of ingratiating words and promises.

"I hear you're a hunter," Minyon had said within minutes after they'd met.

Balzic had gone to Troop A Barracks of the state police as much out of courtesy to the new chief of detectives as to look

him over. Such protocol was expected, and to violate it was to
ask for trouble. But after five minutes with Minyon, Balzic
knew he was going to miss Lieutenant Phil Moyer—the man
Minyon replaced—more than he'd ever imagined.

"Yes, I hunt," Balzic had said. "But nothing big. What I
really like are pheasants. Maybe because I get lucky every
once in a while and hit one."

"You know," Minyon had said, "I've got a dog."

Minyon had a way of leaning close and lowering his voice
when he thought he was saying something important that gave
Balzic the feeling he was talking to an insurance salesman who
had taken the Dale Carnegie course out of desperation.

"You have a dog, huh?"

"I'll say. Weimaraner. Paid four hundred bucks for her.
What a lady she is. What a nose. Maybe we can get together
sometime," Minyon said, his large, florid face opening for the
invitation. When it didn't come, he forced it. "Tell you what.
Let's make it official. Opening day's only a week off. I'll pick
you up, and you can show me the hot spots. I hear you fellas
have a club."

"Yeah, we lease some farms and stock a few birds. Nothing
big."

"Ever hunted with a dog?" Minyon said. "I mean a real
dog?"

Balzic committed himself then with a simple negative
motion of his head. It had been such a slight movement, he
asked himself later whether he had even made it.

Now, here he was, suffering one aggravation after another,
beginning with the first one in Minyon's car. Balzic had just
got settled in the front seat, had taken one brief, envious glance
at the dog in the back seat, and then slid his left hand up on the
back of the seat. Minyon was still in low gear when the bitch
reached her long, smoke-gray snout up and nipped Balzic's
hand. Not hard. Just hard enough to leave teeth marks, but
Minyon thought it was all very funny.

"Just her way of letting you know what's what," Minyon had said.

Balzic should have known right then.

In the field, there was one disgrace after another. The bitch flushed starlings, had to be put on the leash and led away from a groundhog's burrow, and stood baying for five minutes at a squirrel she'd treed. When Minyon finally coaxed her away from that, she'd immediately pointed another starling—only because this one had a broken wing—and Balzic, in a fit of temper at both Minyon and his dog, blew the starling apart from less than ten yards.

"Would've just starved to death anyway," Minyon said.

And Balzic, pocketing the empty and loading, wanted to turn the twenty gauge on them both, one barrel for Minyon and the other for his four-hundred-dollar bitch.

Minutes later, the bitch was into a copse of crab apples, whining, ripping back and forth through the brambles, her tongue flying and sides heaving, and Balzic could not guess what she'd come up with this time. She ignored every signal Minyon gave, and then, in what seemed a final display of contrariness, started digging in a shallow swale in the middle of the copse. Grass and dirt flew, and Balzic broke open his gun and sat in the timothy and rubbed his neck.

Minyon tried everything to get the bitch away from her digging. Nothing worked. Every time he dragged her away and started her in another direction, she wheeled around and headed back to the swale. The third time, he put the leash on her and took her nearly two hundred yards away, but the moment he unleashed her, she made a line for the copse, clawing at the same spot in a frenzy.

Balzic could hear pheasants all around. They sounded to him as though they were calling each other to come get a closer look at the two fools with the lunatic dog.

Just as Minyon reached the dog, Balzic got to his feet and started thinking of a polite way to say they ought to pack it in.

At that moment, the dog took a gulping lunge in the earth and came up with what looked to Balzic from where he was to be a short stick.

The dog ducked around Minyon and took off, bounding and snarling, the stick firmly in mouth, and shot past Balzic, looking for all the world as though she wanted to give them both a chase. Then she stopped and let the stick fall between her paws.

"Play time, is it," Balzic muttered, advancing on the dog, but when he got within a few feet, the dog snatched up the stick and spun off, only to stop twenty yards or so farther away, there to turn, drop the stick, and plop on her haunches, saliva dripping from her lips, ears back, and sides billowing.

Then, as capriciously as she had run from Minyon, she picked up the stick and went loping up to him and dropped the stick at his feet.

"Good girl," Minyon said, patting the dog's head. "Good girl."

Balzic approached them, man and dog both seeming curiously smug, and had to tell himself to say nothing sarcastic. The only way to do that was to say nothing at all.

Minyon examined the stick a moment and then smelled it. "Anybody ever find any Indian burial grounds around here?" he asked as Balzic came up.

"Oh, there've been a couple. Last one I know of was over on the McKelveen farm. About two miles from here. Why? She dig up an Indian?"

"Well, this is just a guess, but this isn't any animal's bone," Minyon said, savoring his words. "And as another guess, I'd say it didn't belong to any Indian—not unless they were in the habit of sawing their people up before they went to the happy hunting grounds."

Balzic took the bone from Minyon's outstretched hand. He looked at the ends of it and then rubbed it on the grass. As the dirt came off, the saw marks were unmistakable. He held it alongside his own leg. "I'll be damned," he said. "Wasn't very big, was he?"

"Now that, I suppose, would depend on how much was sawed off," Minyon said, looking quite satisfied with himself. "Think maybe we better have a look where she was digging."

They went into the copse of crab apples and found the spot. All they could do was scrape around with the sides of their shoes and they soon saw the futility of that. Minyon called the dog over, but she just sniffed the ground a couple of times and then started barking and leaping after the bone in Balzic's hand.

"What do you think?" Balzic said, raising the bone above his head and using his knee to fend the dog off.

"I'll tell you what I think," Minyon said, his face assuming what Balzic would soon come to recognize as his professional expression, "I think you ought to run that bone over to the coroner, and I think I ought to call Hershey and tell them to send out the dogs. We could dig around here for a year, but those dogs they got, hell, they'll put us on to the right spot in a couple hours. One thing though."

"What's that?"

"Be sure to tell the coroner not to do anything to disturb the smell. Anything else he has to do, okay, but no fooling around with the smell." Minyon walked off without another word, heading for the car, and Balzic, following a half dozen steps behind, knew this was going to be the order of things if he hoped to get along with Minyon.

The new chief of detectives at Troop A hadn't thought to call his dog, and they were nearly to the car before she came trotting past Balzic. He had to tell himself that grown men don't kick dogs, or at least not for the reasons he wanted to kick this one.

Dr. Wallace Grimes always struck Balzic as being wholly unsuited to his elected job. He seemed the sort who should have been tending to miners and their families in one of the coal towns of the county, taking his pay as much in trade from the miners' gardens as from their wages. He looked to Balzic better suited to saving life than to investigating the causes of death, though Balzic could not say why he had that impression. It may have come from the deep frown Grimes always seemed to have imprinted on his narrow face, as though he felt some part of the responsibility for the death of the corpses he had to work with.

Balzic thought about it as Grimes disappeared with the bone into the laboratory he used at Conemaugh General Hospital and decided he really had no reason for believing anything about Grimes one way or the other. He had never discussed anything personal with Grimes, and what seemed a frown of responsibility might be nothing more than an expression of professional curiosity.

Grimes was back from the lab in less than fifteen minutes. "There's much more to be done, Mario," he said, "but right now I'd say with some certainty this is the femur, the thigh bone, of an adult somewhere between five eight and six feet. As a guess, I'd say it's been in the ground between a year and eighteen months. Remember, I'm still guessing at this point, but if you can guarantee that I'll have it for another four hours, I'll be able to tell you practically to within the week it was buried."

"That's all right with me," Balzic said. "Minyon might have other ideas, but that's his problem."

"I assure you," Grimes said, his frown deepening, "I could not tell you anything really useful before four hours."

"Take whatever time you need. Just give me a call soon as you know something."

Balzic drove home to change clothes. The heavy wool shirt he'd put on under his hunting jacket in the morning was causing him to perspire freely, and he looked forward to a shower and a cold beer. He was just pulling into his driveway when the radio came on with his call signal. It was the state police.

"Lieutenant Minyon requests info regarding bone found on farm, over."

"Who the hell is this?" Balzic said.

"Sergeant Rudawski, Mario."

"Rudy, hell, man, you sound like something out of the movies." Balzic pulled on the hand brake and waited. "What have you got, Mario?"

Balzic guessed then from Rudawski's tone that Minyon was standing close by and thought better than to kid Rudawski again. "Tell Lieutenant Minyon the coroner needs the bone for at least four more hours to make sure, but his first guess is it's the thigh bone of an adult somewhere between five eight and six feet. Probably been buried for a year to a year and a half. Over."

"Roger."

"Any word on the dogs?" Balzic said.

"Dogs on the way. Estimated time of arrival eleven hundred hours tomorrow. Repeating, ETA eleven hundred hours Thursday."

"Tell the lieutenant I'll see him then. Out," Balzic said, hanging up the mike and getting out of the car. He went up the steps of the porch to the front door and let himself in, wondering why it was that men like Minyon weren't satisfied unless they were making everybody work according to the letter of regulations. What a story they'd give you if you asked them about it—no matter what the people who worked for them would say about it. He remembered a lieutenant on Iwo Jima, an honorable-mention all-America tackle from some Big Ten school, always riding his platoon aboard ship. Two days after the landing, he remembered crawling past that lieutenant's body, face down in the black ash, with twenty-seven holes in the back of his jacket. Balzic remembered forgetting everything else to stop and count those holes. . . .

He started to shut the door and caught sight of his mother in the recliner in the living room. She was nodding, her mouth slightly ajar, the TV section of last Sunday's paper in her lap. On the screen in front of her, a pleasant-looking man was asking some cub scouts if they were ready to sing the song they'd prepared.

Balzic tiptoed over and turned the sound down and then walked softly into the kitchen. He could hear the shower running upstairs and went over to the steps and called up: "Ruth, you up there?"

Before he could tell whether he'd been heard, the phone started ringing and he bounded over to answer it before it woke his mother.

"Balzic."

"Just a moment, chief," a female voice said, "Mayor Bellotti wants to talk to you."

"Now what," Balzic said to the wall.

"Mario?"

"Right. Angelo?"

"Who else? Listen, Mario, I just wanted to make sure you were coming to council meeting tonight."

"I wasn't planning on it. Why?"

"I just had a citizen here, a Glenn Hall, who claims your people put up some no parking signs and painted a yellow line on a curb in front of a property he owns on South Main. Next to H & T Transport—you know that trucking outfit?"

"I know it," Balzic said. "But I can tell you right now my people didn't have anything to do with it. That had to come from the street department, so if the citizen has a complaint he better take it up with Councilman Maravich. He's still in charge of streets and roads—"

"Mario, a moment. Maravich says he doesn't know anything about it, besides which, Mr. Hall here claims somebody in your department has some kind of grudge against him."

"Aw, come on, Angelo."

"I know, I know," Bellotti said, "but Mr. Hall says somebody in your department is responsible."

"Well, what's the friction anyway?"

"The friction is that H & T's trucks are breaking down the curbs and making it tough for his tenants to park their cars, and his insurance company is giving him fits about—"

"Okay, Angelo, okay. Tell the citizen I'll be there tonight to officially deny that anybody in my department ordered the signs, how's that?"

"That's what I wanted to hear, Mario. See you tonight. Eight sharp."

"Right," Balzic said, hanging up. "Oh, brother."

"What was that all about?" Ruth said, tiptoeing barefoot into the kitchen with a towel wrapped turban-fashion around her hair, clutching her terry-cloth robe to keep it from falling open.

"Who knows?" Balzic said. "Some clown says one of my people has a grudge against him and put a yellow line in front of his property and stuck up some no parking signs. So now I have to go to council meeting tonight and make funny noises. It's going to be the perfect end to a perfect day."

"Was hunting bad?"

"Don't ask," Balzic said. "Listen, you're through in the shower, right?"

"No. I'm still in it," Ruth said. "I only look like I'm standing here."

"Oh, funny. I just keep running into funny people today. Minyon's bitch—that four-hundred-dollar bitch I was so goddamn anxious to get out with?—I'm not in the car five seconds and it bites me, and Minyon thinks that's very cute. He gets a real charge out of that, and now there's this citizen who thinks I go around at night painting yellow lines—"

"Aw, poor baby," Ruth said, snuggling close to Balzic, "do you want to go outside and eat some worms?"

Balzic gave her a healthy whack on her backside. "Out of my way, woman, before I really take the heat."

Ruth backed up and went into her Scarlett O'Hara act. "Why, Rhett, honey, I didn't know you felt this way." She made her eyes flutter and let out a long sigh.

"Will you be straight for a minute?" Balzic said but then had to laugh. "Okay, okay, I know when I'm licked." He went up the steps to the bathroom, unbuttoning his shirt as he went, telling himself he was lucky to have married a woman with a sense of perspective, otherwise he could start to like feeling sorry for himself.

The council meeting started smoothly enough and went on that way until all the old business had been attended to. Bids for salt for the streets for the coming winter, submitted at a previous meeting, were approved; two zoning ordinances, recommended for approval by the zoning authority, were approved; the negotiating commission engaged in bargaining with the garbage drivers and mechanics reported that the new three-year contract was submitted to the rank and file with the unreserved endorsement of the union negotiators; and bids for sandblasting the exterior of city hall were tabled for further study. A retirement dinner and gift for a woman clerk in sanitation were approved by voice vote but not entered in the minutes.

Balzic was looking at his watch for the third time in five minutes when the meeting was opened for new business and the chairman of the new human relations commission, Councilman Paul Steinfeld, introduced a Reverend Luther Callum from among the sparse group of spectators. Mayor Bellotti agreed to let the reverend speak, and just as he started—he opened a briefcase and took out a substantial stack of papers—someone tapped Balzic on the shoulder.

It was Vic Stramsky, Balzic's second-shift desk sergeant.

"The coroner just dropped this off, Mario," Stramsky whispered, handing Balzic a large manila envelope.

Balzic nodded and opened it and read:

Subject: Bone examination
To: Mario Balzic, Chief of Police, Rocksburg, Pa.
From: Wallace Grimes, M.D., Coroner, Conemaugh
      County, Pa.
Copy to: Lt. Harry Minyon, Chief of Detectives, Troop A,
      Rocksburg Barracks
The bone examined by me this 18 Oct. 1970 is undoubtedly a left human femur. It was severed by a fine-toothed saw just below the lesser trochanter and just above where it would have joined the patella. It was also unquestionably a healthy bone at time of severance. Because of its size the assumption must be that it was the bone of a male or an unusually large female. Age of bone estimated to be between forty and fifty years. Deterioration of cells in the marrow indicates the bone was severed approximately fifteen months ago, mid or late July 1969.

So, Balzic thought, that tells us something. He looked up in time to see the reverend gesturing in his direction and saying, ". . . times in the past month, I have tried to arrange a meeting with that man, and four times I have been given a polite but clear runaround. I have yet to speak to that man, and, gentlemen, I for one am getting very weary of being told the chief is out, the chief is busy, the chief is working on this, that, or the other case. That, gentlemen, is why I bring my case to you tonight.

"Three instances, gentlemen," the reverend went on, "three in the past six weeks of clear and unmistakable harassment of black juveniles for no other reason apparently than that they were on the streets after midnight and, though I hesitate to say it, gentlemen, that they were black."

Balzic put the coroner's report back in the envelope, let out a very audible sigh, and started looking around for an ash tray.

"The chief may sigh all he wants, gentlemen," Reverend Callum said, "but facts are facts, and I have the documented facts here in my hand." He held up the papers in his hand and then went to the table where the mayor and the four other members of city council were sitting and began to pass out copies.

Balzic found an ash tray and, after lighting a cigarette, put up his hand. Mayor Bellotti recognized him just as Reverend Callum handed out a set of papers to the last councilman.

"Mr. Chairman," Balzic began, but was immediately interrupted by Reverend Callum.

"Mr. Chairman, I didn't relinquish the floor. I still have plenty of things to say—"

"All I wanted to ask," Balzic said, "was if you had a copy of those facts for me, that's all."

"Well if you'll check downstairs in your headquarters, chief, you'll find you already have several copies, because every time I tried to see you and was told you weren't in or were busy or whatever, I left you a copy."

"Yeah, well, for right now, do you mind passing me over a copy?"

"Not at all," Reverend Callum said, handing a copy to one of the spectators to pass back to Balzic. The reverend could not restrain himself; he had to smile at his triumph.

Balzic tried to ignore the reverend's smile as he reached for the copy but found his face tightening anyway. He scanned the pages, looking for names, and found two that brought situations quickly to mind. "Mr. Chairman," he said, "I can settle a couple things right now. For instance, this James Ronnie Dawson, listed in the reverend's report as a juvenile, is not a juvenile—"

"The Dawson case," Reverend Callum said, "is a classic example of police harassment of members of minority groups—"

"Will you wait a minute," Balzic said. "I'm trying to tell you something, man, that you need to know. Just answer me one question first, will you, please?"

"I'll be more than happy to extend the courtesy to you, a courtesy, I must say, you have never extended to me."

Balzic let that go and asked, "How long you been in Rocksburg?"

"I resent your implication," the reverend said. "You're implying that because I'm new here in your city, I'm something of an outsider. The outsider is invariably the scapegoat for all problems, especially racial problems. When you've got a problem that suddenly is brought to light—never mind that it has existed all along—it is because some outsider came in and stirred up the residents. Well, it may be true that I am new in my ministry here—"

"How new?" Balzic said.

"I accepted the call here five months ago."

"That was simple enough," Balzic said, doing his best not to smile. "Now, what I want to tell you is this Dawson, this guy you claim is a juvenile, is, in fact, twenty-three years old. The reason I know that is I personally checked his birth certificate with the state because every time he gets in trouble, not only here but in Pittsburgh and Erie, among other places, he's always using the line that he's a juvenile.

"But the facts, reverend, facts you don't have on these pages as far as I can see, are that Dawson has a yellow sheet dating back to age thirteen, everything from truancy to auto theft, and on the night you have down here, September seventeen, Dawson was arrested on suspicion of burglary, and when he was apprehended he, uh, resisted arrest, to say the least. The fact is he put up one helluva fight before he was subdued, and when he was finally subdued, he was found to be carrying a twenty-five-caliber automatic.

"I was present at his arraignment, and he was booked on charges of resisting arrest and violating the firearms act. Two days after he was remanded to Southern Regional Correctional, he was released on five-thousand-dollar bond, a bond I argued against for all the reasons you can think of. As a matter of fact, I got a call from the narcotics division of the Pittsburgh police yesterday, asking me what I knew about him. It seems they picked him up and he just happened to be carrying about seven, eight hundred Benzedrine tablets on him in a paper bag and gave them the story that he was working for a drugstore as a delivery boy.

"As for this Maurice Williams," Balzic continued, talking fast so as not to be interrupted, "well, his story isn't too much different except that he *is* a juvenile—I think he just turned eighteen—but he also has a yellow sheet going back five or six years, only the charges against him are mostly assault in one form or another, including one against his mother and one against his stepsister. Then there was the complaint made by his stepsister for rape, and the date you have down here, October first, is the day we picked him up for assaulting his stepsister, which was two days after she'd made the complaint against him for rape. And when we did pick him up, we also brought in his sister, and I have photographs downstairs, reverend, if you want to see them, of the way his stepsister looked that night. That was also the night the stepsister dropped the complaint of rape against him. We booked him for assault and battery and aggravated assault, and a couple, three days later, somebody posted bond for him. So he's out on the streets now, and I guarantee within a month, six weeks at the most, somebody else is going to get hurt.

"Now, as for the third instance, this Roland Bivins, I have to tell you straight, his name doesn't ring any bells with me, and I'd like to have time to check it out. That's all I have to say now, Mr. Chairman," Balzic said, and sat down, putting the ash tray in his lap. He stood again and said, "One more thing, Mr. Chairman, I have to apologize for this, because it is true that I knew the reverend was trying to see me, but I did have other things to do, things which seemed more important to me

at the times he wanted to see me, and I probably should've
made the time to see him, if for no other reason than to save
everybody a lot of time in this meeting."

Mayor Bellotti nodded to Balzic and said, "Reverend
Callum, I don't doubt your sincerity for a minute, and I give
you my word that we're going to read your report, but I think
I speak for all the council here when I say the best thing is for
you and Chief Balzic to get together and iron this thing out.
And I'll be happy to make a resolution to that effect and
somebody else can second it. . . ."

While council decided about the resolution, Balzic studied
the Reverend Callum. The reverend looked suddenly a
disillusioned young man, and Balzic, as much as he thought he
ought to be annoyed about the whole thing, could not help
feeling sympathetic for the way Dawson and Williams had
gulled him. It was very easy to be lied to when you had as
much faith in a conviction as the reverend obviously had. Of
course, Balzic had to admit that because he knew nothing
about this Roland Bivins, the reverend might well have a case
there. Balzic knew there was more than one man on his force
who hated blacks on sight. He thought he had succeeded in
keeping them out of the blacks' district, but the chances were
probably no better than even that he'd missed somehow and
sent the wrong man on the wrong beat.

The resolution was made, seconded, and approved without
dissent, and Balzic was directed to meet with Reverend
Callum at their earliest convenience. The reverend expressed
his satisfaction to council, though Balzic thought the reverend's
face showed more resignation than satisfaction.

The Reverend Callum had no sooner found his seat than a
short, paunchy man with diminishing hair and wearing an
expensive suit jumped to his feet and demanded to be heard.
He turned out to be Glenn Hall, and, after a series of
exchanges among Mayor Bellotti, Councilman Joe Maravich,
and Hall, most of them concerned with whether Hall was out

of order, it was agreed to let Hall speak his piece. He went into a long, rambling tirade about the yellow lines and no parking signs in front of his property on South Main, a situation he said reduced itself to the city providing a free parking lot for the trucks of H & T Transport, which in turn was causing the curbs and sidewalks in front of his property to crumble, causing his insurance company to raise his rates, and causing his tenants in the four-apartment building to pester him to death with pleas for relief, and on and on.

Balzic listened half attentively until Hall made the charge that someone in the police department had a grudge against him and had put the yellow line on the curb and the no parking signs up as a way of "getting" him.

"That's ridiculous," Balzic said, without either standing or asking to be recognized.

"That's what you say," Hall shouted.

"I think Councilman Maravich ought to reply to this," Balzic said. "He has more to say about restricted parking than anybody in the police department ever had or has. As far as I know, any time my department wants to have a parking zone changed, we still have to apply to the streets and roads department. Hell, I've been trying to get Burroughs Street made one way for five years now, and I haven't been able to convince Mr. Maravich that it's necessary. Just how in the hell could I restrict parking in front of your place without first going through a formal application in a public meeting?"

"Well that's exactly what I'm trying to tell you," Hall shouted. "It wasn't done in a meeting. It wasn't done in public. It was done in some backhanded—"

"Now wait just a goddamn minute," Councilman Maravich said. "I admit that my clerks are having a little trouble finding the original requisition for that parking restriction, but I've been doing a little checking myself. Number one, the mortgage of the property you're talking about is held by Rocksburg Savings and Loan, and the property you're complaining about—H & T Transport—also happens to be mortgaged by Rocksburg Savings and Loan. . . ."

Balzic's mind began to wander then. He knew what was coming—a long, tedious explanation about the possibilities of mortgage payers competing with each other for special favors from mortgage holders—and he wasn't particularly interested in any of it. He had had his say, brief as it was, and he knew the whole thing would be settled out of his hands anyway.

His mind was going back to the envelope on his lap, to the bone, the left femur of the male or unusually large female, age forty to fifty, severed and buried some fifteen months ago. He searched his memory for someone being reported missing. Nothing. He thought about the place, the Addleman farm. Nothing there either.

The woman, Mrs. Addleman—he couldn't remember her first name—lived there with her invalid mother. He had seen them both that morning when he'd gone up to the house to tell her that he and Minyon were going to hunt on the place. Mrs. Addleman was just pushing her mother's bed over to the sun window in the living room when Balzic walked up on the porch, and the old woman had waved at him through the window.

Howard Addleman had been a member of the Rocksburg Rod and Gun Club, and, in fact, had been the spokesman for a group of farmers who approached the club with the idea of leasing their land to the club for small-game hunting. But Howard Addleman had died two years ago, and Balzic recalled clearly going to the funeral home to pay his respects. Addleman was a short, burly figure even in death, a strong, quiet man whose only vice had been chewing tobacco and who seldom smiled except when somebody made a difficult shot. The rest of the time, he seemed not to enjoy himself, but Balzic knew him well enough to know that he reserved his emotions, saved them almost, as though he was fearful of wasting them on things that didn't deserve more than mere interest or curiosity.

So there was nothing there. But there had to be something somewhere.

". . . so what I'm suggesting to you, Mr. Hall, is unless you have proof of what you're saying, you better be careful what you go around accusing people of," Councilman Maravich was saying, and Balzic thought he ought to be paying attention again.

Glenn Hall reached behind him on his chair for his raincoat. He left the meeting then without another word, giving Balzic a heavy glare as he passed him, a look with a "just-you-wait-buster" menace to it. Balzic halfheartedly told himself to look into it. Who knew? Somebody in his department might be married to this guy's cousin or something. There were thousands of reasons for people to be angry with the police, most of them imagined out of proportion to the facts, but Hall might have one that wasn't. And if somebody in his department was married to his cousin and not treating her right—well, Balzic thought, there were people mad at the police for less nutty reasons than that. . . .

Balzic caught Mayor Bellotti's eye and asked him with a couple of gestures—the finger tips pressed together, palm up—if it was all right if he left. The mayor nodded, and Balzic slipped out of the council room and went downstairs to police headquarters.

Sergeant Vic Stramsky was hammering away at a typewriter, stopping after every five or six violent jabs at the keys to roll the paper and erase a mistake.

"What's that?" Balzic said, standing behind Stramsky and trying to read over Stramsky's shoulder.

"A letter to my insurance company," Stramsky said, blowing away the grit from the erasure.

"What did they do to you now?"

"It's what they won't do, the bastards. They want my payments on the button, brother, but try to get them to send a check."

"You mean this is still the same thing? Hell, that was six weeks ago."

"Seven weeks and two days," Stramsky said, jabbing away again.

"Good luck," Balzic said, walking back to the coffee urn and pouring himself a cup. "Hey, Vic, you know a guy named Hall? Short guy, about forty, getting a little thin on top, talks loud?"

"Shouts, you mean?"

"Yeah. Wears pretty flashy clothes."

"Yeah. I know him. He's a pain in the ass. What about him?"

"Anybody here got anything against him?"

"No more than you have against any pain in the ass. Is that what he says?"

"Yeah. Upstairs in the council meeting he was saying somebody down here had a grudge and ordered a yellow line in front of his property."

"Ah, he's goofy. One time, I don't know, must've been a year ago, I was in the bowling alleys, having a couple beers, you know, and he comes in and starts hollering that I tagged his car. I just look at him. Finally I say, 'Hey, pal, I haven't tagged a car—anybody's car—in four years,' and he calls me a liar. I mean, right there, in front of my brother and his wife's cousin and about twenty other guys. I had to leave. If I'd've stayed, I don't know . . ."

"Well what's with him?"

"Who knows? I heard, I don't know how true it is, but I heard one time he went all the way to the state finals in wrestling in high school and got his ass whipped. Maybe he's still trying to win that one."

Balzic thought that over and then asked, "Anything happening tonight?"

Stramsky shook his head. Then he wheeled around suddenly in his chair, his face beaming. "Hey, I didn't tell you. Got two ringnecks today! Two!"

Balzic turned his back on Stramsky and stared out the window and watched traffic on Main Street.

"What's the matter with you?" Stramsky said.

"I was out today," Balzic said. "With Lieutenant Harry Minyon. All I got was a starling with a busted wing and a goddamn bone."

The dogs arrived a half hour early. Six bloodhounds with their three handlers, and Balzic thought he saw a faint resemblance between dogs and handlers, a long-faced, sad-eyed impatience to get on with the job.

Lieutenant Minyon, in uniform, came in the lead car and parked beside Balzic in the front of the Addleman barn, a building beginning to develop a saddle in its roof.

"You have the bone, I hope," Minyon said.

Balzic produced it, still wrapped in plastic, from the front seat of his car.

"You told him not to foul up the smell?"

Balzic nodded. "I told him. Whether he did or not isn't for me to say. Maybe the dogs'll know."

"Can't tell you how surprised I was to find out Grimes was an M.D.," Minyon said. "Most of these small county coroners aren't."

"Grimes is a good man," Balzic said, and let it go at that. He was going to add that Grimes had been a pathologist in a large university hospital in Philadelphia for years before he'd moved here, but he didn't feel like getting into anything with Minyon this early in the day, or in the case, for that matter.

Minyon looked the dogs and handlers over to see whether they were ready and then set off toward the copse of crab apples where they'd found the bone. They had to pass through what had been prime pasture when Howard Addleman was alive and tending his dairy herd. It was flat for the first couple of hundred yards and then started rising. Minyon set a brisk pace, and for the first few minutes was far ahead of the rest, but by the time they crested the small hill, he had fallen off his pace so that Balzic could hear his breathing. Minyon's dress uniform hadn't made the pace any easier. Circles of sweat were starting to show on his tunic under his arms and in the middle of his back.

"Right down there," Minyon said, stopping to tell the dog handlers and to point at the copse of crab apples. "What I think is you ought to let the dogs get the smell of the place first before we let them have a sniff of the bone."

If the dog handlers objected to Minyon's plan, they gave no indication of it. The more Balzic looked at them, the more they came to resemble the taciturn and docile manner of their dogs. But there was something about them, something just under the surface that belied the surface, something that said to Balzic they were going to conduct their search the way they wanted, no matter who was giving what orders.

The search began around noon Thursday and lasted as long as there was daylight until afternoon Monday. Dogs and men covered six farms, each abutting the other and three abutting the Addleman farm, an area totaling nearly seven hundred acres. Each day's search produced part of a bone except for Sunday, when three parts were found, and each day the parts were turned over to Coroner Grimes. When the handlers agreed to a man that the dogs were exhausted—even Minyon admitted the dogs' foot pads were in dangerous shape—they packed them in and headed back to Hershey.

Minyon was frustrated to say the least. Furious might have been a better word for it, Balzic thought.

"They looked at me like they knew their business," Balzic said to Minyon as they were about to enter the tiny cubicle Wallace Grimes used for an office in Conemaugh General Hospital.

"Hell, man, a search is a search," Minyon snapped. "You don't stop until you've got all the pieces."

Balzic was going to say that he thought they'd got as much as they could hope to get, given the condition of the dogs, but thought saying anything to Minyon at this point was a waste of words.

Grimes was sitting behind his desk when they came in, his fingers pressed together and his eyes wide in thought.

"Afternoon," Minyon said. "Well, what have you got?"

"I was about to ask you the same thing. Not that we need much more," Grimes said. "I mean, not to determine that what we have all fits the same person."

"How about identification? What about that?" Minyon said. "Without that, what do we have?"

"Let's see," Grimes said, picking up a report scrawled in his own hand. "We have both femurs, sawed in practically the same place. We have both left and right humerus, left and right ulna and radius, and the right tibia and fibula, each severed in pretty much the same place as its opposite—excepting the tibia and fibula of course—and with unquestionably the same kind of instrument."

"Two arms, two thighs, and one calf," Minyon said. "Wonderful. And all you can tell us is that they're all from the same body. A male or an unusually large female, I think you said."

"That's right," Grimes said. "Between forty and fifty, dismembered approximately fifteen months ago, unquestionably healthy when dismembered. That's as much as I can tell you. That's as much as anybody could tell you. And I won't be able to tell you any more than that unless, of course, the skull is found, hopefully with the teeth still in place. If we had that, it would simplify matters considerably."

"Yeah. Well, we don't," Minyon said. He shoved some papers away from the corner of Grimes's desk and sat on it. Grimes frowned his disapproval but said nothing, instead arranging the papers nearer to him. "And nobody's found anything in any of the dumps or landfills either," Minyon added. "How much water is there around here?"

"A helluva lot," Balzic said. "I wouldn't want to start dragging it. Tough enough when somebody drowns and we know where they drowned. I'd hate to have to tell a bunch of divers they got to find pieces when nobody even has the first idea which water to start in."

"Then just what the hell do you suggest?" Minyon said.

"Well, it wouldn't be a bad idea to start going over the membership list of the Rod and Gun Club."

"Why?"

"Because all those farms where we found what we've found were leased by the club. Somebody had to be familiar with them."

"Well why in hell didn't you say this before?" Minyon said.

"You didn't ask before," Balzic said, swallowing once to get the phlegm down.

"How many other farms are there?"

"I'm not sure. Six. Eight, maybe more. I used to be involved a lot more with the club than I am now. I don't often even go to meetings now. Vic Stramsky is treasurer. He'd know for sure."

"A Polack," Minyon said. "Jesus, I thought I'd seen the last of them when I left Wilkes-Barre."

Balzic walked out into the hall, knowing that if he stayed in the room with Minyon one more second, he was going to say something he'd doubtless regret.

"Where are you going?" Minyon called out.

"I'm going to see Sergeant Stramsky," Balzic said, pronouncing "sergeant" very explicitly.

"He one of your men?"

"Yes," Balzic said. He did not wait for another exchange but walked quickly down the corridor to the exit leading to the parking lot. He laid rubber pulling out just as Minyon came barging through the door waving his arms and shouting something Balzic did not bother to try to acknowledge.

Balzic parked in the alley behind Vic Stramsky's small frame house in South Rocksburg and made his way around the garbage cans and up the walk to the door leading into Stramsky's kitchen. Stramsky, barefoot and wearing faded denims, answered the knock and let Balzic in with barely a nod and something akin to a grunt. His eyes were bloodshot and the left side of his face was red and creased. He returned to a black cast-iron pan on the stove where he was frying kolbassi and peppers and onions, motioning to Balzic to pour himself some coffee. Then he broke a couple eggs in a small red bowl and began to beat them, pouring in some buttermilk as he did.

"You look like you had a good one last night, Vic," Balzic said, sipping his coffee.

"My brother . . . him and his wife's cousin came out to go hunting and they hung around for me until I got off. They were into the beer pretty good, and when I got here they broke out the bourbon. Jesus . . . I didn't get to sleep until about five. Just woke up a little while ago. Those goofy bastards, they drove home. That isn't what you came to tell me, is it? I mean, nothing about my brother?"

"Nah. I came down to check the membership list for the club."

"What for?" Stramsky said, pouring the beaten eggs and buttermilk into the pan. He turned the gas down and worked the eggs around with a wooden spoon.

"It's about the bones. We found them all on club farms, and I'm just trying to put two and two together."

"You don't sound too goddamn excited about it."

"It's that goddamn Minyon. I don't know what it is with him, but the thought of working with him for the next three years doesn't exactly make my day."

"You mind if I eat first, or do I got to get the list for you now?"

"Hell, take your time. The sooner you give them to me, the sooner I have to get back beside that overstuffed egomaniac."

"All pumped full of piss and vinegar, huh?"

"That's him. Minyon—what kind of name is that?"

"Christ, could be couple things. Could be French. Could be dago, too. Lots of them around. How's he spell it? The dagos I know spell it m-i-n-g-n-o-n-a—something like that."

"Nah. He's no dago. I know a dago when I see one."

"Oh sure. The Pope and Rocky Graziano, they look like twins. You act like there ain't any arrogant wops around," Stramsky said, spooning the eggs onto a dish.

"Who you talking to? Man, I've seen every breed of dago there is, from my mother to Dom Muscotti and all the ones in between," Balzic said, sniffing. "Hey, that smells pretty good."

"Eat your heart out. Polack soul food, that's what this is. Them niggers can have it, so can us Polacks." Stramsky started to eat, swallowed a mouthful, and then said, "You know my brother and me were talking about that last night. You hear all these jokes about Polacks now, but you don't hear no jokes about niggers any more. Who's the groom at the Polish wedding? He's the one in the clean bowling shirt, he's the one with the new bowling shoes, ha, ha, ha. 'Bout time somebody started a Polack anti-defamation league."

"Maybe," Balzic said, "but who would you get to write the charter?"

"Oh, that's funny," Stramsky said, diving into his eggs again, saying nothing until he'd finished and put the dish, utensils, and pan into the sink and run hot water over them. Then he went into another room and returned in a couple of minutes with a large loose-leaf notebook. He handed it to Balzic. "All in there," he said. "The founders, charter members, paid-up members, plus the ones that still owe for this season, which includes you."

"Yeah, well," Balzic said, opening the book, "I'm good for it."

"Don't it ever bother you? I mean, don't it ever get to you once in a while?"

"What?"

"Owing people."

"Never has so far. I always pay."

"Christ, it drives me nuts. I can't stand to owe somebody for a week. Anybody."

"Well, that's your problem," Balzic said, skimming over the list of names. "You know, there's a helluva lot of names in here I don't recognize."

"If you'd come around once in a while, maybe you would."

"I guess. Listen. Save me a lot of time. How do you mark the ones that quit or died?"

"I just draw a line through the name. The ones with the small check beside them still owe this year's dues."

"I see I'm not alone."

"That reminds me. I got to get some stamps today. Send out second notices. I don't see how you guys can feel right out there, knowing you owe for the privilege."

Balzic snorted. "Who's this Louis Amato? He quit or die?"

"Moved. Ohio someplace."

"What about this Francis Banaczak?"

"That was Frankie Banaczak. You remember him. Got killed on the turnpike last year."

"Oh yeah. What happened with his wife?"

"She's supposed to be going a little nutty. Least that's what I hear. Probably just gossip." Stramsky stood and poured more coffee.

"How 'bout this one—Edward Corpin?"

"Got transferred. U. S. Steel sent him to Birmingham."

"Anthony DeRamo? That's not Crackers, is it?"

"Yeah. His old lady made him quit."

"Boy, there's one for you. I remember him when he was the biggest skin hound in Norwood. I'll bet it's been five years since I've even seen him."

"He's walking straight now. Talking straighter."

"Shit, don't believe it. He'll make a comeback. He'll get the urge again. Just give him time. Who's this Gallic? Frank Gallic?"

"That's the butcher. Owns a freezer beef place south of here. Close to the river. You know him."

"I don't think so. At least I can't place him. Well?"

"Well what?"

"He quit or die or what?"

"Quit. Said he was going to a pheasant preserve up around Indiana. You know, they charge by the bird."

"I'm starting to place him now," Balzic said. "Wasn't he the guy got his picture in the paper couple times? Shot a polar bear or something. Then another time he got a Kodiak."

"That's him. He went to Africa once, too, and something tells me he also went to Mexico. Big-game hunter. Went with a couple other guys."

Balzic made a note of Gallic's name and address. "Is his place on Route three thirty-one or fifty-one? It's typed over here."

"Three thirty-one. Backed right up against the river. Used to brag how he could fish right off his property. You know his partner for sure. Mike, let me think, Mike, starts with an 's.' "

"Samarra?"

"Yeah, that's him. The one they call Mickey, Mizzo, something."

"Hell, I know Mickey from way back. But I didn't even know what business he was in, never mind who he was partners with. Last I heard he had a store up in Norwood, but I never dealt there."

"Oh, hell, Mario, him and Gallic been partners ever since they got out of the Army after World War Two. Sure. First, they had a grocery up in Norwood. Then they got a butcher shop and grocery on the other hill across from the old Mother of Sorrows grade school. The one they tore down. Then about ten years ago they went into this freezer beef thing. All they sell is halves and quarters, you know, real cheap, but you got to buy at least a quarter or a half."

"What's the name of their place?"

"Galsam's. They took the first three letters of their last names and put them together. Just go straight south on three thirty-one till it starts to run along the river and then start looking. About six miles, maybe seven. There's nothing around it. Just the place and a couple house trailers."

"Gallic's a World War Two vet, you said. That would make him somewhere between forty and fifty, right?"

"Yeah, he'd be about forty-five or so."

"Okay. So what about this Ippolitto?"

"Is his name still in there? Hell, he died three years ago."

"Janeski. Richard Janeski."

"He's one of Gallic's buddies. One of the guys went to Alaska with him. He quit. Said he was going with Gallic to that place by Indiana. Just as well. Real contrary bastard. Got a real bad face. All screwed up from some kind of accident when he was a kid."

"How long ago did he quit?"

"End of last season. Same time Gallic did. No, wait a minute. Gallic quit before. Yeah, he quit before last season started. I don't remember when exactly, but it was before, I'm sure of that. Janeski quit after."

"Janeski's address right? Rear 214, Church Street?"

"Unless he moved."

"Okay. What about Henry Kozal? Is that the old man—Hank?"

"Yeah. Poor bastard. He just sort of sits around now and drinks a lot. I didn't even bother sending him a first notice. Christ, first his wife and then his kid. That had to be rough."

"Somebody said his kid got the Silver Star in Vietnam."

"I don't know about that. Louie Antal went up to the house one day, see how he was doing, and the poor bastard was just sitting in the kitchen, stoned, with the flag in his lap. Just sitting there. Wouldn't even talk to Louie."

"His kid was pretty old, wasn't he? I mean, he was career Army if I remember right."

"Not so old. Thirty maybe. But he was career Army, yeah."

"Yeah, well—what about this one? Mumai. Theodore."

"He's another one got transferred to Birmingham."

"Peluzzi. How about him?"

"Another one of Gallic's honchos. You know him."

"I know Freddie Peluzzi, the bartender in the Sons of Italy, but this one, Axal, I don't."

"This one ain't like Freddie. Just the opposite. A real prick. You have to remember him. We picked him up couple times for beating hell out of his wife. The last time, it was back in sixty-six, he did ninety days."

"Oh yeah. Now I got him. What happened with her?"

"She finally wised up and dumped him. She's still around. Waits tables down the SOI Saturdays and Sundays. I don't know what she does the rest of the time."

"She the one used to be a blonde? She let her hair grow in black again?"

"Yeah. Rose, Rose Mary, something."

"Didn't he have a nickname? This Axal doesn't register with me."

"Wheels."

"Ah, that's why I couldn't place him. Now I got him for sure," Balzic said. "Wheels Peluzzi. He's another buddy of Gallic's, you said."

"Yeah. Him and Janeski and Gallic. Three of a kind. All big-game hunters. All had trouble with women. Janeski's wife is still collecting child support, from what I hear. I shouldn't say that about Gallic though. I don't even think he was ever married. Somebody said he was messing around with Mike Samarra's sister. She used to work for them. Cashier. Maybe

she still does. But that doesn't sound right to me. I mean, I
don't think Samarra would've gone for that."

"Why's that?"

"I don't know for sure, understand. What little I knew of
him, he was a funny guy. Kept to himself pretty much. Didn't
drink, didn't smoke. A bachelor. About the only thing he did
that was out of the ordinary was sing."

"Yeah, he had a helluva voice all right."

"I never heard about him being in any kind of trouble, and
like I said, I only saw him a couple times, but he gave me the
impression he was a guy you didn't fool with. You know the
breed—one of those old-school dagos. Real religious, and you
don't mess around with their sisters. Hell, Mario, you know
the breed better than I do."

"I knew his old man was like that, so I guess it figures he'd
be like that."

"Well, that's what I'm saying. I mean, I can see him having
a business with Gallic, but I can't see him letting Gallic fool
around with his kid sister."

"You know her?"

"I met her a couple times. Tough-looking little broad.
Looked like him in the face. Short, but built good. Little on the
stocky side. Course it's been a while since I've seen her. Any
of them for that matter. Can't remember how long ago it's
been since I've seen Mike. And I haven't seen Gallic or Janeski
or Peluzzi since they told me they were quitting the club."

"This address still right for Peluzzi? Box 12, Pine Hollow
Road?"

"I can't say, Mario. He moves around a lot."

"Where do these two work—Janeski and Peluzzi—case I
don't catch them at home?"

"Janeski's a steamfitter down at the can factory. Peluzzi, I
got no idea. He used to be a brakeman for the PC&Y, but you
know how those railroads are. Might still be with them."

"They about the same age?"

"No. Janeski's younger. Maybe thirty-five. But Peluzzi's got to be around forty-five, forty-six."

"Okay, what about this Scaglione. Egidilio. Is that Joey?"

"Yeah. He's in the VA Hospital in Pittsburgh. Stomach trouble, I hear."

"Testa I know," Balzic said. "Anybody stopping in to see his wife?"

"You got me. I think he had pretty good insurance though. If she wasn't okay, you'd be hearing about it, as big a mouth as she got."

"Let me see. That leaves Woznichak. Old Nick."

"Yeah, boy, was that awful. He didn't weigh a hundred pounds. You didn't go to see him when he was laid out, did you?"

"No. I didn't really like the guy that much."

"Christ, he looked like a shriveled-up baby in the casket."

"He was a big man all right. You know he was one of the original Pittsburgh Steelers?"

"No, I didn't know that. I knew he played pro a long time ago, but I didn't know that."

"Yeah. He was a real son of a bitch when he was young. My old man used to tell me about him. Used to play the game, go out and get bombed, and take on anybody that looked crooked at him. Course he got his lunch, too. My old man told me one time he came in the Armenian Club, the one that used to be down behind Lockhart Steel. Remember, it used to be right across the street from the old police station?"

Stramsky nodded.

"Yeah, well, here comes this big guy, two-forty-something, drunk and running his mouth about he did this, that, and the other, and there's this little nigger sitting against the back wall. For some reason Woznichak really hated the coons, so he starts hollering at the little jig. My old man's taking it all in, not saying anything, but he knows the nigger. The guy shovels the coke furnaces all day six days a week and on

Sundays he comes in the Armenian Club to get a load on and forget the shovel. Meantime, he doesn't know Woznichak from a bar stool, so he's definitely not impressed. Anyway, Woznichak goes over and says something like, 'I know Armenians are black, but you got to be the blackest Armenian I ever saw,' and the little jig, he doesn't say a word. He doesn't even get up. He just brings his foot up, and while Woznichak's going down, he lets him have it across the ear with the beer mug. One of those real heavy ones."

"I know the kind. You don't see them too much any more."

"Yeah. So Woznichak spends the next couple weeks in the hospital waiting for his nuts to quit looking like baseballs and telling everybody what he's going to do to the jig when he gets out."

"So what did he do?"

"Not a goddamn thing. He goes back to the club the Sunday after he gets out of the hospital and the joint is packed. Everybody's there. They all want to see him kill the jig. And the jig comes waltzing in at his usual time, orders his beer, and goes and sits where he usually sits. Woznichak starts hollering at him, but the jig says nothing. He just sits there drinking his beer until Woznichak starts for him. Then the jig stands up and lifts up his shirt and he says, 'You want to die, just keep coming.' He got a forty-five in his pants."

"It's a wonder he didn't get lynched."

"What's the wonder? Who was going to start?"

"Yeah, but still . . ."

"Still nothing. Who doesn't know how many big ones are in a forty-five?"

"Yeah, I guess."

"But the best part is Woznichak got to save a little something, so he offers to shake hands and forget the whole thing. The jig won't go for it, so then Woznichak says he wants to buy him a drink. The next thing you know, they're into a drinking contest, matching shots and beers, and Woznichak's paying, and the windup is, this little skinny jig drinks Woznichak flat—on Woznichak's money." Balzic thought a moment. "I don't know. It always tickles me to think about that. Even though the guy died bad—I mean, who'd wish cancer on anybody?—but that always tickles me to think he got his lunch that way. Hell, three ways." Balzic stood. "Well, that's it. There's nobody else you know of, right?"

"You got them all."

"Are all the farms listed in here too?"

"Yeah. In the back. There's copies of all the leases."

"Good enough. Hey. Where's Mary?"

"Up her mother's washing down the kitchen. I was supposed to help her. I'll catch hell for two days. . . ."

"Good luck on that," Balzic said. "See you tonight probably." He let himself out the kitchen door and made it down the walk and around the garbage cans to his car, driving back in the middle of quitting-time traffic. The day shift in South Rocksburg's mills was over.

Indian summer was hanging on. Balzic would have enjoyed it had he not stayed too long at Stramsky's and allowed himself to get caught in this line of cars and buses. He'd also drunk too much coffee and felt that he'd probably talked too much. He'd noticed a certain distance in Stramsky's eyes when he was telling that one about Woznichak. Had he told it before? He couldn't remember, but he probably had. He loved the story too much not to have told it before.

He tried to think where he should begin with the information he had. Minyon would have to be told. Balzic's mind focused on Minyon and then slipped quickly to thoughts of a cold bottle of beer, sweat streaming down its sides, a frosted glass . . .

He'd call Minyon. That was where he'd start. Give Minyon what he could use over the phone and then to hell with him. It was too hot, traffic was too bad, home and the refrigerator were too far away.

On the sidewalk, at the intersection by Grant's Five and

Ten, there was a flash of tanned bare legs above sandals and below a short crimson skirt, and Balzic tried to catch sight of the face as the legs weaved through the clusters of straphangers waiting for the northbound buses. Then the legs were around the corner of Grant's and gone.

Ah, well, Balzic thought pleasantly, moving on when the light changed, the face might have been bad and then what. . . .

Balzic called Minyon from home and gave him the list of remaining farms leased by the club. He said nothing about the names.

"You're going to have to show me around," Minyon said.

"You've got people up there who know those farms as well as I do. Better maybe. Ralph Stallcup for one."

"Sergeant Stallcup was temporarily assigned to narcotics."

"Well, get him reassigned," Balzic said. "You're the chief of detectives."

There was a pause during which Balzic could hear the teletype. Then Minyon said, "That's right. I am."

Another pause. Balzic waited.

"I'm also in charge of this investigation," Minyon said, clipping off each word.

"There was never any doubt of that. So when are you bringing the dogs back?"

"I haven't decided that yet."

"Okay," Balzic said. "I'll be around if you want anything."

"I do want something."

"What?"

"Some names."

"Oh, I'm having them typed up," Balzic lied. "Should be up to you sometime tomorrow afternoon. Anything else?"

"Why can't I just have the membership rolls your man—what's his name? The Pol—the sergeant?"

"Stramsky. Because he's in the process of sending out bills and he needs the book."

There was another pause. "Wouldn't you say this was more important?"

"That's why I'm having the list typed up for you. Special." Balzic had to bite the inside of his cheek to keep from laughing. "Anything else?"

"Can't you get the list over here any sooner than that?"

"I'll do the best I can, Lieutenant. Is there anything else you can think of for me to do?"

"No," Minyon said, and hung up.

"Good-bye," Balzic said into the dead line. He hung up and was still laughing when Ruth walked into the kitchen from the back-yard patio.

"What's so funny?" she said.

"Ah, it's not as funny as it is pathetic," he said. "I was just pulling some monkey's chain. Just a couple short jerks to let him know somebody was on the other end."

"Whatever that means," Ruth said. "You ready to eat?"

"Let me take a shower first. Where is everybody?"

"Ma's on the patio taking a nap, and Marie and Emily are still at school. Aquatic club practice. You're home early."

"Feels like I been gone a month."

Balzic turned the car off North Main and headed north on Pine Hollow Road. The hollow was off to the right, hardly more than a deep gully, and if there ever had been any pines in it, they had long since been cut and sold as Christmas trees. Now it was a tangle of brambles and sumac trees with occasionally a locust tree breaking the monotony. The box numbers of the houses, all on the western side of the road as Balzic continued northward, grew smaller the farther he got away from town.

He found Peluzzi's house after backtracking twice and

stopping at two other houses to ask directions. Peluzzi's mailbox, bearing neither name nor number, tilted precariously at roadside.

Balzic could not place the square, shabby bungalow in his memory. He recalled Stramsky saying that Peluzzi moved around, and he was sure then that Peluzzi had been living somewhere else when he'd been arrested the last time for assaulting his wife.

Balzic parked behind a recently polished maroon Pontiac, the car contrasting sharply with the bungalow, its white paint blistered and dirty, the yard a mass of ankle-high grass and pigweed. Balzic stumbled on a loose cinder block that served as a step from the berm to the yard.

Though perhaps an hour's daylight remained, lights shone out from both the windows facing the yard, but when Balzic knocked, one of the lights went off. He could hear a radio or a record player blaring and then being turned off.

Peluzzi answered the door in his underwear. He was carrying a towel, and his thick graying hair was wet. Balzic was surprised to see how short he was; somehow he remembered Peluzzi as being much taller.

"I don't want nothing, I don't need nothing," Peluzzi said, "so whatever you're hustling, go hustle it someplace else."

"Peluzzi?" Balzic said, producing his identification.

Peluzzi peered at the ID case and then at Balzic's face. "What the fuck do you want?"

"You remember me."

"How could I forget you? That mess cost me—never mind. What do you want?"

"I want to ask you some questions. Mind if I come in?"

"Do I have a choice?"

"Yes."

Peluzzi searched Balzic's face a moment, then stepped back out of the doorway. Balzic understood then why he'd had the impression that Peluzzi was much taller: he was thick through the neck, shoulders, and chest, and had long, heavily muscled arms.

"Lemme go put some pants on," Peluzzi said, and disappeared into the only room in the small house that seemed to have a door. The other three rooms—the living room, a room that must have been intended to be a dining room, and the kitchen—were connected by open archways.

Peluzzi returned wearing canary yellow slacks and carrying a pair of shined shoes and rolled-up socks. He sat on a wooden folding chair in what was supposed to be the dining room and put on the socks and shoes. There were five other chairs, none of which matched, and a round table that looked better suited to poker than to eating.

"Okay," Peluzzi said, picking up the towel he'd thrown on the table when he went to get his pants and wiping his hair, "so what's on your mind?"

"Where are you doing your hunting these days?"

"My what?"

"Your hunting."

"You come out here to ask me that?"

"I have a reason."

"I bet you do."

"Well?" Balzic said.

"I don't hunt too much any more."

"Why not?"

"Couple of reasons."

"Let's hear them."

Peluzzi wadded up the towel and tossed it into the kitchen. Then he bent down and retied one shoelace. "What the hell's this all about, Balzic?"

"Just give me the reasons."

"Okay. Number one, I ain't working. I missed three payments on that Pontiac out there and I had to sell most of my guns. I mean sixty bucks a week unemployment ain't exactly living. So how you supposed to hunt without a gun?"

"You sell them all?"

"Everything I could use around here. I still got my three thirty-eight Winchester, but that ain't exactly a squirrel gun."

"Sell your shotgun, too?"

"Gun? I didn't have *one*. I had three. I had a Winchester auto and a couple Italian jobs. A double over and under for skeet and a single for trap. I had to unload them all. I could've cried when I sold that trap gun. That mother cost me close to six bills, and all I could get for it was three bills."

"When was the last time you went hunting? I mean, you don't belong to the Police Rod and Gun Club any more."

Peluzzi laughed. "Is that what this is about—a membership drive? Or do I owe you bastards something too?"

"No."

"Well what then, Balzic? What's with all the questions? I got a date, man."

"A date?"

"Yeah. A date. What's wrong with that? I'm supposed to dry up and blow away or something? So I'm forty-six. I ain't dead yet for crissake."

"Somehow it just sounded, uh, never mind."

"Sounded how? Funny? So have a big laugh. My pleasure."

"When was the last time you hunted on club farms, Peluzzi—let's get back to that."

Peluzzi thought a moment, chewing his lip. "Season before last."

"Why did you quit?"

"Some guy told me about a preserve up around Indiana. Shoot as many pheasants as you want. Guaranteed. Good dogs and everything. Cost a helluva lot but it was worth it."

"Which guy? Gallic?"

Peluzzi's face lost its color. It lasted only a second, and then he regained both color and composure. But he stood abruptly and went into the kitchen. Balzic could hear the refrigerator opening and then a bottle being popped open. Peluzzi reappeared with a bottle of beer and stood in the doorway and drank from the bottle.

"Yeah, it was Gallic," Peluzzi said. "So?"

"He was a pretty good friend of yours, wasn't he?"

"We bummed around together, yeah."

"You did a lot more than bumming around. You went to Alaska with him. More than once."

"If you know, how come you're asking?"

"Whose idea was that?"

"Whose idea was what?"

"Whose idea was it to go on those trips?"

"What do you mean, whose idea? It was all our idea."

"All whose?"

"Mine. Gallic's, Richie Janeski's."

"How many trips did you make?"

"Where?"

"Anywhere. How many trips did you three make together?"

"I still wish the fuck you'd tell me what this is about."

"Just answer what I asked you."

"Why? I don't have to. You said when you came in I had a choice."

"You do. You can answer here or down at the station."

Peluzzi's eyes narrowed. Like the moment when his face had gone white at the mention of Gallic's name, the squint lasted only an instant, but it was intense and unmistakable. He turned sideways and let out a deep belch.

"You know, Balzic," Peluzzi said, facing Balzic again, "I can remember you from Mother of Sorrows?"

"You can?"

"Yeah. I only lasted till the second grade up there, and then my old man couldn't go the freight no more. But I remember you. I was in second grade and you were in first. You were a nosy prick even then. You used to come around asking everybody what they had for lunch."

"I guess I'm just naturally inquisitive. Now which is it going to be—here or at the station?"

Peluzzi took another gulp of beer. "So what was the question? I forget."

"How many trips did you three make?"

"I don't know how many Gallic made by himself or with other guys. But me, him, and Janeski, we went to Alaska twice. Then we went up to Ontario fishing a couple times. Once we went fishing up in Manitoba. Then another time we went hunting in Mexico."

"You planning anything this year?"

"No."

Balzic studied Peluzzi's face. "Why not?"

"I told you, man. I'm busted out. I'm lucky I can go down Main Street. They're going to repossess my car for crissake. How am I going anyplace?"

"Is that the only reason?"

"What's that supposed to mean?"

"I mean, well, you three still buddies?"

"No." Peluzzi's eyes clouded over and then went wide. Again, he regained his composure quickly.

"What happened?"

"What happened—nothing happened! You buddy up with some guys for a while and then you don't. Nothing happened."

"You sure?"

"Aw, what is this? Sure I'm sure. I just don't see those guys no more. I don't know what for. Maybe we all got tired of hearing the same stories. Who knows?"

"When was the last time you saw them?"

"Summer before last. We went fishing up at Tionesta. Then I went hunting with Janeski couple of times. And that was it."

"You haven't seen them since? Neither one?"

Peluzzi shook his head.

"Isn't that a little strange? I mean, you three guys were pretty tight from what I hear."

"From what you hear. So what else do you hear? Come on, Balzic, cut the shit. What's this about?"

"I'll tell you the truth, Peluzzi, but you're not going to believe me."

"So give it a shot."

"I really don't know."

"You don't know! So what are you doing jerking me off like this? Jeeeezus Keeerist . . ."

Balzic turned for the door. "Listen, Peluzzi, I can't stop you from going anywhere, but just in case you should get a job in Cleveland or someplace, you be sure and let me know. I mean, right now I don't know what I'm doing, but pretty soon I might, understand, and if I do, I'll want to know where you are. Understand?"

"Yeah, yeah, I understand. You and my ex-wife's lawyer. Shit."

"See you around," Balzic said, and stepped outside. He was almost to his car when he heard the bottle smash against the wall, and he got in his car wondering how Peluzzi had managed to restrain himself for as long as he had.

It was shortly after eight when Balzic turned up Church Street in search of Rear 214. The street—named after Rocksburg's first superintendent of schools—began on North Main and led up a 10 per cent grade to a low-income housing project built by the government shortly after World War Two. Two blocks from the crest, Balzic spotted the number on a two-storied building, its exterior covered with imitation brick, a building, like the others on the street, which seemed to cling to its foundation out of spite for gravity.

Balzic turned the wheel to set the tires against the curb and got out, going to the rear of the building on a walk of flagstones between 214 and 216. Creaking wooden steps led up to a porch, and, at the top, Balzic took a guess and knocked on the first door he came to.

A pan-faced woman, her head mushrooming with plastic

curlers, opened the door with an uncooked frankfurter in one hand and a large pickle in the other.

Balzic showed his ID and said, "I'm looking for a Richard Janeski."

"Next door," the woman said. "But I can tell you right now he ain't there."

"Do you happen to know where he is?"

"At work."

"Do you happen to know when he gets off?"

"Twelve. Same as my old man. But he won't come home."

"Do you know why not?"

"Sure. After they quit, they'll be down at Pravik's Hotel. Him and my old man. And they won't be home till they're good and stiff."

"Thank you. Sorry to trouble you," Balzic said, going down the steps wondering what reason Janeski had for not coming back. The reason why the pan-faced woman's husband didn't come home until he was stiff was fairly clear.

Balzic sat in the car a minute, thinking. He didn't want to spend four hours waiting for Janeski to show up in Pravik's, and he didn't want to go home. At either place he knew he'd start into the beer, and the way he was feeling, a start would only lead to an end: in Pravik's he'd get bored drunk; at home he'd get listless drunk. He could afford neither. He had to see Janeski tonight and Gallic tomorrow morning if he hoped to find out as much as he could by himself and still have the list of names to Minyon by tomorrow afternoon as he'd said he would.

There was no place else left. He turned the car around and headed it for the station.

He walked in, thinking he might talk Stramsky into some gin at a penny a point. Thinking that, he was unprepared for the Reverend Callum, who was pacing, head down and hands in his pockets, in front of the counter.

"You're a difficult man to locate," Reverend Callum said.

"I guess I am. Did we, uh, have an appointment?"

"No. As a matter of fact, we didn't. But I've been here twice today."

"Oh? What for?"

"I want to settle some of these things. The things I've been trying to settle for six weeks now. The things I brought up in council meeting."

"Let's go back here," Balzic said, nodding to Stramsky in passing and leading Reverend Callum to one of the interrogation cubicles in the rear of the squad room. He directed the reverend to a chair and took one himself. "Well," he said, "so what's on your mind?"

"This is not going to be easy for me to say," Reverend Callum said.

Balzic could see that it wasn't: the reverend couldn't stop rubbing his palms together and he was having a hard time looking at Balzic.

"I guess the only way to say it is to say it," Reverend Callum said. "I've been doing a little detective work of my own, and, well, I'm more than a little ashamed to say that I may have been seeing things that weren't there."

"Oh, listen, Reverend, if that's the way it is, just forget it. Those guys you were talking about, guys like Dawson and Williams, hell, they fool a lot of people. That's how they survive. That's their trade."

"I know that now, but in my first discussions with them, they seemed so sincere. And Williams's mother—now explain to me why she would go to such lengths to corroborate his stories after he'd beaten her. That's what I can't understand. It just doesn't make sense."

"Well, Reverend, I think what you mean is it shouldn't ought to make sense. Sense would be her admitting what he was. But it doesn't work that way. I'll tell you, I've been dealing with people like Williams—liars, bullies, mean, spiteful guys—I don't know, must be close to twenty-five years now.

And you get a bully in here, a real mean kid like this Williams, and you won't find one mother out of a thousand who's going to say, 'Yeah, he's a no good sonuvabitch.' Excuse my language, Reverend, but, well, what do those words mean? I mean, what mother is going to say that about her son, no matter what words she uses? 'Cause you know what she'll be saying."

"Even after he beat her? And threatened to do worse?"

"Not even, Reverend. Because. Oh, they'll come in and make the complaint and they'll be raising all kinds of noise for a while about their kid, but then—well, take Williams and his mother. You know what happened after we arrested him that time—the time you were talking about?"

Reverend Callum shook his head.

"She went through everything, the complaint, the arraignment, the grand jury, but when it came to trial, she'd had some time to think about it. So when she gets on the stand, she refuses to say anything. She got on that stand and she wouldn't say anything except who she was and where she lived. She wouldn't even answer the question whether the defendant was her son or not. The trial lasted something like ten or twelve minutes. The judge threw it out. He had to. The stepsister wouldn't testify either."

"But why? I don't understand that."

"Aw come on, Reverend. They were scared. The worst kind of scared. That woman was scared of her own blood. She went through labor to have that kid. You think she's going to admit to the world—to herself—that she went through labor to produce a rat? Some women, they can do it. They can turn their back. They're not exactly rare, but they'd make a pretty small crowd. The rest, the Mrs. Williamses, well . . ."

"But surely the stepsister should have had other feelings. He wasn't her son."

"Yeah, but you got to remember what he'd already done to her. You ask any lawyer or any judge, they'll tell you, rape is one of the toughest cases to try. It's tough as hell to prove and it's just as tough to defend against."

"But he wasn't being tried for that. She'd dropped that charge."

"That's right. But the fact is she dropped it after we picked him up for assaulting her. Now you couldn't go to court with this, but the fact that she'd dropped it after he'd worked her over only proves to me that he had raped her. And I'll tell you what, a woman that's been raped—unless she's some kind of masochist—well, you give her time to think about it, she just don't want to have anything to do with the guy that raped her. Hell, most rapes, most real rapes, don't even get reported. 'Cause the victims just don't want to ever see that guy again. Now as far as the stepsister goes, she has that on her mind, plus she *has* to look at the guy all the time. He's around. And not just around, Reverend, but he's around working her over. I'll tell you straight. The only thing that's surprised me about the whole thing is the fact that she hasn't tried to kill him. Of course, nobody knows that she hasn't tried. Maybe that's what started him in on her the night we picked him up. Maybe she tried and missed. So, to make a long story short, Reverend, that poor female has got a hundred things going through her head, none of them easy to live with, and it's no wonder at all that she didn't testify against him. I don't think she could even if she wanted to. She could kill him a lot easier than she could talk about him to strangers."

Reverend Callum shook his head again. "I suppose I should apologize."

"Nah. No way. Forget it. What the heck, you make a mistake, that's all."

"So I did." The reverend straightened in his chair. "Have you, uh, checked into the other case I mentioned?"

"The Bivins kid? Was that his name?"

"That's the one."

"No, I haven't. I've had something else on my mind. Give

me a minute and I'll get his file." Balzic left the cubicle and
went to the live file next to the teletype. He motioned to
Stramsky to come over and asked him, "The name Bivins ring
any bells, Vic?"

"Huh-uh. What's the preacher man bitching about—police
brutality?"

"Something like that. He got some bad information,
though."

"Wait a minute," Stramsky said. "You passed it. Back up a
couple."

Balzic flipped the folders back and came up with the one
bearing the name: "Bivins, Roland M." He opened it and
scanned it quickly.

"Look at this. Arrested October 2, twenty-three forty-seven
hours. Romeo's Lunch and Diner. Making threats and using
abusive and obscene language. Arresting officer, Lawrence
Fischetti." He turned to Stramsky. "Where the hell's the rest
of it? Didn't he book him or what?"

"Beats the hell out of me," Stramsky said.

"Fischetti on tonight?"

"Huh-uh."

"Well call him, will you? I want to know what this is about.
And tell him I don't want to hear any bullshit either. Christ
almighty, he doesn't even have down here who made the
complaint."

Balzic returned the folder to the file and went back to the
cubicle where Reverend Callum was staring at his hands.

"How about some coffee, Reverend? Can I get you a cup?"

"No, thanks. I don't drink it."

"Ah, well," Balzic said, lighting a cigarette, "I think you
may have a beef, Reverend. I'm not saying for sure, understand, but I've read Bivins's file and there are a couple of things
out of sorts. Only thing is, the arresting officer isn't on duty
tonight, so it may take a while."

"Are you trying to tell me that you'll call me?"

Balzic felt himself flush. "Listen, I give you my word. As soon as I know something, I'll let you know."

"What can I say?" the reverend said, standing. He extended his hand.

Balzic shook it and said, "As soon as I know, you'll know."

"That's all I can ask for," Reverend Callum said, and walked quickly through the squad room and was gone.

Balzic watched him go and then turned to Stramsky. "You get Fischetti?"

"His mother says he went out. She doesn't know where."

"Went out," Balzic said. "Shit. He doesn't come up with something good about this, he will be going out. And I'll be the one holding the door."

Balzic looked at the clock behind the bar and checked it with his watch. Three after midnight. He'd been in Pravik's Hotel long enough to have one draught and to order the second. He did not recognize the bartender and was trying to place him when the bartender returned with the second beer. Balzic asked if old man Pravik was still around.

"He's around all right," the bartender said. "Just barely. He had a stroke three weeks ago. Why? You a friend of his?"

"I know him," Balzic said, "but we're not friends. So who's taken over the place?"

"Me. For the time being." The bartender didn't seem at all pleased about it.

"You a member of the family?"

The bartender looked suspiciously at Balzic. "Yeah," he said. "I'm his son-in-law. One of them anyway. Why?"

"Just curious. I like to know who owns things."

"You with the Liquor Control Board?"

"No. I'm chief of police here."

The bartender thought about that. "Something wrong? I mean, I never saw you in here before."

"Nothing's wrong here. I'm just waiting for somebody I've been told comes in here pretty regularly. Name's Janeski. He works second trick at the can factory. You know him?"

"I haven't been here long enough to know last names. I'm from Farrell. Only other time I've been here was when I got married. The wife said we had to get married here. So we did, but except for then and now, I don't know anybody."

"What do you do up there? I mean, how are you able to take off and come down here and run this place?"

"That's a good question. Maybe you should come over to the old man's house and ask the rest of the relatives. They don't seem to understand when I ask them."

"Well, you must have a bar up there, right?"

"Right. So they just naturally think who better than me to run this one. In the meantime, I'm getting robbed blind up there, and they're sitting around waiting for the old man to die so they can divvy up this place. A real bunch of sweethearts, and what kills me is they don't think anything at all about it. My place, I mean. Christ, I'll be lucky the stools are still there when I get back." The bartender shook his head.

The door opened then and a group of six or seven men came in.

"Here comes a bunch from the can factory," the bartender said. "What was that guy's first name? Maybe I'll know him by that."

"Richard—Richie."

"Oh yeah. That's him. The one in the T-shirt with all the muscles and the messed-up face." He walked down the bar to wait on them.

Balzic didn't recognize any of them. Though the night had been chilly enough for Balzic to feel comfortable with a raincoat over his suit, all of them were in short-sleeved shirts or T-shirts. It was plain from their hands, wrists, and forearms they all were used to heavy labor.

Balzic watched them a minute or so. Four of them, after getting their beers, immediately began to play the bowling machine. A couple others settled into an argument begun elsewhere about the merits of players the Pittsburgh Steelers had traded away in recent years. The one identified by the bartender as Janeski sat by himself at the bar and took a newspaper from his back pocket and started to read it. He had the neck, shoulders, torso, and arms of a man who had spent years lifting weights.

Balzic went over to him with his ID cupped in his hand. "Janeski?"

"Yeah," Janeski said without looking up from the paper. Then he caught sight of the ID case Balzic held out, shielded from anybody else who might have been looking.

"I'd like to talk to you," Balzic said. "How about if we go sit in the back booth?"

Janeski hesitated, then folded his paper and jammed it into his back pocket. He swept up his glass of beer and followed Balzic to the booth. "So what do you want to talk about?" he said.

"I want to talk about your hunting."

"My what?" Janeski's nose had been broken and his mouth had been cut, probably a long time ago, but it had been bad when it happened. The scar of the cut was very wide, beginning on his left nostril and running diagonally across both lips and ending at the right side of his chin. It made him appear to be constantly sneering. Even his smile now at Balzic's question had what seemed a contemptuous twist to it. The injury had also left him with a slight lisp.

"Your hunting. Where are you going hunting these days?"

"Tell you the truth, I don't do much hunting any more."

"Any particular reason?"

"No time. I been working a lot of overtime. Can't get off."

"You used to hunt pretty regular with a couple guys, didn't you? Peluzzi and Gallic?"

Janeski took his time answering. "I used to hunt pretty regular, period."

"You seen those two lately?"

"What were their names again?"

"Peluzzi. Wheels, they call him. And Frank Gallic."

"Oh yeah, I used to hunt with them. Sure."

"You also belonged to the Police Rod and Gun Club."

"That's right."

"Why'd you quit the club?"

"I don't know if I had any special reason. I just quit."

"Wasn't it because Gallic talked you two, you and Peluzzi, into going to a preserve up around Indiana?"

"That might've been it. I don't remember now."

Janeski's gaze was steady, but his replies were as much questions as answers, and Balzic knew that he was going to have to pull everything out of him. The curious thing to Balzic, curious and suddenly absurd, was that he didn't know exactly what it was he was trying to pull out. First Peluzzi and now Janeski were both very much alive. What more could he learn? Still, the fact that both Peluzzi and Janeski had quit the club soon after somebody had been killed and scattered over club farms seemed to be reason enough to go on questioning Janeski. Nonetheless, Balzic had to admit that the matter of time could be pure coincidence.

"When was the last time you saw either of them?"

"Who?"

"Come on, Janeski. Who've we been talking about?"

"Peluzzi and Gallic you mean? Oh, it's been a while."

"How long a while?"

"I don't know. Year maybe. Maybe longer."

"Didn't you go hunting with Peluzzi last year? And didn't the three of you go fishing—I think Peluzzi said something about going fishing up around Tionesta."

"Well, I remember going hunting with Peluzzi couple times. But I don't remember being on no fishing trip with them."

"Never? Or just the one at Tionesta?"

"Oh, we went fishing together. Up in Canada. Three or

four times. I just don't remember this time you're talking about. At Tionesta."

"Peluzzi says you were there."

"Yeah? Well if he says it, maybe I was, and maybe I just don't remember it. Maybe I didn't catch anything."

Balzic's glass was empty, and Janeski's nearly so. "You, uh, ready for another one?" Balzic asked.

"You buying?"

"You go get them, I'll pay for them."

"Can't beat that," Janeski said, picking up the glasses and going to the bar. When he returned he said, with a lopsided grin, "Isn't every day the chief of police buys you a beer."

"My pleasure. Now to get back to this other thing—tell me again the last time you saw Gallic."

Again Janeski took his time answering. "A long time. I don't know."

"You think maybe it was that fishing trip to Tionesta?"

"Maybe. But I can't even remember being there. But if Peluzzi says so, maybe that was the last time."

"You didn't go hunting with him last fall? Not even once?"

"If I did, I can't remember." Janeski's tone had grown sharper.

"But wasn't it a fact that he's the one who talked you and Peluzzi into going up to that preserve?"

"I don't know if I'd call that a fact. He might've told us about it. Yeah, he probably did."

"Two people say he did. Peluzzi's one and Vic Stramsky's the other. Vic said that was the reason you gave him for quitting the club."

"Well, if he says it, it must be true, right? I mean, he's a cop, isn't he? A sergeant, too, if I remember right."

"What is it with you, Janeski? Why all the reluctance to talk about this?"

"Talk about what?"

"Come off it. You know what I mean?"

"Look, man. I just walked in here to get the taste of that mill out of my throat, and you start asking me all these questions. I don't even know what you're talking about. You haven't said a word yet about what this is all about. I keep waiting, but you just keep asking questions. But I'll tell you what it sounds like to me. It sounds like you think you know a lot of answers, so what I'm thinking is, if you know, man, what are you asking for?"

"I'm trying to put some things together, that's all."

"Oh, that's a good reason. That's a real good reason. I mean, now I understand everything." Janeski was sneering this time. There was no mistaking the effort from the perpetual sneer caused by the scar, and his face took on an even more ugly mien.

Balzic studied him a moment. He didn't know what he was going to say next; the idea suddenly occurred to him. "What happened that time you three were at Tionesta together?"

Janeski had been sloshing the beer around in his glass, watching the foam arc up to the rim. At Balzic's question he became suddenly quite still. His gaze remained fixed on the beer, but he seemed to be making a considerable effort to control himself. "I told you, man, I can hardly remember even being there, never mind what happened."

"A little while ago, you said you couldn't remember being there at all. Now you say you can hardly remember, but you can't remember what happened. I think you're lying."

Janeski's head swung up. "How do you know? You know so fucking much—how do you know what I remember and what I don't?"

"I know when somebody's trying to hide something."

"Yeah? So what do I have to hide, man? You tell me. I mean, you getting ready to arrest me or something? 'Cause if you are, man, you better tell me what for, and if it's for something that is supposed to've happened on this fishing trip, why don't you just tell me what it was? 'Cause I'd like to know."

"I don't know what happened. That's why I'm asking. I just know—"

"What?" Janeski said, his voice breaking. "What do you know?" He stood up, bumping the table with his legs and nearly spilling the beer. "I'll tell you what I know, man. I know I don't have to talk to you. I don't have to tell you a goddamn thing. I didn't do anything, so don't bother me no more. I don't have to tell you shit. You want to know what happened? Then you go back and talk to Peluzzi some more. Better yet, go talk to Gallic. Ask him to tell you what happened, that . . ." Janeski hurried to the bar, banged his glass down on it, and pushed his way through the group playing the bowling machine to the door and out.

Balzic sat there a moment rubbing his mouth. He'd struck a nerve, there was no doubt of that. But which nerve? And what was Janeski going to call Gallic—that what? The way Janeski had fought back the urge to call Gallic that name—whatever it was—convinced Balzic that something had happened among those three. But what of it? What did anything that happened among them have to do with anything? So there had been a falling out among cronies, an argument, a fight even. Suppose it was something more; suppose that—what did it have to do with those bones?

He left Pravik's then, telling himself that maybe Gallic would be more co-operative. But if Gallic wasn't? What if Gallic reacted the same way as Peluzzi and Janeski? But what difference would it make how any of them reacted? What did their reactions—no matter what they were—have to do with the bones?

Had there been somebody else with them, somebody whose name wasn't on the list of membership, somebody who wasn't even from around Rocksburg? And had they had their falling out over that somebody? Or had they had it with that somebody? Maybe the friends who thought they'd always been friends had turned out to be something other than friends?

Hell, Balzic thought, what am I trying to make out of two guys getting steamed about a fishing trip? Suppose they had gotten into a fight, suppose they had killed somebody—what possible reason could they have had for bringing the body all the way back here to take it apart and bury? Tionesta was over a hundred miles away.

If I had any sense, Balzic thought, getting into his car, I'd dump this whole mess right in Minyon's lap. That was what Minyon wanted anyway, and he'd be doing himself a bigger favor than he would Minyon.

If it hadn't been for that damn dog of his, Balzic thought. "Bitch," he said. "Stupid, fat, contrary bitch . . ."

Balzic slept fitfully at best. Twice his mother, flushing the toilet, woke him, the first time at three and the second at six. The second time he tossed about for some minutes and then, fearing that his tossing would wake Ruth, he got up and went out into the kitchen.

He put water in a pan on the gas, and, while searching through the spice jars and cans for the instant coffee, the thought came to him as though he'd never slept: that fishing trip; Peluzzi, Janeski, and Gallic fishing the Allegheny River around Tionesta . . .

Something had happened: Peluzzi's face losing its color when he'd heard Gallic's name; Janeski first claiming not to remember even being there and then storming away in a barely controlled rage.

What name was Janeski going to call Gallic?

Balzic gulped two swallows of the coffee, dumping the rest in the sink and hurrying to the bathroom, there to lather himself under the shower and to shave, mindless of the strokes of the razor.

By seven o'clock he was at the station and by seven-thirty he had cleared up the routine matters. At a quarter to eight he was pulling off Route 331, seven miles out of Rocksburg, onto the gravel parking lot of Galsam's Freezer Meats.

It was a low, square building with the front right corner of it reserved for customer service, the facing of that portion all white tiles and large square windows. Scotch-taped onto the insides of the windows were signs painted in red and blue tempera on white butcher paper: "CHARGE ACCOUNTS WELCOME," "WE CUT FIRST, THEN WE WEIGH," "MASTER CHARGE HONORED," "ASK ABOUT OUR BAR-B-QUER'S SPECIAL," "DEER HUNTERS, DEER SEASON WILL BE HERE BEFORE YOU KNOW—WE CUSTOM SLAUGHTER DEER, $12.95 PLUS HIDE."

There was only one small light burning in the customer service area. For some reason Balzic expected to see meat cases, but there was only a Formica-covered counter extending the width of the room. A cash register sat in the middle of the counter. Beyond the counter, he could make out dimly two stainless-steel doors leading, no doubt, to walk-in freezers. In the back wall on the right was a wooden door.

As Balzic got out of his car and stepped around the side of the building he could hear the soft mooing of cattle. The smell came to him then, too.

Off to the right, about fifty yards away across a drive, a large mobile home sat on a permanent foundation of cinder blocks and mortar. Seventy-five to eighty yards behind that one, beyond a weeping willow and a row of poplars and a pair of short, thickly branched evergreens, was another mobile home. It, too, appeared to be on a permanent foundation.

In front of the nearer mobile home was parked a double-cab International pickup truck bearing the same sign on its door as was across the front of the building. Beside the building was a Ford truck fitted with a bed for hauling livestock. In the drive beside the second mobile home was a sedan, but, because of the trees, Balzic could not make out the model or year. Between the two mobile homes, sitting on four jacks on the grass, was a camper designed, Balzic guessed, to fit the pickup truck.

Lights had been on in the second mobile home since Balzic had arrived, and, as he stood now, listening to the cattle and to what he thought was the Conemaugh River, lights came on in the near trailer. He could make out a shadow, just the top of somebody's head, moving around inside. Then the shadow went out of sight, apparently into another room.

Balzic lit a cigarette and went back to his car to wait.

At eight o'clock exactly, fluorescent lights came on in the customer service area, the wooden door opened, and Mike Samarra, wearing a starched white coat and carrying a clean apron, came into the room.

Though it had been years since Balzic had seen Samarra, he recognized him at once. Except for the gray hair above his ears, Samarra seemed not to have changed. He was a bull of a man, with very little neck and large, rounded shoulders and wrists thicker than an ordinary man's ankle. He moved about in the same firm, no-nonsense gait that struck Balzic as characteristic, even at this hour of the day. Even as a kid, Mickey Samarra had had little nonsense about him. Balzic remembered him delivering ice in the mornings before school when most of the other kids were still trying to figure out how to stay warm just a minute longer.

Samarra came to the front door and, without so much as a glance at Balzic's car, unlocked it, then returned to the counter, going through the levered door to the cash register. After unlocking the register, he appeared to Balzic to be filling the cash drawer with money taken from his pockets. Only after he'd done that did he pause and take note of the car in his lot.

Balzic got out of his car and went inside and crossed the small room to Samarra with his hand out. "Mike, how are you? Remember me?"

"Mario?" Samarra's face twisted into a puzzled frown and then broke into a broad grin. "Mario Balzic. I'll be a son of a gun."

"You remembered. How about that. How are you, Mike?"

Balzic shook Samarra's hand, a hand with black hair like wires on the backs of the fingers. Though Balzic was more than a head taller, his hand was lost in Samarra's.

"I'll be darned," Samarra said. "Jeez, it must be ten years since I saw you."

"Yeah. Pretty long time, Mickey."

"Ha. I'll be darned. You know how long it's been since anybody called me that—Mickey? Son of a gun." Samarra grinned again. "Well, heck, what brings you out here? You looking for a good buy? Believe me, I've got them. I've got some terrific beef back here, Mario. Been hanging for almost six weeks. A guy was supposed to pick it up last week and he called yesterday and said he's leaving town or something. It's just right."

"Well, I'll tell you, Mickey, what I'm really here for is to see your partner."

"My partner?" Samarra's grin faded into an incredulous frown. His eyes began to dart about.

"Yeah. Gallic."

"Oh, Mario, you want to see him. I want to see him. Tina wants to see him." Samarra's voice was on the edge of despair.

"Tina?"

"Tina's my sister, Mario. Don't you remember? No, I guess maybe you wouldn't. She's a lot younger than us. She's twelve, no, thirteen, years younger. She'll be thirty-four the tenth of next month."

"Ah, just what do you mean you want to see him?" Balzic said.

"Just what I said, Mario. I haven't seen Frank for—wait a second. I'll tell you exactly." Mickey reached under his white coat and pulled out a wallet bulging with papers and cards. He took out a paper smudged with the color of the wallet. "Here it is. He went fishing on Friday, twenty-sixth of July a year ago. He came back the following Sunday night, and that was the last I ever seen him."

"I'll be damned," Balzic said. "I'll be damned."

"Mario, do you know something? I mean, if you know anything about this, Jeez, I hope to God you're going to tell me."

"Mickey, you forget. I came here looking for him, remember?"

"Oh. That's right." Mickey's face screwed up in thought. "But why? Why'd you come out here looking for him?"

Balzic picked his words carefully. "Oh, I just wanted to ask him some questions. Had to do with the Rod and Gun Club. Our treasurer got his records fouled up and said Gallic would know what he needed to know. I wasn't doing anything, so I said I'd come out and find out for him."

"Oh," Samarra said, and Balzic knew he'd accepted the explanation. "Mario," Mickey said suddenly, his words coming in a rush, "I tell you, it's the darndest thing. I knew that guy since 1942. I mean I knew him a little bit before when we were kids in school, but I really didn't know him, if you know what I mean, until we went into the Army. Then we got to know each other pretty good. You know, we sort of got thrown together. And you know how it is when you have to go away from home, all those strangers around, you don't know what's going on half the time. Anybody that's from your home town is like a cousin or something.

"Well, we went through everything together—training, we went through Africa, through Italy, the whole shooting match. And a lot of the times the thing that kept us going was what we were going to do when we got out. We were always making plans. You'd be surprised how much just making plans can keep you going. I'd've never believed it myself if somebody told me.

"Well, we did get out—God knows how. Without a scratch, neither one of us. And so we just naturally tried to do what we planned all those times. It just seemed like the thing to do. First, the grocery up in Norwood, then the butcher shop across from the old Mother of Sorrows grade school, and then, finally, this place. We went through hell together, Mario. All kinds of hell. But good times, too.

"But then one day—phffft—he takes off. Not a word. Not so much as a post card. Nothing. My God, Mario, we were together nearly twenty-seven years. Imagine! Jeez, I thought Frank was my best friend. It turns out I didn't know him at all. I can't get over it. If I could understand it, maybe—ah, what's the use talking?"

"Mickey, did he, uh, beat you out of anything?" Balzic said.

"No! That's the real puzzle. That's what I really can't understand. He didn't take a penny. Jeez, he didn't even take what was his. And he never has, either. I just called the bank again two days ago. Eleven thousand dollars, Mario. Still in his account! Mario, I tell you, it doesn't make sense. Heck, he didn't even take his truck."

"The pickup?"

"Yes. The camper, too. He left everything. My God, all his guns. You know, for a long time I thought maybe he drowned. He used to drink sometimes. Sometimes he drank way too much, but it didn't interfere with the work, so I never said anything about it. But, anyway, he used to fish sometimes at night, and I was always telling him to watch out. The river's shallow back there, but it's pretty fast. You go off those rocks, you're gone. You know, I hired three—what do you call them?—scuba divers? Yeah. I paid them out of my own money, not out of the business money. I had them for a week. My God, I don't know how far down the river they went, but they didn't find a thing. Nothing."

"Mickey, why in the hell didn't you call us?"

"The police? Mario, I know you'll think I'm crazy, but when you're in business, dealing with the public, boy, I'll tell you, people are funny. They think something's wrong, boy, they stay away. And the police, well . . ."

"Yeah, I know. The police always mean something's wrong."

"That's right. Even if nothing's wrong, your customers will think there is and, boy, once they go away, they don't come back."

"You still should've called us, Mickey. Me, anyway. I'd have kept it quiet."

"Ah, Mario, I didn't know what to do. I'll tell you who I did call, though. I called the Missing Persons. About a month after. Right after I had those divers come in. And I asked them to please keep it quiet—which they do anyway, I found out—but they never came up with anything. Nothing. I just called them again last week. It's like—Mario, I'll tell you. It's like Frank was never even here. And my God, Tina—she was, they were supposed to get married. Tina, boy, I wish I knew what to do for her."

"Is that who lives in the front trailer?"

"Yeah. That used to be Frank's. I have the one in back. Tina, my God, Mario, she just mopes around, don't say anything, won't talk to the customers. I don't know what to do with her. I mean, sure, it's a real blow, but to me, too. Not just to her. But I guess it's not the same."

"How tough is it on you?"

"Mario, are you kidding? Never mind the work, I'm going nuts trying to keep the figures straight. The taxes. My God. And then we were having trouble with a new inspector. I knew he was a grafter the second I seen him. He wanted something in the back pocket just to give us the same rating we always had."

"When was this?"

"A year ago last April. We had troubles back and forth with the federal people, and everything was just about to get cleared up when Frank leaves. Now it's still hanging fire. Frank could deal with those people. I mean, that was what he was really good at. He could really talk. But with me, those guys start throwing those legal words around, I'm like a clown. Mario, I tell you, I don't know whether I'm coming or going sometimes."

"What's the problem with the taxes?"

"Oh, God," Samarra said, throwing up his hands. "We pay taxes to everybody. The city, the county, the state, Washington. We pay quarterly, you know. All along, right from the beginning we made a rule both of us would sign the checks. Everything except personal income tax. And ever since he's been gone, well, I've been signing everything. I've even been paying his income tax."

"What the hell for? He's not around."

"I—I don't know. I just want everything to look right. Just in case."

"Just in case what?"

"Well, I mean, in case he comes back."

"Hell, Mickey, his taxes would be something he'd have to settle."

"Yeah, but what if—I mean, the government's tough, Jeez. You screw up with the Internal Revenue, I could go to jail."

"Oh, come on, Mickey. Anybody else wouldn't even think twice about it. Hell, half the country is trying to beat Uncle out of every cent they can, and you're paying double. What's your lawyer say about all this?"

"I don't have a lawyer. We never needed one. We didn't cheat."

"God, Mickey, I don't know how you do it. My advice to you—get a lawyer, man. Put your mind at ease about these things. I'm no expert on tax law—hell, I have to go to H. & R. Block myself, that's how dumb I am about it, but I can't believe that you'd have to pay income taxes for a partner that isn't there. Not even Uncle's that greedy. Tell you what. How about I call up Mo Valcanas and make an appointment for you?"

"Isn't he the criminal lawyer?"

"He does everything."

"But I'm not a criminal."

"Forget that, will you? Listen, if nothing else, what happens if Gallic never shows up? No matter how legal you've been, no matter how straight you tried to keep everything, you've still got problems. You need somebody to advise you about these things."

Samarra hung his head. For a second Balzic thought he was going to break down. Then his head came up and he looked squarely at Balzic. "I'd appreciate it, Mario, if you'd get this Valcanas for me, but what I want you to know—honest to God—I haven't done anything wrong. Everything I did, I did to keep the business going. I don't know. I wanted it right when Frank came back."

"You really think he's going to?"

Samarra sighed. "Oh, God, what do I know? I keep hoping, that's all. I mean, if he does, ah, what the heck do I know?" He put his hands on the counter and supported his bulk against his stiffened arms. "You know what I think, Mario? I mean what I really think?"

Balzic waited.

"I think something bad happened that weekend he went fishing, that's what I really think."

"What makes you think that?"

"Those two guys he went with. Ah, I don't know. I never liked them. And Frank, he was always going off somewhere with them. Canada, Alaska, Mexico. You know, this place used to be full of stuffed heads? My God, there used to be a polar bear right over there in that corner, and over there, in the other corner, there was a brown bear. A Kodiak. Huge things. That darn polar bear was almost nine feet high."

"What happened to them?"

"They're all in the back. All his stuff is. He must've had fifteen heads. Animals I don't even know the names of, never mind the deer heads and racks."

"Whose idea was that?"

"To put them in the back?"

Balzic nodded.

"Tina's. She made me. She said she couldn't stand to look at

them no more. I thought it would help her. She thinks I threw
them out, you know—gave them to the garbage men. That's
what I told her, but I couldn't bring myself to do that. So I put
them where she doesn't go. They're in the back of the big
freezer. Both bears, everything. I got them covered up with
dropcloths."

"Where is she now?"

"Over in the trailer. She's supposed to come over about
eight-thirty, quarter to nine. But more and more she doesn't
come over until she hears a customer's car. Even then,
sometimes I have to call her on the intercom. I tell her, Tina,
you got to quit moping around. You're young yet, you got to
get out of here once in a while. She just looks at me. My God,
yesterday she told me to shut up. The first time in my whole
life she ever said that to me. She's my sister, Mario, but ever
since our parents died, I been, well, you know, more than just
a brother. And my God, it's breaking me apart to see her like
she is now. It's like, God forbid, it's like she don't care whether
she lives or not. God forgive me for saying that, but I never
said it before. . . ."

"Mickey, uh, think a minute. You said you think something
bad happened that weekend, right?"

Mickey nodded.

"But then you said Frank came back on the Sunday after he
left, right?"

"Yeah."

"And the truck's his? The pickup?"

"That's right."

"Well, how could he have got back here if something
happened during that weekend?"

"That's another thing I can't figure out. The truck is here,
but Frank ain't."

"Do you mean you didn't see him? I mean actually see him?
That Sunday night."

"No. Did I say that? No. I didn't see him. I just woke up

Monday morning to start work and I saw the truck. Parked right where it is now."

"You mean it hasn't been moved?"

"Oh, no, no. It's been moved. Sure, I take it down to the gas station every once in a while to get the battery charged and keep air in the tires. And all last winter I used to start it up every day and run it awhile, you know. I made sure there was antifreeze in it. And I keep the inspections up to date. But I don't drive it around. It's Frank's."

"Does Tina?"

"Oh, God no. She won't go near it. I swear, I don't even think, I mean, this is going to sound funny. Sometimes I'm in here with a customer, and she'll be coming over from the trailer, and she has to walk right by the darn thing. She looks like she doesn't even know it's there. I can't explain what I mean. Do you get what I mean?"

Balzic nodded. "You think she'll be coming over pretty soon?"

"I don't think so. Lately, I don't know." Samarra hesitated. "Ah, what the heck. I may as well tell you. Yesterday when she told me to shut up, you know what that was about?"

Balzic waited.

Samarra pushed away from the counter and started to pace about, pulling and tugging at his thick fingers. "Those two guys, the ones Frank used to pal around with, well, I never liked them. They never did anything to me, understand. It's just that when Frank was with them, I'd know about it the next day. Sometimes for the next couple days."

"How do you mean?"

"I can't explain it too good, Mario. But he'd be different. Even when he'd just go around town drinking with them during the week. When he'd wake up, he wouldn't just be hung over. He'd, well, he wouldn't talk to me for a while. And then when he did, he wouldn't say no more than he absolutely had to. He'd act like I was the dumbest guy in the whole world. Now, you know me good enough from when we were kids, Mario. I mean I never was any brainstorm. But I know my work. I know how to get along with the customers. And I'll tell you, I kept the books in every business we had. Every one, and there never were any mistakes. Oh, the register might be off a couple bucks, but heck, that happens in any business no matter how close you watch it. But never anything big."

"I understand," Balzic said.

"Okay. So what was I starting to say?"

"About those two guys and Tina telling you to shut up."

"Yeah, that's it. Well, Frank was usually real nice to me most of the time. Not that we carried on any big conversations. Heck, you work together as long as we did, you don't have to talk much. You know everything that has to be done. But lots of times we'd be in the back working and we'd be singing. Singing like crazy. I like to sing, you know. I been singing in church since before my voice changed. And Frank had a nice voice, too. He could only sing melody, but I'd sing harmony, and it made the day go, too, you know? But when he'd be out with those two, I don't know, two, three days, sometimes a week would go by before he'd want to sing again. And if I tried to start, he'd just give me this look, like, why don't you dry up? You know—I mean, he never said it right out, but you see what I mean?"

"I see. So what happened yesterday?"

"Well, yesterday, I don't know. I couldn't stand it. I was thinking about the taxes, about everything, and I said to myself, I got to talk to those two guys—"

"You never talked to them before?"

Mickey shook his head.

"Never? Not even once? In all this time?"

"Never. I told you, I didn't like those two. I knew Peluzzi from way back. He ain't a good person, Mario. Never was. I remember the way he used to talk to his father when he was a kid. God, if I ever talked to my father like that—ah, never mind. Anyway, I thought about it—calling them up—and I thought and I thought. So, finally I decided to ask Tina about it, to see, you know, if she thought it was a good idea, and if she did, then I was going to do it."

"This was yesterday?"

"Right. I couldn't sleep the night before with thinking about it. So when she comes in, I tell her what I'm thinking. My God, I thought . . ."

"What?"

"I thought, wow, the way she looked at me. And did she ever tell me off. Mind your own business, she says, and what do you know, she says. She's not hollering or anything, but, boy, I know she's really mad. Then she says she never wants to hear those two guys' names again. Never. And I tried to interrupt her to tell her maybe they know something, and that's when she tells me shut up. My God, Mario, I could've cried right there."

"Is that what makes you think something happened that weekend?"

"Huh? I don't follow you."

"Well, I mean you said you were thinking that before Tina acted that way."

"Oh yeah. Sure."

"So what do you think now?"

"Now? I'll tell you. Now I'm convinced. I mean, ain't you?" Mickey continued to pace about, pulling and tugging at his fingers. "Mario, this'll maybe sound funny, but I'm really glad you came. My God, you don't know what a relief it is to talk to somebody else about this. I haven't been able to talk to anybody about it. It's all inside—Frank, Tina, the business. It's like I'm in a pressure cooker and something's wrong with the valve. I think sometimes I'm going to explode. My God, I didn't get two hours' sleep last night. And without the pills I wouldn't even get that much . . . but the thing that really convinced me, to get back to this thing I started to say, well, how did Frank get out of here? I mean, the truck's here. He never had a car. Always a truck. Used to get a new one every two years. So how'd he leave from here if it wasn't with those two guys?"

"Did you ever stop to think that he never came back?"

"What?"

"You said yourself you never saw him after he left that Friday, right?"

"My God, I never thought of that." Mickey stopped his pacing and clasped his fingers together on top of his head. "You see what a real smart guy I am."

"Course that wouldn't explain how the truck got here," Balzic said.

"Huh?"

"Nothing. I was just thinking out loud. Say, do you think I could go over to talk to Tina?"

"Huh? Oh no, you better not."

"Why not?"

" 'Cause she told me never to come in there. And if she won't let me in there, Mario, well . . ."

"Uh, Mickey, how long's she been living there?"

"About three months. I'll tell you exactly." He reached into his pants again for the thick wallet. He found another scrap of paper. "Yeah. Here it is. She came back three months ago yesterday."

"Where was she living before that?"

"Well, you know, I held onto my parents' house in Norwood, and she lived there. Then about a month after Frank didn't come back, she said she had to get out of here. So I said—"

"Get out of here?" Balzic interrupted.

"Oh you know. Not out of that house. I mean here. Every place. She said this place was making her crazy. She said she couldn't stay around here any more. So I said, where you going to go? And she said she wanted to go to Theresey's for a while. In Toledo. Theresey's the oldest girl, Mario. You remember her."

"Yeah. I remember. She married Tony Ianni. Did she go? Tina?"

"Yeah. I drove her up. And she stayed there a year. Then, like I said, she came back. I didn't know she was coming. She just showed up here three months ago yesterday. I don't even know how she got here. She must've took a bus."

"And she moved right into the trailer?"

"Yeah."

"Didn't you think that was a little strange?"

"Tell you the truth, I did. But she was acting so funny for so long, I thought if that's going to make her feel any better, let her. The place was just sitting here. What could it hurt?"

"She ever in it before? I mean when Frank was here?"

"Oh yeah. Sure. I told you, they were getting ready to get married. She was in it lots of times."

"Mickey, don't get mad when I ask you this, okay?"

"Don't get mad about what?"

"Well, she's your sister. . . ."

"Go ahead, Mario. I won't get mad."

"She ever spend the night there?"

"Ah, Mario, none of us are kids. She was no kid either. What they did, I didn't think about. I didn't ask about it either. And what I saw, I pretended I didn't see. Besides, they were talking about marriage. Anyway, it was with Frank. It wasn't with some stranger, some guy she met someplace. I mean, until this, you know, I thought he was, ah, never mind what I thought."

"So she did spend some time with him?"

"Sure. What do you think? But I'll tell you what. I thought it would be good for them. Frank, he used to bring some real floozies home sometimes. I used to wonder where he found them. Real skags, you know? I never said anything to him, understand, but I'll tell you, there were times when I'd find myself praying a little bit that he wouldn't catch nothing. My God, there would've went our license. . . ."

"How long were they going together?"

"You know, Mario, it was real funny. Tina worked for us since the summers when she was in high school. And Frank, he never looked like he knew she was around, and then all of a sudden, it's like he can't think about anybody else. That was about three years ago. Then they were always together, I mean, except for the times when he was with Peluzzi and Janeski. Frank took her hunting, fishing. Heck, he even taught her how to dress game. That was real funny. She was around this business practically all her life, and she never once so much as asked how you do it. Then, deer season two years ago, she even helped out in the back, you know, when we got jammed up."

"She helping you now?"

"That's another funny thing. I asked her to help me, 'cause, you know, now I really need the help, but now she's like she was before. She don't go near the back. Otherwise, I wouldn't've felt free to put Frank's stuff back there."

"I see," Balzic said. "Well, listen, Mickey, I'll get in touch with that lawyer for you. I have to go now. But I'll be in touch, okay?"

"Mario, before you go, I mean, you been asking a lot of questions. What do you think?"

"Not much of anything right now," Balzic lied. "I just wish to hell you'd called me when Frank didn't show up. Fifteen months is a long time. But don't worry. I'll be thinking about it. And I'll keep in touch," he said, going out to his car.

He sat in the car for a few seconds, looking at the pickup and the trailer where Frank Gallic had once lived and where Tina Samarra was now living. "I'll be damned," he said, and then turned the car around and drove back along Route 331, heading into Rocksburg until he came to Five Point Intersection, there turning up Willow Creek Road to go the back way to the state police station.

He parked in the area reserved for people taking driving tests and went in through a back door, nodding to troopers he knew as he made his way into the duty room. A portly female typist Balzic didn't know was transcribing something from a recording machine; a trooper Balzic had seen once or twice was seated at the radio console directing extra mobile units to an accident; and Corporal Ed Bielski was talking to a citizen at the front counter.

Balzic stood by the counter and smoked until Bielski finished with the citizen.

"Mario," Bielski said, "how goes it?"

"It goes. Sideways, backwards, but it goes. Where's Minyon?"

"The lieutenant," Bielski said, "is hard at it, doing his duty behind a bunch of bloodhounds."

"He got fresh dogs in already? I'll bet the handlers liked that."

"Thrilled beyond belief. At least that's what I heard. I wasn't here."

"They got here before you came on?"

"An hour before I came on to be exact. And Lieutenant Minyon was waiting for them. He also had a certain sergeant with him. I think you know the man. Stallcup? Seems he was up and about at that hour because you recommended him to the lieutenant. Least that's what I hear."

"Stallcup pretty hot about it, huh?"

"I hear he wants to speak many words with you."

"What the hell," Balzic said. "It'll do him good to chase Minyon around the boonies. He's putting on a little grease."

"I'll tell him you said that," Bielski said. "So, Mario, what can I do for you?"

"I just want to borrow a typewriter for a while, that's all. I promised Minyon a list of names."

"Help yourself. You know where everything is. Anything else?"

"Yeah, there's one thing you could do, if you would. Call Rocksburg Savings and Loan. Tell them it's routine but confidential. Here's the names. Find out what these two got, what's been taken out and put in and approximate dates for, say, the last year and a half." Balzic wrote on a pad the names of Michael Samarra and Frank Gallic and pushed the pad around to Bielski.

"That's easy enough. Anything else?"

"Well, you might ask if they happen to know who these two carry insurance with. They might know, they might not. It's a long shot."

"Good enough. You know where the typewriters are."

"I'll find one," Balzic said, and set off through the maze of offices and cubicles to find a machine not in use. He located one after a minute or two and, using his index fingers, he pecked out the three names and addresses of Janeski, Peluzzi, and Gallic. When he'd finished, he wondered why he'd even bothered, just as he wondered why Minyon was out with the dogs.

Minyon, of course, didn't know what he knew and so would naturally be out looking for what he could find, trying in his own way to establish identity. Still, Balzic couldn't help thinking it was a waste of time and energy: a positive identification of the bones would only prove what he already knew.

He walked back into the duty room as Bielski was hanging up the phone.

"What did you come up with, Ed?" Balzic asked.

"Couple of pretty rich guys, these two. This Samarra had over twenty grand in his account. Twenty-one thousand, one hundred and fifty-three bucks, give or take some change. What the hell's he do?"

"He's a butcher. Just a dumb butcher. Nice guy, but dumb."

74 K. C. CONSTANTINE

"The other one, Gallic, he's not too bad off either. He's got eleven thousand and four bucks and change. He a butcher too?"

"He was."

"Regular deposits for Samarra," Bielski said, reading from his notes, "but the other one hasn't made any deposits since the June before last."

"Figures. How about withdrawals?"

"Every three months for both of them. The amount varies, but never more than three hundred bucks."

"They say who made the withdrawals?"

"Apparently this Samarra."

"Also figures. They say anything about who they have their insurance with?"

"Yeah. We got lucky there. Their agent just happens to be one of the directors of the savings and loan."

"So?"

"Seems they're partners—"

"Yeah."

"—so they had a big fire, theft, storm, and liability policy on the business, a Galsam's something or other."

"Freezer Meats."

"Yeah, that's it. Anyway, it's all-inclusive and pretty big. This Samarra had life insurance, fifty thousand worth, with his sister, a Christina Marie Samarra, as beneficiary. The other one, Gallic, seems he didn't believe in it. Both of them had medical insurance which, in addition to covering all the usual expenses including major medical, also paid them fifteen bucks a day so long as they were unable to work. That's about it."

"It's about what I expected," Balzic said. "Thanks, Ed."

"Don't mention it. What have you got there?"

"This is the list Minyon wanted. Tell him it's here when he gets back."

"Is this about the bones?"

"Yeah."

"Just yeah? Nothing else? You don't want me to tell Minyon anything else?"

"Why? Do I look like I got something else to tell him?"

"I don't know, Mario. You sort of look like you know something."

"Oh, I know lots of things, Ed. Trouble is, none of them makes too goddamn much sense right now." Balzic headed for the back door. "Listen, Minyon wants me, tell him I'll be down my station until eleven or so, then I'll be out the club range until noon. Afterwards, back at the station until four-thirty or so and then home for a while. Okay?"

"Okay, Mario. He'll be asking. See you later."

Balzic went out to his car thinking that he'd hate to be in Bielski's place. Bielski had to have learned by now how Minyon felt about Polacks; Minyon wasn't nearly subtle enough to hide his prejudice, and Bielski wasn't due for a transfer for at least a year. If that wasn't enough, Bielski should have made sergeant six months ago, and it was common knowledge that he was smarting about his test result. Given those preconditions, Balzic wished he could observe Bielski when Minyon returned: how much of what Bielski learned in the past half hour would he tell Minyon? how would he say it? would he say anything at all without being prodded? Poor Bielski, Balzic thought. The best he could hope for was an early transfer, and with luck, he'd get sent to Wilkes-Barre, to where Minyon had just come from.

Balzic pulled into the space reserved for him at city hall and went into the station just as Patrolman Larry Fischetti, in street clothes, was parking his car.

Desk Sergeant Angelo Clemente was busy at the radio. A mattress fire in somebody's attic was tying up traffic in The Bottoms, the section of Rocksburg on the flat by the Conemaugh River where a half dozen truck terminals and the larger mills and fabricating plants were located. From Clemente's face, Balzic could see what a mess it was, but he didn't interfere, proceeding instead to the live file. He rooted out the file on Roland Bivins and took it back to one of the interrogation cubicles, there to wait for Fischetti.

"Back here, Fish," Balzic called out.

Fischetti, in his early twenties, recently returned from Vietnam, a heavyweight wrestler in high school, came into the cubicle looking, Balzic thought, too intimidated for anybody's good.

"Sit down, Fish," Balzic said, pushing the Bivins file around so Fischetti could read it. "Okay, so explain this."

"I screwed up," Fischetti said, without looking at the file.

"Hey, goddammit, I ain't a priest. I don't want a confession. I want an explanation."

"I did everything wrong. I lost my head. The kid got me hot and I just forgot everything."

"More interpretation I don't want. Will you just tell me what happened?"

"Well, I was on my beat and I made my call in from the box and Stramsky tells me to check out a disturbance in the diner. Romeo's place. It's late. I'm getting ready to go off. I'm tired. I'd been out with my dogs all morning—"

"So?"

"—so anyway, I go in and there's this little fart hollering his head off. I can't make sense of what it's all about, but as soon as he sees me, he starts in on me. 'Here comes the pig,' he says. Now meanwhile, there are about four or five others in a booth, and I'm thinking, hell, man, watch yourself. You do this wrong, you could really screw things up. So I walk back to him, you know, easy, and I haven't said a word. I stop about three, four feet away from him, and I ask him what's going on. He says, 'None of your business, motherfucker,' and he calls me a pig again, and I look at him and I think, Christ, he's just a kid. Can't be fifteen. Meanwhile Romeo is going nuts. He's hollering at me, the kid's hollering at me, the other spooks in the booth, they're laughing, and everybody else in the place—I don't know, I could just feel everybody watching me to see what I was going to do."

"So what did you do?"

"Chief, honest to God, I don't remember what I did. All I know is, the next thing I had him outside. I had a real good take-along on him. He couldn't move. Which was no big thing. I mean, I had him by forty pounds at least."

"And?"

"Well, he wouldn't shut up. He just kept calling me names, motherfucker and pig and honkie. I think I told him to shut up or he was going to get hurt."

"Beautiful," Balzic said. "So then what?"

"Well, I got him to the call box and I tried to call in for a mobile unit, but he's hollering at me so loud, cars are stopping and Stramsky can't hear what I'm saying and I'm getting hotter by the second. So the only way I can figure to get him to shut up is to make the take-along tighter. You know, put it on him so it hurts."

"And you did."

"Yeah. I put the phone down and I got a new grip. I really wanted to break his arm."

"What then?"

"I told him if he didn't shut up I would. Break his arm, I mean. And he did. The mobile got there, and I put him in and brought him down here."

"What time was that?"

"Well, it was after twenty-four hundred. I knew that because Stramsky was gone and Royer was on the desk."

"Then what?"

"Then I put him in the lockup."

"And?"

"That's when I really screwed up. I was shaking so bad, I just filled out the report half assed and I went home."

"Half assed is right. What did you tell Royer?"

"I don't even remember talking to Royer."

Balzic rubbed his mouth and sighed. "Christ . . ."

"Chief, I've been thinking about it ever since it happened. I was going to come and tell you about it every day, but I couldn't. . . . I think I ought to quit. I don't think I'm cut out for this."

"That's right," Balzic said, "add self-pity to it. That makes it perfect. Listen to this, goddammit, you're not quitting. But I'll tell you what you are going to do. You're going to explain this to a certain black preacher. And then you're going to spend some time talking to somebody else I know. Goddammit, there's no excuse for what you did. None. I mean I can understand taking the heat because a snot calls you names. That I can understand. But that doesn't mean you forget everything you know. This report is absolutely inexcusable. And Christ almighty, not bothering to arraign the kid—Jesus, Fish, what the hell were you thinking about? You don't even know what happened to the kid."

"Royer told me a couple days later he held him for a couple hours and then called his mother and let him go."

"Yeah. A couple days later you find out!" Balzic took out his notebook and wrote down two names. "Here. You call these two people and you arrange to see them. At their earliest convenience, you got that?"

"Yes, sir." Fischetti looked at the names. "Who are they?"

"That Callum is the black preacher. He's the one who brought this mess to my attention. I had to hear it from him in a city council meeting, for crissake. The other one, Higgins, is a psychologist."

"A what?" Fischetti looked deeply injured.

"You heard me right. A psychologist. He's a little, skinny, light-skinned spook. Maybe, if you pay attention, he'll teach you something about dealing with spooks. If nothing else, maybe he'll convince you they're just people, because right now I have the feeling you don't think so. And don't worry about paying him. That'll come out of department funds. But you're going to have to arrange your own transportation and you won't get reimbursed for that. He's in Pittsburgh. And I want to know by tomorrow—no later—that you arranged to see these guys. You hear me? No later than tomorrow."

"Yes, sir."

"All right. Now get out of here and do it. One more thing."

"What's that?"

"Forget about quitting, understand? 'Cause I won't let you."

"Yes, sir."

"And get your chin up off your chest, for crissake. Everybody fucks up once in a while."

"Yeah. Sure."

"Change your tone, goddammit. Everybody does fuck up once in a while. How do you think I feel? I didn't even know about this until last week, and then I had to stand there like a jerk and tell the whole damn council I didn't know anything about it. And you think that spook was calling you names? What the hell do you think they're calling me? And you know what? I rate a few of those names. Not all of them, understand. But a few."

"Yes, sir."

Balzic made as though he was going to punch Fischetti. Instead, he gave him a light slap and then pinched his cheek. "Get out of here now," he said. "Go have a beer and call those two guys. And learn something from this," he called out as Fischetti was heading for the door.

"What's the matter with the kid?" Clemente said.

"He's a kid, that's what's the matter with him. But keep your fingers crossed anyway, Angelo. If we're lucky, we won't get sued."

Driving out to the Rod and Gun Club rifle range, Balzic tried to empty his mind of all the questions crowding in and yammering to be answered. He succeeded as long as he was shooting. The demands of the Springfield 30.06, aiming, breathing, squeezing off the shots, took all his concentration. It was the primary reason he liked to shoot. As much as he was shooting to keep himself proficient and prepared, he fired his twenty rounds at the silhouette targets to forget whatever else was pressing in on him. It was impossible to shoot well and think about anything else.

The moment he bent down to pick up the last empty cartridge case, the questions started to form, and by the time he'd taken down the targets and rolled them, his mind was again a jangle.

Gallic. Frank Gallic . . .

The name kept rushing to the front of his mind, so that Balzic, without being aware of it, was saying the name aloud as he put the targets in the trunk of his car and slipped the Springfield into its case. He stood with his hand on the trunk lid and asked himself who Frank Gallic was.

As defined by Mickey Samarra, Frank Gallic was hardly more than a shadow. The words Mickey had used to describe him: "best friend," "used to drink a lot sometimes," "used to bring some real floozies home sometimes," "used to fish at night," "must've had fifteen heads . . . animals I didn't even know the names of"—what did all that add up to?

And how had Janeski described him? Hell, Balzic thought, Janeski hadn't described him—he'd just reacted to his name. The closest Janeski had come to describing him was with that name he'd almost called him.

And why had Peluzzi's face lost its color at the mere mention of Gallic's name?

And why did two men who spent as much time with a third as those two had with Gallic suddenly stop seeing him?

". . . he must've had fifteen heads," Mickey Samarra had said, meaning, of course, the animals Frank Gallic had killed, but Balzic couldn't help wondering how many heads Frank Gallic had. How many and which ones did he show to Mickey

Samarra? How many and which to Janeski and Peluzzi? How many and which to Tina Samarra?

So we come back to that, Balzic thought. No matter how many other questions rocketed around in his mind, that one always returned to push aside the others: how many heads did Gallic show Tina? How many, that she should insist that all those other heads, those mounted ones, had to be thrown out? How many, that Gallic's pickup truck should appear to her—according to her brother—not to exist? How many, that, after a month after Gallic had not appeared after that fishing trip to Tionesta, she should go to Toledo and stay for a year? How many, that she should come back, again according to her brother, without announcing her intention to come back? How many, that she should move into the place where Gallic had lived, into the trailer where the two of them had spent how much time together and how many nights?

Balzic slammed the trunk lid and got behind the wheel of his car.

Mickey, he thought, she's your sister, and I respected your wish not to bother her before, but, dammit, I have to talk to her. Maybe she won't let me in that trailer, but in the yard, in the business, in this car, somewhere, she's going to talk to me. Somewhere, somehow, whether she wants to or not, she's going to tell me why she's living in that trailer.

It was ten minutes after twelve when Balzic pulled into Galsam's parking lot. He had just put his hand on the door handle to get out when his call signal came over the radio.

"Balzic here," he said into the mike.

"Lieutenant Minyon here, Balzic. We got lucky today. I thought you might be interested."

"How so?"

"The dogs turned up another bone a little after eight this morning, and I had one of my people run it over to the coroner."

"Same fit?"

"The same, but not the same. This one, the tibia, Grimes calls it, the left calf bone—turns out it was broken once, fairly recently. Within the past four or five years. That was Grimes's first guess."

"And?"

"Grimes X-rayed it and that confirmed the break. Then he checked with all the orthopedic surgeons in the area—turns out there are only six who specialize. Well, he just called me." Minyon paused.

Balzic could picture the expression of satisfaction behind that pause. "So what did he come up with?"

"Our bones finally have a name," Minyon said. "And strangely enough, that name is on the list you left with Bielski for me."

Balzic could not put up with Minyon's dramatic pauses any longer. "It was Gallic, right?"

The pause this time, if such could be said, was filled with disappointment. "How the hell did you know?"

"He was the only one it could've been," Balzic said. "Everybody else was accounted for."

"And just what else do you know that you haven't told me? What have you been doing?"

"Not much. Just sort of driving around. Why?"

"Well do you think you might be able to drive in here and tell me what this information you asked Bielski to get for you—what it has to do with everything? I'd like to know."

"So would I. I mean, I don't know what it means. I'll be in in a little while. I have to do some shopping now."

"Some what?"

"Shopping. You know, buying food for the table. I don't know about you, but I eat every once in a while. See you when I get there. Out." Balzic replaced the mike on its hook and got out while Minyon was still demanding him to come in.

Up yours, Jack, Balzic thought, and got out of the car. He went into the service section of Galsam's—where he'd talked to Mickey Samarra earlier—just as Tina Samarra was leaving her trailer.

He watched her come across the gravel drive. Stramsky had described her well: her face, though feminine and more comely, had as many hard edges as her brother's; she was short and sturdily built; she wore a white dress of the kind worn by waitresses and beauticians; and the white, low-heeled shoes and flesh-colored stockings she wore accentuated her very muscular calves. There was not a suggestion of make-up on her face, and her hair was cut short enough so that she probably never did anything but run a comb through it in the mornings. Pulled around her shoulders was a heavy wool sweater which she clutched at her throat. She passed the pickup truck—as Mickey had earlier tried to explain to Balzic—as though it wasn't there.

She paid no attention to Balzic until she'd gone through the levered door in the counter and put her sweater on a shelf under the counter. "Yes, sir," she said, "can I help you?" There wasn't a trace of a smile of salesmanship.

Balzic produced his ID. "I'd like to ask you some questions," he said after allowing her time to study the picture on his ID and compare it to his face.

Just then Mickey Samarra, his apron and sleeves smeared with blood, came through the wooden door in the back wall behind his sister. "Oh, you're here, Tina. I didn't—Mario, I didn't know it was you," he said.

"How would you?" Tina said. "You just got here. You got a peephole in the wall?" She had not turned around. Her gaze, curious about Balzic yet somehow remote, had not left Balzic's face.

Mickey shrugged as though to say to Balzic, you see? You see how she is? What did I tell you?

"I'd like to talk to Tina awhile, Mickey," Balzic said. "That okay with you?"

"If you want to talk to me, why don't you ask me?" Tina said. "Why are you asking him?"

"Because he's your—"

"My what? My brother?"

"Yes."

"That's right. That's what he is. No matter what he thinks he is, he's just my brother."

Mickey shook his head behind her, held up his arms, and let them drop to his sides. He turned, still shaking his head, and went out through the door he'd come in. Only then did Tina turn around, as though to be sure he'd gone. When she turned back, she folded her arms and waited, her eyes unwaveringly focused on Balzic's eyes.

"Mickey tells me, uh, you were supposed to get married."

"I was."

"You mind telling me what happened?"

"Yes, I mind. But that won't stop you. I can tell that. So the answer is you can't marry somebody who isn't there."

"Yes, but what I mean is, what happened? How come that somebody wasn't there?"

"That I wouldn't know."

"I'd ask him, you understand, but it seems he's not around."

"Looks like you're stuck then."

"You mean you have no idea why he's not around? You mean there was never any indication that he was going to not be around?"

"Oh, there were some indications all right. I just didn't pay attention to them. You never do, I hear. That's what it's supposed to be like, isn't it? Being in love? You don't see what's there? At least that's what I was told." For the first time, her face lost its stony composure. She smiled, but there was no pleasure in it. It had the suggestion of something more than irony, Balzic thought, but he hesitated to give it a name, thinking he might be seeing more than was there.

"How long did you know him?"

"Since I was a kid. Seven, eight, I don't know. He was always with Mickey. Since after the war."

"Mickey said you two didn't pay much attention to one another until just a couple years ago. I think he said it was three years ago."

"Mickey must've told you a lot."

"Well, not a lot, but some things."

"You talked to him long enough."

"Why? Were you watching us?"

"Watching other people is not my thing," she said. "I just heard your car this morning. When you came, when you left."

"Yeah, I guess it would be pretty hard not to hear. Your trailer's pretty close."

"It's not my trailer."

"Yeah, I was going to ask you about that." Balzic watched her face for some change, some twitch, some flicker of apprehension. She remained impassive.

"I've been living in it since I got back from Toledo. Mickey would've told you that. He probably knows to the hour how long. Probably has it written down on a little piece of paper in his wallet."

"As a matter of fact, he has. Three months ago yesterday, I think he said."

"Then he also told you I was living with our sister for a year."

"Yeah, he told me that, too."

"I guess he told you just about everything."

"No, not everything."

"He wouldn't. He wouldn't tell you how many times I slept with him."

"No, not how many times exactly. But he told me you did."

If that surprised her, she did not show it.

"Funny," Balzic said, "neither one of us has even said his name. For all we know, we could be talking about two different people."

"At least two different people," Tina said, "and there's nothing funny about it."

"No, I suppose there isn't. But just to keep things straight, I'm talking about Frank Gallic. That who you're talking about?"

"Yes."

"Just yes?"

"You asked me a question, I gave you an answer."

Balzic had to smile at that. He leaned on the counter and loosened his tie. "You know, there's a funny—well, not funny. Curious. There's a curious thing about this guy Gallic. I've talked to a couple of people about him, and all the people I talk to—except for Mickey, of course—they all don't seem to want to tell me one thing more than just exactly what I ask. You know what I mean? All except for Mickey."

"That's Mickey for you," Tina said, giving the faintest hint of a shrug.

"Mickey seems really baffled about the whole business. Hurt. And not just a little bit. Seems he's been hurt bad."

"No worse than anybody else. He just thinks so. Mickey just can't get over the idea he could do anything wrong."

"You knew better?" Balzic said quickly.

"I didn't say that. I—"

"I know what you said. What I asked you was whether you knew better."

"Any woman knows a man better than another man."

"Maybe so. But I'm not talking about any woman. Or any man. I'm talking about you and Frank Gallic."

"Then I'd still say the same thing."

"Which means, if I understand you, that you knew Gallic a lot better than Mickey did."

"Oh my God, anybody would know him better than Mickey did. Mickey's my brother, but he's dumb. All he knows is business. He's in his trailer, he's in here working, he goes to pick up the animals, he goes to the gas station, he goes to church. His whole life is right there."

"Yours isn't?"

"Now? I guess I'm no different, so I shouldn't talk."

"But it used to be different. When you were with Gallic?"

"You know the answer to that."

"Was it good?"

"What's that supposed to mean?"

"Just what it sounds like. Was your life good with him?"

"For a while, yes, I suppose."

"What changed it?"

"I don't know. I saw some things."

"Like what things?"

"Things things. I don't remember. I just saw some things."

"For somebody who claims a woman knows a man better than any man, you aren't too specific."

"I don't like to talk about it. When you don't like to talk about something, it gets sort of fuzzy. You forget the things you don't want to talk about, and pretty soon you don't even remember what you were trying to forget—if you're lucky."

"Well, if you don't mind, I'd like you to try and remember those things."

"Sure you would. That's what all you . . ."

"All you what? All you men? That what you were going to say?"

"What if I was?"

"Well, just because one man goes bad on you, especially when you thought he was good, that doesn't mean all men are bad, does it?"

"I'd like to hear what the women you know would say about that."

"I've got a mother, a wife, and two daughters. They all live with me, and I don't think they think I'm too bad. I could be kidding myself," Balzic said, smiling.

"You probably are."

"Oh, you got it bad. He must've been a real bastard. Underneath, I mean."

"You wouldn't have had to go too deep."

"But there was something about him. There must've been something good about him, otherwise, you wouldn't be as mad as you are."

"Mad isn't the word for it."

"What is the word then?"

Tina's gaze for the first time left Balzic's eyes. She looked out the large plate-glass window in the direction of the trailer. Then she turned back to Balzic, but she said nothing, looking at him again as she had all along, directly in the eyes.

"What's the word, Tina?"

She said nothing.

"Okay," Balzic said, "so when was the last time you saw him?"

"Over a year ago. Fifteen, sixteen months, I don't know. Mickey would know. He has it written down in his wallet."

"He left to go fishing on the twenty-sixth of July. It was a Friday. The following Monday morning, the truck was here, but he wasn't. That's what Mickey told me. Now when was the last time you saw him?"

Before she could answer, a state police cruiser wheeled into the parking lot. The doors flew open and stayed open. Two troopers got out of the front seat and Lieutenant Minyon got out of the back. He led the troopers in.

"Lieutenant," Balzic said, nodding to Minyon.

Minyon ignored Balzic and spoke to Tina. "I'm looking for a Michael Samarra. Would you please get him."

Balzic looked at the paper folded in Minyon's hand. He knew what it was, but he didn't want to believe it. "What do you have there, Lieutenant?"

"I asked you to please notify Michael Samarra that I want to see him," Minyon said to Tina. To the two troopers he said, "Check around back and in the trailers."

"Just a minute," Tina said, "I'll get him." She reached under the counter for a small intercom phone and said into it, "Mickey, come out front."

"What do you got there?" Balzic repeated to Minyon.

"That should be obvious," Minyon said. "Later on, chief, you can explain to me why you didn't come back to the barracks when I asked you. For now, I'll tell you that I didn't appreciate your little joke about shopping. I'll also tell you there are a couple of things you better tell yourself."

"Oh yeah? Like what things?"

"Like who you are and who I am."

"Oh? I, uh, thought I had a pretty good idea who—"

He didn't get to finish. Mickey Samarra came in then, wiping his hands on his apron, looking quite stupefied at the sight of the three state policemen.

"What—what's the matter?"

"Are you Michael Samarra?" Minyon said.

Mickey swallowed and nodded. "Yes—yes. I am."

"I have a warrant for your arrest. It is my duty to inform you that you are entitled to remain silent, that you are entitled to legal counsel, and that anything you say may be used against you in a court of law. Do you understand the rights I've just explained to you?"

"Mario," Mickey said, "what's he talking about?"

"Do you understand your rights as I have explained them to you?" Minyon said, emphasizing each syllable.

"Just tell him you understand, Mickey," Balzic said.

"Okay. I—sure," Mickey said. "I understand. But how come? What for?"

"You're under arrest for suspicion of the murder of one Frank Joseph Gallic."

"The what?" Mickey said, blanching.

Balzic kept watching Tina. She didn't move, she hardly blinked while the two troopers, at Minyon's direction, led Mickey out to their cruiser.

Minyon said at the door, "You've still got some explaining to do, Balzic."

"Don't I know it," Balzic said.

"Men," Tina said, picking up her sweater and thrusting her arms into the sleeves. "Well," she said to Balzic, "what are you waiting for?"

"I was waiting to see what you were going to do."

"Jesus Christ," she said, "what do you think I'm going to do? I'm going with him." Before she could arrange the closed sign in the window of the front door, the state police cruiser was backing out of the lot. She jerked open the door and shouted, "Wait!" but Minyon ignored her and ordered the trooper driving to get going.

"Come on," Balzic said, "I'll drive you."

"You bastards probably had it planned this way," Tina said.

"You can think what you want," Balzic said, going out to his car, "but I give you my word, I didn't have anything to do with this. I'm as surprised as you are."

"I'll just bet you are." She made sure the door was locked and then hurried over to the trailer. In a few seconds she was out, carrying a small black purse. She stopped to make doubly sure the trailer door was locked, pulling on it and twisting the knob each time. She had barely closed the car door when she said, "Well? What the hell are you waiting for? They'll have him talking in circles in five minutes."

Balzic knew better than to try to pick up where they'd been when Minyon came marching in on them. At first he wanted to try, but when he could hear the noises she made smoking, he knew it would be less than useless. He could only aggravate her into a deeper resistance, and that was the one thing he did not want to do.

In the parking lot at the state police station she turned to him and said, "If you know a lawyer—a good one—I'd appreciate it if you'd get him."

It surprised him. He had assumed she didn't allow herself the luxury of asking favors. "For Mickey?" he said.

"For who else?" she said, slamming the door and breaking into a run across the lot and up the steps into the station.

Balzic got Sergeant Angelo Clemente on the radio and told him to locate Mo Valcanas. "God knows where he'll be," Balzic said. "If he isn't in court or in his office, try Muscotti's or the back room of the bowling alleys. Rocksburg Bowl. When you get him, tell him an innocent citizen is being persecuted by the state police. That should get his ass in gear."

Balzic could have tried himself to locate Valcanas from inside the station, but he didn't want to miss more than he had to. It was going to be interesting to see how Minyon handled this. For a very brief moment, Balzic almost felt a twinge of sympathy for Minyon. The pompous ass had no idea what he had let himself in for with Tina Samarra. Ah well, Balzic thought as he went inside to the duty room, it'll serve him right.

Corporal Ed Bielski was standing at the front counter rubbing his eyes when Balzic walked in.

"S'matter, Ed," Balzic said in a low voice, "got something in your eye?"

"Yeah," Bielski said. "A lieutenant."

"Where are they?"

"In his office, I guess."

"Ed, a couple of things. What kind of warrant did he have?"

"John Doe."

"So he hasn't notified the DA's office yet?"

"Hell, no."

"One more thing. How did he manage to jump to the conclusion that his man was Samarra? Was it from what the savings and loan said?"

"How he jumps anywhere is something you have to ask him. But if you mean did he get the idea from that, I'd have to say yes. He stood around for a couple of minutes after he called you, then he snapped his fingers, and he was off."

"Thanks, Ed," Balzic said, ducking under the counter. He

leaned close to Bielski in passing and said, "Just keep in mind there's always the chance he could get killed in the line of duty."

"His kind never gets killed for crissake," Bielski said. "What I'm hoping for is somebody'll offer me a job as head guard at a hospital or something."

Balzic made his way around the desk and down the short corridor to Minyon's office. He opened the door quietly and stepped inside and took an unobtrusive position in a corner next to a filing cabinet.

Tina Samarra, arms folded and clutching her purse, her face as impassive as ever, had stationed herself at her brother's side. Minyon sat on the front edge of his desk and worked a pencil in his hands as though it were a swagger stick. Mickey Samarra, still in his work clothes, the smell of blood and cow dung fresh on him, sat stiffly on a straight-backed chair, his thick hands on his knees.

". . . and you're trying to tell me that your partner has been missing for more than fifteen months and you never once thought to call the police?" Minyon said.

"You don't have to answer that," Tina said, as the stenographer worked to keep up.

"Tina, please," Mickey said, his eyes rolling.

It struck Balzic that Mickey may have been around cattle too long; his eyes had taken on the bovine cast of dull apprehension.

"This is the last time I'm going to warn you, miss," Minyon said, holding his gaze on Mickey as he spoke, "you interrupt again and I'm going to have you put out of this room, bodily if necessary."

"Sure, that's right. Threaten me," Tina said. "But I heard what you said about his rights, and you can't promise him those things one minute and take them away the next."

"Tina, please," Mickey said. "I know what he said. I got nothing to hide."

Minyon pressed a button on his intercom. "I want two men in here," he said.

"Sure!" Tina snapped. "Get two more. That's just perfect. Why don't you bring all your friends in? Give everybody a chance!" Her face twisted in fury.

Again Balzic was surprised. He had not thought her likely to lose control. Yet the more closely he watched her in the next few seconds, the less certain he was that she *had* lost control. If anything, her fury seemed fully under control, and the more furious for it.

The door opened and two troopers, both over six feet tall, came in.

"You better not let them touch me," Tina said to Minyon, "or so help me God, you'll be sorry."

"Get her out of here," Minyon said, turning his back on them and walking around his desk to look out a window.

The first trooper reached out to put his hand on Tina's arm. She whipped her purse across his face. Before he could back away, she kicked him in the shin and started him hopping. The second trooper had started to move toward her, but apparently thought better of it.

Balzic glared at Minyon's back, swore to himself, and stepped between the two troopers and Tina. Mickey by this time was up and confronting the troopers, the cow-like glaze in his eyes turned to something bullish.

"Hold it!" Balzic said. "Everybody just hold it. Sit down, Mickey. Everything's all right." Balzic bent down to pick up Tina's purse and handed it to her.

"I said to remove her," Minyon said, his back still to them. "And remove Balzic too."

"Uh, lieutenant," the second trooper said, "which one is that?"

Minyon spun around. "Who's in charge here?" he shouted. "I am! Get that woman and that man out of here!" His right arm shot out, the pencil quivering at Balzic.

"That's right. I'm Balzic and he's in charge. Tina, come along. We don't want to make things more difficult than they are. Come along, it's all right. Mickey doesn't have anything to hide. He'll be all right."

"Out!" Minyon roared. "And you. Samarra! Sit down!"

"Come on, Tina," Balzic said, holding out his hand to guide her out the door but being careful not to touch her.

"Mickey," Tina said as she started for the door, "you remember what he said before, this big man. This real big man. You don't have to say anything."

"Tina, I don't have nothing to hide," Mickey said, his eyes going soft again.

"After you," Balzic said to the two troopers, the one having a time trying to walk and rub his shin.

"And book her for assaulting a police officer," Minyon said as the four of them left the office.

"Don't bother," Balzic said after he'd closed the door.

"What do you mean, don't bother?" the first trooper said. "She could've put my eye out with that damn purse."

" 'Cause I'm a witness," Balzic said, "that's why don't bother. You'll tell one story, your partner'll tell one, she'll tell one, and I'll tell another. And believe me, I know the magistrates in this town better than you two do. Better than Minyon does. Believe me, it won't get past the magistrate's office, so what's the point?"

"He's the point," the second trooper said, pointing with his thumb toward Minyon's closed door.

"Ah, forget him. You two hang around here long enough, you'll be looking for something to book him on, so let's just forget it, all right? Let me worry about him. Go talk to Corporal Bielski. He'll tell you about me. In case you don't know, I'm chief of police here."

The troopers looked at one another. The trooper Tina kicked said, "I hope you know what you're doing. As for you, sister, you better thank somebody I got a lot of patience."

"I'm not your sister, and from the looks of you, I'd say patience was all you had."

Balzic winced. "Okay, Tina, that's enough. It's over now. Let's just forget it, okay? What do you say?"

"Tell them," she said.

"Go on, fellas. Go talk to Bielski. He'll tell you I know what I'm doing. And if you don't believe him, go talk to Ralph Stallcup."

"I don't know," the first trooper said, rubbing his face where he'd been hit by the purse and glaring at Tina.

"I say we go talk to Bielski," the other trooper said.

"Okay. But I'm telling you, lady—"

"You can't tell me anything, buster. You ever put your hands on me again, you'll get a lot worse."

"For your information, dearie, I didn't touch you."

"Like hell you didn't. You grabbed me. Right here," Tina said, holding up her left arm.

"Enough, for crying out loud," Balzic said. "Tina, here. Sit down over here. Go on, you two. Go talk to Bielski."

The troopers shrugged at one another and walked off toward the duty room, the one still favoring his leg and rubbing his face.

Balzic pointed to one of the three chairs along the wall outside Minyon's office. "Have a seat, Tina. Go on."

"I'll stand."

"Okay, suit yourself. I got to tell you something, though. That trooper was right. He never touched you."

"He was going to. That's the same thing."

"Uh, maybe you think so, but I'll tell you what. If it ever really came down to it in a magistrate's office, I couldn't lie about it."

"Then why'd you tell them you would? You looking for something?"

"Oh for crissake," Balzic said, sitting in the chair closest to Minyon's door and putting his face in his hands. "You don't quit, do you?"

"I will," she said, looking straight ahead. "When I'm ready."

"What does that mean?"

"I'll tell you that, too. When I'm ready."

Balzic tried again to study her face, and again had to give it up without coming to any satisfactory conclusion. An idea was beginning to form though, murky and with only a few clear edges, and he was trying to help it along without knowing what it was when Minyon's voice carried through the door.

"You're lying!" Minyon shouted.

Balzic turned in the chair and put his ear close to the door.

"I swear to you on my mother's grave I wouldn't do that to Frank," came Mickey's voice. "Frank was my friend. We went through a war together . . . we were partners for twenty-five years—"

"And you were tired of having a partner!"

"Why? Why would I get tired of that? I didn't want nothing. I had everything I want. My God, you said you checked our savings. You had to see I had more than Frank. . . ."

"That son of a bitch," Tina said.

Balzic thought at first she'd meant Minyon, but when he looked up at her, he wasn't so sure. Had she meant Frank? He didn't know. All he knew for certain was that he had never met a woman before who was so able to conceal her thoughts. Had she worked at that? Or had circumstances forced the ability on her?

". . . had everything you want. Had! That's your word, Samarra," Minyon said. "I'm telling you, you didn't have everything you wanted. You wanted the business. All of it. All for yourself."

"But that's crazy. I paid taxes for Frank. I kept up his end. If I wanted the business, if I didn't want Frank for a partner no more, how come I did that? Mario told me I was nuts for doing that. And now you're telling me that's how you know I did . . ."

"Did what? What did you do? Murder your partner? And then saw him up in little pieces? I know that much, Samarra. I know how your partner was taken apart. It was with a butcher's saw."

Balzic stood up. "Listen, Tina, I'm going out front and make a phone call. Do yourself a favor. You and Mickey. Don't go back in there, will you?"

She said nothing for a moment. Then, as though she had not heard him, she asked, "Did you get a lawyer?"

"I didn't call him, no, but I told somebody to call him. He's a tough man to find sometimes. But he'll be here, don't worry about that. Okay? Just don't go back in there."

"Go make your phone call and leave me alone."

"All right," Balzic said. "All right. I'll leave you alone." He went out to the duty room, saw the two troopers huddled with Bielski in a far corner, and went to the opposite side of the room and dialed the coroner's office. A secretary answered.

"This is Mario Balzic. I'd like to ask Dr. Grimes some questions."

There was a click, a pause, and then Grimes said, "Mario, what can I do for you?"

"Answer a couple questions. Number one, how are you so positive the bones used to be Frank Gallic? I mean, I don't doubt it for a second, but I just want to know how positive you are."

"His tibia was fractured, Mario. I called all the orthopedic people I knew and had them check their records. Joe Statti was the one who came up with it. He remembered setting a tibia on about that approximate place four years ago. He brought his X rays over, and it was a simple matter. We just put one picture on top of the other and they matched."

"No possibility that somebody else could have had a break just like it?"

"Like it, yes. But not exactly like it. I imagine a professional oddsmaker would give you a million to one that two fractures would occur in the same way on the same place on the same

98   K. C. CONSTANTINE

bone, but he'd be leading a sucker on. The odds are more like a couple hundred million to one. There's no question about it. Even a layman would recognize it. All he'd have to do is look at the pictures."

"Okay. The second thing is, have you figured out what kind of instrument was used to saw them? Could you be sure of that?"

"No. All I can say with certainty is that it was some kind of fine-toothed saw."

"You wouldn't say it was a butcher's saw?"

"Mario, if you sent that question to the FBI, and you gave them enough time and enough different saw blades and enough bones to make a statistically satisfactory comparison, maybe you could get one of their people to testify to that effect. But I'm not going to get on any witness stand in any court and make any such statement. Even if I wanted to find out, I just don't have the equipment here or the time to make such an investigation."

"Then where the hell is Minyon getting the idea that it was a butcher's saw?"

"I suggest you ask him," Grimes said. "All I can tell you is that he didn't get it from me."

"Okay, Doc. Thanks. Sorry to bother you."

"No bother. Sorry I can't tell you what you want to know."

Balzic hung up and started past Bielski and the two troopers.

"What's General Minyon doing now?" Bielski said.

"The general. Yeah," Balzic said. "I guess that's what he's trying to do—make general. But I'll tell you what. All he's doing is making an ass out of himself. Which won't take too much doing."

Balzic was about to start down the corridor when he was hailed from behind. Myron Valcanas, listing a couple degrees to the right, his black fedora askew, eyes flecked red, a bandage across the brow of his right eye, put his hands on the counter and let out a long, ginny breath.

"Mario, just where the hell is this citizen who's being persecuted by these boy scouts?"

"Oh shit," Bielski said.

"Who's that?" the trooper who'd been kicked asked.

"That, young buddy, is the champion drunk of Conemaugh County, and he just loves us," Bielski said.

"He a lawyer?"

"Yeppie. And oh would I like to be there when he gets hold of Minyon."

"Back here, Mo," Balzic said.

Valcanas came through the counter door in the shuffling gait of one whose nerve ends had long since been burned ragged by alcohol. He tipped his hat to a typist. "Madam," he said, "how nice to see a flower among so many weeds."

The typist, a plain, plump woman, blushed and chewed her lower lip.

"Gentlemen," Valcanas said to Bielski and the other troopers, "how reassuring to know there are still weeds."

"Afternoon, Mo," Bielski said.

"Is that you, Bielski? Christ, you're so drunk I can hardly see you."

"What happened to your eye?"

"What else? A woman happened to it," Valcanas said, grinning. "What else ever happens to a man's eye? In the South, they call it reckless eyeballing, and you can get thirty days for it. Ten years if you're a nigger. Since I'm only a Greek, all I got was some knuckles. Only in saloons is justice so swift."

"Down here, Mo," Balzic said, trying to steer him.

"I heard you before for crissake. I'm coming."

Balzic led the way down the short corridor to where Tina Samarra was standing.

"This is the lawyer you sent for?" she said.

"Occasionally, madam, I am a lawyer. And what can I do for you, whoever you are?"

"This is Miss Tina Samarra, Mo. Her brother's inside with Lieutenant Minyon."

"I asked you to get a good lawyer," Tina said. "The least you could've done was get a sober one."

"Madam," Valcanas said, "let's get a few things straight. Number one, nobody says you have to hire me, and number two, nobody says I have to work for you. Since I seem to recall something a moment ago about somebody's brother being somewhere with some lieutenant, I'm presuming that you don't need to make any decision about hiring me, nor do I have to decide whether to work for you. In other words, keep your opinions regarding my sobriety to yourself. I've taken enough crap from women today—from them, about them, and because of them."

"Mo, a minute," Balzic said.

"Men," Tina said, turning away.

"Take two minutes, Mario. Just try to be concise is all I ask."

"Okay. Her brother Mickey is under arrest for suspicion of the murder of his business partner, one Frank Gallic. . . ." Balzic went on to summarize the case to this point. He did not elaborate on the presence of Peluzzi and Janeski, nor did he offer a theory of his own about the murder. He ended by saying, "All I'll say for certain is Gallic has been dead for fifteen months, give or take a couple weeks, and her brother didn't do it."

"Just how are you so sure he didn't?"

"I know him, that's all."

"That's going to impress the hell out of a jury, Mario."

"That wasn't meant to impress any jury. That was just meant for you."

"Nonetheless, I hope to Christ you have more to base your opinion on than just your feeling about her brother."

"I do."

Valcanas started to say something else but stopped when

Minyon's voice came resounding through the door: "You're lying! When are you going to stop lying?"

"The lieutenant?" Valcanas said, nodding toward the door. "That's him."

"Madam," Valcanas said, "until such time as a decision is made to the contrary, I am your brother's lawyer." He stepped to the door and was about to knock. He turned to Balzic and said, "Christ, that sounded almost biblical, you know? If my mother could hear me now." He pounded on the door with his palm.

There were some impatient, heavy steps, and then the door was jerked open. Minyon stood there, flushed and sweating, looking Valcanas up and down.

Valcanas spoke very softly. "Sergeant, my name is Myron Valcanas and I'm an attorney. I believe you have just called my client a liar, and I'd like to speak with him. What I want to speak with him about is this: you have apparently been calling him names for some time without benefit of counsel, and I'd at least like to be able to explain to him the meaning of those names. Just a minor technicality, you understand."

"In the first place, it's lieutenant," Minyon said. "In the second—"

"Lieutenant? How dumb could I be?" Valcanas said. "Here I was, looking at your face, when all I had to do was look at your uniform. Now what was the second thing you wanted to say?"

"Are you drunk?"

"I'm hardly ever anything else. Is that the second thing?"

Minyon's mouth started to work as though he were chewing a sentence and didn't know whether to swallow it or spit it out. He stood a full five seconds like that and then stepped back slowly out of the doorway, allowing Valcanas to enter, shutting the door quickly behind him.

For fifteen minutes, Valcanas's voice could be heard, never loud enough for his words to be understandable, but without interruption. Then there was a pause, the door was jerked open again, and Valcanas led Mickey Samarra out of the office.

Balzic got a glimpse of Minyon before he slammed the door. Minyon, poor Minyon, Balzic thought. He looked as though he needed to see a doctor about his blood pressure; his face was an unhealthy splash of blotches.

In the parking lot Balzic asked, "How the hell'd you get him out of there? He didn't have to let him go."

"That's right, he didn't," Valcanas said. "All I did was explain to him that anything my client had said under those circumstances wouldn't count for anything anyway. I mean, it wouldn't have mattered if he had made a full confession—assuming he had done it. As long as he didn't have legal counsel when he made it, it wouldn't be worth the paper it was written on."

"But hell, he knew that much."

"Certainly he did," Valcanas said. "But I have yet to see one of these boy scouts behave as though they really understood those rights they have to proclaim every time they make an arrest. They say all the words, but then they go right on as they always have, like they're in a goddamn Jimmy Cagney movie from out of the thirties. They make my ass tired. But the son of a bitch didn't understand me anyway."

"So what did you say that made him understand?"

"All I asked him finally was why he hadn't bothered to have the man arraigned. I mean, if he was all that goddamn sure the man was lying and had, in fact, done this terrible thing, then, hell, why not file the information against him? Of course, he had no answer. Thus, here we are in the parking lot. Now, who the hell's going to buy the next round?"

Mickey and Tina were standing beside them taking it all in, and Mickey, his face purest bovine befuddlement, said, "I told him I didn't do it. What was he hollering at me like that for? Jeez, I never been called a liar so many times in my life. My God, how does he think it feels—one minute I find out my partner's dead. The next minute he's screaming at me I killed him. My God, I loved Frank." With the last, he started to cry.

"Stop it," Tina snapped. "Jesus Christ, stop it!"

"Tina, don't talk to me like that. He was like my brother," Mickey sobbed.

"I know what he was like," Tina said, taking Mickey's arm and shaking him as though he were a child. She looked at Balzic. "Well. How do we get home? Do we have to walk?"

During the drive out to Galsam's Freezer Meats, Mo Valcanas asked to be filled in on the rest of the details. "As long as there's a possibility I might have to defend you, I ought to know what I'm going to defend you against," he said.

Mickey, sitting in the front seat with Balzic, did most of the talking, digging into his wallet to find the corroborating dates to his account of what had happened to Frank Gallic. Balzic glanced now and then into the rear-view mirror and saw Valcanas taking it all in. Once when Balzic glanced at the mirror, he could see Valcanas, still listening to Mickey, giving a long look at Tina. Balzic could not pick her up in the mirror. Apparently she had pressed herself against the opposite door, and because she said nothing during the entire drive, Balzic found himself wondering momentarily whether she was still with them. A foolish thought, he knew.

". . . was I wrong about the taxes?" Mickey was asking Valcanas as Balzic pulled onto the gravel of Galsam's parking lot.

"Not at all," Valcanas replied. "You were just trying to keep the business going. It's not exactly the way I would've done it, but if anything, it speaks in your favor. What doesn't, though, is the fact that you didn't call the police. Course you said you attempted to find him through Missing Persons. There again, that isn't, as some assistant DA would say, the act of a prudent, reasonable man who has nothing to hide. But at least you made that much of an effort."

They got out after a moment when nobody said anything.

Tina, after nodding to Balzic in what he supposed was an expression of gratitude for getting her brother out of the hands of the state police, turned without a word and went immediately into her trailer. After she was gone Balzic wondered whether her nod had been intended to mean gratitude or simply good-bye.

Mickey hooked his stubby thumbs in the pockets of his butcher's coat and shuffled about. "What do I do now? Just go back to work? How can I do that? My God . . ."

"I don't think you have anything to worry about," Balzic said, knowing as the words left his lips how asinine they must have sounded.

"Nothing to worry about!" Mickey cried out. "How can you say that? My partner is dead. Murdered! A crazy man, a state police—he accuses me! My God . . ."

"I didn't mean that the way it came out," Balzic said. "What I meant was I know you didn't have anything to do with it."

Mickey stopped shuffling. "How do you know? Tell me, my God. I want to hear. I have to hear!"

"I just know, that's all," Balzic said, taking Mickey's hand and shaking it. "Take my word for it." He nodded to Valcanas and they got back in the car.

As they drove off, Mickey seemed to Balzic to be standing like a bagged tree in a nursery, its roots close to the ground but surrounded by burlap; Mickey knew where he was supposed to be but seemed to have no comprehension of how to do what he knew he ought to be doing.

"What do you make of it, Mo?"

Valcanas shook his head. "The only thing I can say right now is that I tend to agree with you about him. He seems as unlikely a murderer as I've ever seen. But there are so damn many things that don't make sense."

Balzic snorted his agreement with that.

"For instance, he—Mickey—claims·something happened on

that fishing trip, but the first question that comes to my mind is how his truck got back here."

"Well, that notion of his about something happening on that trip doesn't hold for a couple reasons. I'm not saying nothing happened, understand, but it's pretty hard for me to believe that somebody would kill this guy a hundred miles away and then cart the body all the way back here to get rid of it."

"Just where did they get rid of it? Or he, or she, or whoever."

"I forgot. You don't know that."

"Hell, I don't know anything. Where was it found?"

"In the first place, it hasn't all been found. And all that has been found was scattered all over seven or eight farms that were leased by the Police Rod and Gun Club."

"You mean it was dismembered."

Balzic nodded.

"Well, then, that explains why that idiot lieutenant jumped on Samarra. You have a dismembered corpse, go find somebody used to dismembering corpses, especially if that somebody is the corpse's business partner."

"Yeah, but the thing about that is, as far as I know, Mickey's never been on those farms. He's not a member of the club. Never was. Hell, I doubt that he ever hunted. Gallic was the hunter."

"How about the other two—the ones he went on that fishing trip with?"

"Janeski and Peluzzi."

"Yeah. Those two. So the guy was fishing with them and that's presumably the last anybody saw of him. Were they members of the club?"

"They were. But they both quit. Said Gallic talked them into a commercial preserve up around Indiana someplace."

"I take it you've talked to them."

"Oh, sure. But it was like pulling teeth. I'll skip the details, but they both gave me the impression that something happened that weekend they don't want to talk about. And they also didn't want to talk about Gallic any more either."

"You don't sound as though you tried too hard, Mario."

"I didn't really. Course when I was talking to them, I didn't know Gallic was our corpse either. So I didn't really know what I was talking to them about."

"Well, I don't want to tell you how to run your business, but it seems pretty goddamn obvious you're going to have to turn the heat on them."

"Oh, don't worry about that. I intend to," Balzic said. "But, uh, the thing I'd like to know is what you think of her. Tina."

"Offhand, I'd say she was one of those puritanical Italian females, the kind that look like they ought to be great in the hay until some poor sap gets in there and finds out he's trying to make love with somebody that should've been a nun. I know a lot of Greek females like that, and to my mind, there's no worse breed than a Mediterranean body parading around under a Victorian head."

"I guess I could learn something from that if I knew what the hell it meant. Mediterranean bodies I understand. Victorian heads I don't."

"Neither does anybody else," Valcanas said. "You understand puritan, don't you?"

"Yeah."

"Well, the best definition of a Victorian I ever heard was a person who looked at his genitals and never really believed they belonged to him—as opposed to a puritan who knew they were his and wished to hell they weren't. Oh hell, I'm starting to sound like some goddamn professor for crissake."

"In other words, you think she's not really happy about being a woman?"

"What do I know? Hell, I've seen her only those few minutes. One thing I'm sure of. The only way she could've been any farther away from me on the way out to their place was to get out and ride on the fender."

"Well, then what do you think of this? She made her brother get rid of all Gallic's trophies—which he didn't do—yet she lives in Gallic's trailer."

"It's odd, no doubt about that. Did I hear somebody say they were supposed to get married?"

"Yeah, they were."

"Hell, it might be something as simple as her not having any other place to live. On the other hand, it might be as complicated as any psychiatrist could make it."

"She does have another place to live. Her brother's still got their parents' house up in Norwood. That's where she used to live. Then about a month after Gallic disappeared, she went to live with their oldest sister in Toledo. Then, three months ago, she came back and moved into Gallic's trailer."

"Who knows?" Valcanas said, stretching. "Who knows what women have in their heads. Freud didn't. And you can see from this patch over my eye that I'm not half as smart as he was. I'm just a small-town lawyer with a bottomless thirst. Speaking of that, how about dropping me at Muscotti's?"

Balzic turned north on Main and pulled over to the curb in front of Muscotti's Bar and Grille. "I meant to ask you before. How'd you get up to the state police?"

"Cab," Valcanas said, getting out. "You don't think I'm dumb enough to try driving in my condition, do you?" He started to shut the door and then leaned back in. "I'll tell you, Mario, if I were you, I'd really turn some pressure on those two Gallic went fishing with. And the other thing I'd do, I'd find out where Tina was living that month before she went to live with her sister. I don't know what there is about her, aside, that is, from what I've already said. But I'd sure as hell check her out. What am I talking about? This is your problem. I work the other corner."

"Exactly what kind of pressure would you put on those two—if you were me? I know what I'm going to do. I just want to see if you'd do something different."

"If I were you? Hell, everything I could think of. I'd make a
real performance out of it. I'd pick them up on a John Doe,
bring them in at the same time, and then separate them. Then?
Then I'd shake my finger at them and tell them I know they're
a couple of bad boys and need a good spanking." Valcanas
grinned. "Can't talk you into a drink?"

"Nah, not now. Thanks anyway. You don't need my
company."

"I don't need anybody's company. I get drunk enough, I
don't even need my own. That's the whole idea." Valcanas
straightened up and shut the door.

Balzic watched him shuffle into Muscotti's and then drove
off to Magistrate Aldo Vallone's office to get a couple John
Doe warrants.

Janeski was picked up just as he was punching the time
clock to begin the second shift at the can factory. A beat
patrolman who knew Peluzzi picked him up as he was coming
out of the unemployment office after signing for his compensation check.

Balzic had Janeski kept in a car outside city hall until Peluzzi
was brought in, and then had Janeski brought inside just as he
was directing Peluzzi into an interrogation cubicle.

"What the fuck's going on?" Peluzzi said.

"Sit down, Peluzzi," Balzic said, shutting the door.

"You can't just grab us like this. What for?"

"Us? Who's us?"

"I didn't say us. Did I say us? I meant me."

"That's your first lie. Now sit down."

Peluzzi thought about it a moment, then took one of the two
straight-backed chairs in the cubicle and straddled it. "You
better watch out how you talk, Balzic, calling me a liar. I ain't
no dummy. I read the papers. I know what kind of rights I
got."

"Peluzzi, in the first place, those rights you're talking about are for people who haven't done anything. But that doesn't include you, 'cause you're in a lot of trouble."

"I ain't in nothing."

"I know otherwise. Your pal's been talking."

"Don't give me that shit. What is this—the movies? Television? My pal's been talking. Shit. What pal?"

"The one that's been in here most of the afternoon. You know, the other one in the 'us' you were talking about a minute ago. Course you can go ahead and still try to make jokes if you want, but personally, I don't see a damn thing funny about Frank Gallic's murder."

Peluzzi had been searching through his pockets for a match. He froze at the word murder and stared incredulously at Balzic.

"What's the matter?" Balzic said. "Isn't it funny any more?"

"Hey, now wait a minute. Wait just a fucking minute."

"What for?"

"Say that again. Whose murder?"

"You heard me."

"I know I heard you. I just don't believe you."

"Okay, I'll say it again. It won't come out any different. Frank Gallic's murder."

"You got me in here for that? Man, I didn't even know he was dead." Peluzzi hadn't moved. Except for his mouth, he seemed locked in time, his hands trapped in his pockets, his unlit cigarette stuck to his lips.

Balzic lit the cigarette for him and pulled over an ash tray.

"You didn't know he was dead, huh? I suppose you didn't even know he hasn't been around for fifteen months, and I suppose you didn't know you and your pal Janeski were the last people to see him alive."

"Hey, come on, man, you're moving too fast."

"You come on. You and Janeski went fishing with Gallic up

at Tionesta, a year ago this past July twenty-sixth. That was a Friday. On the following Sunday night Gallic's truck appears at his trailer beside his business, but that's all that shows up. Nobody's seen him since—nobody until a dog digs up one of his bones. That was on the first day of pheasant season. Now you tell me."

"Now, wait. Okay, so we went fishing. I'm not going to say we didn't. But that other thing, man, forget it. I didn't kill nobody. Never. Not even in the war. I was a radioman. I never shot at nothing in my life except animals."

"I didn't say anything about shooting anybody," Balzic said, letting it hang there.

"I didn't say you did. I'm just telling you I never did, that's all. What're you trying to do—get me all mixed up?"

"I don't have to try, Peluzzi. You're mixed up enough without any help from me. Now let's just see if you can get yourself unmixed enough to get your story straight."

"You mean you want to see if my story matches up with Janeski's."

"Did I say that? Now who's trying to get things mixed up?"

"Well what the fuck, man. You bring us both in here, you tell me he's been talking—about what I don't know—and then you hit me with this other noise. What am I supposed to think?"

"I don't care what you think, Peluzzi. Right now all I care about is what happened on that weekend you three were supposed to be fishing."

Peluzzi took a long drag on his cigarette and then tried to take it out of his mouth, but the paper stuck to his lips. The smoke curled into his nose and eyes, and his head jerked back.

Balzic, who had been standing, took the other chair and sat, removing his coat and loosening his tie before he did. "I'm waiting, Peluzzi."

Peluzzi picked at the paper on his lips and then went into a short spell of coughing. "Give me a second, man."

Balzic slapped the table and leaned forward. He said very loudly, "Give you a second! That's a laugh. Peluzzi, you're in trouble. We got some bones. Those bones used to be a man. That man used to be Frank Gallic. And you and your friend Janeski are the last two people to see Frank Gallic. We got a pathologist's report that says Frank Gallic, the guy you two went fishing with July twenty-six a year ago—a pathologist has it in writing that Frank Gallic's bones have been in the ground for fifteen months, and you sit there saying, 'Give me a second, man.'

"I'm tired of jokes, Peluzzi, and you damn well better get tired of them pretty quick, 'cause the way it stands right now, pal, you're up for this one."

"Balzic, honest to God, man, I didn't have nothing to do with that, I swear."

"You swear. Janeski swears. Both of you walking around with your hands on Bibles. Forget the swearing. I want to know what happened."

"What happened," Peluzzi said, his head going up and down and from side to side. "Nothing happened. We went fishing—"

"When? Exactly!"

"I don't know exactly. Late afternoon. Four, five o'clock. I don't remember."

"Janeski says it was three," Balzic lied.

"Okay, maybe it was three. I don't know. Christ, man, that was a long time ago. I can't even say for sure where I was three o'clock yesterday."

"Yesterday you got nothing to worry about. But from Friday to Sunday fifteen months ago you better start remembering. Okay, so you left. You say it was four or five. Janeski says three. So then what?"

"So we got there."

"When?"

"Nine, ten, I don't know. We stopped a couple places."

"Janeski says eight."

"Christ, I don't know," Peluzzi cried out. "I'm trying to tell you, man, that was a long time ago."

"So then what?"

"So then—so then we must've went fishing."

"Where?"

"I don't know, man. On the river. Somewhere. Christ, it was dark. Gallic was the one driving. I don't know where he parked."

"What—it stayed dark the whole time you were there? The sun didn't come up the next morning? Janeski says it was right in the middle of Nine Mile Run," Balzic said, making it up as he went along.

"Maybe it was. I'm not too good at places. Directions. If he says that's where we were, I guess it was. Tell you the truth, I was drinking beer all the way up. We could've been parked in New York for all I know."

"All right, so you don't know where. So you'd been drinking. So what do you remember?"

"I remember fishing and drinking, that's what I remember."

"The whole weekend? Just fishing and drinking? That's not what Janeski says."

"Yeah? Just what the fuck does he say?"

"You tell me. We both know something else went on besides fishing and drinking, Peluzzi. I know it. Janeski knows it. And you know it. You didn't spend the whole time up there just opening beer cans and tossing in a line. You did something else. What?"

"I don't remember."

"Janeski remembers. Why can't you?"

"Janeski, Janeski, Janeski! What's he remember? What?"

"That's what I want to hear from you."

Peluzzi said nothing. He took long drags on his cigarette, several in quick succession, and stared at the wall behind Balzic.

Balzic stood abruptly and put on his coat. "You think about it awhile, Peluzzi. I'll be back." He stepped out of the cubicle and shut the door behind him.

He went to the radio console where Vic Stramsky was sitting. "How much could he hear, Vic?"

"Probably a little less than I heard. And all I heard was you and him shouting a couple times. But I couldn't make out the words."

"You leave the door open?"

"Yeah. He tried to come out once. I told him to get his butt back in there and sit down."

"Good enough," Balzic said. "Do a favor, Vic. Two favors. One, call my wife and tell her I won't be home until pretty late. Two, if Minyon calls, I'm out chasing an accident."

Stramsky nodded and was reaching for a phone as Balzic walked into the cubicle where Richie Janeski was standing, head down, making a circle on the floor with the toe of his work shoe.

Balzic shut the door and took off his coat. "Have a seat, Janeski."

Janeski sat, folded his hands in his lap, and leaned back. His left knee started to bounce. He looked openly at Balzic but said nothing, his face locked into a sneer, making Balzic wonder how his life had been shaped by that.

Balzic reached around him on the chair and took his notebook out of his inside coat pocket. He pretended to read it for a minute and then put it back into his coat. He put his elbows on the table and said, "You married, Janeski?"

"Separated."

"Got kids?"

"Three."

"How old?"

"One girl's going to be fourteen, the boy's going on eleven, and the other girl's ten."

"How long you been separated?"

"Three years, give or take a couple weeks."

"That's a long time."

"It's three years, two weeks, and one day's worth of time, if you want to know."

"Oh," Balzic said. "It's like that?"

"Yeah, it's like that."

"Get to see your kids very much?"

"Yeah. Every week."

"I wonder what they're going to think when they find out about this."

"When they find out about what?"

"Frank Gallic's murder."

Janeski's knee stopped bouncing. His gaze, which had been fixed on Balzic's face, suddenly began to fly about the room. Otherwise, he remained motionless.

"You got nothing to say about it?" Balzic said.

"Hey, man. I told you before in Pravik's. I haven't seen that guy in over a year. I—"

"He's been dead over a year, Janeski. Fifteen months, more or less. The fact is, you're one of the last two people to see him alive. You and Axal Peluzzi."

"Well, what's that mean? Just 'cause we're the last to see him doesn't mean I killed him."

"I didn't say you did. Did I say that?"

"Never mind what you said. I can see what you're thinking. But I'll just tell you something you don't know. We weren't the last ones to see him. How about that?"

"I don't believe you."

"You can believe anything you want, man. I'm telling you we weren't the last."

"That's funny. That's not what Peluzzi says."

"I don't give a rat's ass what he said. How the hell would he know anything anyway? He was stoned."

"Then suppose you just tell me who this last person was to see Gallic."

Janeski started to chew his lips, his tongue flicking out and running over the scar that crossed his mouth. "I don't remember," he said after a long moment.

Balzic laughed. "Janeski, I'll tell you. I've seen some liars in here. All kinds. Real pros and real amateurs. But that one, that lie you just told, has got to rank right down on the bottom of the novice class. Maybe you don't understand some things, Janeski, and maybe you better start understanding.

"You and your friend Peluzzi, you're up for this. We have no other possibilities. Just you and him. You're it, pal. You're sitting there telling stupid lies, and you're about to stand up in front of a judge and hear that man say something terrible.

"Nobody's been in that chair down in Rockview for a couple years, Janeski, but I'll tell you, the way a lot of people are talking these days, hell man, certain people get themselves elected, they just might plug that chair in again. I'll tell you, I wouldn't want to be where you are, and I sure as hell wouldn't be sitting there telling dumb-ass lies."

Janeski's eyes had quit darting about and had fixed again on Balzic the while he was talking. For another long moment, Janeski said nothing, his tongue continuing to slide over his scar. Then he let out a long sigh and said, "There are worse things than dying, man."

Balzic waited nearly a minute before he spoke. "What's worse?" he asked softly.

"Lots of things, man," Janeski said barely above a whisper. "Lots of things . . . being lonely is worse. Being in a whole bunch of people and knowing they don't give two shits about you—that's worse. Not having a family is worse, man. And even worse than that is knowing you had a family and knowing you fucked it up, all by yourself, all because you acted stupid, that's worse. . . . I'll tell you straight, man, there've been plenty of nights I've been laying in bed and I'll be saying, 'Go ahead, get it over with. What the fuck, if this is what it's like, who needs it?' You don't know how many times

I laid in bed and said that, man. . . ." Janeski's voice trailed off and his lips began to tremble.

"Why would you say that, Richie? What would make you want to say that? You do something wrong?"

"Aw, man. Wrong! Shit, I did a lot of things wrong. A ton. But one thing I didn't do, Balzic, and you can take it or leave it, man, 'cause I don't give a shit. I know what I did and I know what I didn't do. But one thing I didn't do, I didn't kill Frank Gallic. Maybe I should've, man. I'd be lying if I said I didn't want to. But I didn't, and those people you're talking about, they can plug that chair in and they can put me in it and when they turn it on, man, I'll be saying the same thing I'm saying now. I didn't kill him."

"You said maybe you should have. You said you'd be lying if you said you didn't want to," Balzic said, still speaking softly. It was not for effect. It had been earlier, but it wasn't now, because he could not recall seeing a man as young, as muscular, as seemingly full of health and strength as Janeski who was so clearly desperate. He could not imagine why he hadn't seen this about Janeski before in Pravik's, and the only reason he could give himself for not seeing it was the horrible and constant sneer on Janeski's face resulting from the scar and twisted nose.

"That's right," Janeski said. "That's what I said, and that's what I meant. 'Cause Gallic was no fucking good. It took me a long time to figure that out. Three years, two weeks, and one day, but I figured it out. I had plenty of time."

"How did you figure it out?"

"Oh man, are you kidding? I just told you. I see my kids once a week. Four hours I get to spend with them on Sundays. They're mine, man. I helped put them here. Four fucking hours a week. And my wife. My wife doesn't even look at me any more. Jesus . . ."

"I understand that, Richie, but, uh, what's that—"

"What's that have to do with wanting to kill Gallic?"

"Yes."

"Aw, shit, man, it's a long story. I don't even know all the parts. All I know is—well, fuck it, man—look at me. Look at my face. You know how long my face has been like this? You know how it got like this?"

Balzic waited.

"My old man did this to me. Yeah. My father. When I was six years old. I don't even remember what for. Maybe I didn't come fast enough when he called me or something. All I remember was one second I was on a scooter, man. Out on the sidewalk. One of those things with just a board on some roller-skate wheels with a handle, and I was pushing myself along and he comes up behind me and raps me across the back of the head and I go flying. The next thing I know I'm all dizzy and throwing up from ether. I'm in a hospital. And when they finally take the bandages off, man, out I come. Like this. And all my life, man, I . . ." Janeski buried his face in his hands and sobbed.

"Easy," Balzic said. "Easy now."

Janeski raised his head after a couple minutes and fumbled through his pockets for a hanky. He blew his nose and wiped his eyes and then kept the hanky wadded up in his right hand and worked it as though he was squeezing a rubber ball.

"You don't have to say any more about that," Balzic said.

"Why? 'Cause you think it doesn't have anything to do with Gallic?"

"No, that's not why I said it. I said it because it's obviously very painful."

"Well it also has plenty to do with Gallic. And I know I don't have to say anything more about it, man. I'm not saying it because I have to. I'm saying it because I want to. I never in my life told another man about this. The only other person I ever told was my wife. I never even talked about it with my mother, and my mother was there. My mother, Jesus . . . You know what I told Gallic, not only Gallic, but any guy that

ever asked me about this? Boy, is this a laugh. I used to tell
guys I got this in a fight. I used to tell them two niggers
jumped me when I was in the Army. And I used to tell them I
kicked the shit out of those two coons, man. Yeah. Feature
that. I haven't been in a fight in my life, since I was a kid,
anyway. And what kind of fights are kids' fights?

"But you know what really hurt," Janeski went on, "I mean
the worst of all? It was my mother, man. My mother wouldn't
even look at me, and every time she did, which was an
accident, she'd turn her face away, man, and I'd run into the
bathroom and look in the mirror and I used to think, God, am I
that ugly? And pretty soon I didn't even have to look in the
mirror, man. I knew. I knew I was the ugliest kid in the whole
motherfucking world.

"And the only thing good about it, man, was my old man
finally left. Don't ask me why. I don't know. I been telling
myself he left 'cause he couldn't stand to look at what he did to
me, but I don't know if that's the truth. I'm probably just
shitting myself. But he left anyway. I really didn't give a shit
why. I was just glad he was gone. 'Cause I could never get
near him, man. Never, without thinking he was going to
maybe rap me and fuck me up all over again. And then there
were times when he was still around, man, that I actually used
to wish he would. Maybe the second time around he'd do it
right. The whole job."

"Richie, you really don't—"

"If you're going to tell me again that I don't have to say this,
I told you before, man I'm not doing what I don't want to do,
okay? Just let me get this out once. I mean, just once, let me
say the whole thing, okay?"

"Okay."

"So anyway, I met this girl. My wife. She was the first girl I
ever met, man, that didn't look at me like I was Frankenstein.
The only one, I swear. Skip the whores. All they look at is
your money and your dick, see if you can pay and don't have
anything.

"So I was out swimming at North Park. North Park was where I could go, you know? I started lifting weights early, man. That was something physical you could do all by yourself. You didn't have to put up with any shit from anybody in any locker room. All that rah-rah shit. I lifted weights for years, man, and when I'd go out North Park swimming, all those pretty boys, they didn't look so good beside me. I mean, swimming, man, when you're walking around in a bathing suit, if you're really built, maybe they don't notice your face so much—least that's what I used to tell myself.

"So anyway, I was out there swimming, and I was trying to see how far I could make it across that pool under water. And I bumped into her. The funny thing was the water was up to my shoulders, so she couldn't see how I was built, and there she was still talking to me. It wasn't until we got out of the pool, man, that I see she only got one hand. All the time we were in the water, she couldn't see how I was built and I couldn't see she only got one hand, you get it?"

Balzic nodded.

"So everything goes along smooth, man. I mean, we understand one another. Why not? Who better than us? So we get married, I got a good job, the kids come along, I'm hunting and fishing when I want. I'm having a good time with my kids. We're living . . . and then about six years ago I met Gallic. I can't even remember how or where. Maybe Peluzzi introduced us. I can't even remember how I met Peluzzi. They're both a lot older than me, ten, maybe twelve years. Maybe it was in the club."

"The Rod and Gun Club?"

"Yeah. It had to be there. I just remember, it was either that time or another time, I was listening to Gallic talk. He just got back from Alaska. Shot a polar bear and he was talking about it. I don't know—he was a real talker. He could tell you anything and make you believe it. The thing was, most of the stuff he'd be telling you was true. But the thing I remembered most that first time I met him was he looked at me, square in the face, man, and he didn't say anything about my face. He didn't ask me about it until a long time later. And I remember thinking, listening to him talk, hey, he ain't such a bad guy. He spread the money around pretty good, and he listened when I said something. But most of all, he always looked at me when he was talking or listening.

"Next thing I know, we're buddying up—me, him, and Peluzzi.

"Then, pretty soon, I'm starting to spend more time with them, with Gallic, not with Peluzzi so much—I'm spending more time with him than I am with my own family. When I get a week's vacation, instead of taking my family somewhere, I'm going someplace with him. Canada four or five times. Alaska once. Christ, we even went to Mexico once. Supposed to hunt jaguars or mountain lions or something. What a joke that was. Cost me damn near a thousand bucks and all we got to show for it was . . ."

"Was what?" Balzic said.

"What? A dose of clap, that's what. From a couple whores in Juárez or someplace. I don't remember where. I just remember getting stoned on that tequila and ending up in this room with these two whores. Jesus, they were just kids. One of them couldn't have been thirteen. But there we were, me and Peluzzi and Gallic, taking turns. Taking turns with the whores and taking turns with the camera."

"With the what?"

"The camera. You know. A movie camera."

"Whose idea was that?"

"Who else? Gallic's. That was his big thing. Everywhere he went, he had a movie camera with him. He was always taking pictures of us, and then we'd have to take pictures of him."

"Everywhere?"

"I don't ever remember seeing him go anyplace without one."

"When you say 'without one,' you mean he had more than one?"

"He had two for sure that I knew of. Probably had another one."

"You ever see these movies?"

"Sure. Everytime we'd go out to his trailer, he'd show them."

"You see the one from Mexico?"

Janeski sighed and then nodded slowly. "Yeah. That one, too."

"Was that when things started to go bad between you and your wife?"

"Nah. That was just the lid. I mean, you stay away from your wife as long as I did after that trip, she got to figure something out. And what could I tell her—that I got the clap from some little whore, one that wasn't as tall as my own daughter? How was I supposed to tell her that? So I just stayed away from her. I didn't even kiss her until I was positive it was cured. I went to three different doctors, man, just to make sure. By that time, she didn't want me to kiss her no more. . . ."

"Listen, Richie, for the time being, let's forget about that part of it, okay?"

"That's about all there was to it anyway, man. You asked me why I would want to kill Gallic. I just told you why. But I'm telling you again I didn't."

"Okay, we'll let that go. But how many other movies did Gallic have like that one?"

"Like the one from Mexico?"

"Yes."

"A whole bunch, man. And he was in every one of them."

"Who took those? Did you?"

"No. That one from Mexico was the only one like that I ever had anything to do with."

"But he had a lot?"

"Yeah. I couldn't say how many, but a lot, that's for sure. You know, at first I used to get my jollies watching them. I mean, they're pretty funny, you know? And when you know the guy, they're even funnier. Maybe I'm nuts, but they were funny to me. At least until he got that one developed from Mexico. That's when it stopped being funny. I mean, I watched it, but then, sitting there, looking at myself and knowing what the result was, man, it was all I could do to keep from throwing up. And I remember thinking that was the first time I ever thought there was something really wrong with that stuff. And then I started looking at Gallic altogether different. Up until then, I don't know, it was like Gallic couldn't do anything wrong. Like whatever he did or whatever he wanted to do, that was okay with me. Up until that, you know, most of the things he wanted to do, hell, I thought it was all great."

"But that changed everything," Balzic said.

"Yeah. But it was too late then. My wife was already gone. The day she left, man, she said something that really pissed me off. I wanted to smack her for saying it. I didn't. But I wanted to. Now, I don't know. I think maybe she was right."

"What was that?"

"She hated Gallic. From the start. Couldn't stand the sight of him. And the day she left, she was almost out the door, she said, 'When you're around him, you act like he's your father.' It really pissed me. I really wanted to smack her for saying that, but all I did was tell her she didn't know what she was talking about."

"Now you figure she was right?"

"I don't know. She said I'd been looking for a father ever since my old man whacked me across the head. I couldn't see it. I mean, I hated that guy, so why would I be looking for somebody to take his place? But thinking about it all this time, I guess maybe I was. I used to ask myself why I buddied up with a couple guys that much older than me, and then I'd think back about it, about everything Gallic said—hell, everything he said to do, I did, just like a kid. Better than a kid. A kid'll give you some steam once in a while. Least mine used to. But I never got smart with Gallic. Even after my wife left, I still never got snotty with him. I just tried to stay away from him as much as I could. It worked for a while, but then, I don't know, I just started hanging around with him again. Just started the same old crap."

"The movies, too?"

"Huh-uh. No way. I mean pictures of us hunting and fishing, yeah. But not that other stuff. I wouldn't even sit still and watch that kind. At least not—"

"Not what?"

"Huh-uh, man. That's all I'm going to say." Janeski's expression and tone had changed abruptly the moment he'd said the word not, as though a circuit breaker had been overloaded and popped out, refusing to carry the current any farther. His gaze dropped to the floor and stayed there. His knee started bouncing again, and he pocketed the hanky he'd been squeezing since he'd cried. He started to knead his hands.

"You can't stop now, Richie."

"Who says?" Janeski said, eyes still downcast. "I spilled my guts enough. Bawling, Jesus . . ."

"I doubt this was the first time. Something tells me you cried a lot, those times you were laying in bed asking somebody to get it over with."

"So what if I did? Ain't I allowed?"

"Oh, I know you are. But something tells me you don't think you are."

Janeski closed his eyes and shook his head from side to side petulantly.

"Men are allowed to cry, you know," Balzic said.

"Yeah. Sure."

"They are. I never knew a man worth knowing who didn't cry once in a while. There's no shame in it. Only the guys who don't know they're men get nervous about it."

Janeski jumped up so suddenly he knocked his chair over

backwards. "What the fuck are you—some kind of head doctor? What the fuck do you know about it?"

"I know a man when I see one."

"Yeah? You also know when you see one that ain't?"

"See one that ain't what?" Balzic asked softly.

"Ain't a man. Do you know when you see a man that ain't a man? Come on. I want to hear the answer to that one."

"Do you mean is there something that shows?"

"Yeah. Just what do you look for? The way he walks? If he walks like a broad—is that what you look for? 'Cause if it is, if that's what you look for, man, I'll give you a hint. You'll be wrong."

"How will I be wrong?"

"You'll be wrong, that's all." Janeski's tone took another turn. He jammed his hands in his pockets and shuffled obliquely away from Balzic.

"Yes, but in what way will I be wrong, Richie?"

"I don't know. You'll be wrong, that's all I know."

"I won't know if you don't tell me."

"Aw, go to the library, man. Go get yourself some books. You sound like a guy that reads books."

"Did you go to the library?"

"That's a laugh. Feature me in a library. What would I be doing there?"

"I don't know. Maybe you were reading about guys that aren't guys."

"That's a real laugh."

"Then how come you're not laughing?"

Janeski looked over his shoulder at Balzic. "Ah what is this, man? You think I did something, then take me wherever you take people that did something. Why don't you do that? Why don't you say something about letting me call a lawyer? Ain't that what you're supposed to do? Why don't you do that? You know what I think?"

"What?"

"I think you don't have the first idea who killed Gallic. And I think you got me and Peluzzi in here because somebody's looking to get himself a little front page. Some headlines."

"As a matter of fact, Richie, there are only a couple people who even know Gallic's dead. The newspaper sure doesn't. Not even the DA knows yet."

"Well what's it going to be then? We just going to stay here and talk until we fall down or what? I already told you I didn't do it. And I also already told you we weren't the last ones to see him."

"That's what you told me all right. What you haven't told me is who was."

"Some broad."

"Which broad?"

"I don't know. Never saw her before or since."

"You're leaving something out."

"No shit, Dick Tracy."

"Look, Richie. I wasn't just talking before when I said you and Peluzzi are up for this one. The DA doesn't know yet, but he's going to know pretty soon. And when he does, he's going to want some names. Because the DA is one of those people always looking to get himself some front page. And I'll tell you what, the fact that you two spent that last weekend with Gallic plus the fact that you told me in plain words that you wanted to kill Gallic, well, you figure it out."

"I also told you in plain words I didn't do it neither."

"Richie, if you walked into any jail, workhouse, reformatory, prison, or penitentiary, and you asked everybody in any one of them, or everybody in all of them, nine-hundred-ninety-nine out of a thousand are going to tell you they didn't do it. And they said it all along, right from the time they were arrested, right on through their arraignment, all the way through all their appeals. More than one died saying that. I'll spare you the sermon, but I'll tell you straight. You know something, you better tell me."

"Why? Why should I do that? Maybe it wouldn't be such a bad idea to let the state take care of me."

"Oh quit talking crap. You're so sorry for Richie Janeski you're starting to make me sick."

"Good. I'm glad somebody else is sick for a change."

"Knock that off. Tell me which broad."

"I told you I don't know. I wouldn't know her name if she walked in here right now."

"Then how do you expect me to believe there even was a broad? Where did you see her? When? How do you know she was the last to see Gallic?"

"She was, all right."

"That tells me nothing."

"Okay," Janeski said. "Okay. You want to know who she was? Then go find the movies. She'll be there, big as life. Gallic made six or seven movies with her. And you know what the joke was? She didn't even know."

"The movies," Balzic said. "The movies. So that's why . . ."

"What?"

"Nothing. Just thinking out loud," Balzic said. "Okay, Richie, let's have the rest of it. All of it. And don't leave anything out."

"Why should I?"

"Change your attitude, goddammit. The game's over. I know you didn't kill Gallic. But there are still laws in this county about having movies like those, never mind being in them. That's one of the DA's favorite misdemeanors. You think so damn much of your kids, you better think how it's going to go for them if people in this town find out you're a movie star. 'Cause there's not a doubt in my mind those movies are still around. Somebody's been looking for them for three months."

Balzic stood up. "I'm going to make a phone call, but when I get back, you better have the rest of that weekend lined up for me. Minute by minute. Otherwise, you're going to wish the state *would* take care of you, as sick as you're going to be when your kids find out about this."

"Wait a minute!" Janeski cried out, but Balzic was out the door and hustling to a phone.

"Hey, Mario," Stramsky said, "Minyon called twice—"

"That's who I'm calling now," Balzic said, dialing.

"State police. Corporal Roman speaking."

"This is Mario Balzic. I want to talk to Minyon."

A click, then a pause. "Lieutenant Minyon."

"Minyon, this is Balzic—"

"Where the hell have you been, Balzic?"

"Never mind. Just go get a search warrant and get your people together. Go out to Galsam's Freezer Meats and do a job on that place."

"Oh really? So you've finally figured out whose side you're on."

"Don't get shitty, Minyon. Just do what I said."

"And just what is it I'm supposed to be looking for out there?"

"Movies."

"What?"

"You heard me. Seems Frank Gallic was a movie nut—among all the other kinds he was."

"Is this another one of your jokes, Balzic?"

"Listen, Minyon, if you don't want to trouble yourself, just say so. The fact is I'd rather go out there myself than have you go, but I'd be doing it alone. You have the people, and there's a business out there, plus two trailers, and at least three vehicles. It'd take me a week. But if you don't want to do it, just say the word."

"I'll do it—in return for a favor."

"I'm listening."

"I'd like you to locate a Richard Janeski and, let me see, an Axal Peluzzi. Your people know this town better than my people, and we've been looking since this afternoon and nobody knows anything."

"Sure," Balzic said. "I'll put it on the horn soon as I hang up. Is that all?"

"That's all. You're sure it's movies you want us to look for?"

"That's what I said. Should be a lot of them. But even a lot wouldn't take much space. They're probably in cans—hell, you know what movies look like."

"All right, Balzic. You'll let me know about Janeski and Peluzzi? I have an idea they'll be able to put this whole thing together."

"Maybe they will. I'll keep in touch." Balzic hung up and grinned at Stramsky. "The big man in the boy scout hat wants us to look for a couple guys named Janeski and Peluzzi. Seems he has an idea they know something."

"Oh yeah?" Stramsky said. "Did he have any clues for us to go on?"

"No. We're supposed to tough it out ourselves. But the big man did admit we know this town better than he does."

"Imagine that," Stramsky said. "Next thing you know he'll be saying kolbassi don't taste too bad."

"Ah, I think I better go easy on friend Minyon. He doesn't have the first idea what I just let him in for. Maybe I should've told him to take along a couple straitjackets."

"Who for?"

"Mickey Samarra. And his sister. I'll tell you, if I was them, somebody would have to put me in a coat."

Stramsky looked puzzled, but Balzic did not bother to explain. Instead, he went back to the cubicle where Axal Peluzzi sat staring at the wall and chewing on a hangnail.

Balzic didn't take off his coat and he didn't sit. He pulled up the other chair and put his foot on it and leaned on his knee.

"All right, Peluzzi," he said, "let's have the rest of that weekend."

"Balzic, why don't you go to hell?"

"Not just yet. Someday maybe. But when I get there, you'll be cleaning the crapper."

"Oh, that's funny."

"I thought so. But it's not as funny as you in the movies."

"Me in the what?" Peluzzi stopped chewing his hangnail.

"The movies. You know—motion pictures. I hear you're almost a star. You're not as big on the marquee as your buddy Gallic was, but you're still pretty big. How's it feel to be almost a star?"

"I don't know what the fuck you're talking about."

"You don't know about taking movies with Gallic? You don't know about Gallic taking movies of you and Janeski? You don't know anything about that?"

"I ain't been to a movie in over a year."

"What's that have to do with anything? Or are you trying to tell me the last time you were at the movies cured you? Is that it?"

"You're not making sense, Balzic."

"You're the one not making sense. I know all about the movies. You and Janeski and Gallic. Frank Gallic, the producer, the director, the man who liked to look at himself. You three fishing. First Gallic takes some shots of you or Janeski hauling in a big one. Couple all-American boys in their fight against nature. Then later on you take a couple shots of Gallic making coffee around the campfire. Tranquil little scene. The hungry heroes settle down to enjoy their catch. How am I doing so far, Peluzzi?"

"So what's wrong with that? So we took some movies. So what?"

"Not a thing. Movie camera's a great invention. Homemade history, somebody said once. You have a picnic, somebody has a camera, and there you are, recorded for all time with your face in a watermelon."

"So?"

"So how about the other kind, that other kind of picnic?"

"What other kind?"

"You know. You and Janeski and Gallic in Mexico, say. You been out hunting something ferocious, and after the hunt, the heroes have a little fun. They find themselves a couple little girls and they all retreat to the hotel for a little good, clean fun. How about that?"

Peluzzi put another cigarette in his mouth and fumbled for a match.

"You didn't have a light before, Peluzzi, remember?"

"So I didn't."

Balzic lit Peluzzi's cigarette and waited. "Well?"

"So what's the big deal? So we got some broads in a room and we took some pictures. Nobody twisted their arms. They got paid. Cost me a small bundle to get rid of what they gave me, so who really came up short? Besides, that don't mean I had anything to do with killing Gallic."

"So you haven't forgotten that?"

"Comedian. How'm I supposed to forget that? I'm still here, ain't I?"

"The time you been having with your memory, Peluzzi, it's a small miracle you remember anything. So maybe we ought to go back over some things. You do remember Gallic having a movie camera, and you do remember the three of you taking turns with that camera, is that right?"

"I remember that, yeah."

"You also remember one movie in particular from Mexico, right?"

"Not so clear, but I remember it."

"Well, suppose you try to remember how many other movies there were like that one."

"I don't remember any more like that one."

"You don't remember being in any more like that one, or you don't remember any more like that one—which?"

"I was only in Mexico once, so how many could there be?"

"Any from Canada like that? From Alaska? Or how about from right here in Rocksburg?"

Peluzzi said nothing.

"Come off it, Peluzzi. I know there were lots. That's Janeski's word. Lots. Lots of movies like that one. Gallic was in most of them. But let's say that was the only one like that you were in. You're still in trouble, 'cause the DA has a special bitch about movies like that. He just loves to tell old ladies how much he's doing to fight corruption and moral decay."

Peluzzi canted his head and squinted through the smoke. "Little while ago you were telling me I was up for Gallic's murder. Now you're just talking about that movie."

"That's right. Right now, that's all I'm talking about."

"Well, which is it, Balzic? I mean, so the DA got a hard on for skin pictures. So what? The most I could get out of that is a couple hundred bucks' fine and maybe thirty days—if I had a dumb lawyer."

"That's right."

"So—so are you still talking about the same thing?"

"The same, but not exactly the same. The way I figure it, Peluzzi, somebody was in some of Gallic's movies and didn't know about it. You knew about it, and Janeski knew, 'cause Gallic showed them to you. You sat around, had a few drinks, and had some laughs. And there were some broads, not only in Mexico and Canada, but from around here, they knew about it, too. Maybe they even had a few laughs themselves. But there was somebody who was in them who not only didn't know she was in them, but who when she found out didn't think they were the least bit funny. In fact, they made her about as mad as anybody gets."

Peluzzi continued to smoke and squint at Balzic.

"What I'm trying to say, Peluzzi, is she thought she knew Gallic pretty good. And then one night she found out she didn't know him half as good as she thought."

"So?"

"Let me put it to you this way. If she didn't know him half as good as she thought, then the chances are pretty good other people didn't know Gallic as good as they thought, 'cause this

female is pretty shrewd. And she knew Gallic a lot better than
a lot of other people who'd been around him a lot longer than
she had. But not good enough."

"What's all this have to do with me?"

"What I'm getting at is maybe you didn't know Gallic
anywhere near as good as you thought you did. I mean, Janeski
thought Gallic was something extra special for a long time, and
then all of a sudden, he thinks maybe he should've killed him.
Yeah. Imagine that, Peluzzi. That's something, isn't it? I mean,
here's a guy who knows another guy as good as Janeski knew
Gallic, and not only knows him but respects him. Admires
him. Does everything the guy says to do, and never gives him
an argument about it. Then all of a sudden he's saying he not
only wanted to kill him, but he should have. Now, that's a
helluva thing to say, especially to a cop, and especially not ten
minutes after he finds out that other guy is dead. Murdered.
And the cop is trying to find out who killed that other guy?
Don't you think that's a helluva thing to say?"

"Why don't you ask Janeski? He's the one said it, not me."

"I already have. Now I'm asking you. How good did you
know Gallic?"

"I knew him."

"How long?"

"Ten years. Maybe longer."

"And you went hunting with him, fishing with him,
drinking with him. You took turns taking movies of one
another—all kinds of movies, Peluzzi. And I probably
wouldn't be far wrong to say you probably slept with him."

Peluzzi's head snapped up. "What do you mean by that?"

"You know. You camped out together, right? So you had to
be pretty close. Those campers aren't too big. Tents—tents
are pretty small things."

"His camper was big."

"I've seen his camper, Peluzzi. It isn't anything out of the
ordinary. It's no bigger than most campers that fit on the back

of a pickup truck. And I've been inside them. I know how big they are."

Peluzzi started to say something and then apparently changed his mind.

"Look at it this way, Peluzzi. There's a guy who knew Gallic for years—twenty-seven to be exact—and you'd think he'd be the one guy to know Gallic better than anybody, but I'll bet you a hundred bucks against a dime, he will be the most surprised guy in the world when he finds out Gallic owned a movie camera, never mind what kind of pictures he took. As far as that goes, all he knew was Gallic used to bring some real skags back to his trailer, and all he was worried about was that Gallic might catch something. But when Gallic did catch something that time in Mexico, he didn't know about that."

"He must not've known him too good."

"Oh, he thought he did. He thought he knew him real good. And not only that, he thinks he knows you real good too. The fact is, he told me he knew you since you were a kid, and he said you aren't a very good person. Those were his exact words. You aren't a good person. You know who I'm talking about?"

"Samarra. Who else?"

"That's right. And he doesn't like you even a little bit. 'Cause he didn't like what you and Janeski did to Gallic when you were out together."

"What *we* did to Gallic? Samarra's head is bent, that's what's wrong with him. I never did nothing to Gallic. Anything Gallic did, it was 'cause he wanted to do it. I never put no ideas in his head. Christ, I knew Samarra was dumb, but that takes it all, brother—what we did to Gallic. Shit."

"Yeah, no doubt about it. Mickey Samarra's a little slow. But he's also, uh, one of the strongest guys I've ever known. Even when he was a kid, nobody would fool with him. And he never wanted to hurt anybody. But just fooling around with other kids, he'd hurt them. You remember that. Who didn't know that about him? Did you ever look at his hands? I mean, did you ever take a good look at them?"

"Why should I? I look funny for hands or something?"

"That guy, short as he is, what a pair of hands he's got. And all he does all day is throw that beef around."

"So he ought to be in a circus. So what's your point?"

"Simple point, Peluzzi. I'm surprised you haven't thought of it yourself. I mean, you said yourself a little while ago, even if the DA does have a hard on against skin pictures, the most you could get is a fine and maybe thirty days. You get a half-decent lawyer, you won't even get that. But just what do you think Mickey Samarra's going to want to do when he finds out about those movies?"

"What are you trying to do, Balzic? That doesn't have nothing to do with me. I wasn't the one with his sister in those movies. That was Gallic. And he's dead, right?"

"So you knew it was Tina Samarra?"

"Sure I knew. What am I—blind?"

"Of course she wasn't the only one."

"Are you kidding? She was just the last."

"What puzzles me is how he managed to bring it off without her knowing about it."

"Simple. He had a camera set up in a closet inside the bathroom. He had a little hole in the wall into the bedroom. Then when he'd get the broad into bed, he'd say he had to go take a shower. He'd tell them he didn't like to make love dirty. He wanted to be clean, and that's when he'd start the camera. When he came out of the shower."

"So most of them never knew?"

"How could they? He'd have the air-conditioner on plus the stereo, so they couldn't hear the camera going."

"But he never said who they were, did he? Especially not Mickey's sister."

"No."

"And naturally you never let on you knew, about her, I mean."

"Why should I? But he knew I knew. 'Cause he used to get a special laugh about her. He used to say, 'This one's fucking wacky. She loves me.' That's what he used to say about her. But I knew all right."

"So there was really only one time and one way she could've found out," Balzic said. "I mean, if nobody told her . . ."

"You're doing the talking."

"It's impossible for me to believe she stumbled on it before. That would have been the end of her and Gallic. Besides, she wasn't living there then."

Peluzzi said nothing.

"So the only time was when she did. Which brings us back to that weekend. You and Janeski and Gallic fishing and drinking beer, you said. That and nothing else."

Peluzzi crushed out his cigarette and said, "I'm tired talking."

"Are you now? Then maybe you better listen better, Peluzzi. 'Cause the way I see it, you got one chance of staying alive once Mickey Samarra finds out about those movies. And that one chance is I give you a long head start and you just disappear. Otherwise, Mickey Samarra'll tear you apart. He'll get those mitts of his on you and, strong as you are, Peluzzi, you won't have a chance. And you better listen good to this part: I'm not going to stop him, and you said yourself the most you could get is thirty days.

"After that, you'd have to come out, and you're dago enough to know what an old-school dago like him thinks about somebody messing with his sister. Especially messing with her like that. And what will really make it worse for you is that Gallic is already dead. Which means, in case you haven't figured that out, is that Samarra won't have Gallic to kill. But he's going to want to kill somebody.

"And here's one more thing for you to think about before you tell me you're tired talking: the state police are out there right now looking for those movies. In other words, friend, you don't have too much time. Because, hell, let's be practical. How long do you think it would be before you came to trial? Couple of months? What are you going to do in the meantime—just keep on collecting checks and walking around like nothing happened? Better think again, Peluzzi, 'cause right now I'm the only person between you and Mickey Samarra, and unless you tell me the rest of what happened that weekend, I'm just going to open that door and let you walk on out of here. How'd you like that?

" 'Cause Mickey won't care if he gets locked up for a hundred years once he finds out about those movies. His life will be over as far as he's concerned. The shame will be a thousand times worse than getting locked up. And the only thing that will make that shame easier for him to live with is the satisfaction that he killed you."

"Why the fuck do you keep saying me? Goddammit, Janeski was in on it, too! I wasn't the only one. Janeski was there too! I wasn't the only one Gallic queered!"

"The only one he what?"

"You heard me." Peluzzi averted his eyes. "And if you think you're going to get me to say any more than that, you're crazy."

"So that was it," Balzic said. "So that's what happened. Your hero, Janeski's hero, the big-game hunter—turns out he was queer. I'll be damned. He must've hid it pretty good all those years."

"Not so good," Peluzzi said, eyes still downcast. "Not when I think back about it."

"How so?"

"Ah, he was always goosing somebody. You'd walk by him, he'd make a grab for your crotch. Stuff like that."

"But lots of other guys do that, right? So you never gave it a second thought. But something must've made you think about it."

"There was something, all right. That time in Mexico he tried to get those two whores to go down on each other. But they wouldn't go for it. Maybe they didn't understand him. But he sure tried."

"And he must've tried with others. And succeeded."

"Yeah, he had a couple reels like that. He really got a boot in the ass out of watching them."

"So when it happened at Tionesta, it surprised you, but not really, is that it?"

"The thing was, we were all pretty drunk, and I remember him saying we ought to circle jerk—you know how when you was a kid—well, not you, I guess. Nah, you wouldn't of gone for that kind of shit. But some kids'll get in a circle and see how far they can leak, that's how it starts. Then the next thing would be to see who could beat off and come the fastest. Well, that's what Gallic thought up. He said we should all throw five bucks in and whoever comes first gets the fifteen. Like I said, we were all pretty drunked up anyway, so we went for it. One thing led to another, and the next thing I know, Gallic's down on me."

"On Janeski too?"

"Yeah, him too. So don't just be hollering at me and telling me what Samarra's going to be doing to me."

"All right, I won't. But then what happened—you start to sober up?"

Peluzzi sighed. "What do you think? Course we started to sober up. That's a long drive back from there. And Gallic was really starting to sweat it. He wouldn't shut up talking about it. He kept saying how lots of guys do that. Real guys, he kept saying, not just them swishers you see in some bars. Said it would probably never happen again in a million years. . . ."

"But he could tell you two weren't buying it."

"It wasn't too hard. I felt pretty shitty myself, so I just kept on drinking. But Janeski, hell, he wouldn't say nothing. All the way back, he didn't say five words."

"Which left only one thing for Gallic to do, right? I mean, if he's still going to be the big man?"

"What else?"

"What I can't figure is how he managed to get Tina out there and get you two out there as well."

"Tell you the truth, I don't know myself how he swung that. All I know is, when he dropped us off at my place, he got us to promise him we'd be there. Christ, he was pathetic. I never saw him like that before. He was practically begging us."

"Did you know it was going to be Tina?"

"He didn't say who. He just said he'd have this broad there and she'd go for anything. He guaranteed it. All we had to do was give him time to get her warmed up and get some booze in her."

"What time was all this?"

"I'm not sure. He must've dropped us off about nine at my place. Then he said to give him a couple hours. So it was probably eleven, eleven-thirty when I got there."

"Janeski was there, too?"

"He showed about five minutes after I did. For a while, he didn't want to get out of his car. He just sat there looking, looking like I don't know what. Tell you the truth, I was a little bit scared of the way he looked."

"Did you talk to him? I mean, did you try to talk him into going inside?"

"No. I tried to tell him to forget it, that's all. He just looked at me. But Gallic's the one that talked him into going in. He came out of the trailer bare ass and he said what the fuck are we waiting for."

"So you went in?"

"Not right away. It took him a couple minutes to convince Janeski. But then we went in. But we didn't stay too goddamn long."

"As soon as Tina find out, it was all over, right?"

"You better believe it was all over. I never seen a broad that mad in my life. Nobody. Never that mad. So if you can't figure out by now who killed him, Balzic, you're some kind of dumb."

"Oh, I figured that out a while ago. Soon as I found out about the movies. I just wanted to know why." Balzic went to the door. "Okay, Peluzzi, all you have to decide is whether you want to chance walking around or whether you want to be locked up until the trial. You think it over."

"Hey! There ain't nothing to think over. You lock me up, man. And then you make sure I get out of this town."

"Don't worry about that. I'll make sure. Just you make sure you don't do anything stupid while you're waiting for the trial."

"I ain't going to do nothing stupid."

"Don't be so sure. You got a history of it," Balzic said, leaving the cubicle and closing the door behind him.

He went out into the squad room and asked Stramsky if there had been any word from Minyon.

"Not yet," Stramsky said.

"Okay. Then put Peluzzi downstairs. He's going to be with us for a while. Make sure he's clean."

Stramsky nodded and got the necessary forms and started filling them in.

Balzic went on to the cubicle where Janeski waited, raw-eyed and cracking his knuckles.

"Okay, Richie," Balzic said, "Peluzzi gave me most of it. Now I want to hear it from you."

"He tell you everything?"

"If by everything you mean the part about Gallic queering you, yeah."

"Oh, Jesus," Janeski said, covering his ears with his hands, his eyes flying desperately.

"Come on, Janeski, get yourself together. Give me some times and the travel arrangements. Peluzzi says Gallic dropped you two off at Peluzzi's place about nine, is that right?"

Janeski dropped his hands to his sides and turned his back to Balzic. "Yeah," he said, his voice breaking, just on the edge of a sob. "It was about then. Little after maybe."

"And Gallic got you two to promise him you'd meet him at his place a couple hours later?"

"Yeah."

"You got there around eleven-thirty?"

"Yeah."

"Peluzzi says you didn't want to go in, is that right?"

"That's right. I didn't even know what I was doing out there with that queer bastard."

"But you finally went in after Gallic came out and talked you into it, right?"

"Yeah. I did. Peluzzi too."

"What I can't figure out is why you even showed up."

Janeski shook his head violently. "I don't know. Honest to God, I thought about it a thousand times. And I still don't know. Sometimes I think I went out there to kill him. At least that's what I like to think I was doing there."

"Did you take something with you? A pistol? Knife?"

"I had my twenty-two with me. In the glove compartment."

"But you didn't take it in."

"No. That's when I knew I didn't have no balls left. I just went on in. Just like I didn't have any brains either. . . ."

"How long were you three in there before she found out what was going on?"

"Couldn't have been more than a couple minutes. Wasn't too damn long, I know that."

"Where was she when you first went in?"

"I don't know. She must've been in the bedroom."

"What made her come out? Did Gallic call her?"

"I don't know. But Gallic didn't call her. He was telling me and Peluzzi to get undressed. I was just standing there, trying to figure out why he was whispering. I mean, if it was the kind of broad he said was going to be there, what was he trying to hide? So I didn't even start to take my clothes off. But Peluzzi, he started to take his pants off, and he was still half shot, and he couldn't get them off without taking his shoes off. So he bent over to take his shoes off and he lost his balance and started hobbling around and knocked over a lamp. That was when she came out."

"Did you recognize her?"

"I told you before. I recognized her from the movies. She was in five or six of them. I spotted her from them."

"But you didn't know her?"

"No. Not then."

"When did you find out who she was?"

"Peluzzi told me."

"When was this?"

"Couple months later. He called me up and asked me if I wanted to go hunting with him. I said if it was with Gallic, forget it. But he said it would be just me and him, so I went."

"And then you found out it was Mickey Samarra's sister."

"Yeah."

"So why'd you lie about it before?"

Janeski groaned. "Man, I've been trying to forget this whole goddamn mess. You didn't get out of me what Gallic did. You got that out of Peluzzi, remember?"

"I remember very clearly," Balzic said. "So what did you think about after you found out who she was?"

"I told you. I just wanted to get the whole load of crap out of my head."

"But you couldn't. Not with those movies still around."

"What do you think? I busted my head trying to figure that out. Once I even tried to make a deal with some guy who was supposed to be a pro. A burglar. From Pittsburgh. But he wanted something out of this world. Five bills. Plus another bill for every time it took him past three times. I didn't have that kind of money."

"So you just went along, not doing much of anything. What were you hoping for?"

"Hoping. That's all I was doing. Hoping everything would

just go away. Then Peluzzi calls me up and tells me she's back living out there, so we know what she's looking for."

"But you still didn't do anything?"

"What was I supposed to do? Go ask her if she wanted some help? If you'd've seen her that night when she walked out and saw Peluzzi trying to get his pants off, you wouldn't be so goddamn anxious to get close to her either."

"So then why hang around? You had money. A car. You weren't strapped in here like Peluzzi. He's got people all over town looking for him with their hands out. But you could've left any time."

"Maybe I wanted to get it over with. Maybe I figured with Gallic gone all I had to do to get myself straightened out was stay away from Peluzzi. Then . . . well, if I went someplace, that'd mean I'd never get to see my kids."

"You knew Gallic was gone?"

"Sure I knew. Nobody saw him. What I figured was it got him worse than it got either Peluzzi or me, so he just cut out. I'll tell you what, when that broad came out and saw us three standing there, man, all I was thinking about was getting the hell out of there as fast as I could move. And I figured Peluzzi and Gallic would be doing the same thing."

"You didn't stay to see if they did?"

"Hell, no. I got that car in gear and floored it. I must've laid a strip of rubber fifty yards long. Then later on, when Peluzzi called me, I figured he got out, so Gallic must've got out too. I'll tell you the truth, I never even thought for a second she'd kill him."

"You must not have been worrying too much about those movies."

"Well, when I thought about it awhile, I figured, so what if she finds them? What's she going to do with them—show them down the Roxian?"

"Didn't you ever think about her brother?"

"He's a jerk. Besides, there again, what was she going to do? I mean, feature it. She calls him in and says, pull up a chair, brother, I got some really good movies I want you to see? Are you kidding? Man, the way I figured it, the best thing that could happen was for her to find them."

"Too bad. 'Cause now you're staring at the worst thing. Her brother—that *jerk*—is going to find out about them pretty soon. He's going to know about everything pretty soon," Balzic said. "I'll tell you what. I'll give you the same choice I gave Peluzzi."

"What's that?"

"You can walk out and take your chances with her brother or you can let me lock you up until the trial. After which I guarantee her brother won't know which way you went or how you were traveling."

Janeski thought about that a minute. "So it still winds up I don't even get to see my kids once a week."

"I'm not going to tell you you should've thought of that before."

"Thanks for nothing. Jesus . . ."

"So what's it going to be? You want to walk, or you want a cell?"

"What do you think?" Janeski said. "Just tell me one thing. How much of this you think'll come out at the trial?"

"If I was her lawyer, I'd turn over every rock there was. You figure it out."

"So my family's going to find out anyway."

Balzic shrugged.

"Jesus," Janeski said. "What do you guarantee them?"

"If you got any money saved, you'd be smart to get them out of here. One of you has to have some relatives someplace. Course, in something like this, friends would probably be better than relatives. If you want me to talk to her for you, I will. And if you're short, I'll see what I can do about getting you a loan. Beyond that, there isn't much I can do. Which is a helluva lot, I might add. But there's one thing nobody could do, and that's stop people from talking."

Janeski hung his head and his shoulders started to jerk.

"Think it over, Richie. Take your time. You'll be here for a while."

Balzic stepped out of the cubicle and went over to Stramsky. "Put Janeski downstairs, Vic."

While Stramsky was doing the paperwork, Balzic took everything from Janeski which he could possibly use to commit suicide, including the plastic buttons off Janeski's back pockets.

"What're you doing that for?" Janeski asked.

"You'd be surprised the edge you can put on plastic if you rub it on cement long enough. It won't cut paper, but it'll cut flesh. And I don't want you doing anything dumb, 'cause if we get lucky, this thing can be hushed up pretty good."

Janeski signed for his personal effects and followed Stramsky downstairs.

In a minute Stramsky was back. "Christ," he said, "you ought to hear the names they're calling one another. I thought I heard them all."

"Naturally," Balzic said. "That's what they been doing all their lives, even when nothing was wrong. Now that something is wrong?" He shrugged and started for the door. "I'm going out to see what Minyon came up with, Vic. Don't know how long I'll be, so if Ruth calls, give her the good news. But gently."

Balzic was in no hurry to get out to Galsam's Freezer Meats. Of all the people and things to be found there, he could think of none pleasant. Only the whereabouts of the movies still piqued his curiosity, and he knew that once they were found, all that followed would be more or less routine. No matter what the papers did with this when they found out about it, no matter how bizarre or grisly they tried to make it, it was downhill as far as he was concerned.

He parked beside the three state police cruisers and sat a

moment watching the shadows moving inside Frank Gallic's trailer, wondering how Mickey and Tina were reacting to it. He imagined a look of betrayal on Mickey's face, and he did not want to confront him. There was no telling in whose direction Mickey would want to lash out.

Balzic got out of his car finally after smoking a cigarette down until he could feel the heat from the ash on his fingers. When he knew he could procrastinate no longer, he went inside and stood just inside the door and watched Minyon's men. They were thorough and efficient, but because they were still in the process of being thorough and efficient, Balzic knew they hadn't found the movies.

Minyon appeared then from the rear of the trailer, probably from the bedroom, and it was only when Minyon stopped to speak to him that Balzic noticed Tina and Mickey. They were sitting in the kitchen, their bodies obscured by the bottom half of a room divider, Mickey's eyes going from one trooper to another as they searched, Tina's eyes fixed on the divider, her head seemingly suspended in a cloud of her own cigarette smoke.

"You sure it's movies we're supposed to be looking for?" Minyon whispered, leaning close to Balzic.

Balzic nodded. "Did you tell them what you were looking for?"

"No. I just let them read the search warrant. Her, rather. He didn't want to look at it. He took her word for it. But we sure as hell haven't found anything that even looks like a movie yet. Hell, we haven't even found any snapshots."

"Well, how about doing me a favor and getting him out of here. I want to talk to her, and I don't want him to hear any of it."

"Balzic, before I go doing you any more favors, I'd like to know what the hell this is all about."

"You get him out of here and you can listen while I talk to her. You'll figure it out as I go along. I don't feel like going through it with you and then going through it with her all over again. I've already gone through it enough as it is. I just went through the whole thing with Janeski and Peluzzi."

"You found them?"

"Sure I found them. You said yourself we know this town better than you do. It wasn't any big thing. Now how about it?"

Minyon sighed irritably. "All right. I'll do it your way, but it better be good."

"It will be, don't worry."

Minyon called one of the troopers over and told him to take Mickey Samarra out on the pretense of looking around the other trailer.

Mickey passed Balzic without a word. It was as though he did not recognize Balzic, or as though he could not associate a name with Balzic's face. The look of betrayal Balzic had anticipated was not there; rather, it seemed to Balzic that Mickey had discovered himself engulfed by some totally foreign atmosphere and could not guess why he was still able to survive.

Balzic stepped beyond the divider and into the kitchen area. He drew up a chair and, nodding to Tina, sat opposite her. She glanced at him indifferently, then crushed out her cigarette and in the same motion took another from her pack and lit it.

If she was disturbed because of the invasion of all these men—there were four troopers still searching in addition to Minyon and Balzic—she showed it only by seeming to draw more deeply into herself.

"Tina," Balzic began, "I think now's the time you tell me what you said you were going to when you got ready."

"I don't remember telling you anything like that."

"You did. Outside the lieutenant's office. When he had Mickey with him, you said you were going to tell me some things when you got ready. I think now's the time."

"You would."

"Tina, I'll put it straight on the line. I know you killed Gallic. I know why. The only things I don't know are how and when."

Minyon's face showed infinitely greater surprise than did Tina's. She looked squarely at Balzic and said, "If you know that, then what difference does it make how or when."

"I suppose how doesn't really make that much difference. But when might make a difference. For your sake, it might make a helluva difference how long you waited to kill him."

"What difference does it make how long you wait before you butcher a pig? A pig is only fit for butchering. Sooner or later, that's all it's good for. When only makes a difference if you're going to sell it."

"It might make a tremendous difference at your trial. I know you're going to find this hard to believe, but I really don't want to see you pay any more for this than you absolutely have to."

"You're right. I find it very hard to believe."

"Then you're just going to have to take my word for it."

"I don't take any man's word for anything."

"I can understand that, but, uh, you're going to have to take mine."

"Why should I? You come in here after these goons come in and start tearing the place apart and you say you know I did this or that—you give me one reason why I should take your word for the time of day. I don't think you know anything."

"Well, I do. Maybe not the same things you know, but I do. And it would be a lot easier for everybody if you'd be more co-operative."

"A lot easier for everybody," Tina said, her face twisting in contempt. "All you have to do is co-operate . . . what that means is all I have to do is what you want me to do. You make me sick."

"Tina, I'm not Gallic, but—"

"Nobody's Gallic. Gallic isn't. Gallic never was. Just what he made me. Just what he tried to make me."

"—I started to say I'm not Gallic, and I'm not trying to get you to co-operate for my benefit, but for yours."

"Are you now? Funny. Seems I've heard that line a few times before. What's good for you is going to make me feel good, too. Isn't that the way it goes? All I have to do to feel good is make you feel good. No matter what. Don't you bastards ever think up anything new?"

"I guess I have to get at it from a different way—"

"Go all the ways you want. Fly around the moon if that gets it for you. Just get it. Get what you want. The hell with what anybody else wants. The hell with what I want."

"I know you don't believe me, Tina, but I have to admit in one sense you're right. I have to get it—the 'it' in this case being the truth—one way or another. So I guess it doesn't really matter whether you think I'm doing you a favor or not. Not in the long run."

"Balzic," Minyon interrupted, "will you quit talking in circles? Say what you have to say."

"There's a big man for you," Tina said. "Don't waste time. Don't find out anything. Don't see what might happen. Demand. Just demand. And you expect me to think you're any different."

Balzic lit a cigarette and thought a moment. "Okay. So here it is. To satisfy you both." He paused to look up at Minyon, a look as full of irritation and contempt as he could make it. "Gallic and Janeski and Peluzzi went fishing on a Friday fifteen months ago. The following Sunday they came back. Gallic dropped the other two off at Peluzzi's house and picked up Tina here. You were living in your parents' house then, the one in Norwood. That was around nine-thirty.

"Gallic brought you out here. I'm not sure how much trouble he had getting you out here, but whether you wanted to come out or not, pretty soon you got the impression something was really bothering him. You probably didn't ask him about it, and he sure as hell didn't say what it was, but there was no mistaking that something was on his mind.

"I, uh, hesitate to bring it up—what was on his mind, I mean—but for the lieutenant's benefit, Tina, I guess I have to. And I guess there's no way to say it but to just say it." Balzic stopped and looked at Minyon. "Gallic queered the other two."

Tina didn't blink, but Minyon's jaw dropped.

"Anyway," Balzic went on, "Gallic had to do something to prove to the other two that he was still all man, so before he went to get you, Tina, he got the other two to agree to come out here.

"About eleven-thirty, eleven thirty-five, after you and Gallic had had a few drinks and spent some time back there," Balzic said, nodding toward the bedroom, "you probably dozed off. You thought maybe you heard a car pull in, maybe two. You weren't sure. But then you noticed that Gallic wasn't beside you, and then you heard something. Voices maybe or somebody stumbling. Then you heard a lamp get knocked over. Am I right so far?"

Tina said nothing.

"Okay, so you got up and you came out and you saw Gallic, naked, with the other two. Janeski was just standing there, but Peluzzi was taking his pants off. It probably took you a couple seconds to figure it out, 'cause I'm sure at first you didn't want to believe it. But then you finally had to believe it.

"You scared Janeski so much, he took off in such a hurry he never found out until a month or so later whether Peluzzi even got out of here. But Peluzzi did manage to get out, so that left just you and Gallic. You and him, the guy you were getting ready to marry. That must have been a helluva moment, especially with him trying to tell you it wasn't what it looked like. From what I hear, he was a very persuasive guy. And something tells me he almost convinced you. How am I doing so far?"

Tina exhaled some smoke. She started to speak, then took another drag on her cigarette, and lapsed once again behind her mask.

"That's all right, Tina. You don't have to say anything," Balzic said. "Not yet anyway. So let me pick it up from there. Gallic was still talking, still trying to tell you you had it all wrong. You knew better, but you were probably starting to cool down anyway. In spite of yourself. Probably at that point all you were doing was berating yourself for being so stupid about him. Or so blind.

"But feeling stupid about him or blind or whatever didn't change how dirty you must have felt. Knowing you and your brother, your family as long as I have, I'd say you probably felt as dirty as you'd ever felt in your life. So the natural thing to do when you feel that way is to want to get clean. And that's when you went into the bathroom. And that's the part I can't exactly puzzle out. All I can do is make a guess, because Gallic would've shut that thing off long before, wouldn't he? So you couldn't have heard it."

"What thing?" Minyon asked.

"The camera. The one that took the movies your people are looking for. Gallic had it set up in the bathroom, focused into the bedroom so he could, uh, have a record of himself as a lover."

Tina shuddered then, an involuntary spasm that began in her hips and ended in a catch of breath.

"What it was," Balzic said to Minyon, "from what I can put together, is the guy needed a whole lot of proof. A sad thing, but there it is . . . but to get back to you, Tina, what I figure is you found it because you were probably looking for a clean towel or a clean washcloth or a fresh bar of soap. I mean, if you really wanted to get clean, as dirty as you felt, you wouldn't want to do it with Gallic's soap or washcloth or towel. Because he'd already taken a shower. That was when he'd turned on the camera. So that was how you found it, right? When you were looking for a clean washcloth or new soap?"

Tina continued to smoke, taking deep drags, blowing out the smoke in heavy breaths, her face as controlled as ever.

"So there was nothing left then," Balzic said. "Nothing at all. And only one way to get clean.

"What I figure is you came out to the kitchen for a knife, most likely, and then you went back into the bathroom, called him in, and told him to explain it. Maybe you didn't even ask for an explanation. And, uh, I'm really guessing now, but something tells me you had the presence of mind to make sure he'd fall into the bathtub."

Tina nodded then, the faintest suggestion of a nod, and she looked at Balzic as though, however grudgingly, she had to admit that a man was giving her credit for something and should be thanked for it. But she said nothing.

"Afterwards," Balzic said, "well, I see no reason to go into the rest of what you did. We all know that. I'm curious about one thing though, only because Mickey told me you never went near Gallic's truck. You used his truck, didn't you, to take the pieces out and bury them?"

"Mickey," Tina said. "Dumb Mickey . . ."

"The question still remains, how long between the time you found the camera and the time you killed him?"

"Not long," she said evenly. "When a pig's time comes, it comes."

"Okay, I'm not going to pester you about that. I'll leave it for your lawyer to convince you it's important. And I guess that leaves only the movies."

"If you find any," Tina said.

"How many have you found?"

"I didn't count them. I just burned them."

"Is that why you came back from Toledo?"

"You know the answer to that."

"You mean you didn't think there might be more until you'd been away for a whole year?"

"For a year I didn't want to think about anything. Then, well, I thought of it."

"Where did you look?"

"Everywhere but the right place until you showed up. Then when you came out asking questions—well, where do you look for shit?"

"In the toilet?"

"The only place I didn't look before. They were in plastic bags in the tank. That's the only good thing I can say for him. Even he knew where they belonged."

"Well," Balzic said, clearing his throat, "unless your people come up with some more, Lieutenant, we've got a problem."

"Such as what? What do we need them for? She just confessed. What more do we need?" Minyon said.

"Her confession here, just now, won't even satisfy the prosecuting attorney. And it damn sure isn't going to satisfy the lawyer that defends her."

"Since when is that our problem?"

"It's always been our problem, the way I figure it," Balzic said. "Or I guess I should say, I've always figured it was part of my problem. You can figure it any way you want."

"I figure it's her lawyer's problem," Minyon said.

"Yeah, I thought you would. But do me—and yourself—one more favor. After you get her booked and locked up, don't bother her until she has a lawyer with her, okay?"

"I don't need anybody's protection," Tina said. "I know what I did. And I'm not ashamed to say I did it. I'm not even ashamed of something else I did. Something you don't know about." She stood abruptly and went to a drawer near the sink.

Minyon lurched after her, but she stopped him with a laugh. "What do you think I'm going to do, big man? I just want you to see something."

She reached into the drawer where the silverware was and lifted a plastic tray and pulled out a square, flat object and tossed it on the table in front of Balzic. It took Balzic a long moment to understand what it was, and only when he made the association with others he had seen like it did it occur to him. It was a tattoo of the American flag with the words

"Death Before Dishonor" below it. He had seen dozens like it when he had been in the Marines.

"That's all that's left of him," Tina said, "and if he hadn't taught me, I wouldn't've known how to do it."

Balzic felt something to start to rise in his throat, swallowed once, and stood. "God, Tina, I'm—I'm sorry." He started for the door of the trailer.

"I don't need any goddamn apology from you," she called after him. "I'm not sorry. Who the hell are you to be sorry for me?"

Balzic did not turn around. Once in the car, he rolled down all the windows, and wheeled out of the parking lot, driving faster than he'd driven since he first got his license, hoping the wind screaming through the car and battering his face would somehow ease the sickness he felt.

After twenty minutes of wild driving, Balzic calmed himself. He had to talk out loud to succeed, but he did, and then he thought he should find Mo Valcanas. He found him in the lounge at the Rocksburg Bowling Alleys.

A saucer-eyed blonde, dressed out of all proportion to the place with a silver brocade dress and silver mules, sat next to Valcanas and kept blowing a contrary lock of silvery-white hair away from her right eye. Valcanas's bandage over his eye had been reduced to a wide Band-Aid.

"Mind if I sit down, Mo?" Balzic said.

"If you're dumb enough to want the company of a wide-awake drunk, who am I to deny you the pleasure?" Valcanas said. "Excuse me. Almost forgot my manners. Mario Balzic, this is, uh, what's your name again, dear?"

"Cindy," the blonde said, huffing again at the lock of hair.

"That's it. Cindy. All you have to think of is cinders."

"Hi," Cindy said. "Can I have another drink?"

"Cinders, *may* you have another drink," Valcanas said.

"May I—can I—I'd like another drink, okay?"

"Charming girl," Valcanas said to Balzic. "Illiterate, but charming."

"So who gets a charge out of reading books? I hated school."

"There, Mario, is a jump in logic not even Freud would have tried to explain. Louis, my good man, bring my charming friend here two of whatever she's drinking," Valcanas called out in the general direction of the bar. "And now, Mario, what can I do for you that you think I ought to, but which we both know I would be infinitely better off not doing?"

"It's, uh, Tina Samarra. You remember. The butcher's sister."

"You're not going to get me another client for crissake. I've got seven right now I don't want."

"Six, dearie," Cindy said. "I can take a hint."

"Sit down and drink your drinks. It's a sin to waste good booze. Besides, you didn't have anything to do with hiring me. Your boy friend did. And he's the only one who can fire me. So just be a good girl and shut up. You know—close your mouth and let your natural charm reveal itself."

"This one needs a lawyer, Mo," Balzic said.

"They all need lawyers. What am I? The only lawyer left?"

"Well, you know about the case."

"You mean that one about the butcher who got himself butchered?"

"I wish to hell you'd put it a little different, but, yes, that's the one."

"You mean she did it?"

Balzic nodded.

"And you want *me* to defend *her*? A female hacks a guy in little pieces and you want me to defend her. Mario, where the hell's your sense of proportion? I should be on the other side."

"That's not all she did," Balzic said. After thinking a long moment, he added, "I figure this guy rated it."

"Listen, Cinders," Valcanas said, "take a walk for five

minutes. I want to talk to this man privately. And I said walk. That means you stay upright and you keep going places. That doesn't mean you keep moving with your feet on the floor."

"Boy, are you ever funny. Where'd Anthony ever find you?" Cindy picked up both her drinks and sauntered off toward the bar.

"She kills me," Valcanas said. "She keeps calling Digs DiLisi Anthony. She thinks he's going to send her to New York. To appear on Broadway, no less. She'll make a hell of a lot of appearances, all right, but there won't be any stage."

"So what's she up for? Rehearsing on her own time?"

"Something like that," Valcanas said, grinning. "Let's get back to this other female—what's her name again?"

"Tina Samarra."

"That's it. Now you said you figured the guy rated it. Did you say that, or am I just getting that impression from the righteousness on your face? Mario, no shit, you have to do something about that. It's boring as hell to have to look at the countenance of a moral defender all the time."

"Yeah, sure. In the first place, I did say it. The guy did rate it as far as I'm concerned. He gave her the best reason any woman could have." Balzic went on to explain, bringing Valcanas up to date in every detail. "So what do you think?" he said finally. "Is it worth your time?"

"That depends how much I get paid—if I get paid."

"Oh, her brother'll pay you. Don't sweat that. But what do you think? I mean, what'll she get?"

"Well, we plead her guilty, I call three witnesses, her and those two her boy friend went fishing with—among other things—and the only tricky part will be making sure those two don't know she burned all the movies. Otherwise, from what you say, they'd have everything to gain by shutting up."

"Both of us together can take care of that," Balzic said. "I just keep them locked up until you talk to somebody in the DA's office to tell somebody else to set their bond so high

156   K. C. CONSTANTINE

nobody'll take a chance on getting walked on it. So then, if you ask all the questions as though the movies are still around, what's the problem?"

"None. There won't be any."

"So what do you think she'll get?"

"That depends on the judge. I'll get it set up in front of Koerner. He's a good, proper Lutheran. He'll be duly horrified. I'd say she'll get eleven to twenty-three months. Good behavior, hell, she'll be out in a year."

Balzic frowned.

"What the hell do you want for crissake? I mean, what the hell, Mario, she's got to do a little time. You know, she's got to reflect upon the error of her ways. The least she can do is spend a year thinking about who she shacks up with from now on."

"I don't know," Balzic said, "seems almost a shame she has to do any time at all."

"Mario, what you need is a drink," Valcanas said. "Louis, a drink for my friend here. The world is too much with him, late and soon."

"What did you say? The world is too much what?"

"The world is too much with you, late and soon," Valcanas said. "That's Wordsworth. You know, poetry. Christ, why am I surrounded by illiterates? I have to start loafing in better saloons."

"If you don't mind, Mo, just save the poetry," Balzic said. "I'll take the drink."

And he did. Many of them.

A FIX LIKE THIS

Balzic waited for the woman to be done. She was in her sixties, her white hair grew in tight curls, and she smelled of garlic. Her floral print housedress was ripped under both arms. Though she'd been talking to the admissions clerk for nearly five minutes, she was still shivering from the cold. She'd obviously left her home too quickly to think of wearing a coat or sweater.

The admissions clerk explained twice to the woman how to file for government health insurance for her husband, who had been conscious but torpid when he was wheeled into the Emergency Unit of Conemaugh General Hospital. Except for her shivering now, the woman seemed calm enough, though every time she asked a question, she put her hand to her mouth and her fingers trembled.

When she'd asked every question she could think of, she turned away from the counter and said aloud to herself, "My God, what am I going to do now?" Then she turned back abruptly to the counter, bumping Balzic

with her hip. "Can I go be with him? I'm allowed ain't
I? My mister, he's all I got."

"Certainly," the clerk said. "Through those doors on
your right. Mrs. Havrilak will show you where he is."

The woman bumped Balzic again as she turned away
from the counter and hurried, her bosom heaving,
through the fire doors leading to the treatment rooms.

"May I help you?" the clerk said.

Balzic held out his ID case because the clerk was new
to him. "I got a call about a stabbing a while ago, and I
got tied up in something or I would've been here sooner.
Who do I talk to about it?"

"Dr. Kamil, I think. He's the very dark-complected
one. Just go through those doors—"

"I know where to go," Balzic said. "I just wanted a
name."

He pushed through the fire doors and walked past
treatment rooms on both sides until he came to the
office. Off to his right he could hear a youngster bawling
and a woman cooing reassurances. In another of the
rooms a man was swearing quietly about a foot, probably
his, though he was cursing about it as though it belonged
to somebody else, somebody not very smart.

The office was empty. Balzic took a seat at one of the
desks and waited. Shortly, a tall, freckle-faced nurse appeared in the doorway. She fumbled through her pockets
while staring at the floor, then stepped quickly to one of
the other desks and began to pat with both hands on
papers jumbled on it. Only then did she notice Balzic,
and she smiled brightly.

"Mario! How are you? I haven't seen you in a month
of bad Saturday nights."

"Hello, Louise. How's business?"

4

"Listen, go get a lab coat. Some of these people you could take care of. I don't know where they came from today. God." She found what she'd been looking for and held it up for Balzic to see. "Around here, pens are more precious than blood." She started out the door but stopped short. "You waiting to see Kamil about the guy who was stabbed?"

Balzic nodded.

"I'll tell him you're here. He's just finishing up with some sutures. At least I hope he is. God, is he slow. I could put a zipper in a dress in the time it takes him to do ten stitches."

"He the only one on duty?"

"No, but the other one's right out of school. Last week, I think. I gotta go," she said, her crepe soles squishing as she broke into a trot.

Balzic took out his keychain and opened the nail clipper and began to clean his fingernails. He pared them over an ashtray, looking up every time he heard footsteps, but none turned into the office.

He closed the clipper and put his keys away and waited some more, looking around the office, mildly curious for a time about a poison chart under glass on the desk where he was sitting. He had just started to read the antidote for copperhead venom when a slight, short man in a lab coat came in. His brilliantly black hair grew in swirls and came very near to his eyebrows.

"I'm Dr. Kamil," he said. His accent was Middle Eastern, Syrian perhaps or Lebanese. "You are the chief of police?"

Balzic introduced himself and shook hands with the doctor. He could not remember shaking a man's hand so delicate.

5

"Ah, yes. So. What do you want to know?" The doctor clipped his words and spoke rapidly in a thin, tenor voice.

"Whatever you can tell me."

"I have the record here. Yes. So. Here it is. The patient is male, Caucasian, forty years of age, and very, very obese. If his brother had not been here to assist us, I do not think we are able to place him on the cart. His brother is also very obese. I have never seen such obesity as you have here in America. But these two brothers are beyond even my belief. Still in all—is that how you say that? Still in all? You have so many idioms here too—"

"Was the guy's name Manditti?" Balzic interrupted.

"Say again please?"

"Manditti. His name."

Dr. Kamil peered at his report. "Yes. Armand. Italian no doubt."

"And his brother brought him in?"

"I suppose yes. I do not know."

"No police officers came with them?"

"I did not see any."

"Where is he now?"

"In surgery most certainly."

"How long ago did he go up?"

"Thirty minutes, more or less."

"Was he conscious? Did he say anything?"

"Oh yes, he was conscious. But he was cursing and crying. If not for his brother to assist us, we would have no information at all."

"Did his brother go upstairs with him?"

"I suppose yes. I do not know."

"All right, Doctor," Balzic said. "Thank you. I'd appreciate it if you'd have somebody type up a report as

6

soon as possible. Mrs. Havrilak knows about the forms and what to put on them. Thanks again."

"There is no need to thank me. It is my duty, is it not?"

"Yeah, but thanks anyway," Balzic said. He shook the doctor's hand, reminding himself not to squeeze.

As soon as the doctor left the office, Balzic picked up a phone on one of the desks and dialed Troop A Barracks of the Pennsylvania State Police.

"State police, Sergeant Rudawski."

"Rudi, this is Balzic. Who's in charge of CID now?"

"Johnson."

"He is? I thought he was going to be transferred out as soon as Minyon passed his physical."

"Well, put an extra quarter in the collection this Sunday, 'cause Minyon flunked his physical, and he is, as they say, being retired with honor." The ironic pleasure in Rudawski's voice was unmistakable.

"Oh beautiful," Balzic said, laughing. "Just beautiful. Well, let me talk to Johnson."

"Hold on." There was a click, then a dead sound, then another click.

"Criminal Investigation Division, Lieutenant Johnson."

"Hey, Walker, old buddy, congratulations. Rudi just told me Shitface flunked his physical and you're going to be with us for a while longer. That's the best news I heard today."

"Mario? Yeah. It looks that way. I almost feel bad for him though. That's a hell of a slice off his pension."

"Don't waste your sympathy. Even his mother had to know he was hopeless," Balzic said. "Listen, Walk, I got a problem. A guy was stabbed. His brother brought him

7

to the hospital, and nobody reported it. I mean, the hospital people called me. And I know them, so it figures they wouldn't report it themselves. But I'm also taking a pretty good guess that it happened pretty close to home. What I'd like is for you to take your people over there and see if I'm right and see what you can come up with, okay?"

"No problem," Johnson said. "From the way you said it I take it he's not dead."

"Yeah, but he's still in surgery so I don't really know what kind of shape he's in. I'm on my way up there now. But listen, don't bother trying to ask any of the neighbors up there anything. They still haven't figured out this isn't Sicily. They see those uniforms, they'll forget how to speak English. Just do a job on the house, okay?"

"Okay, what's the address?"

"You remember where Norwood Hill is?"

"Yeah."

"Well, it's the last house on the right on Norwood Hill Road. Never mind about a number. It sort of sits off by itself. It used to be a half-decent house when their old man was alive, but there's just the two brothers living there now and they're both slobs."

"What's the name?"

"Manditti. Armand is the victim. He's a runner and gofer for Muscotti. His brother's name is Tullio. He runs Muscotti's dump. Couple of real beauties. They call the one Fat Manny and the other one Tullio the Tub. You'd need a truck scale to weigh them."

"Okay, Mario. I'll see what we can do, and I'll let you know."

"Really appreciate it, Walk. Just remember that I'm

8

guessing. It could've happened anywhere. Thanks, buddy."

Balzic hung up and then made his way to the main elevators and up to the seventh floor, where the operating and recovery rooms were, waiting in the corridor by the nurses' station. He looked around for Tullio Manditti but did not see him. Off to his left in an adjoining corridor he could hear a woman mumbling and giggling in that euphoria brought on by preoperative chemicals. Nurses in green surgical caps and gowns bustled about. A doctor in street clothes got off one of the elevators and hurried past Balzic, stripping off his tie as he disappeared through fire doors on the right.

Presently, a plump, middle-aged nurse in white appeared from yet a third corridor. She carried a cup of tea and smiled at Balzic. He held up his ID case, but she waved it away.

"I know who you are," she said. "And you want to know about Mr. Manditti, right?"

"You're a good thing," Balzic said. "What else you going to tell me so I don't have to ask?"

"Well, Dr. Ayoub did the work and he was assisted by Dr. Mitchell. They finished about five minutes ago. I'll go get Ayoub for you."

"Wait a second. Where's Manditti's brother?"

"Oh, God, he smelled up the place so bad I told him to leave. He wasn't supposed to be up here anyway. I told him to go home and change clothes. But the way he was carrying on, he probably didn't. He's probably downstairs in the lobby driving everybody crazy."

"He was still in his work clothes?"

9

"Well, I hope he doesn't sit around the house like that. Where's he work anyway?"

"Where could you work and smell like that? A dump. Excuse me. Sanitary landfills they call them now."

A doctor in surgical clothes appeared then, thin, short, very dark, his black hair glistening from perspiration. "You are from the police?"

Balzic nodded.

"I'm Dr. Ayoub."

"Where they getting all you Syrians and Lebanese?" Balzic said, laughing.

"From Syria and Lebanon, I suppose," the doctor said. His smile was forced.

"Well, uh, yeah. I guess they would," Balzic said and coughed.

The nurse busied herself with some charts.

"So what can you tell me, Doc?"

"He had nine wounds, all of them simple puncture wounds except for two. Those were made presumably by the blade being thrust in and then pulled down. Like so." The doctor demonstrated on Balzic's chest. "The instrument was not very large. None of the wounds was deeper than six inches. The procedure was simple."

"He's going to live?"

"Oh yes. Barring infection, which is unlikely, he will die of heart disease. But for the time being his obesity saved him. It required every nurse in all three rooms to lift him onto the table. And off again."

"How long will he be in the recovery room?"

"How long before you will be able to talk with him sensibly?"

"Yeah, I guess that's what I mean."

"The anesthesia was very mild. We were concerned

10

about his blood pressure. Forty-five minutes. Perhaps not even that long."

"Uh, Doc, would any of those wounds have been fatal to somebody built like me or you?"

"It's difficult to say. Most were in the area of the heart. Two were lower, near the stomach. To someone built like me, surely four or five would have been lethal, that is to say, each of four or five."

"So somebody wasn't just trying to cut him up. Somebody was trying to kill him."

"As I said, if the wounds had been inflicted on me I would be dead. Whether someone was trying to kill him is, I think, your department."

"Can you tell me anything about the kind of weapon?"

"Some kind of simple knife blade. No more than six inches. But I can say nothing more specific than that. I am a resident in general surgery, not in forensic pathology."

"Sure, I understand. Well, thank you very much."

"You're welcome. Good day," Dr. Ayoub said, turning at once and walking briskly away.

Balzic looked at the nurse, who was trying not to smile. "I guess I didn't score too many points with him."

"Oh, he's all right," the nurse said. "He's just all business."

Balzic thanked her and went with a wave over his shoulder to the elevators. In the lobby he looked around, trying to locate Tullio Manditti, but he didn't see him. Balzic approached one of the hospital security guards and held out his ID case. The guard nodded.

"You seen a short, fat guy, really fat, in dirty clothes?"

"In the coffee shop, feeding his face—as if he needs it. He chased everybody out."

"Coffee shop still in the same place? Every time I come up here they're moving things around, putting on all these additions and wings."

"Well, they haven't moved that yet. But give them time. They will."

"Yeah. So how's it going? They treating you all right?"

"No use complaining."

"Okay, pal, take it easy." Balzic oriented himself and then set off for the coffee shop. He found Tullio Manditti more than occupying a stool at the counter. Both waitresses were smoking in the farthest corner away from Tullio and whispering to each other, their eyes darting toward Tullio as he took a third of a glazed doughnut in one bite. One of the waitresses asked Balzic if she could help him.

"Just coffee. Black." He took a stool two away from Tullio. He wouldn't have sat closer to Tullio if he'd been able to.

"Tullio, why didn't you go home and take a bath and get cleaned up like the people asked you?"

Tullio stuffed the rest of the doughnut in his mouth in two bites and chewed rapidly. He turned to look at Balzic but spoke to the waitresses. "Give me two more. And another milk shake."

"We don't have any more doughnuts."

"You got any pie?"

"Just apple and cherry."

"I hate apple and cherry. Ain't you got no banana cream?"

"No."

"Then forget the pie. Give me a couple cheeseburgers with everything. Extra onions. And grill the onions." Tullio had been looking at Balzic while he spoke to the waitress. Now he turned back to the milk shake container in front of him. He looked inside, sloshed the last of the liquid around, and drank directly from it, letting out a thunderous belch when he finished.

"What did you say, Balzic?"

"You heard me."

"Why don't I go home and take a bath, huh? Is that what you said?"

"That's what I said."

"So tell the people to give their garbage a bath, don't tell me. Tell them to put deodorant on their garbage, then maybe I don't smell, how's that? Huh? What's the matter with you, Balzic? You stupid or something? My brother's up there dying and you want me to leave here and go home and get a bath, Cheesus."

"Well, I see it didn't interfere with your appetite."

"Eating, my brother understands. But going home and taking a bath, he wouldn't understand. He'd never forgive me."

"Come off it, Tullio. Your brother's not dying. Not yet anyway. He'll croak from a heart attack pretty soon, just like you. But he's not dying from those holes he got in him."

"That's what you say. Huh! What do you know? You some kind of doctor?"

"I just talked to the doctor. He'll live."

"When the doc tells me I'll believe it. What you tell me I stick up my gazoomey."

"Have it your way," Balzic said, shrugging. "So what happened?"

13

"What do I know what happened? I come home from work and there he was, bleeding all over the porch. Blood all over the living room, Cheesus."

"And you didn't talk to him about it?"

"What talk, you kiddin'? I'm trying to save him, I ain't worrying about no conversation."

"So how'd you get him here? He had to be conscious. You couldn't have brought him here if he's unconscious."

"So he was conscious a little bit."

"Conscious enough to walk, right?"

"Look, Balzic, I can see where you're going. If he's conscious enough to walk, he got to be conscious enough to talk. But I ain't asking him nothing. I'm just telling him to be cool, don't exert himself, we'll be there in a couple minutes."

"And naturally, that's what he did."

"That's exactly what he did."

"He didn't say one word about what happened or who or how or why?"

"He didn't say nothing."

"Okay. So he didn't say anything. So tell me what he's been doing lately."

"He ain't doing nothing. He's unemployed."

"What? He don't carry bags around for Dom Muscotti anymore?"

"What bags? Dom who?"

"Will you stop it. Who're you talking to? This is me, Tullio. And I know you and your brother since you were in Mother of Sorrows Elementary. You're not talking to some state horse or the FBI. I know how long you and your brother been working for Dom and I know what you do, so don't give my head a pain, all right?"

14

"I'm telling you my brother is unemployed."

"Wait a minute, what is this? You trying to tell me your brother doesn't pick up and deliver for Dom Muscotti anymore?"

"How many ways I got to say it? Cheesus."

"Tullio, you know just as soon as I leave here I'll go straight to Dom and ask him."

"I can't stop you from going nowhere."

"What happened with Dom and your brother?"

"What're you asking me for? What do I look like—the labor relations board? I don't know nothing about it."

"Tullio, that's two lies. You tell me one more I'm going to bust you as a material witness, and then I'll go to the DA and tell him you need to be locked up for your own safety. I can fix it so you stay in the slam for six months."

"You got to have a hearing before that, Balzic. Don't shit me."

"Hey, Tullio, you think I don't know the magistrates in this town? You think I can't have a hearing postponed as long as I want? You think about it, Tullio. And while you're at it, think about something else. Think about those twenty-two hundred calories you'll get every day down at the hotel . . . and lookee here. Here comes your milk shake."

Tullio sneered and swiveled around slightly on his stool, the plastic and metal creaking. He started to say something in Italian.

Balzic waved his index finger from side to side. "Easy, Tullio, easy. You don't want to say anything you're going to have to apologize for."

"What was I going to say? Was I going to say something, huh? Me? Nah. I was going to ask you to loan me a deuce, that's all. I'm a little short, and I didn't want to make no speech for the United Nations. So now you made me make one anyhow."

Balzic snorted and shook his head. He brought his money out, stripped off two bills, and pushed them toward Tullio. He stood and said, "Don't even thank me. Just go home and get cleaned up. Your brother'll understand. And everybody here'll love you."

Tullio drank his milk shake and seemed to be thinking, but he said nothing and did not look up as Balzic walked out.

Balzic debated with himself in the lobby whether to try to talk to Armand Manditti or to go straight to Dom Muscotti. An elevator opening in front of him made up his mind as much as anything else did. He rode up to the seventh floor, there holding the door open with one hand and calling out to the nurse he'd talked to earlier. "Is Manditti out of recovery yet?'

"He's on the third floor."

Balzic waved, stepped back inside the elevator, and pushed the button for three. Once there, he asked at the nurses' station for the room number. On his way, he chatted briefly with one of the charwomen, a friend of his mother's.

He found Armand Manditti in the first bed inside the door of a ward with four other beds, all empty. Balzic stopped in the doorway and laughed. The mound of white on the bed gave him the feeling that he was going to try to talk to a snow drift.

He stepped inside and saw Manny staring sleepily at the tube taped to the back of his hand. Manny blinked incredulously, the blinks coming very slowly. Every time his eyes opened, they would roll, and then Manny would

16

shake his enormous head slowly from side to side, once each way.

"Manny? You hear me?"

"Huh? Am I dead?" The words came as ponderously as his blinks.

"You're not dead, Manny. At least you don't look it."

"Huh? Good . . . I'm glad . . . I thought I'm dead. . . ."

"Who stabbed you, Manny?"

Manny muttered something and closed his eyes and let out a long sigh. Balzic started to ask again, but Manny's sigh had turned into a snore and then another. Balzic took off his raincoat and threw it across the foot of the opposite bed. He looked around for an ashtray, found one, and then settled onto a straight-backed chair just inside the door. He smoked and hoped Manny wouldn't stay under the effect of the anesthetic too much longer.

He should have known better. An hour later, he was still waiting. He had talked to some nurses, then briefly to Dr. Ayoub, who had stopped on his way home. Manny continued to snore, the mattress, springs, and sheets groaning and rustling with each breath. Balzic inspected the bed and then the others in the room. Manny's bed was the same as the rest, and Balzic wondered how long it could take the strain.

Balzic could hear Tullio coming as soon as the elevator doors closed. With each heavy step came a breath as heavy. Tullio, freshly shaved and wearing clean coveralls, huffed into the room carrying a paper shopping bag. He stopped upon seeing Balzic and rolled his eyes toward the ceiling.

"Cheesus Christ, Balzic, state cops all over the house and you here. Whose idea was that—them state cops, huh? Yours? What's the big fuckin' idea? They come in

17

there, they didn't have no search warrant or nothing."

"They don't need one."

"What do you mean, they don't need one? You cops can't just go busting into people's houses. Us people got some rights."

"Tullio, don't make my ass tired, okay? Don't say stupid things."

"Don't make my ass tired. Don't say stupid things." Tullio mimicked him, looking around for a place to put the shopping bag, deciding finally on the dining table at the foot of his brother's bed.

Out of it he took a loaf of Italian bread, two long pieces of pepperoni, a thick slab of provolone cheese, a jar of green olives stuffed with pearl onions, a can of black olives, a jar of banana peppers, and a transparent half-gallon bottle with no labels on it that obviously contained wine. Then he brought out a folded dish towel and opened it up. A small paring knife, a can opener, and a fork rolled out. Tullio took those and the towel and put them in the drawer in the stand beside his brother's bed. He looked around, as though thinking where to put the food.

"Tullio, why don't you just eat it yourself? Your brother's not going to be allowed to eat anything like that for a couple days."

"That's how much you know, Balzic. I know what you get in this place. I been here. You can die in here from the food. Half the cooks are niggers. When they find out the food's for a white person, they spit in it. You think I don't know that? They bring up a lunger, a real oyster, and they let you have it. My brother ain't eating in here, period."

"I don't know, Tullio," Balzic said, smiling. "I can

18

remember the time Manny scarfed up seven barbecued chickens in about an hour. That was at the Sons of Italy picnic a couple years ago. Looks like all you brought him was a snack."

"Don't sweat your head, Balzic. My brother'll do okay in here, I'll take care of that."

"Tullio, Tullio. . . ." Manny's eyes opened wide.

"I'm here, Manny. Right here. What do you need?"

"Oh, Tullio, I ain't dead . . . that prick . . . I thought I'm dead."

"What prick, Manny?" Balzic said, going immediately to Manny's side.

"Aw take a hike, Balzic, willya!" Tullio said. "Can't you see he don't know what he's saying? Everybody's delirious when they wake up for crissake, everybody knows that . . . listen, Manny, don't try to talk. You just get some rest, okay? I'm here now. I brought you something to eat when you wake up. But keep sleeping now. You need it. You look bad, Manny. You look all green and yellow. You got to sleep that crap out of your system —that crap they put you out with. Just keep sleeping."

"Okay, okay. Just give me some water, okay? My throat's dry."

"Sure. How 'bout some wine in it? It'll make you sleep better."

"Yeah, sure . . . wine too. . . ."

"You better ask a nurse before you give him any wine, Tullio. It might make him really sick if it doesn't mix right with the anesthetic."

"What do you know? Go on, Balzic, take a walk. You don't think I know my brother's system better than any nurse? Go on, hit the bricks. You're making him nervous. Me too." Tullio peeled the wrapper off a glass, filled it

19

half with wine, and added a little water. He rooted through the drawer of the bedstand behind him until he found a flexible straw. "Here, Manny, here you go. Take a couple big sips. It'll do you good. Really make you sleep good."

Manny raised his head and grimaced. "Holy shit, it hurts. . . ."

"Don't raise up. This straw bends. You don't have to raise up. Just lay there. I'll put the straw in your mouth . . . there, like that. See? Listen to Tullio. He'll take care of it."

"You going to take care of who did it too?" Balzic said.

"Listen, Balzic, I told you to take a hike. He don't have to say nothing and neither do I."

Balzic laughed. "Tullio, you been in trouble so much in your life you don't understand. Your brother's the victim. Get it? He's the victim, and the victim don't need a lawyer. The victim isn't supposed to keep quiet. The victim doesn't get any guarantees. I can stay here forever if I feel like it and ask as many questions as I want."

"Yeah? And what's to stop us from staying here forever and not answering any of them, huh? Tell me that, wise guy."

"Not a thing, Tullio, not a thing," Balzic said, reaching for his raincoat. "But there's one guarantee I will give you. I guarantee I'm going to keep asking until somebody gives me some answers. Your brother gets cut up, something is bent out of shape, and six will get you five it had something to do with somebody else's money. And I'll tell you something else, Tullio, and you better pay attention. Somebody else winds up in this hospital with so much as a split lip, I'm going to collar both of you. There isn't going to be any bullshit like that, you hear me? There hasn't been as long as I've been the man here, and it isn't going to start now. And just to make sure, I'm going to give the same message right now to Dom Muscotti, you hear me?"

"I hear you, Cheese, I hear you. What am I? Deaf? But I don't know what you're talking about."

"Oh you know all right. You know." Balzic pulled on his raincoat and walked out.

Balzic eased his cruiser out of the hospital parking lot and drove just fast enough to keep up with traffic, all the while trying to comprehend what had happened and why. . . .

Armand Manditti had worked for years for Dom Muscotti as a runner. He picked up and delivered—money, betting slips, payoffs, layoffs, special case-lot orders of wine from state liquor stores for Dom, groceries and household necessities for Dom's mother—whatever Dom wanted or needed. Now, by Tullio's words, he was unemployed.

As for Tullio, he managed Muscotti's garbage dump. It was the third part of Muscotti's Rocksburg-bound empire. Since Muscotti's father before him, every piece of garbage collected in Rocksburg and in Bovard Township to the north, Westfield Township to the west, and Kennedy Township to the south and east—all public and private refuse—wound up on land owned by a Muscotti. It made no difference which collection outfit bid for the right to collect the stuff; they all paid Muscotti for the privilege of emptying their trucks. And long before anybody publicly talked about recycling waste, Dom's father and then Dom paid a squad of pickers, usually true wops —that is, Italians without papers—to swarm over each load as it was dumped and cull every tin, steel, or aluminum can they could find, then to separate, clean, and pulverize them into one-foot cubes to be sold wherever the market was best.

World War II guaranteed the family fortune in that third of Muscotti's empire; each load of garbage since only added to it, and the uproar over ecology did nothing in Rocksburg so much as show Muscotti the potential of paper and glass. Muscotti persuaded friends in Rocksburg's Sanitation Department who in turn prevailed upon Rocksburg's City Council to pass two ordinances: the first required that newspapers be bundled separately from other garbage; the second required that bottles and jars be placed in separate cans at each residence and business, public or private. While compliance with the two ordinances was far from total, it was sufficient to make life easier for Tullio's squad of pickers to turn garbage into money.

Garbage turned into money so fast that Muscotti had to start giving it away to keep from going into higher and higher tax brackets, and his philanthropy so charmed the Rocksburg Chamber of Commerce that in 1971 they named him Rocksburg's Man of the Year. It seemed not to matter to them that for fifteen years out of the last twenty Muscotti had been summoned to the Pittsburgh office of the Internal Revenue Service to explain his income, or that at least every other year for the past twenty-five Muscotti had been subpoenaed by county, state, and federal grand juries and assorted crime commissions to testify about the sources of his income. It also had not seemed to matter that Muscotti had been indicted six times, tried five times, and convicted three times since 1945 for operating lotteries and bookmaking establishments. What seemed to matter was his charity, though it had been rumored around town that the Chamber of Commerce was more concerned and greatly more relieved by the fact that there had been no violence even remotely attributable to Muscotti for sixteen years.

Bodies may have turned up in the trunks of cars in other parts of Conemaugh County, certain small newsstands and confectionaries in other towns may have suffered unexplained explosions, but nothing like that had happened in Rocksburg for sixteen years.

Balzic had to smile thinking about it. I been chief for sixteen years, he thought, and those Chamber guys never gave me a phone call. Maybe it was all just a coincidence. . . .

Balzic parked his cruiser beside Muscotti's side door on State Street, and the smile left him. He was back to Armand Manditti again, Fat Manny who was alive only because of his fat, and to Tullio Manditti, who was behaving as though his brother was anything but a victim.

Balzic paused outside Muscotti's door and told himself that he had to control the anger he felt rising in him. There was no reason to believe that Manny's unemployment—if that were true—had anything at all to do with his being stabbed. Still, Balzic was getting a bad taste from fuming over that possibility, and he didn't want to blow the opportunity of finding out by losing his temper.

It was nearly five o'clock when Balzic came down the back stairs into Muscotti's. The bar was lined elbow to elbow with the mill and construction workers who habitually stopped after work to drink and learn the day's winning numbers. Shortly, the office brigade from the courthouse would be coming in, as would the merchants who kept shops in the vicinity. Some students from the county community college sat drinking beer out of quart bottles at one of the tables. At another sat Tom Murray, managing editor of *The Rocksburg Gazette*, with two of his reporters—Dick Dietz, who covered the courthouse, and Bob Armour, who covered City Hall. Surrounding the end of the bar nearest the side door were three of Muscotti's closest friends, Dom Scalzo, Tony DiLisi, and Bruno Cercone.

At the other end of the bar nearest the front door, Vinnie the bartender was arguing fruitlessly with Iron City Steve.

"If the war's over," Iron City Steve was shouting, his elbows flapping and his head bobbing, "how come we got all this combat?"

"Enough already!" Vinnie shouted back. "Just sit down and shut up a while. I had you up to my eyeballs today."

Steve's shoulder jerked and twitched. His hand sawed under his nose and then he pinched the corners of his mouth to wipe away beads of saliva. "You had enough, but who do I get enough of? I don't even see anybody I want a little piece of. . . ."

Balzic walked to that end of the bar, exchanging greetings with everyone he knew—which was everyone except for the students—and wondering why Dom Muscotti wasn't in sight.

"Are we approaching or proceeding?" Steve said to Balzic.

24

"Can't say for me, Steve. How 'bout you?"

"As for me, I approach a little, then I proceed a little. It all comes out the same—I don't go backward."

"Go sit down," Vinnie said. "Sit down and shut up or else go upstairs and go to sleep."

"See there?" Steve said, his hands flailing in all directions. "For every doer there's a teller. Comes out even that way. Gives everybody something to do."

"Shut up, I'm telling you. Jesus Christ, you been going since nine o'clock this morning."

"If I could just believe that," Steve said, picking up his beer and his muscatel and shuffling to the table nearest the front door.

"What'll it be, Mario?"

"Beer. Where's Dom?"

"He had to go someplace," Vinnie said, drawing the beer and setting it in front of Balzic. "He should be back pretty soon. What's the matter? You don't look too good."

"I don't feel too good right now, to tell you the truth. You hear about Fat Manny?"

"No. What about him?"

"Somebody tried to kill him."

Vinnie stopped wiping the bar, his face expressing genuine disbelief and surprise. "No shit. Who? What the hell for?"

"Pretty good questions. I thought maybe you might know something."

Hey, Mario, honest to God, this is the first I heard about it. When'd it happen?"

"Sometime this afternoon. Tullio came home from the dump and found him on the porch. Somebody really carved him up. Whoever it was wasn't fucking around."

"No-o shit. Man, oh man. Mario, I—I don't know what to say."

"What's the meeting about down the other end?"

"You mean Soup, Digs, and Brownie?" The names he used were the nicknames of Muscotti's friends.

Balzic nodded.

"Nothing special. Usual stuff, you know."

"Yeah? Well, do me a favor. Go down there and tell them what I just told you. I want to see what happens."

"Hey, Mario," Vinnie said, leaning close over the bar, "don't even talk like that. That ain't right."

"Just go tell them, will you please?"

"Okay, I'll tell them, but I'm telling you right now, Mario, you're thinking wrong. Those guys don't have nothing to do with Manny. Or Tullio either. If they got some bitch with either one of those two, I'd know about it, believe me. And they don't."

"I believe you. Just go tell them."

"Hey, Vinnie," someone called out. "Couple more here."

"Take it easy, take it easy. I only got two legs."

"Yeah? Well how 'bout using them?"

Vinnie shrugged at Balzic. "See what I got to listen to every day? Comedians. This should be Hollywood, and I should be Cecil B. DeMille. I got a cast of thousands in here every goddamn day." He hurried away to fill that order and then went to the far end of the bar, where he talked briefly with Scalzo, DiLisi, and Cercone.

Balzic couldn't see DiLisi's face too clearly, but Cercone looked like he was going to choke on his drink and Scalzo's face went slack. Scalzo shot a glance toward Balzic, then said something to the other two. He bent his head forward to hear their replies, then picked up his

26

beer and came down the bar toward Balzic.

Scalzo, heavy-lidded, squatly built, indifferent about his appearance, and without pretensions about himself or his work, seemed more and more disturbed the nearer he came to Balzic. It figured, Balzic thought, that he would be the one to talk. He was much older than DiLisi or Cercone—he was sixty-four—and had been with Muscotti longer, since 1945, right after his discharge from the army. That had been his last legitimate employment and was the reason for his nickname. He had been a cook.

He set his beer on the bar and stood very close to Balzic. "What's this about Manny?"

"Well, it's this way, Soup. If it wasn't for all that grease on him, you'd be drinking to his memory."

"Now who the fuck'd want to do that? He's a pain in the ass, Mario. You know that better than I do. But you got to admit, he never hurt nobody. He's just a slob, that's all."

"Well, he must've hurt somebody."

"Nah, I don't believe it. Somebody must've went nuts. Why? Why him? What do you think? You think something else?"

"Right now I'm not sure what I think. All I know is the same thing you know. He's been Dom's gofer for a lot of years, but in the hospital Tullio tells me he's unemployed."

Scalzo laughed. "Come on, you kiddin'? When wasn't he unemployed?"

"You know what I mean. Tullio says he don't work for anybody, though I got to admit he didn't say he wasn't working for Dom anymore exactly, but that was the impression I got—"

"Ah, Tullio's pulling your chain. He don't know what he's talking about. That was nothing. Dom sets him down every once in a while. It's no big deal."

"Yeah, I know Dom's set him down occasionally before, and I got a pretty good idea why. But what was it for this time?"

Scalzo took a moment to reply. "Listen, Mario, I know you for a long time, right?"

Balzic nodded.

"Have I ever fucked around with the rules? Huh? Have I?"

"Not with me. No."

"Well, listen. Neither has Brownie and neither has Digs. I don't know what you're thinking, but I can see you're pissed off. But believe me, you got no right to even start thinking like, uh, well, you know, like sending Vinnie down there to tell us. Like you're going to watch us, you know? You shouldn't've done that, Mario. In fact, I'm a little surprised you did it."

"Well, maybe that was a little chicken-shit on my part, but it's been a long time since anything like this happened, and I'll be goddamned if it's going to get any bigger."

"Hey, I can see your point," Scalzo said. "I know what you mean. But me and Brownie and Digs got nothing to do with those two. They do whatever they do for Dom. We don't have nothing to do with them, believe me. I don't like Tullio. Never did. I used to go up their house when their old man was alive. I liked the old guy. We used to sit around and drink his wine and play *morra*. Even then I didn't like Tullio. He was always a smart-mouth. Even when he's three, four years old, he was a wise little prick. And all the trouble Manny got in, all the

28

trouble he ever got in, it was 'cause Tullio put him up to it. And Manny always got caught. See, Manny ain't too swift in the head, and the old man used to look out for him, and Tullio, he didn't like it. So he was always trying to get Manny in the heat with the old man. It's the same way now. They're the same way with Dom. Tullio tells him, 'Hey, don't turn all them numbers in. Who's going to know?' Shit like that. But Manny always fucks up somehow, you know."

"Is that what happened this time?" Balzic said.

Scalzo shrugged. "Hey, maybe I said too much already. I think maybe you better ask Dom. I'll tell you what. Ask Vinnie. He knows more about that than I do. Believe me." Scalzo picked up his beer and took a sip. "Mario, I been around a long time. Believe me, don't try to make nothing out of this. Somebody went nuts. Had to. Couldn't be nothing else."

Balzic shrugged. "Well, I'll tell you this, Soup. I'm going to keep asking until I find out you're right, how's that? And believe me, I hope you are right."

"I'm right. You'll see," Scalzo said, turning away and walking back down the bar to where Cercone and DiLisi were waiting for him.

Balzic stared moodily at his beer, then picked it up and drained the glass in four swallows, holding it up when he finished for Vinnie to refill it.

Vinnie refilled his glass and set it on the bar. He took some moments wiping the bar and the stem of the glass. "So what'd they say?"

"Soup says they don't know anything about Manny or Tullio."

"Ain't that what I said? Huh?"

Balzic nodded. "He also said to ask you. He said you

29

knew more about those two than he did. Or Digs or Brownie."

"I already told you, Mario. They couldn't have any bitch with those two fat-asses or I'd know about it. Ain't that what I said?"

"That's what you said, all right. So tell me. Is Manny still running for Dom? Tullio says he isn't."

"Listen, Mario, I could tell you, but I think it's better you hear it from Dom, you know?"

"So he isn't."

Vinnie nodded with his eyes downcast and then shrugged. "I don't think it's any different this time than it was all those other times, understand. But you talk to Dom. I got enough aggravation with him lately. He even thinks I'm putting any more of his business in the street, I won't be able to live with him—which ain't to say I been putting any of his business in the street. But he thinks I have."

"What's your aggravation with him?"

"Oh, Mario, honest to God, you don't know?"

"I don't know what you're talking about."

Vinnie nodded for them to move to the very end of the bar. He faced the window overlooking Main Street and spoke very softly. Balzic had to lean over the bar to hear him.

"How old is he?" Vinnie began. "Fifty-seven, right?"

Balzic nodded and shrugged.

"You know how long since he could get it up? Five years. All that Canadian Club. Why do you think I quit drinking? I take maybe two shots of brandy a day. One in my coffee, the other one around noon. He told me to quit. *He* told *me*, get it? So what do you think now?"

"Oh don't tell me."

"Yeah. Younger than his daughters for crissake."

"Hey, it happens, Vinnie. It happens. It's happened to better men than him."

"Hey, those better men ain't got his wife. She ever finds out for sure, I'm going to be the second one she buries."

"You mean she asked you?"

Vinnie shook his head and winced. "She called me at home last week. You know the last time she called me? When Dom's father died. Twenty-two fucking years ago, that's the last time she called me at home. You know what she asks me? She wants to know how's business. How's business! Are you kiddin'? You should've heard the lies I told her. Jesus Christ, I should get an Oscar for that performance."

"What's wrong? How's she know something's up?"

"The register's down a yard, a yard and a half every week for like two months now." Vinnie shook his head and sighed. "This fucking Tuscan, what is he? A medical miracle? He got to get a hard-on now? And me, I'm in the middle. I got to be nice to the broad, you know. Whatever she wants. Booze, bread, food—oh, Christ. I'll tell you, Mario, I wasn't this scared when Sammy Weisberg was still alive. Dom's old lady is something else. Ah, what am I telling you for?"

"Is he dipping into the other stuff or just the register for her?"

"What do you think? I'm telling you, I'm ready to go to California or some fucking place. This has got me nuts. And him, he's like in junior high school, the way he's acting. Twenty, thirty beans every day. Oh, brother.

You know what really scares me? Sometimes I think the bastard really wants to hear how big the bang's going to be."

"It'll make some noise all right."

"Hey, Vinnie, you working today or not?" someone called out down the bar.

"Keep your pants on, what is this?" Vinnie shouted back. He started to hustle away but came back. "You know what I did last Sunday? Go ahead, think about it."

"I can guess."

"Uh-huh. First time since I buried my mother. On my knees, with a candle, in front of Mary yet. Holy fucking Christ. . . ."

Balzic shook his head sympathetically and then resumed staring at his beer between sips. He drank that one and another before he heard the door open behind him and heard Dom Muscotti's voice speaking in Italian to someone still on the sidewalk.

The first person Muscotti saw after he closed the door was Balzic, and he smiled broadly and extended his hand, asking in Italian how Balzic was.

"I'll know better after we talk."

"In the back?"

"In the back."

Muscotti had held Balzic's hand until then. It was a strong grip but with no attempt to show strength, for Muscotti, in spite of his age and perpetual drinking, was somehow still a powerful man. Except that his once-red hair was now iron gray, the only obvious signs of aging about him were the deepening creases in his face and neck and the increasing paunch below his belt. He had given up driving an automobile years ago, and no matter what the temperature or the weather, he walked everywhere without an outer coat. He would ride in an automobile only when he had to leave Rocksburg, asking for a lift from whoever happened to be in his saloon and paying for it with drinks. His shoes were handmade in Philadelphia, and he joked that he would live only about a year longer than his shoemaker.

Speaking to everyone by name, Muscotti led Balzic to the second of two small rooms beyond the kitchen. He held the door for Balzic, flipped the switch for the light over the round table in the center of the room, then closed and locked the door behind them. There were ten chairs in the room, seven of them around the table, and two ancient, wooden filing cabinets in one corner. Muscotti went to the nearest of those and brought out a bottle of Valpolicella and two thick-stemmed glasses.

"Sit, Mario, sit," Muscotti said, screwing out the cork and pouring the wine to within a half-inch of the tops of the glasses.

Balzic picked up one of the glasses and toasted Muscotti's health while still standing. Muscotti returned the toast and then they both sat, pulling out the chairs and sitting obliquely facing each other.

"How's your mother, Mario?"

"Fine. How's yours?"

"Oh, couldn't be better. She's a little mad at me though."

"Why's that?"

"I made her put her money in the bank. She says to me, 'All of it?' And I said, 'Well, you can keep a little in the house.' So how much you think she wants to keep?"

"How much?"

"Five grand. 'Just in case,' she says. Can you beat that? I said to her, 'Hey, what kind of emergency you

33

think you're going to have?' She just laughed. I laughed like hell myself." Muscotti drank the rest of his wine and said, "Drink up, Mario. Have some more."

"Thank you," Balzic said, drinking his and then watching the color of the wine as Muscotti refilled the glasses.

"How's Ruth? Emily, Marie—they okay?"

"They're fine," Balzic said. "Your family?"

"Oh, you know. What do they got to complain about? Hey, did I tell you what I got my daughters for last Christmas? I think I must've told everybody but you."

Balzic shook his head.

"Telephone credit cards. They're better than all the rest of those cards. You can get anything on those AT&T cards, d'you know that? I told them, I said, 'Hey, don't you do it. Just phone calls, that's all,' " Muscotti said, laughing. "Those credit cards, Christ, what a friggin' hustle. I wish I'd've thought of them. They're better than football. Better than boxing used to be."

Balzic coughed and crossed and uncrossed his legs.

Muscotti had been sitting back in his chair. Now he straightened up and put his hands on his knees, looking directly into Balzic's eyes. "Okay, Mario, I'm listening."

"You know about Fat Manny?"

Muscotti nodded. "I heard right before I came in. Young DeNezza told me out on the street."

"Well, what's going on?"

"I don't know," Muscotti said, shrugging.

"Is he still running for you?"

"No."

"Why not? What happened?"

"He did something he wasn't supposed to do."

34

"Hey, listen, Dom, maybe you don't see what I see—"

"Oh, Mario, wait a minute. I see plenty. I knew you were going to be here as soon as young DeNezza told me. I said to myself, I'll bet a hundred to one Mario's waiting for me when I get inside."

"Okay, so you won. So what's going on?"

"Mario, I'm telling you, I don't know."

"But for sure he's not working for you anymore."

"Oh, you know, it wasn't nothing permanent. I just had to sit him down a little while, that's all. He'd've got his job back."

Balzic sipped his wine and thought a moment. "Dom, sixteen years ago next month, we made some rules, remember?"

"I remember," Muscotti said, nodding vigorously.

"No whores, no dope, no muscle, right?"

"That's right."

"And it never cost you a penny tax, right?"

"Not to you, that's right."

"Or to any of my people either."

"I can't argue with that."

"So all of a sudden we get some muscle and you're telling me you don't know anything about it?"

"Mario, honest to God, I don't. It shocked me to hear it. I mean it. I don't know where it came from or why. On my father's grave it didn't come from me. What the hell do I want with muscle? What am I—one of those crazy New York guys? All muscle does is bring heat. Who the hell wants heat? Right now, look what's happening. Somebody goes Hollywood, and here you are, looking at me like I'm a crazy. Christ, Mario, how long's it been since we talked back here like this? You think I want

35

this?" Muscotti threw up his hands. "Over Fat Manny?"

"Okay," Balzic said. "So why'd you sit him down? Was he booking on his own?"

"What do you think?"

"I'm asking. Was he?"

"Yeah, sure. What else? The sonofabitch, I should've had him out the dump. That was my mistake. Giving him something better because my mother likes him. I should've put him out there."

"Why didn't you?"

"I just told you. My mother likes him. He brings the groceries, they sit around and gossip. He knows just what to tell her. She feeds him, he eats like six plates of pasta, he tells her how she's the best cook in the world since his mother died, and she loves him. Then he tells her who he saw coming out of church, who was in the A&P, who was buying zucchini, who was buying eggplant, and she wants to know all that stuff. I tried other guys. They don't know how to talk to her. She gets mad and I got to put him back on. She's really been hollering at me since I set him down this time."

"How long's it been this time?"

"A week."

"Okay, so he booked something and he got beat. You don't think there could be any other reason?"

"What else? He books a winner, he can't pay, the guy takes the heat. What the fuck—I'd do the same thing myself." Dom shook his head. "I told the goddamn dummy a hundred times. I said, 'Manny, you can't do this. One of these times you're going to get burned, and everybody's going to think I'm backing you. And I ain't. And you're going to have to take the weight, and where the fuck are you going to get the five-forty if you take a buck on a solid hit? You ain't getting it from me; not even at five percent a week, you ain't getting it.' I told him that so many times I can't count them. You think he listens? Huh? What am I talking for?

"What kills me, you know when he does it? Five minutes after he passes a bakery. He sees all those jelly doughnuts and cream puffs in the window and right away the eraser starts going. He got twenty, twenty-two bets, he turns in eighteen. And that friggin' Tullio, he tells Manny, 'Don't worry about it. Dom got so much paper the government's coming to him. What's a buck and a half to Dom?' And friggin' Manny listens to him and thinks it's all right. I'd like to kick Tullio's ass myself. Manny's too. But see, Manny ain't as smart as Tullio. So as mad as I get at him, I really can't get too mad, you know? 'Cause he's dumb . . . I should've kicked his ass the first time he did it. I knew this was going to happen. . . ."

"Well, you kick both their asses if you want to, but there's two things you better do first."

"Me? What do you want me to do?"

"First, tell Tullio not to get any ideas. 'Cause something happens, I'm going to come straight to you."

"Aw, Mario—"

"Aw Mario nothing. We made the rules. You and me. You get the action, you keep the odds right, you pay no taxes. Everybody who wins gets paid, and no more than five percent on the shylocking to the losers. Did I leave anything out?"

"No."

"Okay. Then convince Tullio."

"Or else?"

"Or else you all go to the slam, and I'll fix it so

37

everybody has to put up cash bonds. All the street people you got. It'll cost you a fortune."

"But, Mario, you know it's not me!"

"I know it's not. But I'm making it you. Because Tullio won't listen to me. He thinks I'm a jackoff. *Your* jackoff. But he does something, and everything stops. And it won't be me serving the warrants. It'll be U.S. marshalls."

"Aw, come on now, Mario. I been straight with you all these years and you're going to talk like this to me? Over something you know I didn't have nothing to do with?"

"All I'm telling you to do is tell Tullio. Because, Dom, this town is not going back to the way things were when Collela was chief and you and Sammy Weisberg were burning each other down. Collela worked both of you pretty good, and from what I heard he paid seventy-five thousand for that place in Florida. Which must've made you and Weisberg feel pretty smart." Balzic stabbed the air with his index finger. "Goddamnit, I don't have any retirement like that to look forward to, and you got a lot more money because I don't. So you tell Tullio."

"Okay, Mario, okay, take it easy," Muscotti said, shaking his head with his eyes downcast. "But I can't make any miracle for you. Some things you just can't control."

"Put somebody on him."

"Like who?"

"Cercone would make a good keeper. Tell him what's going to happen."

"Brownie? At the dump?"

"Hey, Dom, how you handle it is how you handle it. All I'll tell you is this: I'll do everything I can to find whoever it was as fast as I can. Which brings up the second thing you have to do. Tell Manny to quit listening to Tullio. As long as Tullio's got his ear, Manny's not going to tell me anything. But he opens up, it's simple. I go collar the guy and that's that. But if Manny keeps shut, then I got to find the guy myself, which is going to take time, which is going to give Tullio time, which means you got to keep somebody on him longer, which means you lose business somewhere else. And if Tullio shakes whoever you put on him and does something stupid, then I guarantee it'll cost you a fortune in bail."

Muscotti shook his head and rubbed his palms together. "That fat-ass. I should've got him on with the county. Dumb as he is, he ought to be working for the government."

Balzic drove immediately to his station after leaving Muscotti's. He was so preoccupied with what he'd said to Muscotti and the way he'd said it that he ran a red light two blocks from City Hall, spinning the wheel wildly to swerve between a pickup truck and a station wagon loaded with cub scouts. He didn't even slow down. He slouched against the seat, tucking his chin into the lapels of his raincoat, and hoped he hadn't been recognized.

Going up the steps, he said under his breath, "You dumb bastard, it's a good thing you got sense enough to have an unmarked car. . . ."

Inside the duty room he found Desk Sergeant Vic Stramsky talking on the phone, taking a description.

"Another runaway," Stramsky said after hanging up. "Cleaned out his old lady's purse and split. Thirteen

39

years old. I wonder how far he thinks he's going to get on four bucks and change."

"Well, put it out to the troops," Balzic said. "Maybe we'll get lucky with this one. What's that, the third one this week?"

"Yeah," Stramsky said, nodding, "but we found the second one."

"Well, that makes it two to one, the kids are still leading." Balzic went to the coffee urn and poured himself a cup. He took a sip and scalded his lips, spitting the coffee on the floor. "What the hell's wrong with this machine? Everything comes out boiling."

Stramsky ignored him, rolling over to the radio console and putting out the name and description of the runaway. When he was finished, he said, "What're you screaming at the machine for? If you know everything's coming out boiling, why can't you wait?"

"Go ahead, give me a lecture about patience. My head's going six ways at once—all wrong—and I'm supposed to improve my character. I burn myself once more, that machine goes in the can, and nobody'll have to worry about my character." He went to the log on the table in front of the radio console and ran his finger down the list of calls. "Some day this is. Two bent fenders, a mattress fire, a runaway, and Fat Manny—and he doesn't even make the log."

"What're you mumbling about?" Stramsky said, rolling his chair over beside Balzic.

"Put down here that Armand Manditti was the victim of felonious assault, sometime between three-thirty and four-thirty. Assailant unknown. Give it the whole treatment."

"Did you say Fat Manny?"

40

"Yeah. Listen, I'm going up to Norwood."

"Why?"

"Because that's where Manny got it."

Stramsky started to smile, but caught himself and turned away.

"What's so funny?"

"You. You're really gunned up about something. If you were going up to Norwood, why'd you come back here? You could've told me that on the radio."

Balzic snorted. "You think that's pretty dumb, huh?"

"Well, you know. . . ."

"Yeah? Well, you should've seen me ducking after I almost took the front end off a station wagon full of kids. You'd've really got your jollies over that. . . . What the hell do I know what I came back for? Maybe to burn my mouth on the coffee, all the weight I tried to lay on Muscotti. I couldn't believe it was me talking."

Stramsky chortled. "What'd you say to him?"

Before Balzic could reply, the phone rang. Stramsky answered it and then held it out for Balzic. "It's Johnson from the state CID."

"Hello, Walk. What do you got?"

"Not much, buddy. But I'll tell you one thing. You weren't joking about those two being slobs. I never saw a house like that. God, newspapers up to the ceiling in, uh, I guess it was the living room; garbage in the kitchen you wouldn't believe; in the bathroom, so help me, there was a radiator and two batteries for a car. And stink! Jesus. You couldn't tell if there had been a struggle or not. My people kept looking at me and saying, 'How would we know?' "

"Yeah. So did you get anything?"

"We scraped up a lot of blood. There was no forcible

41

entry. We got a couple sets of prints, but that's really the best I can offer."

"How about somebody stepping in the blood—any chance?"

"No. There was a lot of stepping and stumbling going on, but not one damn thing clear."

"How about tire tracks?"

"All over the place, but we could only make out one matched set, and then when this Tullio showed up, it didn't take any expert to see they were all off his car." Johnson paused and chuckled. "That Tullio, is he something. He came in and started screaming where was our search warrant. I tried to tell him that his brother was the victim and that his residence was the scene of a crime, but I wasted my breath. He raised holy hell for about ten minutes, then all of a sudden he says, 'I got to take a bath. Don't bother me no more.' And off he goes and takes a bath."

"So, uh, you really didn't get anything, huh?"

"Sorry, Mario. I wish I could give you something more, but about the only thing I have are the prints. I sent our print man up to the hospital to get the victim's, and we got Tullio's. Once we get a comparison we might have something, but that's about it."

"Well, thanks, Walk, I appreciate it."

"Listen, you also weren't kidding about the neighbors. I didn't find one who could speak English."

"Oh, they can all right, don't kid yourself. But they won't. Not even to me." Balzic sighed. "Okay, Walk. So let me know how the prints turn out."

"Will do. Take it easy."

Balzic hung up and swore.

"I take it they didn't come up with anything," Stramsky said.

"You take it right, brother."

"So now tell me what you said to Muscotti."

"Huh? Oh. Nothing much. I just told him that if anything happens because of Manny getting chopped up, I was going to guarantee his whole operation was going to the slammer, that's all. Just the goddamnedest threat I ever made in my life. And then I sat there with all the face in the world and tried to make out like it's no threat. Like it's a sure pop. Christ, I must be watching too much television or something. But you know the real capper?"

Stramsky shook his head.

"I think he bought it, how's that grab you?" Balzic shook his head and snorted softly. "Now can you feature me walking into the U.S. Attorney's office in Pittsburgh, bigger than shit, and I'm trying to convince those guys that I let the second biggest banker and lay-offer in the county—I let him run for sixteen years, and not only did I never bust him or anybody connected with him, but I never took a penny from him. Now just what do you think they're going to say? They're not going to be able to say anything. They'll all be laughing so hard they'll have hernias."

"Don't you think Dom knows that? Or don't you think he's going to think of it?"

"I don't know. The look on his face, I couldn't believe it. But maybe all that Canadian Club finally got to his brain. Then again, maybe he got himself in too deep in something else."

"What's that?"

"Something Vinnie told me. Seems that old Tuscan

43

is going to do adolescence over again. He got Vinnie so shook up, Vinnie went to church last Sunday and put up a candle in front of Mary. Dom's wife finds out for sure what's going on, everybody'll be putting up candles in front of St. Jude."

"You mean Dom got himself a broad?" Stramsky threw back his head and roared with laughter.

"Yeah, it's funny now, but what do you think's going to happen when his old lady starts asking him how come the register's down a yard and a half every week? How many stories you think he can come up with?"

"Is that what he's throwing at the broad?"

"According to Vinnie. I'll tell you, I never saw Vinnie so rattled. Which, the more I think about it, the more I think is the reason Dom bought my bullshit." Balzic sighed heavily. "Which just gives me another thought. Holy Christ!"

"What's the matter?"

"The matter is, Dom's old lady blows the whistle on him, we're right back in the U.S. Attorney's office, are you kidding?"

"So? You're clean. The whole force is clean."

"Come on, Vic, you know better than that. There's two ways to be dirty. Everybody knows the first way. The second applies to us. We don't do what we get paid to do, we're dirty, brother, and that is all she wrote."

"Hey, Mario, don't you think you're getting a little carried away? Hell, Dom's wife never goes near his joint. And who's going to tell her?"

"Nobody has to, Vic. She's already wise. She called Vinnie at home last week and asked him how business was. She knows something's up. She goes through

Dom's pants every night as soon as he starts snoring. Hell, Dom'll tell you that himself. She just hasn't figured out how come he's been short—oh, Jesus Christ." Balzic clapped his hands and threw them upward and then held his head. "No wonder he bought it! He's looking at me and listening to me, but he's hearing his old lady."

"I don't get it," Stramsky said.

"Dom. I'm thinking he bought *my* bullshit. But that's exactly the same story his wife's going to give him. The only difference is I was bitching about Manny. But he's already been through this in his head with his wife. In his head, he knows that's what she's going to say. I could've been talking about the broad for all the difference it makes. He knew goddamn well I can't put him in the slammer without taking a lot of heat myself, but she can put him away forever just on the income taxes alone. Ho, boy, what an ego I got. I wish I had a brain to match." Balzic pounded his fist on a desk and then walked quickly toward the door.

"Hey, where you going now?"

"Someplace. Wherever I can find somebody smarter than me. Wherever the hell that is. Hell, right now that's practically anyplace."

Balzic took the alleys to avoid traffic, pulling in ten minutes later to the rear parking lot of Rocksburg Bowl. He hustled inside to the lounge and bar, looking around for Mo Valcanas. It had to be ladies' day at the bowling alleys because the only man Balzic saw was the bartender, an aging and overweight one-time pretty boy who brushed his hair with his hands and straightened his tie each time he filled an order. He seemed to have found paradise serving alcohol and stale jokes to leagues of

45

women bowlers. Balzic surmised this in a minute, then started for the room behind the bar where the gin games were played daily.

He found only Mo Valcanas and Dick Gervasi, the owner of the alleys, playing cards. Gervasi was writing on a small pad, and Valcanas was shuffling the cards while trying to read the score upside down. Both looked up at the same time.

"Mario," Gervasi said. "Long time no see, buddy. Where you been keeping yourself?"

"It should be longer," Valcanas said. "He comes here, he's got something in mind for me."

"Gentlemen," Balzic said, drawing up a chair and straddling it. "I'll come right to the point."

"The day any cop comes right to the point will be a first in American history," Valcanas said. "And that includes you."

"Oh, you're so sweet. I could just give you a big kiss."

"You want something to drink, Mario?" Gervasi said, standing.

"No, thanks. What I really want is to talk to the Greek for a couple minutes. You mind?"

"What the hell are you asking him for? You want to talk to me, why don't you ask me if I mind?"

"Oh, you're so lovable. I'll bet your mother just beamed the whole nine months, just beamed and glowed waiting for you to pop your cute little bald head out."

"Hey, I'll be glad to let you two alone, Mario. This Greek's killing me today. I need a breather."

"I see you got a new bartender," Balzic said. "What happened to Jimmy?"

"He's in the hospital. He'll be back in a couple weeks.

You sure you don't want something to drink?" Gervasi went for the door.

"Nah. I had plenty already today."

Gervasi left then, closing the door firmly behind him.

"Okay, Mario," Valcanas said, "I hesitate to ask, but what is it this time?"

"Just a couple questions about the law, that's all."

"And naturally these couple answers I'm expected to give will be for free. You couldn't ask in my office, where I might feel justified in sending you a bill."

"Naturally. Besides, every time I walk into your office I start to feel like I'm really in trouble, like I really need a lawyer."

"Uh-huh," Valcanas grumbled. "I ought to set up an office in all the saloons I go into. I might start making some money."

"Boy, there's a contradiction for you. You set up offices in all the saloons you go into, you couldn't afford the light bills."

"Well, let's quit fucking around. It'll cost you two drinks. I got to get that much out of you."

"Fair enough. So here it is: now I know that a wife can't be forced to testify against her husband, but how about if she volunteers? What's she worth on the stand?"

"That depends. Give me a situation."

"Well, the woman, after a long and faithful marriage on her part, finds out that her old man's screwing around, which he's never done before. In the meantime, he's been involved for most of his adult life in illegal activities. She may not be an accomplice exactly, but she's the closest thing to it there is. She knows everything, in other words."

47

Valcanas grinned and then broke up laughing. "Christ, don't tell me you're getting worried about Dom too? Half the goddamn courthouse is walking around on eggs about that. That's all I've heard down there for the past two weeks."

"Well, I guess I must be the dumbest guy in town then."

"You said it, Mario, I didn't."

"Aw fuck you too. Well, what about it? How much damage can she do?"

"That would depend on a couple of things. First, it would depend on whether she has access to records or had been keeping records herself. I mean, her credibility goes down to practically zero if she just walks into the U.S. Attorney's office and says, 'I know my husband did this or that or whatever.' That's for openers. Then suppose she has records, enough to get the whole thing to trial. It would depend on the attorneys—how good the prosecutor was in leading her through her motivation for coming forward at this late date in her life—and on his lawyer—Dom's—for trying to wreck that motivation. But the big thing would be the jury. The prosecution would want as many old ladies in the jury box as they could get, preferably Italian Catholic, and the defense would want as many dirty old men as they could get. Whoever wins that battle wins the war, that's what it comes down to."

"So given the worst suppositions, Dom's wife could really raise some hell."

"If you have something to be concerned about, sure. Hell, Corcoran is so rattled that yesterday he called a recess in the middle of a drunk-driving trial. Two more minutes and it would've been over. But he called a recess. I thought his tipstaff was going to faint. But, hell,

Corcoran's got reason to be nervous. All the fines he's laid on Dom's people in the last eight years wouldn't add up to two thousand bucks. That time the state boy scouts caught Digs DiLisi with forty-two-thousand bucks and about ten pounds of numbers slips, Corcoran let him off with costs. Just what do you think that was worth?"

"I don't even want to guess," Balzic said.

"Well, you ever get curious, you go ask Digs how much was in the briefcase when he went to pick it up. He came bitching to me afterward, and I told him, I said, 'You dumb bastard, you ought to be glad you got that much back. Maybe now you'll think of something better to do with those slips than leave them laying around on your kitchen table.' "

"But I thought you beat that for him."

Valcanas smiled. "Come on. I filed a motion to suppress evidence on the grounds that the boy scouts' information was based on hearsay. The law's changed now, you know that. Now the so-called confidential informant has to appear himself in front of the magistrate. But then, Christ, a cop's hearsay was good enough.

"Anyway," Valcanas went on, "if I hadn't known that Corcoran was going to hear the damned thing, I wouldn't even have wasted my secretary's time typing up the motion to suppress. But I knew what he'd do. Exactly what he did, which was give Digs a speech about how the tentacles of gambling reach into all sorts of nasty nasties, and then fine him a hundred bucks and costs. But Digs, that egotistical ass, he can't get it through his head that you put forty-two big ones on the wheel of justice, somebody pushing is going to think lifting is easier. And to this day, he thinks that if it had come up in front of some of Dom's other friends, my motion to suppress—to put it mildly—would've been received with anything more than a smile. He thinks those other guys would've hit him with a fine and costs—and let him walk out with a full briefcase.

"Christ, sometimes these wops make me laugh. He gets half a briefcase back, and he gets pissed at me. He says—and I quote—'It would've been cheaper to go to jail.' I said, 'Why you stupid sonofabitch, you go to jail and you don't get anything back.' But do you know, to this day he's never paid my bill. Not only that, he refuses to speak to me. Christ. . . ."

Balzic chewed his thumbnail thoughtfully.

"Besides which," Valcanas said, shifting around on his chair, "this has got to be the biggest joke in this county since Froggy ran for judge."

"Why's that?"

"Dom's not screwing anybody for crissake. He can't. You can't drink as much as he drinks and still grind your organ. If anything, his genitourinary tract is in worse shape than mine—if that's possible."

"Well, I wouldn't pretend to know whether he's screwing anybody," Balzic said. "But a hell of a lot of people seem to think so. And his wife know's the register's short in his saloon. What difference does it make whether he is or isn't or can or can't—if she thinks he is, what's the difference?"

"None. If she acts on what she thinks. If that is what she thinks. Why don't you ask her and be a real cop—prevent a crime instead of waiting until it happens and then trying to prove that whoever you caught is the person who did it? Hell, what could be more salutary than that?"

"Oh, up yours. What do I say? 'Hey, Gina, there's

something I been meaning to ask you—is that how I start?"

"How you ask is your problem. I'm not interested in the answer myself. All I know is, the most Dom can do is rub bellies. And that would be pure nostalgia. I'll make you a bet though."

"What bet?"

"I'll lay twenty against one that all he's doing with that broad—whoever she is—is talking. And giving her money for being kind enough to listen. People are waiting in line to talk to the brain strainers, either because it's fashionable or because their families can't stand them anymore. But can you feature Dom going to a shrink? Hell, I can imagine him exposing himself to a little girl sooner than I can see him admitting that there was something going on in his head he couldn't handle.

"And what about a priest?" Valcanas went on. "You know what a priest is to Dom? He's a guy in funny clothes who read too many books when he was a kid because the nuns scared the shit out of him. And all he's good for is saying the words that make your wife feel all right about screwing you, or that make the family feel okay when somebody dies. But most of all, he's good for saying the right words in front of a jury when you get busted for running a book. And unless he's had some genuine change of mind, those are the reasons he takes up the collection every Sunday at twelve o'clock mass. Go ask Marrazo if I'm not right. Better yet, go ask him if Dom ever came to him with a problem—any problem."

"I don't have to ask," Balzic said. "Most of what you said I agree with, except for that part about paying the broad just to listen."

"Oh, come on, Mario. Hell, I had a client once who

51

used to pay a whore fifty bucks an hour once a week, sometimes twice, just so he could cuss her out and call her names. He never went within three feet of her. What do you think he was doing?"

"You tell me."

"He was telling her everything he didn't have the guts to tell his wife. The whore used to sit around doing her nails, listening to records, and all she was required to do was look up every ten minutes or so and say, 'What do you know about it, dummy?' Then he was off for another ten minutes. But do you think his wife believed that? Especially after she went to the trouble of hiring a private dick to find out where he was going? And you want to hear something really stupid? I actually arranged a meeting in my office."

"Oh, are you kiddin' me?" Balzic said, laughing. "With the wife and the whore?"

Valcanas scratched his throat slowly. "I was a lot younger then. A lot younger. God, when I think about it, I can't believe I was ever that young."

When Balzic finally quit laughing, he said, "I still can't get it through my head. I—"

"Look," Valcanas said, "I know you talk with Marrazo a lot. And I think I know you well enough to be reasonably sure that if something was really bothering you, you'd go to a shrink. But what do you think would happen in this town if word got around that the chief of police was seeing a shrink?"

"I wouldn't tell anybody about it."

"Then what's so hard to understand about paying a broad to listen to you?"

"I don't understand it because I can't see myself doing it, that's all."

"Well, Christ, you just said that if you had to go to a shrink you wouldn't tell anybody about it. Now you say you can't see yourself paying a broad for practically the same thing. You're as bad as the people you'd be scared of."

"That's not what I mean."

"Oh, hell, I'm starting to get thirsty. You owe me two drinks, don't forget."

"I didn't forget."

"Then let's go get them," Valcanas said, standing and going toward the door. He stopped short of it. "Think about this, Mario. You wouldn't tell anybody about going to a shrink; now just try to imagine what happens to the *padrone*. I mean, who's he have to talk to? Don't forget, you and I both know where Dom fits in the scheme of things in this part of the state, but most people around here have a vastly inflated notion of who he is and what he can do. And the ones who work for him? Christ, they think he's got a bulletproof soul, except for Vinnie. Vinnie knows that's a crock. He knows Dom better than anybody."

"Well, okay," Balzic said, "but just for the sake of argument, if he does need somebody to talk to, why wouldn't he go to his *padrone?*"

"How should I know? I don't know their rules. For all I know they may play as many silly word games as the Shriners. Maybe there are some things they just don't talk about. Hell, I don't know what's ailing Dom—if anything is. Maybe he suddenly found out he's mortal. Maybe he started paying attention in church. I don't know. Go talk to the broad, I'm telling you. Find out what she's like. See what her angle is. Or go talk to Marrazo. Maybe he knows something. But if you really want to know what's going on, talk to the broad. That's what I'd do . . . come on. You owe me two drinks."

They went out to the bar and Balzic ordered for Valcanas.

"Don't you want anything?" Valcanas asked.

"No. I'm trying to think where I should go, whether I should go talk to the broad or to Father Marrazo."

"You know, Mario," Valcanas said after his drink came, "I'm starting to wonder why you're so concerned about this in the first place."

Balzic shrugged. "Something happened today that is really giving off a bad odor. If I don't get it straightened out in a hurry, it might stink all the way to Pittsburgh. And believe me, the last thing I want is for that U.S. Attorney to get his nose open—no matter what causes it to get open . . . I'll see you, Mo. Try not to hurt anybody driving home."

"Aw go pound sand. Hey, what about the other drink?"

"I owe you one," Balzic said, laughing and clapping Valcanas lightly on the shoulder as he turned to leave. He heard Valcanas cursing in Greek as he left.

Balzic went in the back door of St. Malachy's rectory. He found the door to Father Marrazo's study slightly ajar and knocked gently. He heard some movement but no answer to his knock, so he pushed the door a bit more open.

The priest was sitting at his desk as though he had just put something on the floor, and when he saw that it was Balzic he reached down and brought up a jelly glass half full of wine and an unlabeled bottle which looked to be about two-thirds empty. He didn't bother to stand or speak, nor did he smile. He simply looked at Balzic and then nodded toward a chair for Balzic to sit. He opened a drawer in his desk and brought out another jelly glass, filling it and his own, again nodding to Balzic to have the wine.

"*Salud,*" the priest said, just above a whisper. He drank half his glass without waiting for Balzic to return the toast.

Balzic sipped the wine, just enough to taste it, then put the glass back on the desk and sat in the chair the priest had nodded to.

"Uh, Father, you sick?"

"Not physically, no."

"Well, uh, listen, if there's a better time for me to come back, you know, just say the word and I'll—"

"No, no. Don't leave. Let's just drink some wine and sit here a little while."

Balzic waited some moments, sipping the wine. Then he asked, "Is it that bad?"

"Mario, it's the worst thing—ah, listen to me. I almost said it's the worst thing that's happened to me since I've been in this parish, but that's how bad it is. It's got me thinking about myself instead of what's really involved, as though—ah, never mind . . . I'm really glad you came. There's nobody I know better able to understand this . . . but, please. Drink up."

Balzic took up his glass and drank. "Is this Mr. Ferrarra's wine?"

The priest nodded. "And when we finish this, I've got another bottle, and if we finish that—if you're still here

—I've got a half-gallon of California chablis." The priest spoke with his eyes closed, and his face was going through the very obvious contortions of a man trying to keep from crying.

Balzic lit a cigarette and sat on the edge of his chair, trying to decide whether to speak or keep silent. He couldn't recall ever seeing the priest so distraught.

Some minutes passed. They emptied their glasses, the priest refilled them, and they drank that. The bottle was almost empty. Father Marrazo looked at it, poured the last drops into Balzic's glass, and then left the room. He reappeared shortly, carrying another bottle of Mr. Ferrarra's homemade wine in one hand and the chablis in the other. He set both bottles on his desk and refilled their glasses from the Ferrarra. Then he sank slowly into his chair, picking up his glass and holding it up to the light. "What a color," he said. "Isn't it beautiful?"

"Lovely."

". . . he taught my introductory course in philosophy, can you imagine? Good Lord, how long ago was that?"

Balzic frowned quizzically but said nothing.

"What a roar he caused over at St. Vincent's," Father Marrazo said. "He was supposed to be giving us Aristotle and Augustine and Aquinas, and there he was, throwing Kierkegaard and Heidegger and Jaspers at us as well. My God, it's a wonder he was allowed to go on as long as he did. But, uh, he left eventually. In my junior year. He was made assistant here, and then when he got to be too much here, out he went to St. Jude's."

"Uh, Father, who're you talking about?"

"What? Oh, I'm sorry, Mario. I thought I said. Father Sabatine. From St. Jude's, out in Westfield Township."

"I think I might've met him," Balzic said, "but I don't know him."

"Oh, he raised some hell in this diocese, believe me. He had old ladies of both sexes running to the bishop every week about something he said the Sunday before. Once, long before the encyclical absolving the Jews of any responsibility for killing Christ—long before that—he said it straight out in a sermon. He said to blame the Jews for the death of Christ was absolute nonsense. Remember, this was twenty years ago at least, but years before that encyclical came out. He couldn't have shaken up this diocese more if he'd walked into Aldonari's office and called him a Fascist to his face—which Aldonari was."

"Bishop Aldonari?"

"Well, you know, Mario, I don't mean that literally. But there was no mistaking Aldonari's sympathy when it came to Mussolini. Anybody who could make the trains run on time in Italy and still let the Vatican alone—hell, according to Aldonari, that was practically the Second Coming. So when Sabatine said what he said about the Jews, Aldonari nearly had a stroke.

"And do you know what started all that?" the priest went on, suddenly quite animated. "It was all over Sam Weisberg. Yeah, can you believe it? The thing was, in those days Sabatine had a real passion for golf. The only two things that could keep him off the course were snow and lightning, otherwise he was out there, swinging away. And it must've been on some public course that he met Weisberg. Of course, Sabatine could play any time he wanted to at Westfield Golf Club.

"Apparently, what happened was that he became

friendly with Weisberg—how I can't even guess—but he did, and Weisberg probably mentioned something about playing at Westfield. So Sabatine took him—can you imagine?—two or three times from what I heard."

Balzic just shook his head.

"Well, then, apparently Weisberg started making noises about wanting to join Westfield. I don't need to tell you what that club was like right after the war. Every Italian beer distributor, saloon keeper, bartender, and cook in the county was a member. Half of them were members of this parish, and all of them were friends of Muscotti's. Some of them real friends. It's a small miracle that Weisberg wasn't killed the first time he set foot in the parking lot."

"And you mean to tell me that nobody told Sabatine who Weisberg was?" Balzic said.

"Maybe it was because Sabatine was a priest and wasn't supposed to know about such things," Father Marrazo said, shrugging. "Hell, I don't know why nobody told him, but it's obvious that nobody did. Anyway, he got tired of the polite runaround every time he brought the subject up, so he took it right to the membership committee—formally. They listened to him, thanked him for taking an interest in their club, drank some wine with him, all courteous as hell. Then they waited a couple days and sent him a nice, neat little note saying they were sorry but their membership was filled.

"Well, Sabatine didn't just jump to the wrong conclusion. He flew. And apparently, it never occurred to him that there might be some other reason besides Weisberg's ancestry. And I know damn well that it never entered his mind that any one of two or three guys on that membership committee would've considered it an honor to kill Weisberg. And I'm equally certain that Sabatine never suspected for a second that Weisberg was anything but sincere. He'd've probably fainted if he'd heard that Weisberg was laughing himself silly every time he thought of the looks on those guys' faces when Sabatine was in there trying to talk them into letting him join their club.

"Looking back, it's easy to say that Sabatine was naive, or stubborn, or just plain stupid—and that's hard for me to say, especially now. But Sabatine apparently never said a word to anyone. He just had a fit, I mean, he just got righteous as hell, and the very next Sunday he really let those golfers have it, all the ones from the club at what we used to call golfers' mass. I think the last thing he said was something like, 'You insufferable bigots, don't you know or have you ever stopped to think that Jesus was Himself a Jew?' He was about as subtle as a kick in the balls. But even worse was what he did to his hair.

"In those days," Father Marrazo continued, "his hair was fiery red, and very curly, kinky, like Muscotti's used to be, and for some reason he combed it so that it looked like he had sprouted horns. The only possible reason I could give for that was that he had a small reproduction of Michelangelo's *Moses*—he'd had it for years, and he loved it and loved to tell the reason why Michelangelo gave Moses horns—or what he said was the reason— which was that somebody had made a mistake in translating the Hebrew word for light, that the Hebrew for beams of light radiating from Moses' head somehow came out 'horns' in Latin.

"I don't know if that was Sabatine's reason for combing his hair that way or not, but the effect on all those

59

golfers was, well, it just stunned them. They rang Aldonari's phone off the wall, and when Sabatine finished high mass Aldonari was waiting for him; he was right there at the side of the altar.

"He gave Sabatine twenty-four hours to pack and present himself to the cardinal in Philadelphia. I can't remember that cardinal's name, but anyway, he kept Sabatine there for almost six months to make sure he'd emptied his head of what was then flaming heresy. But the day Sabatine came back, he called me, and I'll never forget what he said. He said—without even bothering to identify himself—he said, 'Well, I ate them. I ate my words and I genuflected like a proper little altar boy, but I'll be damned if the Jews are responsible. Who the hell was responsible for all those Jews in Germany—the Lutherans and Communists I suppose?' And then he hung up, just like that. I remember holding my stomach I was laughing so hard. I was thinking, well, hang on to your crucifix, Sabatine's back." Father Marrazo sank back into his chair and shook his head. He seemed to grow smaller. "But now, oh, God. . . ."

"What's the matter now?"

"Well, part of it is that he's got cancer."

"Oh, that's rough," Balzic said. "That's really rough."

"Mario, my friend, that's not the half of it. Not even the half."

Balzic frowned. "I don't know what could be worse—"

"Ho, Lord, Lord, Mario, let me think how to tell you." The priest drank the rest of his wine and motioned for Balzic to do the same, then he stood and turned away from Balzic. When he turned back, his eyes were brimming with tears. He didn't bother to wipe them. He

60

sniffed a couple of times and refilled their glasses, sitting again with a thump.

"Last week, Bishop Conroy called me and ordered me to form an *ad hoc* committee to oversee the auditing of the financial records of St. Jude's parish. He told me to call Kelly from St. Mary's and Marcellino from St. Francis' and to drop everything everybody was doing and meet with the diocesan auditor immediately. All Conroy said was that we were supposed to be there when the auditor went over Sabatine's books and that we were supposed to verify any irregularities. He said he'd gotten some, uh, disquieting information was the phrase he used—yeah, some disquieting information about the mortgage payments from the bank which holds the mortgage on St. Jude's. And that's all he would say.

"So I called Kelly and Marcellino and we met with Jack Raymond, the auditor, and about nine-thirty this morning the four of us went out to St. Jude's unannounced—as Conroy had specified. Well, as soon as I saw Sabatine I wanted to get back in the car. I hadn't seen him in six months or so, and he'd lost so much weight I almost didn't recognize him. And the pain in the man's face, oh, it was awful to look at. It was so obvious the man has only months to live. Maybe not even that long. Weeks perhaps. Shaking hands with him was like grabbing a handful of kitchen matches.

"Well, I stuttered and stammered all over the place, but I finally managed to say why we were there. He never took his eyes off me the whole time I was trying to tell him, and when I finished he took my hand in both of his and he said, 'Anthony, why did he send you? He had to know how much you'd take this to heart. But don't.' And then he just turned around and let us follow him into his office, and he pointed at the books. They were all laid out as though he'd been expecting us.

"And I asked him if he had been expecting us, and he said, 'No, not you necessarily, but somebody.' Then he said he was very tired and he had to lie down, but if we needed him all we had to do was knock on the wall and he'd come over.

"Now, remember, we still had no idea what we were supposed to be looking for. I suppose I shouldn't be speaking for the others, but I had not the slightest idea. So Jack Raymond went to work, and Kelly and Marcellino were right with him, but I didn't even want to look at the damn stuff. I just kept pacing around, looking at the books on his shelves. He has a fantastic library, the library you'd expect to belong to a man who loves ideas and words. Really great stuff. And I kept looking at his books and remembering what he'd been like in that philosophy class I mentioned earlier and about the hell he'd raised—not for the sake of raising hell. Not at all. He really loved the Church, and he always wanted Her to be better so the people could be better, more loving, more giving, more gracious. And there we were, picking over his books like he was some damn embezzler. It just didn't make sense.

"I mean, what the hell would a man, one of the most honest men I've ever known, certainly the least ambitious for church office—he didn't give a rat's can to be anything more than he was. He never disgraced the Church after he'd been dismissed from the faculty at St. Vincent's. I don't mean that he didn't fight like a tiger for the ideas he discussed with us, but when it was finally decided that he had to go, he went gracefully. The same that time he had to recant to the cardinal in Philly. He went. He ate his words. And he came back still believing that his idea was right—not that he was right but that his idea was—but there was never, never a word out of him about leaving the Church or, or about doing anything to disgrace the Church by disgracing himself. That just wasn't like him. So what the hell were we doing there?

"I mean, would this man who had never disgraced himself when he was young and healthy—what would he be doing now that he's dying of cancer? About his mortgage payments? It didn't make sense. And the longer I stayed there, the less sense it made and the worse I felt. . . ."

Father Marrazo paused to drink some wine. He had been speaking quickly and rather loudly. His face was flushed and there were traces of perspiration on his forehead and upper lip.

"And then I started to think about St. Jude's," Father Marrazo went on suddenly. "Do you know, Mario, what that parish was when he took it over? When he was practically exiled there?"

Balzic shook his head.

"Mass, Mario, he said mass in a garage! A three-bay garage owned by Melago's, that trucking outfit. And the parish was so small that if you put every member of every family in the parish in that garage for one mass, there would still have been room to park a truck in the third bay.

"His altar was a workbench. Think of it, Mario, a workbench! Tools, cans, tires, chains, dirty rags, oil and grease on the floor—the first collection went to buy tarpaulins to cover the floor so the people wouldn't get greasy when they kneeled.

63

"Hell, he didn't break ground on this building until 1954. He practically begged for the money. And there wasn't one person in the diocese, bishop on down, who didn't know what the man was doing or how hard he was working. He didn't have an assistant until a couple years ago when his health started to go. Now he's got two. But what work he did by himself . . . and there we were, going through his books like he was a thief. I thought I was going to be sick. The idea that he could, or would, do anything for his own gain was absolutely ludicrous.

"And I said so. I told Kelly, Marcellino, and Raymond that we had no right, no reason, no matter what Conroy had said. And I'd no sooner got the words out when Raymond looked up and said, 'We may not have the right, but we have a reason.'

"And do you know what Raymond showed us? He showed us that for the last five months the mortgage payments had increased by twelve hundred and ninety dollars a month. Since November, the payments increased each month by exactly that amount. And we all looked at the figures Raymond showed us and we could see it was true. But I said, 'Well, what the hell's wrong with that? That's great!' But Raymond said, 'There's no explanation for it. There's nothing here to show where the money's coming from.' And I said, 'So the hell with the figures. So it's irregular. So it's unusual. The man's doubled the mortgage payments on his church building, what the hell's wrong with that?' But Raymond kept insisting. 'You don't understand,' he said. 'There's no explanation where he's getting the money.' And I said, 'But why do we have to assume there's something suspicious about it?' And he said, 'Suspicious is your word, Father.

64

All I know is the bank is concerned and the bishop is disturbed.'

"And I just started to howl. It was ridiculous. We go out there looking for who knew what and we find out that Sabatine's doubled his mortgage payments and this damned auditor is talking as though he'd just got the evidence on the greatest swindler in history. And I'm laughing my head off. I'm looking at this pompous-assed auditor and I can't stop laughing, and Kelly and Marcellino are starting to laugh too, and then, uh, I feel someone touch my arm.

"It was Sabatine. I hadn't even heard him come into the room. And he looked awful. Just terrible. And everything got quiet, and I finally managed to stop laughing. And he—Sabatine—he looked at me with those eyes so full of pain that it hurt me to look at them, and he said, 'Anthony, the bank has every right to be concerned, and the bishop has every right to be disturbed because it's all a fraud. All that money, that twelve hundred and ninety dollars every month since November, all of it was obtained through a fraud I instigated.'

"Mario, I thought I was going to be sick. . . ." The priest leaned back in his chair and covered his face with his hands and began to sob very quietly. "Damn it!" he cried out, and his shoulders shook.

Balzic jumped up and hurried around the desk and behind the priest. He put his hands on the priest's shoulders. "Let it go, Anthony," he said. "Let it go."

They remained like that for some minutes, Father Marrazo sobbing in his chair and Balzic standing behind him and rubbing and kneading the muscles in the priest's neck and shoulders. Then Father Marrazo began to speak, his words coming in bursts between gasps. "It's so easy to say it's all pride . . . an old man getting old because he starts to think he's indispensable . . . so easy to say he fell for the duty . . . but only 'cause he found out he was dying . . . that's crap, Mario, real crap . . . that man is more than that . . . he just saw his work unfinished . . . he knew it would be done, he knew it . . . but he didn't lose hope . . . and he didn't get smug and arrogant . . . it's not the same, Mario, if you lose your patience, that's one thing . . . if you misplace it, it's not the same as thinking you can't be replaced—or that you won't be . . . my God, Sabatine was too smart for that . . . he hadn't succumbed, he'd surrendered . . . he hadn't given up, he gave himself up—Mario, for Christ's sake, there is a difference . . . he just lost his perspective . . . it wasn't even that he lost his patience . . . it was his perspective . . . he got out of joint with himself . . . he dislocated his spirit, Mario, that's all. . . ."

Father Marrazo broke down completely. He wept until his eyes were puffed and mucous and spittle dribbled over his fingers. He looked helplessly at Balzic several times, each time trying unsuccessfully to speak. Balzic kept kneading the priest's neck, stopping once to give him his hanky, and then continuing while the priest blew his nose and coughed up phlegm, all the while baffled about the sort of fraud Sabatine had committed which Marrazo was trying so desperately to explain away. Balzic debated with himself whether to ask questions in order that Father Marrazo could get everything out and be done with it or whether to keep silent and let the priest decide if there was more he wanted to say or felt he could say.

Soon, the priest waved his hand and leaned forward, signaling to Balzic that he was feeling better, and Balzic stopped rubbing and went around the desk and back to his chair.

"I'm sorry, Mario."

"For what?"

"For acting like a kid."

"Hey, that wasn't any act and you ain't no kid and don't ever apologize to me for crying over a friend."

"Thank you," the priest whispered.

"Aw come on, Father. I'm going to get embarrassed if you don't cut it out. Here, have a little wine. Make you feel better."

"I think I had too much already. You shouldn't drink when you're depressed. It just makes it worse."

"Yeah, but sometimes it also makes it better. Go ahead."

"Maybe you're right." The priest picked up his glass and sipped what was left in it. Balzic stood and filled both their glasses, still debating with himself whether to prod the priest to talk more about what Sabatine had done. When he sat down again, he had decided against it. If Father Marrazo wanted to say more, he would, and if he didn't, nothing Balzic could say would persuade him to say anything. The priest could be as close with his thoughts as any man Balzic had ever known. He might let his emotions go now and then, as he had just done, but he was very careful with his thoughts. Now that Balzic thought about it, he was sure this was the first time he had ever heard Father Marrazo reveal anything about another priest or about priests in general. Perhaps he had had too much wine.

"Mario, I think I've said enough for one night. I know I don't have to ask you not to repeat anything I've said. There is one thing though."

"Name it."

"There are bound to be rumors. His housekeeper, Sabatine's, was in and out all the while we were out there. We tried to shoo her away, but she's a, well, never mind what she is. You know her. Mrs. Tuzzi. Gatano's widow. So I'm sure there are going to be rumors. If you hear anything, just do your best—hell, you know what to do."

"Say no more, Father. Anything comes my way, I'll handle it."

"Thank you." The priest paused. "Mario, I really am sorry to put you through this—"

"Forget it, Anthony."

"No, let me finish. You came here obviously with something on your mind. You never just come to pass the time of day. You always have a reason. I'm sorry I couldn't listen to you. But I couldn't. Tomorrow I'll be able to, but tonight I just can't. This has, uh, this has really thrown me. I mean, I just can't imagine Sabatine doing this. And I've really got to sort things out. I have to be able to say something coherent to the bishop. I can't understand why he hasn't called me. . . ."

Balzic stood and drank the last of his wine. He felt suddenly quite drunk. He knew full well that nobody gets suddenly drunk, and the only explanation he could give himself was that he had managed somehow to ignore the gradual sensations of it because he'd been engrossed with what the priest had been saying and going through. He had to hold onto the back of the chair to keep from weaving. "Listen," he said slowly so as not to slur his words, "you don't have to say anything. I understand.

68

And listen, if there's anything else I can do, you know I will."

"I know."

"Well, good night, Father."

"Good night, Mario. And thank you."

Balzic pulled into the driveway of his house and sat in the cruiser for a minute or so after he'd turned off the ignition, trying to comprehend how he'd gotten as drunk as he was. Then he remembered the beer he'd drunk at the bar in Muscotti's, the wine he'd drunk with Dom Muscotti in the back room, and all that wine with Father Marrazo. "Hell," he said aloud, "it's a wonder I'm alive." He stumbled getting out of the car and tripped twice going up the steps to the porch. While he was fumbling for his house key, the door was jerked open by his daughter Marie, and she was smiling wryly.

"Oh, hell, Marie, don't do things like that."

"Hi, Daddy. What things?"

"Never mind. You going to let me in or do I have to stand out here till you tell me what you're going to tell me or whatever?"

"Daddy, are you drunk?"

"Can I come in first?"

"Sure." She backed out of the doorway, and Balzic slid by her, kissing her hair as he passed. Marie closed the door and began taking off his coat. Balzic resisted at first but then let her.

"Are you happy drunk or sleepy drunk?"

"I am definitely not happy drunk. Where's your

69

mother? Where's my mother? Where's your sister?"

"Mom and Grandma are in the kitchen talking. Emily's in bed watching a movie."

"Ho, boy, why don't I ever hear she's in bed reading a book? How come it's always she's in bed watching the tube? I ought to throw that thing—ah, never mind."

Marie stood behind him with his raincoat draped over her arms. "I don't know why she's always watching the tube, Daddy."

"Well what are you so full of? You look ready to bust with something."

"Can't I just meet you at the door and help you take your coat off?"

"Huh, the last time you met me at the door and helped me off with my coat, it cost me forty bucks. Not that I don't appreciate your help. It's your sincerity I can't stand."

"Ohhhh, Daddy."

"Oh Daddy my rump. Come on, what's it going to cost me this time? On second thought, don't tell me. Wait'll I get some coffee, okay?"

"I can wait."

"Okay? Some coffee first, okay?" Balzic slung his arm around her neck and headed wobbily toward the kitchen. "I'll even let you pour it for me. That way, you'll have two things going for you."

She wriggled free of his arm and hurried away, saying, "Wait'll I hang up your coat."

"Okay, so hang it up, hang it up." Balzic loosened his tie and unbuttoned his collar, sputtering out a long sigh.

Marie bounced back into the room, ducked under his arm, and started steering him toward the kitchen.

"Easy now, not so fast, somebody might've moved it.

We get going too fast in the wrong direction, it might wind up taking us twice as long to get there."

She giggled. "Daddy, sometimes you're really funny when you're drunk. Especially when you're trying to be serious."

"Ho-ho, backhanded compliments yet. Go 'head, keep working your hustle, daughter. It's a little crude, but it's not bad. Smoothe out the edges, you'll be pretty good in a couple years."

They bumped into the door frame going through the dining room and then came to a halt by bumping into the door frame leading into the kitchen.

"Hello, ladies," Balzic sang out to his mother and his wife. He hoped he didn't look or sound as drunk as he felt.

"Mario, are you all right?" Ruth said.

"Yeah, sure. Just had a little too much to drink, that's all. I'm okay."

"Hey, kiddo," his mother said, "you better sit down before you fall down."

"Hey, I'm not that drunk."

Ruth stood and took him by the arm and pulled him toward the chair she'd just left. "Sit down, Mario. Marie, turn the water on. Come on, Mario, sit down, sit down. My God, look at your eyes. There's no white left at all."

Balzic slumped into the chair Ruth held for him. He rubbed his eyes with his palms and yawned noisily. He shook himself and stretched and then twisted around to look at Marie who was waiting for water to boil so she could make instant coffee for him.

"So whatta you want, Marie? You meet me at the door —you hear that, Ruth? Ma? She meets me at the door, she helps me off with my coat, then she tells me she just

71

wants to meet me at the door and help me off with my coat. D'you believe that? So come on, Marie, let's have the words, I already got the music."

Marie was nearly finished preparing the cup of instant coffee. "It's just nineteen ninety-five, Daddy." she said.

"Ouuu, just nineteen ninety-five, Daddy, that's all. For what? For what am I gettin' grabbed this time?"

"A blazer."

"A which?"

"You know what a blazer is, Mar," Ruth said. "The girls' athletic teams don't get jackets the way the boys' teams do, so the girls decided to buy them for themselves."

"What jackets? What're you talking about?"

"Mar, you know how the school gives jackets with letters on them to the boys who play football and basketball. But the girls don't get anything except a letter. So they got together and decided they'd buy them to shame the school board into doing it from now on."

"Oh, wait a minute. This is goofy. Marie, you mean to tell me you got to have a jacket to remind you of all the time you spent in that swimming pool?"

"Daddy, that's not the point," Marie said, setting the coffee in front of her father.

"What's the point then? I don't need a jacket to remind me I'm a cop. If it was up to me, the only cops in uniform would be traffic duty. Everybody else would be in civvies."

"Daddy, we aren't cops. We're girls who compete for the school and all we get are letters. The boys get letters *and* jackets. We just think we ought to get the same as the boys."

"Ho boy, that's how it starts. Equal strokes for equal

folks. He got a pretty uniform, I got to have a pretty uniform . . . next thing you know it's everybody get in step and the next thing after that is you need a bulldozer to make the cemetery—"

"Mario!" Ruth said. "What're you talking about?"

"Nothing, everything. I was just thinking of all the cemeteries scattered all over the world, all of them full of guys who happened to get the privilege of wearing a uniform."

"Aw, Mar, now wait just a minute. This is a school jacket we're talking about, and that's all we're talking about."

"Sure. And all I'm talking about is that's how it all gets started." Balzic stifled a yawn. "School jackets, letters, aw, forget it."

"Mario, it's only right," his mother said. "If the school gives to boys, they should give to girls too."

"Yeah, Ma, I know, I know. But how come I got to be part of it? Marie wants the jacket, the blazer or whatever, why don't she do something? She thinks it's right, then she should do something."

"Like what, Daddy? Like what should we do?"

"What do those band kids do? They want to go march in the Miss America parade or down the Orange Bowl, what do they do—sell pizzas, hoagies, wash cars, stuff like that. Hold a raffle, raffle something off, a TV or something. But I don't like uniforms, and I think to want a uniform is wrong. But I'm not you. You want something to wear to make you special, go ahead, but don't ask me to get it for you—and it doesn't have anything to do with money."

There was silence, the women glancing uncomfortably at each other while Balzic stirred his coffee.

Finally Ruth said, "Maybe that's not a bad idea, Marie, holding a raffle I mean."

Marie frowned and scratched her ankle with her other foot.

"Hey, kiddo," Mrs. Balzic said brightly, "you talk about raffles, guess who won seven hundred dollars."

"Who won seven hundred? I don't know, Ma. Who?"

"Rose Abbatta. Nicolao's widow. You remember."

"Oh, yeah, yeah. I remember her. Good for her. She could use it. She had a lot of rough luck in her lifetime."

"Ho boy, Nicolao was sick so long with that black lung. And then Rosalie, all her life with that poor girl."

"What's wrong with her?" Marie asked. "I don't even know her."

"The people Ma's talking about are old friends of hers," Ruth said. "You've never met them. And the girl she's talking about, Rosalie, she's very retarded."

"Yeah. Is born with brain damage," Mrs. Balzic said. "Have to take care all the time. They got schools for them now, but then it was like a sin to have that happen for you. God was punish you for something. So they never can do nothing without the girl, never go nowhere, all the time have to watch for her. But they been let her go places by herself now. Rose told me Nicky bought her a bike even."

"How old is she?" Marie asked.

"Oh, yoy-yoy, she must be thirty-six, thirty-seven anyhow."

"At least that," Ruth said.

"Is she a mongoloid or something?" Marie asked.

"No," Ruth said. "You can't tell anything from look-ing at her, except she's sort of, you know, she doesn't

74

have much of a shape. But she had to be watched all the time. A couple times she set fire to the house just playing with matches. And her mother, well, she just never could relax. Except when young Nick got old enough to help her."

"I was just going to say," Balzic said, "he really took care of them after old Nick died."

"Oh sure," Mrs. Balzic said. "He work very hard. Never marry. Always looking out for his mother and sister. He's a good boy."

"Is he still working for the paper, the *Gazette*?"

"He must be," Ruth said. "I don't know why he wouldn't be. He has a really good job there. He's a, oh, what do you call them?"

"Linotype operator," Balzic said, yawning.

"Yeah. That's right. He makes good money."

"Well, yoy-yoy, I tell you something," Mrs. Balzic said, "that's some kind of luck, huh? All those ladies win all that money."

"Huh? What ladies?"

"Well, first was Amelia Motti. You remember, Mario. She's Alfonso's widow. Then was Flora Ruffola, she was marry to Amadie—you know her, Mario?"

"No, Ma, I don't know her."

"Well, okay, then was Sophia Cafasso, she was marry to Domenico—you know her?"

"Uh-uh."

"Sure you do."

"Maybe I do, Ma. I just can't think too clear right now."

"Well, okay. So then was Olivia Tuzzi, Gatano's widow, and now is Rose Abbatta." Mrs. Balzic laughed and slapped the table. "Son of a brick, how you like that? Alla win seven hundred bucks. Yoy-yoy, I like to win sometime, don't you think, kiddo?"

"That'd be nice, Ma."

"Hey, lady, you do all right at bingo," Ruth said.

"Yeah, sure. But seven hundred bucks? How nice!"

Balzic sipped his coffee and scratched the inside of his thigh. "Hey, Ma, d'you say Mrs. Tuzzi won seven hundred too?"

"Yeah. Why?"

"I don't know. I haven't heard her name in a long time, and I could swear I heard it before today someplace. I'll be damned. I can't remember where, but I thought—"

"Mar, I think you better go to sleep," Ruth said. "You look like you're getting ready to fall off the chair."

"Huh? Oh yeah. I better . . . listen, Marie, go tell your girl friends to wash some cars or something. And I'll tell you what. I'll make up the difference, whatever you're short. But if you want that blazer, if you really want it, then I think you ought to try to get it for yourself. Start it anyway. Okay?"

Marie came behind him and hugged him and kissed the top of his head.

Balzic patted her hands and then pulled them apart as he lurched to his feet. He reached out for Ruth's arm and let her direct him into the bedroom. He plopped on the bed and didn't argue when she pulled off his shoes and socks and undid his belt. She struggled to get his pants, coat, and shirt off, giving up finally when Balzic kept falling backward. She left his shirt on.

Balzic was asleep before she left the room, and his last

conscious thought was an effort to remember where he'd heard Mrs. Tuzzi's name before today. He couldn't. His mind was flooding with flags and crosses and Stars of David and school monograms and acres and acres of graves. . . .

Balzic awoke with an oppressive fog in his head and the feeling that he had tried to eat tissue paper sometime during the night and hadn't been able to swallow it. He hoisted his feet over the edge of the bed and tried to focus on the alarm clock. He looked at it between rubbing his eyes and yawning, each time disbelieving what he saw. It was twenty minutes after ten.

He could hear pans being washed and rinsed in the kitchen, the sound of soap pads against metal alternating with sudden rushes from the faucet.

He found fresh clothes and went out to the kitchen, hugging his mother as she bent over the sink, and then started up the stairs to the bathroom. He stopped on the third step and asked where Ruth was.

"She's get her hair fix. She just leave."

"How come you let me sleep so long?"

"We try to get you up, kiddo. Ruth try. Me too. But you just no want to get up, that's all."

"Oh." He turned and continued up the stairs, holding onto the wall. He brushed his teeth first to get rid of the tissue-paper taste and then stood in the shower for ten minutes, letting the hot water beat on the back of his neck. By the time he'd finished shaving, the fog in his head was starting to lift.

Downstairs, his mother had coffee and tomato juice waiting for him.

"You want eggs, Mario?"

"No, Ma. I couldn't eat anything. This is enough right here. Just the juice and coffee. Wow, I was really blown away last night. Hope I didn't say anything out of line."

"You?" His mother laughed. "Since when?"

"I don't know. When you get that drunk, you can get out of line anywhere. Even here."

"No, sonny. Not you. Not last night." She was smiling and chuckling as she wiped the pans and put them away.

Balzic drank the juice slowly, savoring it. He was half finished with the coffee when he remembered what he wanted to ask his mother. "Hey, Ma, last night you said something about Mrs. Tuzzi. Remember? When you were talking about somebody winning a raffle or a lottery or something?"

"Yeah, sure I remember. What about?"

"What was it again—four ladies—"

"Five."

"Okay, five. And Mrs. Tuzzi was one of them?"

"Yeah. That's right."

"Well, I was trying to think where I heard her name before."

"What you mean where you heard her name before —you know her all your life."

"Yeah, I know that, Ma. What I mean is, yesterday I heard her name mentioned before you said it, what you said about her. And I really can't think where."

"Well, what difference it makes, huh, kiddo? She no do nothing bad, that's for sure."

78

"It doesn't make any difference. I'm just trying to remember."

"Well next time, don't drink so much. Maybe your head work better."

"Ho boy, you're beautiful, you are." Balzic finished his coffee and stood. "Did anybody call me?"

"No. Only one call. I call Rose Abbatta, tell her how good I feel for her."

"How good you feel for her? What for? What happened to her?"

"Boy, kiddo, you really was drunk last night. You forget that too? She win seven hundred dollars, don't you remember?"

"Oh yeah. That. Yeah, sure. Well, she pretty happy, huh? So what's she going to do with it?"

"Oh, she very happy. But I don't ask what she's going to do with. She tells me, but I don't ask. She thinks maybe she buy a new icebox."

"A new icebox? Hell, that's no present. She ought to take a vacation. Ah, that's none of my business where she spends it. It's her money." Balzic started out of the kitchen but came back. "Hey, Ma, I don't know why this is bothering me, but it is. What's Mrs. Tuzzi do?"

"She keep house."

"Doesn't she have a job? I thought she had a job."

"Yeah. That's her job. She keep house."

"For who?"

"For Father Sabatine."

"Out at St. Jude's?"

"Yeah, yeah, that's right. Why?"

"Nothing. I just remembered where I heard her name before. Yesterday I mean. Father Marrazo mentioned her. Okay. That settles that."

79

"You happy now, you remember?"

Balzic kissed her on the cheek. "It doesn't make me happy or not happy. I just couldn't remember and it bothered me. You know how that bothers you when you can't remember something you know you know. Listen, I got to go now. I'll see you later, and if I'm going to be late, I'll call you."

"Okay, Mario. Be careful. And be nice. Give somebody a break."

"Give somebody a break? Why today?"

"Oh, I don't know. I just say that, that's all."

"Okay, Ma. I'll give somebody a break today. You and Ruth. I'll stay sober, how's that?"

Balzic learned upon arriving at the station that nothing was going on which couldn't be handled by Desk Sergeant Angelo Clemente. He also learned that Lieutenant Walker Johnson had called to report that a set of fingerprints belonging to someone other than Armand or Tullio Manditti had been found on the door frame of their house and that those prints were being forwarded to the FBI in Washington. That was all the information Johnson had. Balzic screwed up his face thinking about it.

He was just starting out the door when the phone rang. Clemente answered it and waved to Balzic to stop.

"It's Eddie Sitko," Clemente said.

"What's he want?"

"What do I know, he wants to talk to you."

Balzic picked up another phone. "Yeah, Eddie."

80

"Good morning, Mario."

"Ho boy. When you start in like that, that 'Good morning, Mario,' I can hear trouble coming. What do you want to do this time, Eddie? You want to burn down the hospital to see if your troops can put it out if they ever have to?"

"Be nice, Mario, be nice."

"Hey, Mr. Fire Chief, the last time you asked me to be nice, you told me you were going to hold a foam drill at two o'clock in the afternoon, remember? At the intersection of Main and Market. Remember?"

"I remember very well. That's what I want to talk to you about."

"Oh, Eddie, say not so. You're not going to do that to me again." Balzic closed his eyes and rubbed his temple.

"Mario, we made a mess last time. I mean a real mess—"

"I know, I know. I remember the mess. Traffic backed up six blocks in every direction, foam like meringue a foot deep, and the goddamn phones had smoke coming out of them. You know how long I heard about that?"

"Mario, I heard about it long after you did. But the complaints don't change anything. We got that foam equipment because as long as the goddamn state highway department won't come up with a bypass for Route 66, and as long as gas tankers are using 66, we're sitting on dynamite—"

"Eddie, what do you want me to do—write my state rep? I know what you're saying, and I agree with you one hundred percent. But why do you have to practice on Main and Market? I practice shooting three times a week, but not on Main Street."

"Mario, we've been through all this before—"

"A hundred times."

"But if nobody can move the state people off their asses, then I want my people ready."

Balzic sighed. "So you're really going to do it?"

"Certainly I'm going to do it. Only this time I'm not going to warn anybody except you. I'm not even going to tell my people. I'm just going to have my wife phone in the alarm, and that way, everybody'll think it's the real thing."

"Oh, Eddie, Eddie, Jesus Christ, don't do this to me."

"It's something that has to be done, Mario. But I want your word you won't tell your people."

"Eddie, for crissake, I'm in the middle of something. I can't fuckin' take time off to go direct the people who're supposed to be directing traffic."

"Mario, it has to be done."

"Look, Eddie, I give you a bad time sometimes, I know I do, but that's because I don't want you to start believing your press clippings. I respect you. I think you're one hell of a fireman. You got more balls than anybody I know. I've seen you do things they wouldn't put in the movies because nobody would believe them, but for crissake, will you do me this favor and hold off for a while? I mean it, Eddie. I'm in the middle of something and I don't even know how big it is yet."

There was momentary silence on the other end. "Is it that bad?"

"I don't really know. I just got a bad feeling. Please hold off for a while. Please? And I promise you, as soon as I get this straightened out, you can hold foam drills to your heart's fucking content—at four-thirty, at eight in the morning, at twelve o'clock Sunday in front of St.

Malachy's. You can hold disaster drills until your joint falls off. You can pour ketchup on my head and make me a victim, I won't care. But not now, okay?"

"Okay, Mario, okay. I'll hold off. But not forever."

"Eddie, what can I say? I hope you have to rescue a widow tonight, and she just can't stand it she wants to be so grateful." Balzic hung up and let out a long sigh. "Christ, I should be selling repossessed cars. What a bullshit artist I'm turning into."

"You talking to me?" Clemente said.

"Huh? No, I'm talking to myself. Hey, I'm going to Muscotti's. I got to do another bullshit job on somebody."

"Who?"

"I don't know."

"Then how you—"

"Angelo, when I know what I'm doing, I'll tell you, okay? In the meantime, try to make sure nobody robs the place, okay? We must have close to seven bucks back there in the coffee can."

"Ouuu, sorry I said anything."

"Angelo, what're you, getting old? I can remember when I used to get wise with you, you'd tell me to bug off. All of a sudden you're sorry? So you didn't retire, so what're you doing? Going senile on the job?"

"Okay, so shove it. You got problems, so do I."

"That's better. That's the Clemente we all know and love. See you later, Ang. Anything happens, I'm at Muscotti's."

It was five minutes to noon when Balzic, following a courthouse stenographer and two sheriff's deputies, entered Muscotti's. The bar was crowded with people eating or waiting to eat one of Vinnie's hot sausage sandwiches. The sausage itself was made by Vinnie's Uncle Lou. What Vinnie did was boil and brown the sausage, combine tomato sauce, tomatoes, sweet peppers, onions, thyme, and oregano into a sauce, and then, as he put it, "let the sausage fall in love with the sauce."

Because Vinnie's Uncle Lou kept no schedule about making the sausage, Vinnie had no schedule about preparing the sandwiches. But when he did; word spread quickly. Within a half-hour after he announced that the sausage was ready, that sausage and sauce had made love, it was gone—pounds of it in four-inch portions sliced lengthwise, dripping with sauce, and served on hard rolls.

The amount was never the same because Uncle Lou never delivered the same amount. One morning he might appear with eight pounds. He might not appear again for three days, and then, as likely as not, he would have ten pounds. A day later he might appear with four pounds. Sometimes two weeks would pass before he would appear at all, and he might come empty-handed and roaring drunk, bellowing popular songs from the 1920s in a quaking tenor until Vinnie called a cab for him and gently told him to go home.

Questioned about the erratic delivery of sausage, Vinnie's reply was usually something like, "Hey, my uncle don't only make sausage, he also makes wine. Sometimes he goes down the cellar to make the sausage, he starts tasting the wine, and he forgets what he went down the cellar for. He makes the sausage when he feels like.

The rest of the time he sits in the cellar and drinks and thinks about the old country. Hey, I hope when I'm fuckin' seventy-six, I still got enough stomach left to eat it and drink it the way he does, never mind make it. . . ."

Balzic had not come for the sausage. He had come to see if he could meet Dom Muscotti's supposed girl friend, and, if he talked right, to learn if she was—as Mo Valcanas had predicted—merely a sympathetic audience for Muscotti. Balzic didn't know how he was going to go about learning this. He had not even thought of a sensible opening line. But he knew that it was something he had to learn. The presence of Gina Muscotti loomed large in his mind, just as he knew she loomed large in her husband's mind.

Gina Muscotti was a grandmother, frail, fair-skinned, with snowy hair, who looked as though she should be making television commercials for floor wax or vegetable shortening, but she was Italian in her heart and Catholic in her soul. Only God would help her husband if she became convinced that he was treating another woman differently from any other female patron. Balzic shuddered to think that giving a woman booze and twenty dollars a day was hardly Muscotti's custom with female bar patrons.

The bar crackled with the cheer of people drinking and eating food they relished. Adding to that cheer was a truck driver for a beer distributor who had hit a number for fifty cents and was buying drinks all around.

Balzic found a place at the bar near the front door and stood alone for more than five minutes before Vinnie got a break to come and ask if there was something he wanted.

"As long as I'm here, let me have one of those sausages."

"Oh, Mario, honest to God, I just sold the last one to that kid over by the radiator. I didn't have much today. Only six pounds."

"Then give me a beer. Wait a minute, don't run off. Tell me if the Tuscan's girl friend is here."

"The who? Oh." Vinnie rolled his eyes. "Down the other end. You want the beer here?"

"Yeah, sure." Balzic pushed a quarter toward Vinnie and glanced down the length of the bar. He could see only one woman, thirty or so, with straight auburn hair and no makeup. She wore a faded denim jacket over a white tee-shirt. As Vinnie set the beer down and picked up the quarter, Balzic said, "That one standing by herself? At the end?"

"That's her," Vinnie said without moving his lips.

"Oh you're shittin' me. She used to be a caseworker down the Juvenile Home. She worked with Dom's daughter, Louise."

"You got it, pal."

"Christ, she's married. She got three kids."

"Wrong," Vinnie said. "She got two kids, but she ain't married no more. She also don't work down the Juvenile Home either."

"Why, hell, she used to come in here all the time with Dom's kid. Nobody paid any attention to her. Then I didn't see her for a long time. Come to think of it, haven't seen her down Juvenile for a long time either."

"That's what I'm telling you."

"Oh, I don't believe it. She was Good Samaritan to the world. Used to take those kids home, all that crap. What's she trying to do—save the Tuscan's soul?"

"Mario, I don't know what she's trying to do. I only know what she does. She drinks bourbon and beers all day long and she walks out with at least a twenty. You want to know what she's trying to do, you got to ask her. As for me, I wish she'd get eyes for me or for you or for Iron City Steve, I don't care for who. But she keeps up with Dom, I'm going to get ulcers in my shit." Vinnie started to walk away, but turned abruptly and came back. "You know where she was all that time you didn't see her around?"

Balzic shook his head.

"Mamont. Uh-huh, that's right. The funny farm. She just got out about two months ago. Six months she was in there. I don't know what you can do with that, but I'm telling you 'cause sometimes she don't make too much sense—that's if you're really going to talk to her."

"I don't know where I'm going yet, Vinnie. But thanks for telling me." Balzic sipped his beer and mulled that one over. Mamont State Hospital. Six months on the farm and out to twenty a day and free boilermakers, compliments of the number-two numbers banker in the county who years ago announced his impotence. A hundred and twenty a week or more and all the booze she could handle—for what? For sympathy? Huh, Balzic said to himself, maybe she's a faith healer. Nah, no way. If she could cure that problem with faith, she'd be filling more stadiums than Billy Graham.

Balzic had not realized it but he'd been staring at her, and when his eyes refocused, he saw that she was returning his stare. There was no hostility in it, nor even discomfort. What he saw was bemused curiosity. He turned his face away and pretended that he'd found an itch on his neck. Then he turned his back and took a long drink of beer. He tried to think how to approach her and then found himself trapped in a debate whether he really had any business approaching her at all. This was personal, he said to himself, but then he said, it could become the worst that Muscotti feared. And if Muscotti feared it, there was good reason for lots of other people to start fearing it. Still, it was personal. And it was one thing to be summoned by neighbors to end a family argument before it turned into assault or worse, but it was something else again to invite yourself into the middle of a potential family argument—no matter that this potential family argument could wind up in the U.S. Attorney's office. Oh, hell, he groused to himself, nobody even knows what Gina Muscotti's thinking about. All she did was call Vinnie to find out how business was at the bar. Who am I kidding? Balzic thought. She calls Vinnie, that's got to be a first. She knows something's up. She knows. . . .

Balzic felt someone brush against his shoulder and then felt someone drawing a stool near to him.

"Hi, Chief," the voice said pleasantly.

Balzic turned around while in the midst of swallowing beer. He nearly choked. It was her. He gagged and coughed and felt his eyes bulging.

"Easy," she said, patting him on the back while he bent over the bar and coughed violently. "Don't hurt yourself," she said, laughing. "If I'd've known I'd cause all this, I wouldn't have come."

"It's all right," Balzic said after his coughing passed. "It just went down the wrong way. You didn't cause it."

"Chief, don't lie. I saw you staring at me."

"You did? Yeah. Well, I guess I was."

"Honestly, you too? Everybody's staring at me lately. I'm going to get crazy again if this keeps up."

"Crazy again?"

"Oh, Chief, come off it. I saw Vinnie telling you."

"You saw Vinnie telling me what?"

"That I just got out of the zoo a couple months ago."

"You could hear that from clear down where you were?"

"I didn't say I could hear it. I said I could see it."

"You could see it?"

She nodded.

"You must be some kind of lip reader."

"I don't mean that. I mean I could see the exchange between you two. I got the vibrations. I saw the auras."

"The what?"

"The auras. Don't you know that people give off electrical charges?"

"I know we got a lot of electricity in us. I don't really understand—"

"Well, it doesn't matter. But one of the definitions of aura is that it's a current of air caused by a discharge of electricity, and when people give off their electricity, they disturb the air around them and create color. Haven't you ever seen a painting of a saint?"

"Well, sure I have—"

"Well why do you think painters put them there? You think it was something the Church invented? To make people think saints were special? I mean, sure they're special now, but see, a long time ago, before painters began to work exclusively for the Church, they used to paint everybody like that, not just saints and martyrs, because, well, a long time ago people believed everybody had one."

"You might be right," Balzic said. "I don't know enough to argue."

"Oh, you can't argue at all. This is true. It's how I got my head together. I used to see auras all the time around people's heads, but then I found out that this was true historically, that people used to believe it, and if I hadn't found that out I'd still be in the zoo wiping old ladies' asses and mopping up their vomit."

"This got you out, got your head together?"

"Sure. Because once I found out it was true a long time ago, then I knew it was still true and I wasn't seeing things. I mean I was seeing things, but—"

"Well, you just lost me there, 'cause a long time ago people used to believe the world was flat, but just 'cause they believed it didn't make it true. I mean, we know it ain't flat."

"Sure, but the world's not flat. I mean, we know the world's not flat because of science. And science is the very thing that drove away the idea that people had auras. I mean, it wasn't scientific. Nobody could measure it, and if you can't measure something, then it's not scientific to talk about."

Balzic shrugged. "I guess so. In some respects."

"Of course," she said, laughing, and then she put her hand, her palm with her fingers together, on the middle of Balzic's back. She kept it there for two or three seconds, her eyes sparkling, her lips parted, her head canted. "Don't be afraid," she said after taking her hand away.

"I'm afraid?"

"Sure. You think I'm going to tell you something destructive. And I am—in a way. I mean, you can't ever tell anybody anything constructive without telling them something destructive. They go together like black and white. But everybody always gets scared at first until they know that."

"Okay, I'll play," Balzic said. "What do I think you're going to destroy that's going to shake me up so much?"

"What else? Your ideas."

"Like which ideas?"

"Well, like the one that I can know you were afraid while you were looking at me with this great stone face that says, 'Hey, I'm tough. I'm imperturbable.' "

"And you knew I was, uh, afraid because of my aura, is that it?"

"Well, I felt your fear in your spine."

"Oh."

"Just oh? Is that all? You don't have to be so damned reserved or polite. You can laugh or argue or do anything you want. Except don't be a goddamn American on me."

Balzic laughed. "That's pretty hard."

"Oh, you don't know how hard. For crissake, a third of the world is American. Everybody who believes that time is a line that goes from left to right and can be numbered from one to ten is American. And you believe that. It's practically in your genes. And you know who are the worst about that? Those goddamn psychiatrists. They're so goddamn wrapped up in their little left-to-right, one-to-ten world, they're convinced that anybody who doesn't believe in that is crazy. And they almost had me believing it! And when I tried to tell them about time being an orbit and a revolution, a circle with no beginning and no end, they put me in the rubber room and shot me full of dope."

"They shot you full of dope? The psychiatrists?"

"Sure. There's no difference between heroin and Thorazine. Only chemically. It's all dope. Anything that makes you not want to find out who you are is dope."

"Uh, what's booze then? I mean, what's in those glasses in front of you?"

"Oh, see what a bastard you are! You look for contradictions," she said, laughing impishly and touching Balzic's back again with her palm. "Just because I use dope in a glass doesn't mean I don't know I'm using it or don't understand why I'm using it."

"Why are you using it?"

"Oh, look how serious you say it! Everything coming off you looks like something Rembrandt painted, all dark brown. If he were here now, he'd probably want you to go home and pose for him."

"Yeah, well, so how come you use it? Come on, don't give me any more stuff about my auras or whatever the hell they are. How come you take dope in a glass?"

She took her hand away slowly and touched Balzic's cheek with the back of her index finger. "You promise not to arrest me?"

"Aw be serious, willya?" Balzic snorted a laugh.

"I won't be serious, but I will be sincere. You have to promise."

"That I won't arrest you?"

"Yes. Absolutely."

"Okay, I promise." Balzic smiled and then caught Vinnie's eye and motioned for him to refill their glasses.

She said nothing while Vinnie was doing this, and

Vinnie said nothing to either of them. He refilled their glasses, took Balzic's money, brought the change, and left quickly without a word.

"See how well Vinnie understands auras?" she said.

"Who? Vinnie?"

"Sure. See how he knew not to intrude?"

"Well, I don't know if it's because he understands auras. But I know he understands people pretty good."

"Oh, he won't admit it, but he understands," she said.

"So, uh, now that I promised not to bust you—what's your name by the way?"

"Oh, my name, my name. We were having such a good talk and now you want to spoil it with a fact." She grimaced. "Now I don't know whether I ought to tell you why I drink dope. Even though you promised." She pressed the heel of her hand against her forehead and hit herself gently twice, thinking for a long moment. "Okay. My name is Mila Sanders Rizzo. Feel better now? Is that enough, or do I have to go through the whole bit—name, age, marital status, social security number, phone number, address? Why does every conversation have to start out like an interrogation, like everything has to start according to the Geneva Convention . . . oh, wow, I hate that. Every time I talk to Dom, the first thing I have to say is where my children are, who's watching them, do I trust them, what time do I have to pick them up."

"Well what do I call you?"

"I don't care. Call me yoo-hoo, only when you say it, think of it as being spelled y-o-u-w-h-o. Think of it as a nickname for my full name, which is you-who-are."

"Does that have capital letters?"

"Oh, God," she said, groaning, "don't you Ameri-

93

cans ever give up? Put capital letters on it if it makes you feel better, I don't care."

They were both laughing by the time she finished talking. She paused to sip her bourbon and followed that with a sip of beer.

"So come on," Balzic said, "I want to hear why you take your dope in a glass."

"Okay, but remember your promise."

"I remember."

"Well, I have certain hangups. One of them, the biggest I guess, is that my father owned a bar."

"So? Lots of people who own bars have children."

"Yes, but you see, I'm—I'm still trying to get my head together. And I keep trying to find out where I came from, what I was before I was. I'm trying to go back in order to get here. I think it's crucial to know what I was before so I can know what I am now."

Balzic rubbed his chin. "And you're finding that out in here? Taking dope in a glass?"

"This is the best place! I come in here, it's like a womb. And then it's like infancy. All these glasses need are rubber nipples on them. And then during the day when I talk to Dom I'm in puberty and adolescence. And then later on, when everybody goes home at night, when there's only Dom and me in here, then I'm almost me— where I am now. And then when I give him some head, it's everything all at once, it's—"

"When you give him what?"

"You heard me. Oh, come on, don't look so innocent. Don't tell me you don't know what I'm talking about."

"Oh, I know what you're talking about," Balzic said, feeling himself blush. "I just never heard anyone say it so matter of fact before, that's all. No, that's not it. You just surprised me."

"Well it's no big deal. I mean, everybody knows it, so what's to hide?"

"Uh, listen, uh, maybe you shouldn't be telling me these things. I mean, they're, uh, pretty personal, you know?"

"Well, Christ, everything's personal! There isn't anything you can say that isn't personal. Talking about the weather is personal. Somebody says, 'You think it's going to rain?'—what do you think they're saying? They're making noises that say, 'Hey, I'm harmless. Let's talk.' And if that's not personal, what is? Besides, you're lying when you say you don't want to hear this. 'Cause this is exactly what you do want to hear. You think I don't know that? I mean, why'd you come in here and talk to Vinnie about me if you didn't want to know what was going on?" She spoke quickly but softly and there was not even annoyance in her face or tone.

"Well, uh, I guess you got me," Balzic said.

"Of course I do. But I'm not trying to get you. I just want you to be as sincere and honest with me as I'm being with you. Is that so much to ask?"

"No."

"Well, then why don't you give yourself a break? I mean, if you want to know how to handle this, then you better know what there is to know, don't you think?"

"How do you know I want to handle it?"

"Oh, stop it, will you please? You're the chief of police. Dom's, well, you know what he is better than I do. Everybody knows his wife. And everybody, including you and Dom, is scared shitless that she's going to find out and want to get some kind of silly revenge or something just because I'm using him to grow up on. Everybody thinks he's using me to prove what a man he still is. But that's a load. I'm using him a hundred times more than he'll ever think of using me. Whose idea do you think it is that he gives me all the money? You think it's mine? He's showing off. And I let him because that's the only way he can make any sense of me. But I don't want his money. I haven't spent a penny of it. It's all in the bank. All he has to do is give me the slightest indication that he regrets giving it to me, and I'll tell him how soon he can have it back. There's no big deal."

"Uh, how about running that down again?" Balzic said. "I'm a little confused."

"Well how many ways do I have to say it? I'm into where my head is. Right now. I have to find out what I'm doing, and I'm using Dom to help me. Because my father owned a bar. Because—"

"What happened to your father?"

"Nothing happened to him. He's still alive and healthy as hell. He just can't help me, that's all. He's always making judgments about what I'm supposed to be. He won't ever just let me be who I am—if I could ever find out. But if I'm ever going to get myself together, then I have to have a substitute. It's called acting out. All those creepy psychiatrists know about it. They're the ones who told me about it. So just because I understand it—no. Just because I really do it, really do act it out, everybody gets excited. And it's really no big deal."

"Not even if Dom's wife decides it is? I mean, suppose she thinks it's the biggest deal there is. Like adultery."

"Oh, come on. Who knows better than her that he isn't capable of adultery? I just told you, giving him head is like sucking shots and beers with nipples on the glass. He never has an erection. He can't! Christ, afterward, he cries every time."

Balzic shook his head and sighed. "Wait a minute. Don't you understand that that might not make any difference to her?"

"Well that's her hangup, not mine. God, I've got enough of my own. I can't handle mine and hers too."

"Well okay then. Just who the hell is supposed to handle it? Me?"

"Isn't that what this whole conversation is about? Isn't that what you want to do? Handle this? Protect everybody? 'Cause if it isn't, then you're sure sending off some funny auras."

"Oh, Christ, we're back to them again," Balzic said. "Vinnie! Hey, Vinnie! Give us a couple more here."

Vinnie approached, grinning slyly. "So how we doin', Mario? Everything okay? How 'bout you, kid? You okay?"

"I'm okay," Mila said. "But I don't know about the chief here. He's confused. There's gray around his head a foot high."

Balzic started to say something but was stopped when he felt someone touch him on the left shoulder. He turned and was confronted by Brownie Cercone, somber and scowling.

"We got problems," Cercone said. "Come here."

Balzic followed him to the far end of the bar.

"Listen, Balzic, I didn't want any part of this, I want you to know that."

"Any part of what? What're you talking about?"

"What do you think I'm talking about? What did you talk about yesterday?"

"With Dom?"

"Sure with Dom. D'you think the fuckin' Pope?"

"So okay. What's the problem?"

"Dom did what you said. He stuck me on Tullio out the dump."

"And?"

"He split. I lost him."

"How the fuck could you lose him at the dump?"

"Not so loud for crissake. Just listen and I'll tell you." Brownie's eyes darted over Balzic's shoulders. "He told me he had to go take a crap. So I'm with him all day, right behind him from the time he wakes up this morning, but I ain't going in the can with him. I mean, Jesus Christ, I got stink all over me from that dump—"

"Forget that. What happened?"

"He goes in the can. I'm waiting and I'm waiting. Ten minutes goes by, and I holler in at him. I say, 'Hey, d'you have a fuckin' heart attack or you jackin' off or what're you doing?' Nothing. So I open up and he's gone. Turns out there's another door in the back so guys can get in from outside without going through the office. So I start running around looking for him, but one of the pickers tells me the fat-ass climbed on the back of a packer when it was pulling out."

"Whose truck?"

"Nobody knows," Cercone said. "What do you think I'm telling you we got problems for? Jesus, don't you think that's the first thing I'm going to ask? There was only one guy saw him going, and that guy's just off a boat last year. He can't read English. He don't know what that fuckin' print means on the truck. He also don't know one truck from another."

"Oh for crissake. Does Dom know yet?"

"No. I ain't been able to find him either."

"Well you're having some kind of day, Brownie, I'll tell you that."

"You can't tell me nothing. You think I don't know Dom's gonna shit hand grenades when I tell him?" Brownie winced and whistled softly. "You know, I thought this was a bunch of nothing yesterday. Real nothing. But being around that fat-ass all day, now maybe I think he's really gonna do something. But listen, Balzic, you got to know this is something those two whales did on their own. The rest of us didn't have anything to do with it."

"I know that."

"Well then what the fuck was all that noise you gave Dom yesterday? What the fuck was that about?"

Balzic turned away without giving Cercone a reply. He paused at the door, turned back to Mila Sanders Rizzo, and said, "I got to go. But I want to talk to you some more."

"I'm right here every day," she said, smiling. Then she put both her hands together over her head and made sweeping motions as though she were doing a breaststroke. Then she pointed at Balzic and laughed.

"Oh fuck," Balzic said under his breath and hurried out to his cruiser.

Balzic scrambled out of his cruiser at the station and trotted into the duty room, loosening his tie as he went. Sergeant Angelo Clemente looked up, startled, and swiveled around on his chair.

"What's up?"

"Get on the phone. Call every fourth guy and tell him to call the other three. Everybody doubles up until further notice; extra shift in plain clothes."

"What do I tell them?"

"Just tell them to get the fuck in here. And I don't mean two hours from now."

"Mario, I hope you know what you're doing. That's a lot of overtime. Council ain't going to go—"

"Do it, Angelo! You let me worry about City Council."

Clemente shrugged and shook his head several times, his eyes half closed, his lips pursed. He muttered something else, but he rolled his chair over to one of the phones and started dialing.

Meanwhile, Balzic went to the radio console and opened the switch to all channels.

"All units, all personnel," he began. "Priority, priority. Apprehend and arrest one Tullio Manditti, male, Caucasian, age approximately thirty-five, height approximately five feet seven inches, weight approximately two hundred and eighty, ninety pounds, build extremely obese, usually wears and was last seen wearing coveralls. Street charge is material witness. Bring him to the station. Repeat, bring him to the station. Do not, repeat, do not remand him to a magistrate. Manditti may be armed. Do not let his build fool you. He is agile and extremely strong. Do not attempt to apprehend him by yourself. Call for backup. Repeat, call for backup . . . and for the rookies and all you other dumb fuckers out there, that means I want Tullio Manditti in here but you ain't supposed to try to make the collar by yourself. One on one, he'll get you off your feet and sit on you. Then you're his. If you do get stuck, mace him, but whatever you do, don't get close enough to use a baton. Guaranteed, you'll lose. . . ."

Balzic repeated the call and asked for and got confirmation of reception from all beat patrolmen and mobile units. Then he stood and went over beside Clemente. "How we doing?"

"I got two more to go. No problems so far. Lot of bitching, but no problems."

"Good. Stay with it. I want them all here."

Balzic went to another phone and dialed Muscotti's. Vinnie answered.

"This is Balzic. Are Soup, Digs, and Brownie there?"

"Just Brownie."

"How about Dom?"

"He won't get here for another fifteen or twenty minutes. Why?"

"If Tullio Manditti should happen to roll in there— which I doubt—you tell him to stay there and then you call me, got it?"

"Yeah, sure, Mario."

"Okay, let me talk to Brownie."

There was a whooshing sound, as though Balzic had had a clam shell shoved against his ear, and then a thump. Then Vinnie's voice called out to Brownie Cercone. More whooshing and scraping followed.

"Yeah?" Brownie said.

"Balzic. You get Soup and Digs and get on the street. Talk to all your people. I want Tullio, you understand?"

"Hey, now wait a minute, Balzic. I ain't no fuckin' beagle."

"Wait my ass. You turn beagle. You get on the street and start looking and talking. And when you find him, you stay with him until you call me, you hear?"

"Oh for crissake—"

Balzic hung up without letting him finish. Then he waited.

An hour later his entire force, except for the men already on duty, was assembled in the duty room. Few of them looked Balzic in the eye. There was much grumbling and subdued cursing until Balzic reminded them of the overtime pay. Then they grew quiet and attentive and some of them even looked eager. Balzic worried about the eager ones but tried to put them out of mind while he told them who he wanted and why.

Two hours later, after calling Walker Johnson of the state police and District Attorney Milt Weigh and asking for whatever assistance they could give, Balzic was still pacing around the duty room. He'd allowed Angelo Clemente to go home because Clemente's feet made it impossible for him to walk more than three or four blocks without having to rest for ten minutes and because his wife was using the family car to take her mother shopping.

Sergeant Vic Stramsky had taken over the desk, and he was being quietly proficient, handling all the nuisance calls without bothering Balzic.

By five o'clock it appeared to Balzic, who had quit pacing and was now sitting at one of the front desks with his feet up, that Tullio Manditti may as well have been in Florida. Balzic scowled up at the clock above the radio console and drummed his fingers on his stomach.

"Hey, Vic, see if my arithmetic's right."

"Huh?"

"Just add something. Right there, on the blotter." Balzic paused and pinched the bridge of his nose. "Me and you and Angelo. That leaves thirty-three of our people. Okay, so then we got Soup, Digs, and Brownie. How many people you figure they got?"

"All over Rocksburg and Southwest Rocksburg, and Westfield Township? Hell, they got to have ten or twelve apiece. More than that."

"I figure it's more like twenty apiece."

Stramsky shrugged. "Maybe so."

"Okay, so if only half of them are out looking and listening, that's thirty, thirty-five more, right?"

"Yeah, that would be about right."

"Okay, so then we got two mobile units from the state, one from Westfield in Westfield, and then we got three undercover narcs plus Carraza and Dillman from Weigh's office."

"Let me add it up here." Stramsky scratched the hair above his ear and started figuring on the blotter. After a moment he said, "I get between seventy and seventy-five, depending on how many of Dom's street people are cooperating."

"Yeah. That's what I came up with," Balzic said. He leaned back in his chair and kneaded his hands. "Just think, Vic. I mean, imagine it. Seventy, seventy-five people looking for one guy, a fuckin' dirigible on feet, in a town this size for—what is it now—three hours?"

"At least that long."

"And nobody sees him. Now what do you figure the odds got to be on that? Hell, I didn't even include the security people at the hospital." Balzic shook his head. "That's three, four more, right?"

"No. There's just two guys up there now. The other two won't come on until the nurses start changing shifts. That's at eleven."

"Even so, Christ, the sun is shining, everybody knows what he looks like. I mean, who could miss a walking mountain, even if it is short?"

Stramsky shrugged and was about to say something when the phone stuttered on the switchboard. He plugged in the line and listened for a short time. Then he said, "Mario, I think somebody seen him."

"Huh?" Balzic lurched forward on his chair and grabbed the phone. "This is Balzic. Go ahead."

"This is Mrs. Kwalick in Emergency."

"Yes, ma'am, how are you?"

"I'm fine, thanks. But I think you better come up here. We just had an admission, a man in his early forties named Francis Dulia, and he's in very bad shape. He has at least a dozen fractures, probably more, but no lacerations or abrasions. The man who brought him in says that he was beaten up."

"I'm on my way," Balzic said, dropping the receiver on the hook and scurrying toward the door. "That fat bastard did it. That sonofabitching lard-ass got him. All these people looking, and he got to him anyway. . . ."

"I did not make a thorough examination," the doctor said. He was Indian, tall, slim, with long, slender hands. His accent was British. He gestured apologetically. "I

104

made really just a cursory examination and then I alerted radiology and the resident surgeons. I then requested that a neurosurgeon be summoned."

"Uh-huh. Well what did it look like to you?"

"There had been severe concussion, and quite possibly fractures of both the left parietal and temporal bones—"

"The skull?"

"Yes. Here." The doctor pointed to two places on his own head, just above the left ear and then slightly above and behind the ear. "His eyes responded very poorly, and there was extensive bleeding from the left ear. From the swelling and from the position of his teeth and chin, it was clear his mandible was fractured—his jaw. Excuse me, I will speak in layman's terms. His left collarbone was obviously fractured. That was visible. I did not even have to touch it."

"What else?"

"The upper left arm was fractured in at least two places, as was the forearm and quite possibly the wrist. Again, that was clear to the eye from the position of the left arm. His left knee was extremely swollen, indicating fractures there. There were other swellings up and down the length of his left leg, from the hip to the foot. But there was something very curious."

"What's that?"

"There were not even abrasions of the skin. I admit that I am relatively inexperienced, but I have never seen anything like these injuries. I do not see how it is possible to have that many fractures without laceration—in fact, very little evidence of trauma except for the contusions. I don't understand it."

"Well, unfortunately I do," Balzic said.

"Then perhaps you can explain it to me."

"Listen, do you know the county coroner?"

"Dr. Grimes?"

"Yeah. You get him to explain it to you. He knows all about it. He's the one who explained it to me. Okay, Doc, thanks. Oh, what about the guy's wife?"

"Understandably, she was quite hysterical. I prescribed Nembutal for her."

"Can I talk to her?"

"Not for three or four hours at least. She was much too active physically and vocally. My first prescription only slowed her somewhat."

"What about the guy who brought him in? Where's he?"

"Oh, I don't know that. You should ask Mrs. Kwalick."

Balzic nodded and patted the doctor on the arm. He headed out of the office to find Mrs. Kwalick, stopping at each of the treatment rooms and leaning in to ask if she was there.

At the last treatment room, he was hailed before he leaned in by a grizzled, powerfully built, elderly man wearing a tee-shirt and green trousers. His soiled green cap was dotted with outdated United Mine Workers union buttons. He had no teeth, and he was rolling a cud of tobacco from cheek to cheek.

"Ain't you the chief of police?"

"Yes. What can I do for you?"

"I brung him in. Him and his missus. The fella that had the hell beat out of him."

"Ah, you're the man I'm looking for," Balzic said, putting his hand on the man's shoulder and steering him gently toward the office where moments ago he'd spoken with the Indian doctor.

"Have a seat, Mr., uh—"

"Harsha. Andrew T. That's for Theodore. Just call me Andy."

"Well, Andy, are you a neighbor?"

"I live next door to them if that's what you mean, but I ain't their neighbor."

"How close is next door?"

"It's twenty-one feet from my house to my property line. It's forty feet from the property line to their house. They say it's fifty feet. *He* says. She never said nothing about it. That's why I ain't their neighbor. I got a lawyer working on it right now. I don't know what the hell he wants with that other ten feet, but he ain't gonna get it, and right now, it looks like he ain't gonna be able to use it even if he does get it, which he ain't, and—"

"Uh, Andy," Balzic interrupted him, "I'm sure your lawyer'll take care of your property rights, uh, so just tell me what happened—if you know."

"Huh? Oh, I know what happened all right. I seen the whole thing."

"Okay. Exactly what did you see?"

"Well, I come home from work, and I was standing in my kitchen just ready to pour myself a shot and a beer, to cut the dust, you know, and then I was going to go out and clean up the mess them goddamn raccoons made. They—"

"Go on," Balzic prodded him.

"Well, Dulia come out the back door of his house, and I thought he was gonna come over and start breaking my hump about the goddamn property line again. So

107

I was getting ready for him. I had a few things I was gonna let him have, but as soon as I could see his face close up, I could see he looked real confused and kinda scared, sorta all flustered like he didn't know where he was. I seen guys coming up out of the shafts like that after old Mother Earth shakes her ass a little bit. You know, they made it out okay, but they're still pretty shook up.

"So, anyway, he starts to look around like he's trying to find something. Then he looks up at the woods behind us. Then he sneaks over to the far corner of his house and peeks around the corner. He pulls back real quick. Then he runs, sorta tippy-toe, over to the other corner, the one closest to me, and he peeks around that.

"So now I'm thinking this is pretty comical, so I'm really watching him. I got a shot in my hand and I didn't even drink it until it was all over. Anyway, all of a sudden he starts to run up toward the woods, and he gets only, oh, maybe four or five steps when this thing come flying from down around the front of his house, I guess, and smacks him right square in the back and down he goes. And, oh, you can see he's hurting. His face is all twisted up, and he's having a hard time catching his breath."

"What was this thing that hit him?"

"Well, I couldn't tell right then. Not until the fat guy picks it up."

"Then what?"

"Well, then I could see it was a bat, you know, a baseball bat, except it had something white wrapped all around the end. Looked like a towel but I couldn't be sure."

"Go on."

"Well, next thing I know this real fat guy, I mean really fat, he comes up and grabs the bat and he whacks

108

Dulia across the leg with it. He don't say nothing. He just whacks him. Then he leans down close to Dulia and says something to him, but I can't hear it. But I heard Dulia say, 'Oh, Christ, don't hit me again,' something like that. But that guy whacked him anyway. Right here." Harsha pointed to his left forearm.

"You heard them through the window?"

"No. I had the window open a couple inches. I just painted my kitchen the last couple days. Just did the last coat on the woodwork yesterday. That's how come I had the window open."

"Okay. Go on."

"Well, the fat guy whacks him again. Right across the side of the knee. Right here." Harsha stood and pointed to the outside of his left knee. "He was laying on his side like this." Harsha got on the floor on his right side and propped himself on his right forearm and held up his left arm as though to cover his face. Then he scrambled up and demonstrated as though chopping wood with an imaginary ax. "The fat guy was whacking him like this, see?"

"I see," Balzic said.

"Then he leans down and says something else to Dulia. But I can't hear that either. All I can hear is Dulia begging him not to hit him again. But the fat guy don't pay no attention. He straightens up and whacks him again. Right here." Harsha pointed to the outside of his left wrist. "And Dulia is screaming like hell and then he starts to bawl."

"And you were just watching all this?"

"Sure I was watching it. What do you think I'm telling you? Oh. You mean how could I just stand there and watch it? Oh, hell, I seen fellas pinned under tons of

109

shale, man. Just their head sticking out. I seen guys with half their face blowed away, their guts hanging out, their legs and arms maybe four, five feet away from them— over in Italy during the war. It don't bother me."

"I understand. Well, go on. What happened then?"

"Well, this fat guy leans over again and says something else. I can't hear him. But this time, Dulia, he starts hollering something which I couldn't make no sense out of. He starts hollering, he says over and over, 'It couldn't lose. It wasn't supposed to lose.' "

" 'It couldn't lose? It wasn't supposed to lose?' He said exactly that?"

"Yup. I heard it clear as a bell. He must've said it, oh, four, five times," Harsha said. "And this fat guy, he whacks him two more times. Right here on the hip. Oh, he's really bringing it to him. And Dulia's screaming. Then it's the same thing all over again. 'Bout five more times. He'd lean down and say something to him, then he'd up and whack him, all up and down his left side."

"How long did all this take?"

"Huh? Oh, not more than a couple minutes. Everything I told you so far. Maybe not even that long. No time at all."

"Okay. Go on."

"Well, by this time Dulia's all cried out. I mean, his face still looks like he's crying, see, but there ain't no noise. So then this fat guy, he puts the bat down, you know, leans it against his leg, and he takes out a hanky and wipes his face and neck. He's really got a sweat going. Then he leans down real quick, and Dulia says something I can't hear. He talks for a real long time, oh, maybe five minutes, and the fat guy's leaning over and listening real intent and wiping his face. Then, all of a sudden, he shoves the hanky back in his pocket and he hollers, 'You motherfucker, I'm gonna beat your fuckin' brains out. I wasn't, but I'm going to now.' "

"He said exactly that?" Balzic said.

"Just what I said. It was only the second time he said anything I could hear. And he kept saying it. And he starts in whacking him again, and he steps over him and whacks him four or five times real fast. Once here"— Harsha indicated where by drawing his thumb downward over his left collarbone—"and at least three times on the head. I couldn't tell where exactly, 'cause by this time the fat guy is between me and Dulia, but I knew where when I went over to Dulia after."

"Then what happened?"

"Well, then the fat guy, he just turned around cool as you please and walked off toward the front of the house. Then I heard a car start up and drive off. That's when I went over to see how Dulia was. Soon as I got close, I could see the blood coming out of his ear, and I knew I had to get him in here real fast. I couldn't wait for no ambulance. So I backed my truck up the lawn and I went and got some blankets and I laid him in the back as easy as I could and I brung him in. Then I went and got his missus from where she works."

"And that's it?"

"That's it. That's everything. I didn't leave nothing out."

"Okay. Now, is there any doubt that you'd recognize this fat guy again if you saw him, I mean positively recognize him?"

"Shoot, you couldn't mistake him. Not that lard-ass."

"Did he ever see you?"

"He never even looked in my direction. Not once."

111

"How far away were you?"

"I told you before. My house is twenty-one feet from the—"

"Yes, I know. But where were they? How far from Dulia's house?"

"Oh, they was maybe ten yards from the back corner of his place and, lemme see, maybe five yards over toward my place."

"And you had a clear, unobstructed view?"

"Sure. There's nothing but the fence I put up 'bout two months ago."

"What kind of fence? How high?"

"Regular chain-link fence. You can see through it. I bought it out at Sears and put it in myself. Three feet above ground and a foot below ground. I was looking over it at the fat guy, but I had to look through it to see Dulia."

"But there was nothing else between you and them, no trees or hedges or anything like that?"

"Not a damn thing 'cept the fence."

"Okay, Andy, that's enough about that. Now what can you tell me about Dulia?"

"Aw, he was okay until he hurt his back. Then he couldn't work no more, and he started to get moody as all hell."

"When did he hurt his back?"

"Oh, must be over a year now. He was in the hospital a long time. Five or six weeks. Oh, he was a mess. They took a piece of bone out of his hip and put it in his back, and then he got an infection or something. He looked like hell when he finally come home. And then it wasn't too long before he had to go back in. But I never had no trouble with him before that. They been living there for

112

ten years, and he never said a goddamn word about the property line till after he come out of the hospital the second time. Then that's all he talked about. One time I said to him, 'What the hell you think's under there, oil or something?' "

"How about the people on the other side of him? Did he have any trouble with them?"

"I don't know nothing about that. There's just an old lady living there, and she ought to be in the county home. But I don't think Dulia could've given her a bad time 'cause his missus used to look out for her, that old lady I mean. I seen her taking food over lots of times and I think she used to wash her clothes."

"Uh-huh. Well, what else do you know about him? How were they living if he wasn't working? Was he on workmen's compensation?"

"Yeah. Then his wife works at that supermarket. She's a checkout. They was getting by, I guess. Not like when he was working, naturally. He was a bricklayer. You know how much those guys make an hour. So it was a comedown, but hell, they didn't have no kids."

"Did you ever hear him talk about gambling, betting on anything?"

"If he did I never paid no attention to it. Course, he might be like a lot of fellas. Play the numbers just like they was breathing, but they never say nothing about it until they hit or until they miss by one number and then you hear 'em bitching."

Balzic nodded. "You ever see the fat guy before?"

"Never."

"Ever see anybody who looked like him, built the same way, only a little taller and a couple years older?"

"Nope."

"Well, is there anything else you can remember about Dulia, anything at all?"

Harsha shook his head. "No. I didn't have much to do with him. I keep pretty much to myself. Ever since my missus died, I don't feel like socializing too much, if you know what I mean. No, until he starts getting this screwy idea that his property goes ten feet more than it does, we never did nothing but pass the time of day. I never even drunk a beer with him."

"Was he a drinker?"

"Well, till he hurt his back, all I ever seen him drink was a couple beers after work when it was hot. But now he drinks a lot. Sweet wine. Buys it by the gallon, least twice a week. I heard him say once it was the only thing made his back quit hurting. Sounded to me like he was trying to kid somebody. But maybe it did. I been pretty lucky. I never had no back trouble, but I seen a lot of guys with it and they ain't worth a fart for working, so it must hurt. But that's all I know about him drinking."

"What about his family, his relatives?"

"Well, I think I already told you they didn't have no kids. Only relatives I ever seen visiting them was an old lady and her son and daughter. The daughter looked a mess. The only reason I even knew they was relatives at all was his missus told me, 'cause she felt sorry for the old lady on account of the daughter. But I don't even know their name. All I know was they was on his side of the family. But how they was related, hell, I don't even know that."

"The daughter was a mess? How do you mean?"

"Oh, I don't know, she just looked all lumpy, like a pile of putty. And Dulia, he used to look out for her. Every time they come, he used to follow her around their

114

backyard like he was trying to make sure she didn't mess around with nothing, or maybe he was trying to make sure she didn't hurt herself. That's the way it looked to me."

Balzic thought a moment. Something struck him, some connection. He didn't know what it was, but he knew he knew what it was without being able to think of it clearly.

Balzic took out his notebook and asked for Harsha's address and phone number. Harsha gave his address but said, "I don't have no phone. I had them take it out after my missus died . . . hey, I been meaning to ask you. I mean, I guess you know what you're doing, but how's come this is the first thing you wrote down? All them detective shows I see on TV, them cops are always writing things down, making notes and all, when they're getting stories from witnesses, I mean."

Balzic smiled. "Andy, I was just about to tell you to come down the station so a stenographer could take your story in shorthand. She wouldn't miss a word, and if I was writing things down I wouldn't be able to read it tomorrow. Anyway, we have to notarize your statement and then we have to take it to a magistrate to file an information against this fat guy; otherwise you'd have to appear before a magistrate yourself, and there's no point in you doing that."

"Oh. I don't know what all that means, but I guess you know what you're doing."

"Well, don't worry about it. The thing is, I won't be able to get a stenographer until late tomorrow afternoon. Can you come in around four?"

"I could get there by about ten after, how's that?"

"That's fine. In the meantime, don't die on me—"

115

"Oh, hell, I'm healthy as a horse."

Balzic laughed. "I can see that. What's really important is that you don't forget anything you saw."

"Oh, shoot, I couldn't forget none of this, no sirree."

"Good. Then go on home and have a couple cold
ones. And listen, if I'm not there tomorrow, just tell the
desk sergeant what you're there for and he'll take care of
you, okay?"

Harsha nodded and left with a shrug and a wave.

Balzic then called Stramsky at the station and told
him to put out the word that Manditti was now wanted
for attempted murder. "There's no question the dummy
did it, Vic. He just beat the hell out of a guy named
Francis Dulia with a baseball bat. Call Muscotti and tell
him he better tell his people to get off their asses. Tell
everybody to get off their asses. Something tells me
Tullio ain't finished yet. I don't know why I got that
feeling, but I do. In the meantime, I'm going to stay here
and try to talk to Dulia's wife and Fat Manny."

Dulia's wife was still deep under the influence of the
Nembutal, so Balzic went up to the third floor to see Fat
Manny. He found him flat on his back gnawing on a stick
of pepperoni, licking his fingers between bites.

"Hello, Manny. How you feeling?"

"I'm going to live. You feeling okay, Balzic? You
going to live?"

"For a while I think."

"Good. We wouldn't know how to act around Rocksburg if you wasn't the chief of police. You keep the

streets safe and everything. Us citizens are really grateful."

Balzic saw that the other beds were still empty. He turned around and closed the door quietly. "Okay, Manny, let's cut the happy horseshit."

"What happy stuff? Am I giving you happy stuff? I thought we was just being nice."

"So okay, so keep on being nice and tell me why you screwed Francis Dulia."

"Huh? Who? Who was that again?"

"You never heard of him, huh?"

"Never heard of him," Manny said ponderously.

"Then why do you suppose your brother would want to put a job on him with a Louisville Slugger?"

"What're you talking about? What job? What slugger? My brother? You must be eating wrong, Balzic. You must be eating too much American bread or something. That stuff messes up your system. My brother would not even hurt a stray cat."

"Manny, I got everybody looking for him. Everybody on my force, plus all of Dom's people, plus state people, plus county people. Your brother's up for attempted murder. And even if Dulia doesn't die, which is unlikely considering that his skull is fractured in two places, not to mention a dozen other fractures—even if Dulia doesn't die, your brother's going away on every assault rap the state ever wrote. And as pissed off as Dom is at you, you have to know that Tullio's going to go it alone. He won't get any of the fringe benefits, not so much as an extra pack of cigarettes a week."

Manny took another bite of pepperoni and chewed it slowly, thoughtfully, but he said nothing.

"I mean, think of it, Manny. When we get him there

117

isn't going to be anybody standing up for him. He's going to go up in front of the man all by himself, and then he's going to do all that time by himself. And he won't do it at the hotel down the road, Manny. He'll be doing it in Pittsburgh, in The Wall, where they keep the bad guys, the crazies. And not a friend, inside or out. So why don't you give your brother a break and tell me where he's going? He turns himself in and maybe he won't have to go to Pittsburgh. Maybe he'll find out he has some friends."

"That don't make no sense, Balzic. I mean, even if I knew what you were talking about, and even if I knew where he was going—hell, who says he's going anywhere? He's probably home. Besides, how could he turn himself in if you had to go get him? And what's he going to turn himself in for anyway? He ain't done nothing."

"You just tell me where he is, Manny, I'll call him on the phone. You let me talk to him for five minutes, I guarantee he'll be begging me to let him turn it over. You know there's about ninety percent spades down there? Do I have to tell you how your brother likes spades?"

"Balzic, you're trying to pump carbon monoxide up somebody's ass, that's what you're trying to do. I don't know what you're talking about."

"You don't know any Francis Dulia?"

"How many times I got to tell you?"

"And you never booked a winner for him and then told him to take a walk?"

"I don't know where you're getting this stuff. I don't book nothing. I'm a chauffeur, everybody knows that."

"Who're you trying to shit? You haven't driven anything anywhere for anybody for over a week. How'd you get those holes in you?"

Manny thought for a moment. "It happened like this. I was carrying a bunch of quart pop bottles in a bag. I was gonna take them back for the deposit. The bag broke and one of them fell out the bottom and I tripped on it. Then I fell down on top of the rest of them. They broke. I mean, I'm pretty heavy, you know?"

"Oh, Jesus, Manny, that's enough. I'm going to ask you just once more not to be dumb. What do you say?"

Manny rolled over on his side, grimacing and wheezing, the bed creaking ominously. He laid the stick of pepperoni on his nightstand. "Hey, Balzic, there's some olives and bread underneath there. You wanna hand it to me, huh?"

"You tell me where Tullio is, I'll go get you a banquet."

"Aw fuck you. I'll call a nurse. Who needs you?"

"I think you and your brother are both going to need me pretty bad before this is over. But with all the static you're giving me, maybe I won't be around."

"Hey, Balzic, all of a sudden I'm tired. I don't want no more conversation. I think I need my rest."

Balzic snorted. "I wish you'd give me a rest. Right now I'm wondering how Tullio's going to take it when I tell him what kind of diet you're trying to put him on. After all the food he brought you in here? And you're not going to be able to take him a pepperoni."

"See you around, Balzic. I'm asleep."

"Have it your way, fatso. You just better start praying that Dulia doesn't die."

"Everybody dies, Balzic. And don't call me fatso. Fat

Manny, that's okay. But I don't go for that fatso stuff."

"Just what're you going to do about it, fatso?" Balzic snarled. "Laying there with your lard full of holes, just what do you think you can do about it? Go call your fatso brother and tell him to put a job on me with his bat? I wish you would. And I wish he would. 'Cause I'm so pissed at you two fat-asses, I'd like nothing better than to have him coming at me with a bat. I keep a three-foot baton in my car, fatso. Your fatso brother ever comes at me with a bat, I'll show him some moves with that baton he won't believe. You hear me, fatso?"

"Blow it out your ass, Balzic. You're giving me a headache."

Balzic turned and left, muttering and cursing under his breath. Once out in the hall, he stopped and faced the wall, making his hands into fists, chewing his lips, and fighting the urge to knock holes in the plaster. The way I'm going, he thought, it'd be my luck to hit a stud. That's all I'd need. My hand in a cast. . . .

He shoved his hands into his pockets and went to the elevators, taking one to ground level, then walking quickly to the Emergency Unit. He found Mrs. Kwalick and had her direct him to the room where Mrs. Dulia was. It was a waste of time; Mrs. Dulia woke in wild-eyes starts only to doze off in midreply to one of his questions. Nothing she managed to blurt out was of any use to him.

Balzic paced around the room for some minutes trying to think if there was something he should be doing that he had forgotten or overlooked, but the more he paced and looked at his watch, the more he knew that the only thing he could do was wait and hope for some good luck. Maybe I ought to get somebody praying, he thought, and went out to the pay phone in the lobby. He dialed St. Malachy's rectory.

Father Marrazo answered gruffly.

"This is Mario, Father. How you doing?"

"The same," the priest said in Italian.

"You having any luck with your problem?"

"You mean about Father Sabatine?"

"Yeah."

"It's going to take more than luck, Mario."

Balzic waited for him to go on, but the priest said nothing. "Well, uh, how 'bout praying? Isn't that helping?"

"Mario, I hope you never hear me say anything like this again, but I'm nearly prayed out. The bishop is so angry he can't talk, and Sabatine is so depressed he won't talk. And I'm getting ready to dump the whole thing on Kelly and Marcellino."

"Oh." Balzic didn't know what else to say.

"Was there something you wanted, Mario?"

"Huh? Oh, no. No, I just wanted to see how you were making out with your problem, that's all."

"Well, what can I tell you?"

"Nothing—I guess. Sorry to bother you. I hope you, uh, I hope it works out." Balzic hung up without saying good-by. Well, he thought, no help there. Not even a little shot of consolation. But there's no use getting worked up about it. He has his own problems. I can't expect him to do my work. Probably wouldn't have done any good anyway to have him praying, but it sure would have made things feel better. "My ass," Balzic said aloud, as he turned away from the phone and looked around. "My ass. . . ."

"Such language," said an old woman with hair so gray it was turning yellow. She was sitting on an imitation leather couch beside the phone. In front of her was a four-legged aluminum walker. She clucked her tongue at Balzic. "What would your mother say?" she said sharply.

Balzic stared down at the woman, but he could not bring himself to tell her that if his mother had been there she would have told the old woman to mind her own business and stay out of other people's conversations.

"Young man," the woman snapped, "if you don't leave me alone, I'm going to call the police." Her eyes were as hard as the set of her mouth.

"Old woman," Balzic said, "I am the police. And right now there's nothing I'd rather do than leave you alone. Good afternoon."

The old woman's face softened suddenly in a crooked smile. "It was so nice of you to bring me here," she cooed. "The people are all so wonderful. Have you met my son?"

"No, ma'am," Balzic said, recognizing at last the woman's senility. "No, ma'am, I haven't."

Her face pinched as she squinted meanly at Balzic. "You should," she hissed. "He's a bastard just like you."

Balzic shook his head and walked away from her. He stopped in the center of the lobby and looked around. Every seat was occupied. He turned slowly and looked at each of the faces, seeing on one confusion, on another irritation, on still another impatience, on still another grim-lipped pain. There was a woman, enormously pregnant, with her ankles and feet so swollen that she had taken off her slippers and stockings and was staring glumly at her feet. There was a teenaged boy with a blood-soaked hanky wrapped around his hand. There

122

was an old man, his nostrils half destroyed by cancer, who was staring blankly at his hands. A black woman, her face stony, was trying half-heartedly to soothe a young girl who would not stop crying though outwardly nothing appeared to be wrong with her. There was another old man, breathing in phlegmatic bursts, who was turning an unlit cigarette over and over in his fingers. There was a young woman with long, frizzy red hair and very fair skin who sat with her chin in her hand. She seemed to be talking to herself, and when Balzic looked at her, she jumped up suddenly and hurried past him toward the exit, saying to herself, "Fuck this place. I mean, this place can just go fuck." And then she was gone.

Balzic could not look at the rest of the faces. He felt suddenly that if he didn't get out of there, if he didn't get outside into the crisp March air, he was going to choke on the confusion and irritation and impatience and pain. He stood transfixed for a moment and then wheeled about and nearly ran out of the lobby.

Outside, he gulped air and loosened his tie and wanted to untie his shoes and undo his belt. He tried to remember when he had felt such an overpowering sense of oppression. Then he asked himself what the point was of trying to remember that. A comparison was senseless. Besides, he thought, what the hell do you expect to see in an emergency waiting room? That's the way it looks every day of the week. And on the holidays? When the solid citizens are out having fun? Hell, man, today that place was practically healthy.

It was eleven-thirty-two in the evening when Balzic got the phone call from the hospital. He had never met the doctor and had to ask him twice to repeat his name. Even then he wasn't sure he could pronounce it. The doctor was another Lebanese.

"Not that it matters all that much," Balzic said, "but when did he die?"

"Eleven-twenty," the doctor said. "I just completed the death certificate."

"Did he ever regain consciousness?"

"No."

"What did you put down as the cause of death?"

"Massive brain damage as a direct result of multiple fractures of the left parietal and left temporal bones."

"Is Dr. Grimes there?"

"Not now, no. He had the body removed immediately to the morgue. I am sure he will have a full report for you in the morning."

"How's Dulia's wife taking it?"

"I'm told she is quite incoherent."

"Well that's natural, I guess. Thank you." Balzic hung up and stared at the phone. He scratched the back of his left hand and thought for a long moment, his eyes wide and unblinking.

"Hey, Vic," he said, looking up to see Stramsky looking back at him expectantly.

"It's murder now, right?" Stramsky said.

Balzic nodded. "Poor sonofabitch never woke up . . . it was probably better." Balzic stood and went to the window overlooking Main Street. He jingled coins and keys in his pockets and listened vaguely to Stramsky calling all units and personnel to change the charge on Tullio Manditti to a general charge of murder. Stramsky then called the state police and told them that the investigation was now officially theirs.

There were only a few cars moving on Main Street and no pedestrians that Balzic could see. The temperature had dropped fifteen degrees since the afternoon, and Balzic fully expected to see snow. Wind lifted bits of paper from the gutters and off the sidewalks and swirled them about, but there was no snow. He watched the paper being blown this way and that, and he found himself thinking that his mind was working the same way: bits of information were coming and going with little apparent sense.

It should have been a simple matter. Manny had booked a winner on his own for Francis Dulia, and when Manny couldn't come up with the money Dulia went berserk. That was logical enough. One guy with an appetite bigger than his brain hustles a guy with a bad back, an unemployed guy who lately was given to moods of surly indignation. Nothing to it. Enter the brother with his bat, exit one guy who thought the world was out to screw him and found out that he was right. What could be more logical than that?

But what was Dulia telling Tullio during that couple of minutes before Tullio straightened up and said he was going to beat his brains out? Tullio didn't go there to kill him. You don't put a towel around the bat if you're looking to kill him. The towel's there to keep from killing him. And Tullio never hit him in the head until after Dulia quit making his speech—whatever it was.

Then there was that thing Dulia said. "It couldn't lose. It wasn't supposed to lose." That's what Harsha said he said, and Harsha had absolutely no doubt about it. "It wasn't supposed to lose." . . . Ah, that's crap.

There isn't a bettor in the world who thinks he's booking a loser. Still, this wasn't the ordinary bettor. This guy was ballsy enough to try to collect his winnings with a knife.

So what the hell did he bet on? It had to be a number. That's the only bets Manny ever carried. But how does this guy think a number couldn't lose? Old stock, new stock, New York race, Brooklyn race—that's all the numbers there are. The stocks come out of *The Wall Street Journal* and the races come out of the *The New York Daily News* . . . every guy who ever tried to fix one of those numbers got dead in a real hurry. And this Dulia, this square from Westfield Township? Who the hell could he know to even begin to fix anything?

So why am I thinking fix? Good question. Why am I? Because it doesn't make sense for a guy who's about to lose his life to say something like that? Okay. So what would he be saying? Oh, shit, I don't know what all he said to Tullio. Just that.

No, goddamn it. He said that because he was sure, that's why. Because he was right. That was a guy looking for what was his, what belonged to him, what was owed. Maybe they weren't much—what the hell is ten feet of property more or less? But if you've hurt your back and you can't work and you feel like the world has just given you the shaft, you start making sure you get what you think is really yours. That was a guy with a grudge against the world, and he was looking for sure things. A guy getting ready to die who cares more that what he bet on wasn't supposed to lose—he cares more about that than he does about living or dying. That guy had to know something. He knew a fix was in. Some kind of fix. Had to be. . . .

Balzic reached for a phone and dialed.

"Yes?" Dom Muscotti answered curtly.

"This is Mario. Dulia died."

Muscotti made growling noises. "That's—that's a shame. A friggin' shame. I'm sorry, Mario, I really am."

"Are you sure you didn't know him, Dom?"

"Sure I'm sure. I told you before when you called. I thought then that I maybe heard the name someplace, but now I'm sure I didn't." Dom paused. "That friggin' Tullio, wait'll I . . ." His voice trailed off.

"Wait'll what?"

"Nothing, Mario. Did I say something?"

"Skip it," Balzic said, sighing impatiently. "You sure this guy didn't book with one of your people?"

"Mario, I asked everybody, honest. Listen, what would I be lying for now?"

"Keep your shirt on. I didn't say you were lying."

"Well, nobody knows him, I'm telling you."

"D'you talk to Manny yet?"

"Not yet. I'm going up the hospital as soon as I close up. I don't know what the occasion is, but I got a bunch of college hot dogs in here and they're celebrating something. I'd've closed up an hour ago if it wasn't for them, but I need the paper."

"You need the paper?" Balzic laughed.

"What're you laughing for? You think I don't take a beating every once in a while? I'll write you a letter. There's some guy killing me. I think he must have something on a couple jockeys or something. Christ, I can't handle him no more this week. I laid him off yesterday to Pittsburgh and today to Buffalo. What do you think that's gonna cost me?"

"I don't want to know," Balzic said. "Well, tell your people it's murder now. And when you talk to Manny, tell him I'm making him an accessory before and after. Conspiracy, the whole bit."

"I'll tell him," Muscotti said. "Don't worry about nothing. I'm gonna talk to him like a father."

Balzic hung up and thought it over. If Muscotti did know Dulia, why would he say he didn't? To protect Manny? Not likely. Muscotti was sore enough a week ago at Manny to give him a vacation despite his own mother's fondness for Manny's company and conversation, and there was no one alive Muscotti tried to please as much as his mother.

What's more, it had been sixteen years since Muscotti had used muscle for anything. Since Sam Weisberg retired to Florida, there had been no reason to use muscle. Muscotti was solid with the old men in Pittsburgh, and nobody would dare provoke him without provoking them.

Balzic could only conclude that Muscotti was telling the truth: neither he nor any of his people knew Dulia, professionally or otherwise.

So what the hell did Dulia fix? Balzic drummed his fingers on the desk and began to think that there was a good chance he was complicating a simple thing.

He shook his head. There was still Dulia's life-and-death insistence that what he had bet on couldn't lose, and try as he might, Balzic could not put that thought out of his mind. He kept rattling it around, thinking that there was something right in front of him that he was overlooking, something everybody took for granted which he just couldn't connect to Dulia. He was sure it had to be something local. Dulia couldn't be anything but a local square who tried to make a local score.

At five to twelve Sergeant Joe Royer came in and took

over the desk from Stramsky. The rest of the shift changed, and everybody brought in the same word: no Tullio.

By one that morning, Balzic had decided that Dulia had been a square, a dumb square who had stumbled onto something.

By one-thirty, Balzic had decided that Dulia had been the most cunning man in the county.

By two o'clock, Balzic admitted that he didn't know a damned thing about Francis Dulia.

He called Romeo's Diner and ordered a cheeseburger. When it was delivered, he took two bites out of it and wrapped the rest of it up and put it in his desk. His tongue was biting from all the cigarettes, his throat and chest were burning, and his stomach was growling from all the coffee.

He drew oblong boxes on a note pad, filling them in until they were solidly black, then drew some more and filled those in. Dozens of questions about Dulia rumbled through his mind, and he fumed that he couldn't get answers to any of them until the workmen's compensation bureau opened in the morning. He'd have to work backward from there, and with any luck, he might know something about Dulia by noon. Until then, all he knew was that he was trying to grab a handful of smoke by even thinking about Dulia until he had some pertinent details about the man's life.

At two-twenty-five the phone rang, and Balzic lurched to answer it.

"Hey, kiddo," his mother said, her voice hoarse, "how come you no come home?"

"Huh? Ma? What're you doing still up?"

"Aw, my ankles hurt. They wake me up. But never mind. How come you no come home, no call or nothing? Ruth li'l bit worried, kiddo. She li'l bit mad too. You should call at least."

"I know, Ma, I know. I'm sorry."

"Better make up with Ruth tomorrow. Not me. Tell her you sorry."

"Okay, Ma, I will. Now go back to bed, okay? Try to get some sleep."

"Oh, Mario, sometime I don't mind I can't sleep. Sometime I just like sit here by myself. I take some wine, and I think about long time ago."

"Well, don't think too much. You can't get it back, that's what you're always telling me."

"Sure, I know that. But I don't feel sad about the long time ago. I just like to think about, that's all."

"Okay. Well, good night, Ma. I don't want to talk much right now, okay?"

"Hey, wait, kiddo. Is you—you stay late because of Frankie Dulia?"

Balzic frowned at the receiver as though it were responsible for what he'd just heard. "Yeah, Ma. But how'd you know about that?"

"Oh, I talk with Rose today. She feel very bad."

"Rose who?"

"Oh, Mario, what's wrong with your memory all of a sudden? Rose Abbatta, that's Rose who."

"Mrs. Abbatta told you about him?"

"Yeah, sure. Didn't I just say?"

"Yeah, but how'd she know about him?"

130

"Mario, he's her nephew."

Balzic straightened his back. "Say that again, Ma?"

"What'sa matter with you, you drunk? Frankie Dulia is Rose Abbatta's nephew."

"No I'm not drunk. Just tell me how Mrs. Abbatta found out what happened."

"Well, Nicky, he buys Rosalie a bicycle couple days ago, last week sometime, and right away she want to take over to show Frankie. But Rose don't let her until today. So Rosalie go over, but nobody's home. So the neighbor man, he tell Rosalie Frankie's in the hospital, got all beat up. And Rosalie come home all crying and wet her pants and, oh, was just carry on terrible. Rose said it took her half-hour to get Rosalie calm down so she can say what's happen. Rosalie really love Frankie a lot. Ever since they was kids, he look out for her, and—"

"Ma, I should've known. I should've known," Balzic said, shaking his head and thumping the desk with the side of his fist.

"You shoulda know what?"

"I should've known to call you in the first place."

"Hey, I call you, kiddo, you forget?"

"It doesn't make any difference, Ma. I got to hang up now. Don't worry. Go to sleep. And thanks."

"For what?"

"I got to go, Ma, honest. I can't talk anymore now. Wait a minute. What's Mrs. Abbatta's address?"

"Huh? What you want that for?"

"Please, Ma, just give it to me, okay?"

"Okay, okay. She live on Pinewood Drive. In Westfield Township. I don't remember number. But she's live in third house on right-hand side."

"From which end?"

131

"From this end. From when you go out from town."

"Oh thank you, Mother. You're beautiful. G'night."

"Hey—"

Balzic cut her off, held his finger on the receiver button, and waved to Royer to come over. He lifted his finger and dialed the operator and then scribbled a note for Royer. Royer looked at it, puzzled, and held up his hands questioningly.

"Tell somebody to get down there and pick him up," Balzic said.

"What charge?"

"Make one up. But tell them to move it. Operator? Operator, this is the Rocksburg police. This is an emergency. I want you to get the residence of a Mrs. Rose Abbatta on Pinewood Drive in Westfield Township. The number may be listed under her son's name. Nicholas or Nicolao. And keep ringing until somebody answers."

The operator said she would and clicked off. There was a long pause. Then the operator came back on. "Sir, that line is busy. If this is an emergency, do you authorize me to interrupt that call?"

"Hell yes. Cut in on it!"

Balzic looked up at the clock above the radio console. "I hope you worked overtime tonight, buddy," he said aloud. "Of all nights, I hope you got some time and again tonight. . . ."

The shriek ripped into Balzic's ear and set his flesh tingling. He thrust the phone outward and then brought it slowly closer to his ear until he could hear without

132

being hurt by the pitiful but piercing cries of Mrs. Ab-batta.

"Please send ambulance! Please, God, my Nicky is hurt! Please, please send ambulance quick!"

Balzic shouted to Royer, "Forget that last thing I told you. Get Mutual Aid and send them over to Pinewood Drive in Westfield Township—hold it till I get the address.

"Mrs. Abbatta, this is Mario Balzic. Listen to me. What's your house number? Mrs. Abbatta, do you hear me?"

She would not stop. She kept calling, pleading, for somebody to help her help her son.

"Mrs. Abbatta, goddamnit, I am trying to help you. This is Mario Balzic. Stop yelling a minute and tell me your house number!"

She sucked in her breath and then coughed violently. It took her nearly a minute to stop and control her voice. "God forgive me," she said. "Mario, I know your mother all my life . . . God forgive me."

"Mrs. Abbatta, never mind about God right now, okay? Just tell me your house number."

"It's all my fault, oh, God," she whispered. Then she sobbed and fought the sob so that she sounded as though she were being strangled. Finally she blurted out, "Number fifteen. Fifteen, you hear?"

"I hear. Fifteen." Balzic called it out loud enough for Royer to hear. And then he repeated the address so there could be no mistake. "Okay, Mrs. Abbatta, you go be with Nick now. There's an ambulance on the way right now. You hear me? Mrs. Abbatta, you hear me?"

"Yes, yes, I hear."

"I'm going to hang up now, Mrs. Abbatta. You just

go stay with your son. People will be there to help him in just a few minutes, you hear?"

"Yes, I hear. Thanks God. Oh, thanks God. . . ."

"Good. Just go be with him." Balzic depressed the receiver button, lifted it, and dialed Troop A barracks of the state police, asking for the duty officer.

"Lieutenant Poli," a voice said after a moment.

"This is Balzic in Rocksburg, Poli. I need a couple mobiles real quick."

"No kidding. Do you now?"

"Cut the crap, Poli. We got one murder tonight and we may have another possible. Same suspect, and he's got to be in the area. I need—"

"Balzic, I can't help what you need. I got three people down with the flu. I was told to assign you one unit, and that's the one you got cruising Norwood Hill. In the morning you're supposed to get another one. I couldn't give you another one if I wanted to because I don't have one to give."

"Okay, Poli, thanks anyway." Balzic hung up and pushed the cuticle back on his thumb, calling out to Royer, "Tell all the mobiles to concentrate on the area between Westfield Township and Norwood. I'm betting a thousand to one that fat-ass is just going to go on home and make out like nothing's happening. That would be his style."

Royer sent out the message and then said, "She was calling Mutual Aid when you cut in."

"Huh? Who?"

"That woman, Abbatta. She was trying to call them herself. The Mutual Aid dispatcher said to thank you. He couldn't get her house number out of her until you cut in."

"Oh. Big fuckin' deal. I did something right."

"Hey, uh, Mario, what's going on? I mean, how'd you know to call that place? And what did you want this Nick Abbatta picked up for down at the paper?"

"Oh, Joe, Jesus Christ, it's a long story. A long, messy story. But to make it quick, it has to do with a lottery. You know the kind I'm talking about. Everybody with a building fund or a mortgage or some fuckin' charity for some guy who broke his leg playing softball runs them. The American Legion, the VFW, the Moose, the Sons of Italy, the Polish Falcons, the Kosciusko Club, the Russian Club, the churches, all those phony athletic clubs, the Amvets, Christ, you name 'em, they've all run them at one time or another. Most of them run off the stock numbers, but lately a lot them are picking the winner from the last three digits of the U.S. Treasury balance . . . hell, I got two in my wallet right now. One from the VFW and another one from the Polish Falcons Stramsky sold me."

"Yeah, okay," Royer said. "I got one from Stramsky myself. But I still don't get it. How'd you know to call that house? I mean, I can't figure what the hell happened up there."

"Tullio got to him, that's what happened," Balzic said, standing and stretching and letting out a long, disgusted sigh that sounded more like a snarl. "What a fuckin' stupid I am. Right under my face. I knew there was a fix, I just fuckin' knew it! But you think I could put it together? Goddamn! . . . I also knew it was a pile of crud, but I never thought it was going to be this big a pile

. . . oh, Jesus, Mary, and Joseph, wait'll the newspapers and TV guys get hold of this—well, at least there's going to be one newspaper that ain't going to be playing it on the front page."

"Mario, I must've left my head out in the car," Royer said, "but I still don't know what you're talking about."

Balzic walked toward the door. He was in no hurry. He knew it was only a matter of time before they got Tullio, and he knew Tullio was finished. Right now he was probably burying his bat or sawing it in little pieces and burning it. "You just think about it some more, Joe. I'm sure you'll put it together. In the meantime, stay on the horn. I want everybody awake out there. That fat-ass can't have gone too far. I'm going up the hospital, see if there's anything I can do for Mrs. Abbatta."

Balzic didn't use his light or his siren to get to the hospital. Because he passed only three other cars, he didn't have to use them. But he wouldn't have used them anyway, not even if he had been in five o'clock traffic. He was feeling so stupid he didn't want anybody to know he was a cop. They'd all bust a gut, he thought. If they knew how much I didn't know, they'd all crawl into caves and get themselves some rocks . . . aw fuck this. What the hell am I thinking about? Christ, if you don't know the relations, you don't know anything. You got to know who relates to who, 'cause until you do, you're as dumb as the day you were born. You got to know who knows who, who has what, who wants what, who can do which for how much—you got to know that or you can sit around all day long picking fuzz out of your bellybutton. . . .

The Emergency Unit waiting room was improbably quiet when Balzic walked in. He had thought an ambulance would have had sufficient time to bring Nick Abbatta in, but he saw in a glance that there was only one person in the room. A middle-aged black man, thin as sticks, sat slumped in the corner of the couch nearest the fire doors leading into the treatment rooms. There was a large swelling above his left eye, his right eye was puffed nearly closed, and his lower lip was split so badly that it looked like beef liver. He was trying to smoke a cigarette, but the paper kept sticking to his lip and he was cursing under his breath about it.

Balzic walked directly to the admissions desk but found no one there. In an adjoining office to the rear he could hear someone talking on a phone. He started to go into the treatment rooms, but stopped when he felt the presence of someone close behind him. It was the black man.

"Ain't you the chief of police?"

"That's right. Something I can do for you?"

"I think maybe you better arrest me or somethin'."

"Oh yeah? Why should I do that?"

" 'Cause I just beat the motherfuck outta my woman."

Balzic sighed, wanting to say, not right now, don't bother me, some other time maybe, right now I got enough people getting worked over, but he didn't. He said, "Is she here? Is she trying to file a complaint against you?"

"Naw, she ain't here. She at her place," the black man said. "And I don't know if she goin' file no complaint. All I know is I come on over her place and she don't say two words, she jus' start into bangin' on me with a skillet. She like to tore my head off."

137

"And then you beat her up, right?"

"Not jus' then. I wait till she asleep. Then I beat the motherfuck outta her."

"Oh, Christ," Balzic said. "How do you know you didn't kill her?"

"Oh I ain't killed her. She was still runnin' her motor mouth when I walked out the house."

"So you think that means she's still alive, huh?"

"Well I ain't never heard no dead person talk, has you?"

"Why the hell did you have to pick tonight?" Balzic said. He was sorry immediately after he'd said it.

"Hey, man, all I'm doin' is tellin' you. You don't wanna do nothin' 'bout it, that's cool with me. That's jus' fine with me. I'll jus' go on back over there and sit down and wait some more till they gets ready to stitch up my lip."

"You know what? That's a good idea. If she files a complaint against you, then I'll be happy to arrest you, how's that?"

"That's fine with me," the black man said, turning away to take a seat again. He took a couple of steps and then turned back. "Say, man, you wouldn't happen to have no cigarette with a cork filter on it. This paper keep messin' over my lip."

"There's a cigarette machine around the corner down that hall," Balzic said, pointing to the hall behind the man's back, but he recognized from the man's expression that he had no money. Balzic rooted in his pockets and found enough change for the man to buy a pack. The man took the money with his eyes downcast.

"I'll pay you this back in the mornin'," he said.

"Forget it. Pay me back by not beating your wife anymore."

"Oh, she ain't my wife. I learned long time 'go, you don't marry no woman. You marry a woman, you wrong with the law right from the go. She can put you out, put you in jail, put you in a mental institution, take your money, take your clothes, your car—she can jus' get over you somethin' terrible. And there ain't a motherfuck you can do 'bout it." The man set off toward the cigarette machine, shaking his head, and saying repeatedly, "She ain't my wife. Ain't no woman my wife. My momma didn't raise no fool. . . ."

Balzic heard the commotion outside then but didn't even bother going to the door because he knew that the ambulance crew knew its business and that the best thing he could do was stand clear.

The attendants, hunched over and scurrying the stretcher along, bumped through the outer swinging doors and past Balzic and then through the fire doors, entering the treatment rooms.

One quick look at Nick Abbatta's face was enough for Balzic. If Abbatta was alive at all, it was only because the paramedics in the ambulance crew had found some dim signal of life and were hurrying more out of duty and hope than sense.

Balzic felt himself going queasy in the stomach and cold across the chest. Then he saw Mrs. Abbatta herding her daughter Rosalie through the outer doors. Rosalie was mumbling something inaudible over her shoulder to her mother, but Mrs. Abbatta paid no attention; instead she put both hands in the middle of Rosalie's back and shoved her forward. Rosalie stopped short at the sight of

Balzic, and her mother cried out, "Go on, move, you, you stupid!"

Balzic walked quickly toward them and held out his arms to embrace Mrs. Abbatta. She fell into his arms and sobbed against his chest. Rosalie scooted clumsily out of the way and dropped onto a couch, bumping her legs against it. She put all four fingers of her right hand into her mouth and began to whimper.

"Shut up, you," Mrs. Abbatta snapped at her. "This my fault, God forgive me, but you—you stupid!"

"Easy, Mrs. Abbatta," Balzic said. "Easy."

"Oh, no," she said. "I can no be easy with her this time. All her life I be easy with her. But no, not this time. This time she should be in there. Not Nicky. Not my Nicky."

Balzic had no doubt that if he hadn't been holding her around the shoulders, she would have attacked her daughter. Rosalie sucked backward against the couch, one foot on top of the other, and she tried to get all the fingers of both hands into her mouth. Tears streamed down her plump cheeks and mucous bubbled from her nostrils.

Balzic tried to steer Mrs. Abbatta toward a chair, but she resisted him. "I want be with Nicky," she cried. She repeated it over and over, and Balzic had all he could do to keep her from tearing loose and rushing into the treatment rooms to find her son.

"Please sit down, Mrs. Abbatta. Please."

"What goods to sit? I got to do something."

"Mrs. Abbatta, believe me, you'll only be in the way in there. These people know what they're doing. They'll take care of Nicky." It was a kind lie to tell, but a lie nonetheless, and from the way Mrs. Abbatta looked at him, he could see that she knew he was just telling one of those kind lies. She glared at him fiercely for it, but then she seemed to droop. She covered her face with her hands and let Balzic ease her into an overstuffed chair.

She began to speak in Italian, but talking so low and quickly that Balzic could not follow her accurately. She sounded as though she was saying something about her daughter, about what a burden God had given her in this life, about how she had been able to stand it until now, but that this was too much. This was the last weight she could—or would—carry. From now on she was no longer going to take the responsibility for her daughter. It was her fault, God knew, but it was Rosalie's just as much.

Balzic wasn't positive about the first part of what she'd said, but he felt sure he'd understood her when she'd said that she was not going to be responsible for her daughter anymore and that it was Rosalie's fault as much as hers.

"Mrs. Abbatta, you can't mean what you're saying."

"About what?" she demanded suddenly in English. Her eyes flashed toward her daughter, still sucking her fingers and whimpering on the couch. "About her? God-damn right I mean. As God my witness. If God forgive me for Nicky, then God forgive me for her too."

"Hey, what's goin' on? I was 'posed to be next." It was the black man back from the cigarette machine and looking outraged.

"You'll get your turn," Balzic said to him, at the same time putting his hand on Mrs. Abbatta's shoulder.

"Ain't this a bitch," the black man said. "This stuff always goin' on. Let a white man get in here and—"

"Sit down and shut up," Balzic said. "You don't have

141

half an idea what's going on. Just find yourself a seat."

"Don't tell me find no seat! I can stand if I want. You can put me in the back the line, but I can damn sure stand if I wants. Huh!"

"I don't care if you hang from the ceiling," Balzic said, moving toward the man. "Just turn it off."

The black man grunted, turned and looked at Rosalie, and said to her matter of factly, "See how they do, girl? Onliest way it ever been. Black men and ugly women always gets in last."

Balzic wanted to knock him down, but in glancing at Rosalie, he saw that what the man had said had had a curiously calming effect on her. She took her fingers out of her mouth and wiped them on her robe. She sniffed and looked up at the black man as though wanting him to say more and as though it didn't matter much what he said.

The black man walked over and stood in front of Rosalie. "You better blow your nose, girl. We both know you a mess, but ain't no use you makin' a bigger mess." He walked off suddenly, disappearing behind the admissions desk, his head bobbing as he looked for something, and then returned carrying a box of tissues. He held them out to Rosalie and said, "Here, girl, clean up your face. You lookin' sorry as a Salvation Army suit."

Rosalie did not hesitate. She took the box of tissues, said "Thank you very much," and wiped her face and blew her nose. When she finished, she giggled up at the black man, her lumpy torso shaking with relief and gratitude.

Balzic turned back to Mrs. Abbatta, whose lips were stretched like wire across her teeth. "She how she does?" she whispered hoarsely. "Anybody treats her li'l bit nice,

142

see how she does?" In Italian, she hissed the word for nigger. Then, still speaking Italian, she said, "Frankie was a nigger too."

Balzic went quickly to her side and sat on the arm of the chair. "What did you say?"

Again in Italian she said, "Frankie was the same. A nigger."

"Mrs. Abbatta, what're you talking about?"

"I'm the worst of everybody," she said, still speaking in Italian, but slowly and distinctly enough for Balzic to understand her clearly. "Nobody is worse than me. I made it come to this. If I had not agreed, it would never have come to this. So who am I to call names, to blame her or Frankie? Who am I to do this? I'm the real nigger in this."

Before Balzic could reply the ambulance crew came back out, and one of them motioned to Balzic that he wanted to talk to him. Balzic hurried to the man's side and listened with his head canted close to the man's mouth.

"I think somebody better get him a priest," the attendant whispered. "His heart's just fluttering."

Balzic cursed to himself as he went through his pockets looking for a dime. All he found were some pennies and one quarter. He went to the admissions desk, stepped behind it, and hit buttons on the phone there until he got a dial tone. Then he dialed St. Malachy's rectory.

Father Marrazo answered on the second ring, sounding as though he had been using wine to get to sleep and had succeeded only in getting a little drunk.

"This is Mario, Father. I'm at the hospital. They just brought in Nick Abbatta, and he needs you fast."

"Give me five minutes," the priest said. "Uh, Mario —never mind. I'll talk to you when I get there."

Balzic hung up, then ducked inside the treatment room doors and asked one of the nurses if the paramedic with the ambulance crew had been exaggerating. He got a somber, negative shrug in reply. He didn't know why he'd bothered to ask; he'd sensed as much when he'd seen Abbatta's face earlier.

He turned away slowly and walked as slowly back toward the doors leading to the waiting room, wanting to kick holes in the walls as he went. He came suddenly alert when he heard the scuffling in the waiting room.

He rushed out to find the black man hanging onto Mrs. Abbatta's left arm and trying to pull her away from her daughter. Mrs. Abbatta, old and portly though she was, kept leaning away from him, staying close enough to slap with her right hand at Rosalie's face but not getting close enough to connect. Rosalie had drawn herself into a corner of the couch and was shrieking wildly, begging her mother to stop.

Balzic darted around the black man and bear-hugged Mrs. Abbatta from behind, pinning her arms to her sides.

"For God's sake, Mrs. Abbatta, leave her alone. She's not responsible for this. Come on, leave her alone. Calm down."

"You think so, huh?" Mrs. Abbatta twisted herself, not to get free from Balzic but to look into his eyes. "Who you think tell Frankie? Her, that's who! This stupid!"

She sagged backward against Balzic and began to rock with sobs. "My God, my God . . . what did I do? . . ."

Balzic eased her across the width of the waiting room and gently pushed her down onto another couch. "Why don't you lay down for a while, Mrs. Abbatta? Really, try to lay down a little while."

She shook her head violently, then closed her eyes and pressed the heels of her palms against them. She began to speak very quietly between sobs. It took Balzic some moments to understand her Italian.

". . . I promise thee, O blessed Jude, to be ever mindful of this great favor, and I will never cease to honor thee as my special and powerful patron and to do all in my power to encourage devotion to thee. Amen. . . ." Then she began to say Hail Mary, finishing in a whisper.

Balzic had been squatting in front of her, holding her shoulders, but he had to straighten up to shake the cramps out of his thighs.

Mrs. Abbatta began to pray again, this time in a voice almost less than a whisper, her hands still pressed tightly against her eyes. She finished just as Father Marrazo hurried into the waiting room, but she didn't look up to see who had come in.

The priest merely nodded at Balzic on his way through the lobby. In five minutes he was back out, shaking his head. His eyes were as near desperation as Balzic could ever recall seeing them.

Mrs. Abbatta took her hands away from her eyes, and instantly upon seeing the priest, she began to wail.

"Do you hear his confession?" she shrieked.

The priest nodded, but when Mrs. Abbatta cast her eyes downward in momentary relief, he shook his head no to Balzic.

"What can we do for her?" the priest asked after Mrs.

Abbatta had cried and shouted for her son until she seemed unable to take another breath without collapsing.

"We can take them to my house," Balzic said. "My mother's really good at this." Balzic glanced over at Rosalie, who was still cringing on the couch. The black man was standing beside her, patting her on the head as he would have petted a puppy.

"The thing is," Balzic went on, taking the priest a few steps away, "she's really got the heat for her daughter. I can't take them alone, and neither can you, so she's going to have to sit up front with me and Rosalie can sit in the back with you; otherwise we're going to have one bitch of a time. We got to keep them apart until my mother can talk some sense into her—if that's possible."

"Well, let's do it," Father Marrazo said.

"Yeah, but I got to do something first." Balzic walked over to the black man and took his arm. The man cursed and tried to pull away, but Balzic wouldn't let go.

They went into the treatment rooms, where Balzic stopped the first nurse they came upon. "Will you see to it that this man is treated? He's been waiting a long time, and he's been damn good about it. And if he doesn't have any insurance, send the bill to the Rocksburg Police Department, you understand?"

Puzzled, the nurse nodded after a moment, then pointed to a room one door away and walked toward it, motioning for the black man to follow her. The black man scratched his head and then shook it, looking as though he couldn't think of anything to say and knowing that he would later regret that he hadn't been able to think of anything.

Balzic left him without another word, going back out

to the lobby quickly. It took some persuading, both by him and by the priest, to convince Mrs. Abbatta that the best place for her to be now was with one of her best friends. She kept saying she wanted to be with Nicky, and then she tried to insist that she ought to be home. Together, Balzic and the priest got them into the cruiser, and Balzic drove to his house as fast as he thought he could without alarming either mother or daughter.

He didn't have to wake his mother; she had been sitting in the kitchen since she'd phoned him earlier. And when Balzic led them all into the kitchen she seemed instantly to sense what was wrong. She began immediately to soothe Mrs. Abbatta, asking nothing of anyone but reading all their faces.

Balzic relaxed then, knowing there was no one more capable of talking some sense into Mrs. Abbatta about Rosalie as soon as Mrs. Abbatta emptied herself of her next rush of grief. He also knew that before he closed the front door Ruth and the girls would be out to help. He and the priest got as far as the dining room when Ruth appeared.

"Mario, what the hell is going on?"

"In the kitchen. Mrs. Abbatta and Rosalie. Nick's dead."

"Oh my God, how?"

"I'll tell you later. Go help Ma, will you? I got to go."

"Oh for Christ's sake," she said and hurried into the kitchen without another word to her husband.

Balzic was checking the lock on his front door to make sure it would lock behind him when he heard his call signal crackling over the cruiser radio. He ducked around Father Marrazo and bounced down the steps two at a time.

"Balzic here. What's up, Joe?"

"Tullio's in his house, Mario," Desk Sergeant Joe Royer said.

"He's in his house? How the hell'd he get past those people up there? Never mind. I don't want to know. Is anybody talking to him?"

"Stramsky."

"Well tell him to tell everybody to sit on it. I'm on my way."

Balzic dropped the speaker on the seat, turned the ignition, and put the cruiser in gear. He looked out his window and saw the priest still standing on the steps. "What're you going to do, Anthony? Where you going? Your car's up the hospital. You can't do anything here. Come on, get in."

The priest shook his head thoughtfully, then trotted down the steps and around the front of the cruiser and got in. He had barely closed the door when Balzic stomped on the accelerator, throwing him against the dashboard.

"Easy, Mario, easy. I don't think he's going anywhere."

"Probably not. But I'm not hurrying because he might try to take off. I want to get there before one of my people decides to play the Lone Ranger."

Balzic made it to Norwood Hill, a distance of four miles, in less than three minutes. Father Marrazo was crossing himself when they got out.

148

All four of Balzic's mobile units were there with their spotlights trained on Manditti's house, as were one mobile from the state police and one from the county detectives, all of whom trailed after him as Balzic approached.

"What's the story, Vic?"

"Well, we got two in the back and two on each side, and the rest of us girls are where you see us."

"How long's he been in there?"

"The state guy signaled Fischetti about twenty minutes ago and he called me. After that it's all confusion. There's something wrong with the fuckin' radios again. Sometimes we can send and we can't receive, and then sometimes it's the other way around. My car radio's all fucked up too. Mario, you got to get some money from Council. We can't keep operating like this. Christ, somebody's—"

Balzic held up his hands. "I know all about the radios, Vic, but first things first, okay? Now, how'd he get in there?"

"He didn't drive in, that's for sure. He must've walked up over the back of the hill. It's a wonder he didn't have a heart attack."

"Who's been talking to him?"

"Just me. I don't know what the state horse said. I don't think anything."

"He said anything back?"

"Just once. He said for us to leave him alone before he got mad."

"Before he got mad, huh?"

Stramsky shrugged. "That's what he said, Mario."

"Okay, give me the horn."

Stramsky handed over the amplified bullhorn, and Balzic walked with it to the end of Manditti's front walk.

"Tullio? You hear me?"

No answer.

"Tullio, it's late, everybody's tired, we got half the hill up already, and the more noise I make on this thing, the more people we're going to wake up. There's lots of old people and babies up here need their sleep, so don't put any frost on my tomatoes, huh? Just get your butt out here. Now!" He turned to Stramsky and handed him the keys to his cruiser. "Go get the gas out of my trunk. I'm not gonna fuck around with this clown, not even for one minute."

A window squeaked open to the left of the front door.

"What're you, kiddin' me, Balzic?" came Tullio's voice from behind the window. "Whatta you want? What're you doing, screaming about old people and babies? What're you doing out there making all that racket and with them lights? You don't hear me making no noise. I ain't the one waking people up. So why don't you take them boy scouts and the rest of them fruitcakes and go on home? Cheesus."

"Tullio, for sure you're putting a frost on my tomatoes. I'm gonna tell you once more. If you're not out here in five seconds, you're gonna think you're in a gas factory."

Tullio let out a long groan and slammed the window shut. In four seconds he was standing in the doorway, shielding his eyes from the lights with his forearms.

"Turn them lights off, for crissake. What is this, Balzic? What're you doing this to me for? What'd I ever do to you, huh?"

"Just shut up and turn around and put your hands against the side of the house."

"Put my hands on the house, Cheesus. Turn them

150

lights out so I can see what I'm doing."

"Go 'cuff him, Vic," Balzic said, "before I go up there and break his head."

Stramsky and the state trooper darted forward and handcuffed and searched Tullio after they'd made him lean his forehead against the side of the house.

"Hurry up, willya?" Tullio kept shouting. "This hurts my head. I got a little weight here to hold up, you know."

"He's clean," Stramsky called back to Balzic, who was leaning against the fender of one of the cruisers. Father Marrazo stood next to him and started to pat his pockets, looking for cigarettes.

"There's some in my glove compartment, Father." Balzic faced the porch again. "Tell him his rights, Vic, and say 'em loud enough for the man from the state to hear."

Father Marrazo got the cigarettes from Balzic's car and began opening the pack in the spotlight from the cruiser Balzic was leaning against. Just then, Stramsky and the state trooper, each holding Tullio by an arm, led him down the walk and stopped in front of Balzic.

Tullio had come peacefully, if not quietly—he had never stopped complaining about the lights—but he took one look at Father Marrazo and went wild, screaming, cursing, kicking, lifting both Stramsky and the state trooper off the ground as he jerked his massive shoulders from side to side, all in a frenzied effort to get at the priest.

"You fuckin' priests! What're you doin' here? You fuckin' goddamn thieves! You're the biggest thieves! You got all them collection boxes, you ain't happy . . . you got to fix things, you motherfuckers!"

"Tap him!" Balzic called out to one of his own patrolmen who had just come from around the side of the house.

The patrolman drew his baton, scurried around the front of the frantic group, and when he'd taken aim, tapped Tullio on the forehead just hard enough to stun him and make him stop thrashing.

"Move again, Tullio," Balzic said, "and I'm going to take that baton and split your goddamn head open, you hear me?"

"I hear you, I hear you, Cheesus. What're you guys getting so rough for? I wasn't doing nothing."

"I'd hate to see you when you're doing something," Stramsky said, breathing heavily.

"I'm just looking out for my rights, that's all. That's all I'm doin' . . . us citizens got some rights, ain't that right, Balzic? . . . What's the priest doing here? Somebody getting married or something?" Tullio rattled on and on, but his jokes were only words.

There was no doubt now in Balzic's mind about who Tullio had really wanted to work over with his bat. Until this moment, until he had heard and seen Tullio's reaction to Father Marrazo's presence, Balzic had not been certain, but now he was absolutely sure. All he had to do was watch Tullio's eyes while he kept trying to make jokes. Tullio's gaze worked the priest over from head to foot and back up again.

It must have been a real struggle for him, Balzic thought, though it was hard to imagine Tullio ever struggling over a matter of conscience. Still, the situation had been the kind that would force even a Tullio into a struggle. Maybe for the first time in his life Tullio had had a real war in himself about who to get after he'd gotten

Frank Dulia, and Balzic wondered how much had been added to that struggle by the thought of all those women . . . ah, it's all a lot of wasted wondering, Balzic concluded. I could ask him about it from now until I retire and he wouldn't tell me a thing.

"I want to see a lawyer, Balzic," Tullio said, his gaze still fixed on the priest.

"You'll get to see lots of them."

"You know what I mean," Tullio grumbled. "My own."

"Don't worry about it, Tullio. I'm sure Muscotti'll make sure you get the best lawyer he can get for you."

"Oh yeah," Tullio said disgustedly. "Write me a letter."

Balzic turned away and started for his own cruiser. "Book him, Vic. And no mistakes. I don't want to lose this clown over some bad bookkeeping."

Stramsky nodded, and he and the state trooper led Tullio off to the state mobile unit.

"Somebody put some locks on the house," Balzic called out to no one in particular. "I don't want to give these good people up here a chance to go bad on me . . . okay, let's go home. Let's everybody go home and think about what we're going to do with all that overtime, all that time and again. . . ."

In the cruiser, driving back to the hospital so Father Marrazo could get his car, Balzic said, "Okay, Father, are you going to tell me, or am I going to tell you?"

"Mario, if we both know, then what's the point? Any explaining either one of us has to do has to be to somebody else anyway."

"I don't know, Father. Maybe we ought to just clear the air with each other, you know?"

The priest shook his head slowly. "This is a real mess, Mario. No matter how much we talk about it, we still won't be able to change that."

"I know it's a mess. But what I can't get through my head is why Sabatine would go for something like this. I mean, sweet Jesus, rigging the Treasury balance—wow. I mean, I remember what you told me before about him. I didn't even know what you were talking about. I mean, I'm not sure I'd understand you now if you told me the same things all over again, but hell, Father, he had to be smarter than this."

"What can I tell you?" the priest said disconsolately. "He did. For all I know it might have been his idea. I don't really know whose idea it was. Something tells me it was Mrs. Tuzzi's. But that's just a feeling. I can't get her to say anything about it, nothing at all. But no matter who approached who in the beginning, Sabatine could have stopped it any time he wanted, and he wouldn't have had to say a word."

"Well why the hell didn't he?" Balzic said, slapping the steering wheel repeatedly.

"You got a cigarette?"

"I thought you got the ones out of the glove compartment. Never mind. Here, take these," Balzic said, handing over a nearly crushed pack he had jammed behind the sun visor.

"There's only one left, Mario. I don't want to take your last one."

"I can get more in the hospital."

"So you want to give me this one?"

"What is this, Anthony? You got the ones from the glove compartment. What'd you do, lose 'em?" Balzic shot a quick glance at the priest. "Oh. Don't tell me. I can feel a homily coming on." Balzic waited, but the priest seemed content to smoke and stare out the window.

"Okay, Anthony, you got me hooked. What's the message?"

"It wasn't any big deal," the priest said. "You had something I seemed to need. We're friends. You gave it to me."

"You trying to tell me that's why Sabatine went for this?" Balzic screwed up his face and sighed. "Come on, Anthony. I don't know, but when I saw you a couple nights ago, before I knew any of this was connected, before I even had the first idea—damn, man, you made it sound a lot more complicated than that. A lot more complicated."

"It is a lot more complicated. But maybe when you cut all the details, maybe it was as simple as one person having something another person needed. You know, of all those women, only two of them had any kind of half-decent income? . . . You know where Mrs. Cafasso's son is? Domenico's widow—you know they only had one son —you know he's in the alcoholic ward in the Vets Hospital in Pittsburgh?"

"No, I didn't know that."

"He is. You know why? Because he was with Graves Registration at Normandy. He—"

"I know what they do, Anthony. They pick up the pieces and try to pair up the dog tags."

"That's not what I was going to say. I know you know

155

what Graves Registration means. What I was going to say was that he hasn't been sober two days in a row since he was discharged. He got something like ninety percent disability, but he spent the whole check every month on booze. She never got a dime from him. And Domenico died of black lung before anybody thought of giving pensions for that . . . God, Mario, she was eating dog food. Imagine it! Dog food!

"And Mrs. Ruffola's story isn't much different," Father Marrazo continued. "Her husband went the same way, same disease. Their only son was killed at Salerno, about three miles from where both of them were born, her and Amadie. You know that Amadie refused to accept the insurance check from the government? He threw the guy who tried to deliver it, threw him bodily off his porch."

"Yeah," Balzic said. "My mother told me about that."

"Did she tell you that he never went out of the house after that? Never worked another day? And that he died less than a year later? Did she tell you that?"

"No, she didn't. But I heard it around."

"Well, do you know what Mrs. Ruffola's social security check was worth? Seventy-two dollars a month. A month, Mario! Imagine trying to live on that."

"Yeah, but—but, goddamn, Anthony, there had to be a better way."

"Sure. The Pope should auction off the Sistine Chapel. He could feed a lot of people with what he got for that."

"Aw come on, Anthony. I didn't say anything to deserve that."

"It wasn't what you said. It was your tone . . . okay, so maybe I shouldn't have made that crack. I apologize.

156

I was out of line. But for a second there, you started to sound a little Presbyterian on me."

Balzic wheeled the cruiser over to the curb and jammed on the brakes. He twisted around to face the priest.

"What the hell is this, Anthony? We going to go through a whole thing about who's supposed to take care of the poor people, the old ladies with all their sad stories? Jesus Christ, there's a thousand stories like that around here, probably more. Anywhere there's a mine or a mill, anywhere there's widows old enough with husbands who never got in on those pension plans or got screwed out of them by some goddamn bookkeeper or lawyer—what do you got? But, goddamn it, you said there were only two women with any kind of half-decent income. Who was the other one? Sabatine's housekeeper, Mrs. Tuzzi? Well what's she going to do now? Who do you think's going to hire her again? After this gets out, who's going to give her a job? The bishop maybe?

"And what's the other one going to do, the one we took to my house a little while ago, what's she gonna do? In a couple days you're going to say the words over her income. I'm sure Abbatta had a damn good insurance policy. That printers' union took care of its own for a long time now. But tell me something, Anthony. You think she's really going to have the heart to spend any of that insurance? After what she set up with him? After tonight?"

"Mario, please don't shout, will you?" The priest opened the window and flipped out his cigarette butt. "I was just trying to suggest some of the motivation, that's all. I don't like it any better than you do. Sabatine was

157

as far out of line as any priest can get. All I'm saying is that if you give him the benefit of some doubt, you have to recognize that he saw a chance to help some people, some old women, who really needed help, and—"

"He also saw a pretty good chance to pay off the mortgage on his church, don't forget that."

"Mario, I'm not forgetting anything," the priest said sharply. "But that man was running out of time, and who knows what was going through his head? All I'm sure about is that never, never did he think anything like this was going to happen."

"Anthony, what're you telling me, huh? For everything there's a price. You pay in money or time or sweat or blood, but you pay, and—"

"I know that, Mario," the priest said, holding up his hands as though to ward off the words.

"Let me finish," Balzic said. "When you get into a fix, when you start trying to make funny things happen, you open the door for somebody else to get in there. And, goddamn it, you know that as well as I do. The pros know it. But they know it before they start. Before they do anything, they add up the taxes they're going to pay, and they're almost a hundred percent sure who they're going to pay them to.

"But what's this amateur doing? Where'd he come from? Why the hell didn't he run a bingo game and give all those ladies a percentage? What—he was too good for bingo? He never had a game in his church as long as I can remember. If he did my mother would've been there, and so would a couple hundred other women. Bingo he can't handle. But he goes for a fix like this? With his eyes open and he doesn't even think to look? You knew who blew it for him? That poor slob Rosalie. She's the one who told Frank Dulia. She figured it. And she isn't supposed to have the brains of a cow!"

"Mario, you're shouting again."

"Anthony, two guys are—aw, fuck it. I'm sorry. I'm sorry for everybody."

"You're sorry," the priest said, laughing feebly. It was a bitter and rueful sound. "What do I tell the bishop? Never mind the bishop. What do I tell Sabatine? He doesn't know anything about this yet."

"I don't know," Balzic said, pinching the bridge of his nose as he drove away from the curb. "But maybe we ought to stop talking for a while. We're both getting a little salty."

"I'll agree with that," the priest said. "But just tell me one more thing and then I'll drop it. How did you know what Sabatine was doing?"

"Huh? Until Tullio started screaming at you, I didn't know. But that's when it all went together. My mother was the one who told me about those women winning seven hundred apiece. And something kept bugging me about that, about the amount, but I didn't even know how to think about what was bugging me until I remembered what you told me about Sabatine's mortgage payments. And even then I didn't figure it went together. But then my mother told me, tonight as a matter of fact, that Frank Dulia was Mrs. Abbatta's nephew. 'Cause at that time, right before she told me that, I was still trying to understand what Dulia said to Tullio."

"What was that?"

"He said that whatever he bet on wasn't supposed to lose. That's when I started thinking fix. But it was all a mess in my head until just a little while ago. Then when Tullio starts on you, I thought, hey, what do we got here?

159

We got a priest, five old ladies, a linotype operator at the only newspaper in town, the paper that puts out the Treasury statement every day, and one thousand tickets at two bucks a pop. So what's the payoff on those tickets —fifteen hundred? Fourteen hundred if whoever is hustling them is greedy. You know the attraction better than I do. They pay seven hundred to one, maybe seven-fifty, which is a hell of a lot better than the five-forty a number pays.

"So if the ladies get seven hundred apiece, that leaves thirteen bills. Subtract ten bucks for printing, and that leaves twelve-ninety, which is what you said Sabatine's mortgage payments went up.

"It would've been a sweet thing," Balzic went on. "It was, until Rosalie told Dulia. And how smart could he have been? He bets with Manny. On a Treasury number! Nobody, but nobody in the world would've taken that bet except Manny. I don't know a bookmaker who would've touched it. They just don't fuck around with those things."

Balzic stretched and yawned at a stop light. "Well, I got Tullio. That's the only part of it I want. The rest is all yours. And believe me, Anthony, I don't envy you."

"Uh, Mario," the priest said hesitantly, "do I understand you? Are you saying you're not going to do anything about Sabatine?"

Balzic looked at the priest. "Anthony, you really surprise me. What do you want, huh? What am I supposed to do, huh? I mean, I know what I'd like to do. I'd like to go kick Sabatine in the ass even if he does have the big casino. But you didn't really think I was going to bust him? The women too? Ho, man, for what? Fraud? Who made the complaint? Uh-uh, Anthony, they're all yours. And if I'm you, I'd just hand it over to the bishop. I'd just dump it on his desk; let him figure it out. That's all you're supposed to do, right? Isn't that all he wants from you? A report?"

"Yeah. A report," the priest said. "It'll be the hardest thing I ever did."

Balzic drove away from the intersection slowly and pulled into the hospital parking lot. "Well, Father, you got two masses to say in the next couple days. I don't think either one of them's going to be what I'd call easy."

"No, they won't. But Sabatine's still alive." The priest got out and started for his car, but stopped after a few steps and came back.

"What's the matter?" Balzic said.

"Your cigarettes. Here." The priest handed them in.

"You want a couple to hold you?"

"Just one. I'll stop someplace and get some. Muscotti's will still be open. I could use a little wine. Maybe even a little competition with the cards."

"Yeah. Well. Maybe I'll stop down myself."

Balzic didn't stop at Muscotti's. He didn't go home either. He didn't want to discuss Father Sabatine with Father Marrazo anymore, and he knew that if he went to Muscotti's they would inevitably begin to fret and fume over the whole sorry business again. And if he went home he would have Mrs. Abbatta and Rosalie to contend with, and he didn't want any part of that either. He didn't even want to know whether his mother and Ruth were handling that well or whether they had had to be reinforced by his daughters.

He drove aimlessly around town for more than an hour, then finally turned the cruiser in the direction of his station, knowing that he was copping out on his family, but he didn't care because he made himself not want to care. He had had enough. All he wanted now was a cot in one of his lockups and a little bourbon out of the pint he kept in his desk for just such times as these, times, as he usually thought of them, when he wanted to become a bug.

Inside the duty room he asked Royer if the booking and arraignment of Tullio Manditti had gone smoothly and correctly.

"Here's copies if you want to read them," Royer replied.

"Did you read them?"

Royer nodded.

"Any mistakes?"

"I couldn't see any."

"Is he down at Southern Regional?"

"Yeah, county guys took him."

"What was the bond?"

"Hundred thousand."

"Well, then he stays until the trial. Nobody he knows is gonna put up ten percent of that. Good. That settles it. We got the bum, we got the motive, we got the witness, and we got the bond."

"We got a witness? Who? I didn't know we had a witness."

"I didn't tell you that? Sure. Hell yes. A guy named Harsha. Lives right next door to Dulia. Saw the whole thing from less than twenty-five, thirty feet, unobstructed. What could be better than that?"

Balzic scratched his chest, pulled his underwear loose from his crotch, and went back to his office, returning in moments with the pint of bourbon. He went toward the door leading to the stairs down to the lockups. "There's nobody down there, right?"

"Not yet," Royer said.

"Well, I'm going to sleep down there. So don't let anybody bring anybody in. Tell 'em to give 'em a lecture and send 'em home. And if anybody calls, unless it's a nuclear attack, I ain't here."

"Okay, Mario. I don't know how you can sleep on those things."

"Hey, Joe, you're not insinuating that we don't provide adequate facilities for our, uh, wayward citizens, are you?"

"Who? Me?"

"Listen, if it's good enough for the rabble, it's good enough for the rousters . . . you know, sometimes I think it ought to be part of the training for the rousters to spend a couple nights in the slammer, and, oh, would it ever be good for the DAs and the judges, and man, oh, man, wouldn't it be terrific for all them fuckin' politicians? Huh? Think of it, Joe. As a requirement for public office, the first thing you had to do after you got elected was spend a weekend in the slam. Man, oh, man, wouldn't those fuckers think a little bit about some of the laws they write? Huh? Wouldn't they now? . . ."

"I don't know if I'd go that far," Royer said.

"Yeah? Well, once I read about a Jap. He built himself a coffin, and every once in a while he used to sleep in it, you know, just to get used to the notion. I think that's a hell of an idea. And that's why I sleep downstairs sometimes. You know, to get used to the notion."

"Well, it's your back," Royer said. "Sleep easy." He turned back to his desk and picked up the newspaper. "I didn't know we had a witness," he said, speaking more to himself than to Balzic.

"Well we do," Balzic said, starting down the steps. "And it's a damn good thing, 'cause if we didn't—well, I don't even want to think about that."

Balzic slept well indeed. And he hadn't needed more than two swallows of bourbon to get him started. When he woke, he accidentally kicked over the paper cup out of which he'd been drinking, and he saw with some surprise how little he had drunk.

He went to the end of the corridor to the shower room, undressed, relieved himself, and showered and shaved. He almost didn't mind putting on the same clothes, he felt so rested and refreshed. When he came up the stairs and walked into the duty room, he was humming.

"Mornin', Angelo," he said to Desk Sergeant Angelo Clemente. "What're you looking so sour about? Christ, man, look outside. It looks like spring for sure. Look at it."

"Yeah," Clemente said. "It might look good to you and me, but it ain't going to look too good to some people."

"Why? What happened? Something happen?"

"Four guys in a wildcat mine out in Westfield Town-

164

ship. Two guys got out, but two of them didn't."

"When'd this happen?"

"Well, the story I get from Eddie Sitko is they were just going to work. They just started in the shaft when the roof let go. They weren't fifty, sixty feet in."

Balzic shook his head and looked at his shoes for a long time, struggling not to remember what had happened to his own father. He could have walked on the ceiling more easily. "Well, that happens, Angelo," he said finally. "That happens a lot with those small outfits. Sometimes they just try to cut the costs too much. They from here?"

"Nah. Both fatals were from Westfield Township. All four of them were. I never heard the names though. Couple of good hunkies. One of them had a wife and five kids. Smolensky. George John, forty-six. The other one didn't have no family. And it might've been time for him. He was sixty-four. Harsha."

Balzic had started to walk back to his office, shaking his head in that immediate gut commiseration he felt for anyone who died as his father had. He stopped as though stung when he heard the name Clemente had said.

"What was that other one's name?"

Clemente read it off the log to make sure. "Uh, Harsha. Andrew Theodore."

"You sure?"

"Well, that's the name I got from Eddie Sitko."

"Andrew Theodore Harsha, sixty-four, from Westfield Township?"

"Yeah. I'm telling you. What's the matter?"

Balzic let out a long groan and then kicked a metal desk and then kicked it twice more until he had put three dents in it. "Jesus fuck!" he roared.

165

"What's the matter? Hey, Mario, Mario, what's the matter?"

"He was our witness! I'm sorry he died. I'm sorry anybody dies that way, but Jesus fucking Christ, he was our witness!"

"What witness? What're you talking about? How come nobody tells me nothing?"

"He lived next door to Dulia. He saw Tullio kill him. You know what kind of case we got against Tullio without a witness? Without Muscotti, understand, without Muscotti's help—'cause Muscotti ain't about to help him —Tullio got cousins scattered all over western Pennsylvania, and those cousins got friends. He can come up with twenty guys who'll say he was playing cards with them or whatever they have to say for him. For crissake, I'm the only person who heard Harsha's story. He was supposed to come in today at four o'clock to make a statement, that's how sure I was—sure, my ass. That's how sloppy I was. Jesus Christ," Balzic said, holding his head, "no worse testimony in the world than second-hand testimony from a cop who got it from a guy who's dead. Agghhh, bullshit! . . ."

Balzic sat sulking at the end of the bar by the kitchen in Muscotti's. He had been drinking for nearly two hours, starting with a double whiskey and then changing to wine, chasing both with large glasses of ice water. He kept telling himself not to get drunk, at the same time telling himself there wasn't anything he'd rather do.

Muscotti's was quiet. It was midafternoon. The lunch

crowd had long gone, but it was still a couple of hours before the afterwork crowd would come in. Solitary customers, the retirees, the lonely, the lushes, had drifted in and out. Now there was no one except for Balzic and Vinnie.

"Mario, you better take it easy," Vinnie said, as he poured still another double wine and refilled the other, taller glass with ice and water. "It don't look good, you know what I mean?"

"What're you worrying about, huh?"

"Hey, you know, take it easy. This ain't like you. You don't look good."

"Which is it now: *it* don't look good, or *I* don't look good?"

"Ah, you know what I mean."

"Well, what are you worried about? How I look to the public? Or how I'm gonna look to the rest of your customers? They're all fuckin' squares anyway, so what's the worry?"

Vinnie sighed and shrugged. "Well, you know."

"Yeah, sure. Well, up the squares, how's that?"

"Look, why don't you stay with the ice water for a while?" Vinnie said. "Dom'll be in in a couple minutes. You can talk it over with him. Maybe he can come up with something. But don't make a mess of yourself. That's not right."

Balzic sipped the wine, then looked at Vinnie and drank it down in four swallows. He knocked over the glass setting it on the bar. "Vinnie, we been friends too long for you to start making like a teacher with me, huh?"

Vinnie threw out his hands and let them fall against his legs. "Okay, Mario. I don't say nothing. No more."

"Then put some more in there."

167

"You got it, buddy. You can drink 'em all day, I can damn sure pour 'em all day."

Balzic stifled a yawn and rubbed his palms together. He spun around slowly on the stool and looked at the opposite wall, then spun back and read the community college basketball schedule for the fifth or sixth time. He took a sip of the chablis Vinnie brought him and then a sip of the ice water. A motorcycle roared by on State Street, its engine noise piercing, causing Balzic to close his eyes and cover his ears.

He felt someone tap him on the shoulder. When he opened his eyes and took his hands away from his ears, he saw Dom Muscotti and heard him saying something about ". . . arresting those friggin' nuts."

"What nuts?"

"Those motorcycle nuts. They make me crazy with all that noise. There got to be something stupid about people who like noise. Ain't there an ordinance about how much noise you can make?"

"Sure," Balzic said. "Three of them."

"Well why don't you tell your guys to enforce them?" Dom screwed up his face and walked around behind the bar. "You know what noise does to you, Mario? I been reading about it. It can send your blood pressure up twenty, thirty points, a real sudden noise, d'you know that?"

Balzic scratched his scalp, rubbed his lips, and took another sip of wine.

"Did you know that, Mario?"

"Yeah I know that. But do you know what I'd have to do to enforce any ordinance about noise? I'd have to have ten more cars and twenty more people. For crissake, I'm supposed to have two lieutenants, one for juve-

168

niles and one for administration, and I been waiting three years for Council to approve the money for them. Do I have to say any more?"

"Okay, Mario, okay. Take it easy. I was just making conversation anyway." Muscotti turned away and went through the letters and bills Vinnie had handed him. He said nothing, put the envelopes and bills in a nook beside the coffee machine, then coughed and leaned under the bar to spit in an empty beer case.

"What're you drinking for now?" Muscotti said when he straightened up. "You know, you look a little drunk."

"Your bartender been giving it to me for twenty minutes, now you're going to start. Maybe you ought to start selling candy."

"Hey, I'm sorry I asked. Just pretend I didn't say nothing, okay?"

"No, I won't," Balzic said. "You want to know what I'm drinking for, I'm going to tell you. You're just the guy who ought to hear it anyway. It was one of your *paisans*—no, not one. Three of them. First it was Manny. Then Tullio. Then Brownie for letting Tullio get away from him. And those three assholes got me in a real bind."

"Let's go in the back, huh, Mario? If you're going to drink wine, you might as well drink good stuff."

"Okay. Fine. That's fine with me. 'Cause I got plenty to say."

"Okay, okay, take it easy. Come on back and say it."

Balzic left his wine and water on the bar and followed Muscotti to the room where they'd talked before when he'd made his senseless threat to shut down Muscotti's operation. He let Muscotti go in first and then dropped woozily on a chair, running his fingers through his hair

169

and then rubbing the back of his neck.

"Hey, Dom," he said, "no more wine for me. I had more than enough about an hour ago."

"Whatever you say," Muscotti said, sitting opposite Balzic. "So, uh, what's the problem?"

"I told you, I'm in a real bind. The worst one I ever been in."

"So tell me."

"I had a witness. He saw Tullio put the job on Dulia, watched—"

"You 'had' a witness?"

Balzic nodded and rubbed his temples. "He got killed this morning. A fuckin' mine roof caved in on him. But without him, the only case I got against Tullio is circumstantial. It's a hell of a case. Any third-rate assistant DA could nail Tullio easy."

"So what're you worrying about?"

"In order to do it that way, I got to open up a real can of worms. I'd have to bust six people, including a priest and five old ladies, for operating a lottery, for fraud, for conspiracy, that whole number. Then I'd have to get the DA, Weigh, to go along with immunity for them so they could testify about the circumstances. And, uh, in any other case, that's no big deal. But this time it might not be so easy. I don't have to tell you Weigh ain't Catholic, and he just might get a hair up his ass because this is all Catholic and it all smells.

"But forget that," Balzic went on. "I mean, even if Weigh played it straight, even if he went along with the immunity, once these people testify, they're finished. The papers, the television, the radio—they'd eat 'em alive. No matter that nobody prosecutes them, they testify and they may as well crawl in their coffins."

170

"Wait a minute," Muscotti said. "You lost me. What priest? What old ladies?"

"Sabatine—"

"What?" Muscotti's eyes went wide and his head jerked forward. You mean the Sabatine from out St. Jude's? The one who tried to get Weisberg in Westfield Golf Club?"

"Yeah, yeah—"

"Why, Christ, I heard he got the big casino."

"Yeah, yeah, that's him. But wait'll you hear who the ladies are. You're gonna shit. Listen to this lineup: Mrs. Motti, Mrs. Ruffola, Mrs. Cafasso, Mrs. Tuzzi, and Mrs. Abbatta. You know what they did?"

"Hey, Mario," Muscotti said, standing suddenly and folding his arms and taking a step backward. "I'm not so sure I want to know. And I don't know if you ought to be telling me."

"Yeah? Well, sit down, 'cause you're going to hear it. 'Cause your fat gofer jumped right in the middle of it. And his brother finished it last night. He killed Nick Abbatta last night—"

"What?" Muscotti had to support himself on the back of the chair he'd been sitting on.

"You heard me. So sit down and—"

"Holy shit," Muscotti said. "And this was because of what the priest done?"

"That's right. They started it, and Dulia heard about it—"

"Yeah. But, Mario, you're still talking, you're still gonna tell me about a priest, and when you start talking about a priest, there's some things you just ain't supposed to say, I don't care what he done."

"My ass. Sit down and listen. Because this priest is

171

going to get a lot more grief if I don't come up with something, you understand?"

Muscotti scowled and chewed his lower lip and paced around the tiny room for nearly a minute. At last he sat and nodded. "All right. I'm listening."

"Okay, so here it is. Now I don't know whose idea it was in the beginning. I don't care. It doesn't matter anyway. But Sabatine went for a lottery. You know the kind, off the Treasury balance at two bucks a throw on a thousand tickets. Then somebody convinces Nick Abbatta to rig the numbers to match up with one of the ones those old ladies had. The women got seven bills apiece when it was their turn to win—or maybe they split it every month, I don't know—but the rest of it went on St. Jude's mortgage. Anyway, Abbatta's sister, the retarded one? Rosalie?"

Dom nodded vigorously. "I know her."

"Well, somehow she put it together. With her brains, I can't see how, but she did. What I figure is everybody was doing a lot of talking about it in front of her, figuring, you know, what does she know? But it turns out she worshipped Dulia, and she spilled it to him, or maybe just told him enough so he could figure the rest out for himself. But he couldn't have been too smart because you know who he booked it with."

Muscotti held up his right hand. "Say no more, Mario. I got it figured from there . . . boy, I see what you mean. This could really stink. And that friggin' Weigh, he collects taxes from me like two sponges. He charges me twice as much as Froggy used to. It took him two years to get around to it. Christ, I have to laugh now. I remember thinking, son of a gunsky, hey, maybe this

Weigh is really an honest square. But, boy, when he got around to it, he really put it to me. And I can't get a goddamn thing on him. I been trying ever since I started to pay, but he's smart, that bastard. Someday, remind me to tell you the ways I got to wash the money before he touches it . . . but never mind that. The important thing, Mario, is you're right. There's no doubt, he's a friggin' Mason all right. He'd love this. He'd prosecute it all by himself. He wouldn't let no assistant get the glory. That fucker'd have it both ways. He'd have my money and he'd be laughing at all us Micks."

Dom paused and shook his head harder and harder as though trying to resolve something very difficult. "That fat-ass. What's my mother got to like him for, can you tell me that? He got more fat between his ears than he got anyplace else. But she likes him. She really does. She calls him twice a day in the hospital. She must've sent him three baskets of fruit already . . . I'm stuck, Mario. I can't do nothing to him. You got to understand that. She'd never forgive me. And I couldn't handle that."

"Okay. So we got your mother and Manny on one side. But what do we got on the other side? Huh? Six widows and a priest with cancer."

"Six? I thought five."

"What's Dulia's wife? Don't she qualify?"

"Okay, okay." Muscotti held up his hands. He stuck his lower lip out and rubbed it thoughtfully with his index finger. "Okay," he said slowly, "okay. I can handle it. I paid enough taxes down that friggin' courthouse. But, Mario, you got to understand, I can't let Manny take too much weight. He can't do no more than three months. My mother can handle that. I'll talk to her. She'll

173

understand that much. But, uh, one thing. Whoever I get, you got to school him. You can't let nobody else do it. It got to be right."

"Don't worry," Balzic said. "I'll make him a genius."

Tullio Manditti was brought into courtroom number four of the Conemaugh County courthouse five weeks to the day after Nicolao Abbatta Jr. was buried, five weeks and a day after Francis Dulia was buried.

There were few spectators in the room and no reporters. Tullio's trial had been docketed for the fall session of criminal court, but for reasons Clerk of Courts Louis Cepola wouldn't have explained to Jesus if He'd come back, the trial was suddenly called for the last day of the spring session. In fact, only Cepola, presiding Judge J. Harold Corcoran, Assistant District Attorney Ralph Manganero, Defense Attorney Louis Harmonich, the witnesses, the prospective jurors, the bailiffs and other court officers, and two spectators knew it was to be a trial. Tullio kept leaning over to his lawyer during jury selection and whispering hoarsely, "How come they're picking a jury? I thought this was supposed to be the preliminary hearing."

"I already told you," Louis Harmonich said back each time, "you already had one of those."

"So how come I wasn't here?" Tullio snapped during the last of these exchanges.

"You didn't have to be here. I was here, Mr. Mandizzi. That was enough."

"How many times I got to tell you? My name ain't

Mandizzi! It's Manditti. Ditti. Like ditto, only with an 'i' on the end."

Harmonich shrugged sheepishly.

Balzic, sitting in the first row between Father Marrazo and Dom Muscotti, leaned over to Muscotti and whispered, "Who found that guy?"

"Corcoran," Muscotti whispered back. "D'you think the Pope?"

"He must've had help."

"What help? That guy was sitting in the public defender's office like an apple waiting to fall off a tree."

"Oh yeah?"

"Certainly. Been in court about three times, all for drunk driving. Flunked the bar exam twice. Finished fifth from last in his class."

"And Corcoran found him all by himself, huh?"

"So? He was looking. What can I tell you?"

Balzic shook his head.

"What's the matter? Even Tullio's entitled to a lawyer. So what's a judge supposed to do if all the other lawyers are busy? He got to appoint one. So he appointed one."

Jury selection took three hours, two before lunch and one after. Court reconvened at exactly one-fifteen—when Judge Corcoran said it would—and the bailiffs and court stenographer were so surprised by Corcoran's attack of punctuality they had to be phoned twice in the basement coffee shop by Corcoran's tipstaff before they believed it. At one-nineteen, when they hurried in, Corcoran had been on the bench turning his gavel end over end for four minutes.

At two-nineteen, the last alternate juror was picked, the jury was sworn, and then Corcoran began to explain their duties and responsibilities. He was just at the point where he usually became loquacious, the point where he usually told juries how the whole system of American justice was based on the common wisdom of twelve ordinary citizens reasoning together, when he and everyone else in the room heard the insistent rapping of metal on wood coming from the first row of the spectators' section to Balzic's immediate left.

Balzic glanced over in time to see Muscotti putting a quarter in his pocket.

Corcoran coughed, drank some water, apologized for the laryngitis he felt coming on, and said, "Just pay attention to the evidence you hear. That's all that counts. The evidence. I'll tell you what you're supposed to do later on. Mr. Manganero, Mr. Harmonich, are you ready?"

Both attorneys stood and said they were, and then both waived making an opening statement.

Manganero began the case for the Commonwealth of Pennsylvania by calling Dr. Aram Sharma, the Indian Balzic remembered as the doctor who had been on duty when Frank Dulia was brought into the Emergency Unit of Conemaugh General Hospital. Dr. Sharma referred constantly to a small note pad, describing vividly in precise English in both medical and layman's language Dulia's condition when he had examined him.

Louis Harmonich said he had no questions.

Manganero next called the Lebanese doctor, who told of witnessing Dulia's death and filling out the death certificate.

Louis Harmonich said again that he had no questions.

Manganero next called Coroner Wallace Grimes and led him through a series of questions designed to illuminate Grimes' qualifications in forensic pathology. Louis Harmonich interrupted him to say that that wasn't necessary. "Everybody knows Dr. Grimes' reputation."

"All right, Dr. Grimes," Manganero said. "Did you perform an autopsy on one Francis Dulia sometime during the early morning hours of March 24?"

"I did."

"And would you tell us the cause of Mr. Dulia's death?"

"Massive brain damage as a direct result of multiple fractures of the left parietal and left temporal bones." Grimes did not have to refer to his own report, which lay in his lap, nor did he have to be instructed to indicate on his own head for the jury's benefit exactly what he was talking about.

"Where there other bruises or fractures or marks on the deceased's body, Doctor?"

"There were. Many of them." Grimes went on to enumerate the fractures. "There were no abrasions or lacerations. Just contusions. No cuts or burns. Just swellings."

"What would cause that, Doctor? In your expert opinion, what would cause the sort of injury to a human body such as you've described?"

"Well, the body is struck with some instrument which has been padded, something like a baseball bat that's been wrapped with a towel. The body receives the blow without suffering laceration or abrasion, but if the blow is powerful enough, something has to give somewhere, and what usually happens is that a bone fractures."

Manganero then repeated all the fractures that Grimes had enumerated previously, asking after each one if Grimes would say that that particular fracture was caused in the manner he'd just described. Grimes agreed after each one that it had.

Louis Harmonich said he had no questions.

Manganero called Balzic next. Right after he asked Balzic to identify himself, Louis Harmonich stood and said that there was no need to elaborate on Balzic's background or on his integrity. "Everybody knows who he is."

Balzic had to look at his shoes to keep his nervous smile from being seen by the jury.

Manganero led Balzic through a series of questions which focused on and skirted the periphery of the fact that Francis Dulia had been transported to the hospital in a pickup truck owned and driven by one Andrew T. Harsha, since deceased, who had witnessed something in the backyard of his neighbor's—Mr. Dulia's—house on the afternoon of March 23.

Manganero began to ask Balzic what it was that Mr. Harsha had witnessed, but Louis Harmonich objected, saying that though Balzic's testimony was obviously the best evidence since Mr. Harsha was dead, it was still second-hand evidence and he wanted the court to instruct the jury in that regard. Judge Corcoran looked sternly at Harmonich and was about to reply to his objection when Manganero said, "It's all right, your honor. We have another witness. I have no more questions for this witness."

Louis Harmonich said he too had no questions for this witness.

"Step down, Chief," Judge Corcoran said.

"Call Mr. Domenic Scalzo," Manganero said.

Dom "Soup" Scalzo passed Balzic on his way to the witness chair as though he had never seen him before in his life. He said, "I do," before the clerk finished reading the oath and took the witness chair with his eyes fixed on Manganero. He looked at no one else while he spoke.

"Mr. Scalzo," Manganero began, "would you state your full name and address and give your occupation?"

"Domenic G. Scalzo. I live at 531 Theobald Avenue, Rocksburg. I'm self-employed."

"At, uh, what are you self-employed, Mr. Scalzo?"

"I'm a business consultant."

"Could you be more precise than that?"

"I advise people about investments and what their chances are of making a profit."

Judge Corcoran had a coughing fit, interrupting Scalzo's testimony for almost a minute.

"Uh, Mr. Scalzo," Manganero said after Corcoran managed to get control of himself, "did you happen to be in the residence of one Andrew T. Harsha, now deceased, on the afternoon of March 23?"

"I was."

"What were you doing there?"

"I was advising Mr. Harsha on an investment he wanted to make. If he'd've listened to me, he'd still be alive today."

"And what was that?"

"I told him to get out of that mine he was in. I told him he was getting too old for that kind of work. It was all right to own a part of it, but he shouldn't be working in it."

"Yes. Well, unfortunately, Mr. Harsha did not take your advice. We all know that he died in that very mine one day later. Well, Mr. Scalzo, will you please tell us if you saw anything unusual that day while you were visiting and advising Mr. Harsha?"

"Yes. I did. I mean, I will. We were in the kitchen having a drink. He just came home from the mine, and he said he wanted to cut the dust a little. . . . "

Balzic could stand to listen to no more. He bumped Muscotti's knee with his own and waved his hand feebly from side to side to show that he was leaving. He had to step in front of Father Marrazo to get to the aisle. The priest looked up at him, and his eyes were disturbingly hard and disbelieving. Balzic rushed from the courtroom, looking at the carpet, avoiding everyone's eyes.

Outside in the corridor, Balzic went to the marble balustrade overlooking the circular stairwell which was directly under the dome of the courthouse. He looked up at the dome and fumbled to loosen his tie and unbutton his collar. He felt himself breathing rapidly and tried to take long, slow breaths. He licked his upper lip and tasted perspiration. He looked at his palms, and they glistened wet in the light of the great globe suspended from the center of the dome.

Someone touched his arm, and Balzic swung his head around so quickly that he nearly became dizzy. It was Father Marrazo.

"Mario," the priest began and then stopped as though he had no idea what he was going to say, but his gaze was so intense that Balzic had to turn away. "Mario, what's—what the hell is going on?"

Balzic leaned his backside against the balustrade to support himself and jerked at his tie and collar. "You know what's going on, so what're you asking for?"

"I don't know," the priest said. "I sat in there and I

180

listened and I couldn't believe what I was listening to. And then you jumped up and your face was white. Mario, I want you to tell me what's going on."

Balzic started to walk away from the priest, but Father Marrazo caught him by the sleeve. "Mario, I've never interfered with you before, and I may not know everything you know, and I may be way out of line, but I know when something is wrong, and there is something really wrong going on in there." The priest was trying to whisper, but his words sounded to Balzic as though he were shouting.

"Aaagh," Balzic growled. "What the hell did you want to go on, huh?"

"The right thing."

"I did the right thing. What do you think I did?"

"Mario, you may think you did the right thing, but it's coming out all wrong. The way you're doing it is all wrong."

"And how 'bout if I did it the right way, huh? I could've done it that way, sure. But do you know Weigh's a Mason? Huh? Do you know—"

"I don't care what he is. That doesn't change anything."

"I don't believe this," Balzic said. "I don't believe this is you talking. After all you know?"

"You don't believe it? Huh? You don't believe it's me? Then what're you doing out here with sweat all over your face? Look at me. You can't even look at me. And you talk about after all I know? That's right, that's right. I hear Mrs. Abbatta's confession every day. The others, two, three times a week. And I heard Sabatine's. He asked for me. He could've asked for the bishop. I wish he had. But I was with him right up to the end and I heard him. Which means I heard everything. But what I haven't heard is what Soup is doing on that witness chair." The priest's face was flushed, and the veins stood out on his forehead and throat from trying to whisper while talking so forcefully.

Balzic took a long time before he answered. As many ways as he thought to say it, he knew finally that it didn't matter how he said it. He could give only one answer. "I know where the confessional is."

"Okay," Father Marrazo said. "Okay . . . okay. . . . " He repeated that word several more times as though trying to find satisfaction in its mere repetition. He cleared his throat and tugged at his own collar. Then he looked at his shoes. "You, uh, you want to go, uh, get some wine? Huh?"

Balzic nodded slowly. "Right now I could drink just about all the wine there is in the world."

They walked in silence to Muscotti's and did not speak to each other until they began to quibble over who was going to pay for the drinks. What little conversation there was took place between Balzic and Vinnie who kept demanding to be brought up to date on the trial. He couldn't understand why they'd both left if it had not yet gone to the jury. Neither Balzic nor Father Marrazo would answer that.

Their drinking was joyless, mechanical, a seeking after the alcohol rather than the wine. It took nearly an hour before they started to feel the wine flowing in them, and by that time they were threatening to drink all the chablis and chianti Vinnie had on the shelves. Balzic even started making noises about going to the backroom to help himself to Muscotti's private stock of Valpolicella.

Mila Sanders Rizzo, sighing giddily, came in then and plopped down on the stool next to Balzic. She leaned close to him and whispered, "I understand you solved your problem."

"Well, that depends," Balzic said, glancing uncomfortably at Father Marrazo. "In a way I did, and then again I didn't. How you coming with yours?"

"Well, I guess that depends too. Dom wants me to manage a store for him."

Balzic started to smile. "What kind of store?"

"Oh, this woman's husband died, and she's sick and she wants to get rid of it. Dom says there's a real market for what they sell." She was smiling impishly, sardonically. She leaned close to him again and whispered, "Religious supplies. Bibles and crucifixes and plaster saints and rosaries and medals and bumper stickers that say all kinds of goopy stuff like, 'God's only dead if you're Red,' and crap like that. Dom says with all the halos I see on people I'd make a million dollars in ten years. I told him I'd do it if he let me put up a big yellow neon cross with a sign on it that said, 'Two million rosaries sold.' You know, like hamburgers. Boy, did he get mad."

Balzic nodded as though it was all the most reasonable thing he'd heard in weeks. "What's his wife say?"

"Oh, you don't think he talked to her about it, do you?" she said, pulling back and laughing loud.

Before Balzic could reply Dom Scalzo barged through the front door, scowling and cursing under his breath until he drew even with Balzic's back. Then he tapped Balzic on the back and started to speak but he was too furious. For some moments all he could do was curse.

183

"What's the matter with you?" Balzic said. "You just did the good deed of your life and you look like you just got robbed."

"I'll tell you what's the matter," Scalzo said. "You wanna hear what's the matter? I'm gonna tell you what's the matter. Jimmie Salio, that bastard—Corcoran's bailiff?"

"I know who he is. Who doesn't?"

"Yeah, well, he thinks it's a big joke. I come down off the stand and I start to walk out. I'm done, what am I gonna stick around for? He's standing back there at the back door and he's looking at his watch. I'm almost past him, and he grabs me and he whispers—you know how he whispers? Like normal people talk that's how he whispers—he whispers, 'You stopped testifying at exactly four-twenty-eight.' And then he hands me six bucks and he whispers again, 'A buck around. Four-twenty-eight. On the new stock.' So I'm going, no, no, you know. I'm shaking my head and I'm not taking the money. So the cocksucker—excuse my language, Father—so the dumb bastard shoves the money in my coat pocket. So whatta you think? Don't you know there's a state cop sitting right there, right in the last row, and he hears everything. And he follows me outside, and Jimmie's following me and I'm trying to give the money back to Jimmie and that goddamn state cop arrests me! Right there in the hall! Jesus Christ, I wanna throw both them bastards right over the balcony.

"I go in there to do something good for once in my life, for justice—for justice, you goddamn Mario, ain't that what you told me? For justice I go in there and tell the biggest lie I ever told in my life and now I'm under arrest for bookin'. Stick your justice up your ass."

Balzic turned to Father Marrazo and both of them looked at Vinnie and then all three roared with laughter until tears were streaming down their cheeks.

"Oh, God, God," Balzic said at last, his eyes, mouth, and stomach aching from laughter. "Vinnie, give him a drink. Give everybody a drink. And keep them coming. I got everybody's."

And Vinnie did. He said later on when he told the story that he'd never poured so many drinks or laughed so hard in an hour's time in his life, and no one who had been there that day ever doubted him. Just as no one ever doubted him when he said that the next day he laughed even harder when Dom Muscotti told Soup Scalzo that he had put Jimmie Salio up to it, had told him to have someone else tip off a state cop and make sure he was there in the last row, and that it was he himself who had given Salio the six dollars Salio kept trying to force on Soup.

"You should've seen Soup's face," Vinnie would tell the story time and again. "Oh Christ, I thought he was gonna choke. All he could say was, 'Why? What'd you want to go and do that to me for?' And Dom looked at him and said, 'Soup, I knew how you were gonna think when you came down out of the chair. Like you did something really good. And you did. But I didn't want you to start thinking you were too good. You start thinking you're too good, you're gonna forget who you are.'"

And no one laughs harder at that story than Balzic.

AFTERWORD

The good people at David R. Godine, Publisher, Inc. gave me the opportunity to write this afterword. William B. Goodman, their Editorial Director, who is also my editor, suggested that I account for the "genesis of Mario Balzic: his character, his style, his milieu." (Robin W. Winks, general editor of the Godine Double Detective series, probably egged him on in this.) Goodman also suggested that I say something about my conviction that I must write under a pseudonym. He says these two subjects would "interest readers." Well, since Goodman is one of the best readers I know (another is Robert V. Williams, and more of him later), I will go with his notions. The question-and-answer format is mine.

* * *

Q. Where did Balzic come from?

A. Immigrant parents, Serbian father, Italian mother. Born in western Pennsylvania, educated in public schools, combat veteran of World War II Pacific Theater, Marine Corps. Father killed in coal mine accident. Married, with two daughters. Mother lives with him. Never wanted to be anything but a policeman.

Q. That can be surmised from reading the books. Where did he come from?

A. He came from a news store on a Sunday morning after I'd been grumbling for days about the latest in a long line of rejection slips for what was then my most serious "straight" novel.

Q. Explain further, please.

A. I was buying a paper in a news store. While waiting for my change, I looked down. There were stacks and stacks of

books by Mickey Spillane, Carter Brown, Ellery Queen, Agatha
Christie, Ross MacDonald, John McDonald, Georges Simenon,
et al., and I asked the owner how many of those he sold. "Can't
keep 'em in stock," he said. I walked out of the store and around
the corner to where my car was parked, and there, straight
ahead of me, were the ruins of the local railroad station. I had
to drive about a block and a half to get to the station and then
had to turn away from it and go another block before I made
my next turn. As I approached the station, I thought, "Now
there would be a good place for somebody to get murdered."
By the time I reached the second intersection, I had conjured
up the basis for *The Rocksburg Railroad Murders*, i.e., a kid
killing a man because he thought the man was somebody else
who had deserted him when he was a toddler.

Q. And you wrote it in three days and were an overnight
success.

A. I wrote it in about ten months and couldn't give it away.

Q. Aren't you leaving something out?

A. Yes, but I'm going to leave a lot out. A friend of mine,
who had introduced me to literary agent Bertha Klausner, told
me of a conversation he'd had with her, oh, perhaps a week before I'd walked into that store. She'd told him, "Why don't you
write mysteries? They always sell," or words to that effect. So
I had that in my head while I was waiting for my change.

Q. Why'd it take you ten months? Georges Simenon never
takes longer than eight days, and Mickey Spillane wrote one in
three days once.

A. Well, see, the thing I learned about detecs, or mysteries,
or whatever you want to call them, is that plots for them are no
easier to put together than plots for straight novels.

Q. Come on, man. Anybody can write a mystery.

A. That's what they all say. But I found out quickly that the
problems of mysteries are no different from the ones you have
in trying to write a straight novel. If you have a problem of
character in a straight novel, you're going to have it in a mys-

tery. You have to answer the same questions: Who is this person? Where did he come from? Where does he live? Where's he been? Why does he talk like that? Why is he doing this, that, or whatever? Why is he not doing this, that, or whatever? How do you present the characters in the story? What point of view? What perspective? What tone? That last one, the tone, that's the knuckle-buster. Get that one wrong, and the book's gone, the story's dead. Nobody will read it.

Q. Then how do you get it right?

A. Best question there is. Also the hardest one to answer. You do it and read it and do it again and read it again, and keep doing it until it starts to *look* like you would want to *hear* the story. Very tricky stuff, this tone business, because you're not writing it to be spoken or acted or even to be read aloud. You're writing it to be read silently. So, getting a tone that *looks* like you would want to *hear* it is a bit of a shadow dance. It's easier done than talked about, but the core is that if the tone offends your own eye and grates on your own ear, then it's probably going to offend strangers' eyes and ears, too. The tone you have to watch out for, as R. V. Williams told me often, is the one that sticks its elbow in the reader's ribs and says, "Look at me, I'm writin'!" The tendency to show off is always there. The tendency to say, in one way or another, "Christ, ain't I wonderful," has to be watched like a sick puppy. Let it get away from you and it will crawl behind the couch and choke on its own vomit. That's an unpleasant metaphor, but the ego of storytellers is no small thing and can't be ignored. Let your ego get out of control and it will crawl behind your story and throw up all over it. The hardest lesson to learn in telling stories is that the story is more important than the teller.

Q. Your digressions are almost celestial. Where did Balzic come from? And stick with it this time.

A. He came from a lifelong ambivalence about cops, ergo, authority figures, ergo, my parents and especially my mother's father.

Q. Lifelong? Really?

A. My earliest memories are of my mother, her father, my father, and the '36 flood. The order is significant. My grandfather was the dominant male in a small tribe. Before he died when I was twelve, I had developed a murderous hatred for him. When I learned that he had died, I asked my mother to take me to see him: I wanted to make sure he was dead. The first chance I got to be alone after seeing him laid out on his bed, I danced around, chanting, "He's dead, he's dead," until I fell down exhausted. When you hate someone and he dies, it's a wonderful feeling.

Q. Out of the wonderful feeling came Balzic?

A. When I said that the order of my memories is significant, I said it to illustrate the fact that I grew up with a profound sense of ambiguity about who was who in my family. I'm still trying to recover from that.

Q. Stay with the question, please.

A. I am. Out of the rubble of this confusion will emerge a pattern, I assure you.

Q. A pattern is not a character.

A. True. But out of the patterns of childhood come the inclinations and aversions of adulthood. Because my early family life was such a jumble, because my grandfather was such a force in my life, because my father was so much at his mercy, I had a hellish time comprehending how one gets around in this world. I'm leaving out an encyclopedia of family history (call that emotional crossfire), but my point is that for a long time I had a tough time dealing with people who thought they were supposed to tell me how to live. A slip here, a slide there, a misperception here, a miscalculation there, and I could easily have vanished into penal obscurity. I was on my way.

Q. Still no word on Balzic, eh?

A. Well, on the way I was on to, I met a few authority figures who didn't have any doubts about who they were or about what places they occupied in the social scheme. (Usually, the only place you find that kind of certitude is among professional soldiers, men who have given up their claim to assert themselves in all but a few clearly defined circumstances.) Out of those meetings came a notion of how cops ought to behave. See, when I was trying to tell the world to mind its own business, nobody had heard of Miranda, Gideon, or Escobedo. In those days (the early '50s), cops could do damn near anything. There just were no brakes, except the one on searches based on the exclusionary rule. But since Miranda, et al., the clamor for a return to "law and order" has been gaining momentum at a scary pace. It appeals to new ears every day, but what it amounts to—no matter how it's phrased—is a return to the days before Miranda, et al. The exclusionary rule is catching flak right now. There is practically a mob who would love nothing more than to break that one. They keep yammering about the "good faith" of policemen gathering evidence. But when the police break into your residence to search for contraband they think you're hiding and they're acting in good faith but without a proper warrant, who do you call? And when a cop decides to stop you and search you and he doesn't like the way you're answering him and he starts to put his billy on your back, who do you call? If you answer, "The cops," you have not seriously given any thought to what it means to return to the days before Miranda, et al.

Q. Are you saying that out of your confused emotional upbringing and your brushes with cops and your fear of people calling for law and order—are you saying Balzic comes out of that?

A. More or less. I told you there was a pattern.

Q. Christ, you ought to be handing out pamphlets on a corner somewhere. You're a closet preacher. Church of the Open Novel. By your own admission, you don't know how to deal with authority figures and here you are writing police parables.

A. Fascinating, isn't it?

Q. Do you agree you're a closet preacher?

A. No. But I will admit that it's another of the tendencies you have to guard against, another of the things that, if you're not careful, can screw the tone of a story.

Q. But you do believe that there are people out there who need to be told some things and that you're the guy to tell them, yes or no?

A. Yes *and* no. I've gone through that soap-box phase in every one of these Balzic stories. It's always there in the first draft. It's usually gone by the third draft—or at least I hope it is. When Writers are young and when they're still aiming to create Literature (observe the capitals), and when they're spending most of their time hanging out with other Writers "discussing" Literature, one of the things they talk about a lot is "having something to say." That phrase has dammed up more than a few people.

Q. Explain further, please.

A. Well, I've known people, quite capable prose writers, who, when they finally got down to pen and paper and tried to write a story or a novel, found out—if we're to take their word for it, at any rate—that they "had nothing to say." What I suspect they discovered is that they didn't know how to tell a story, but, because they have never gotten over that "having something to say" crap, they could not get on to the recognition that a story can be told about things that were said three thousand years ago. They confused the subject with the telling, in other words. A good painter can make an astonishing portrait of a dull, homely, seemingly insignificant man or woman, just as a competent storyteller ought to be able to present a good story about one, or a whole clan of them, for that matter. Witness Flannery O'Connor or Andre Dubus, among others.

Q. We're running out of space. What about the anonymity stuff? Why the alias?

A. Many reasons. I want to be able to live as normally as anybody else. I want my family to be able to do that also. I don't want to lose the protection ordinary people have because of their ordinariness. When I go out and about I don't want to waste time avoiding people who would try to make me special. I don't think my family ought to be forced to change their lives because of something I do. I also do not want to change the way I write or what I choose to write about because I have to worry about how other people may react to it. Personally, temperamentally, I am not a social person. I do not meet people easily or mix well, as they say, even with people I know. Professionally, I spend much time watching other people and eavesdropping, and I can't very well snoop in other people's lives if I have to spend time getting them to quit snooping in mine. And if you think people will not snoop in your life because they've decided you're special, then you have just never done a public thing. I had a very brief, singularly mediocre career in professional baseball. One of the things I learned from it was that some people who pay to watch you do something they think they know a lot about also think you owe them more than your work, and they try to collect at every opportunity. By the time organized baseball had retired me, I'd had all the fame I'd ever wanted.

Q. Anything else you want to say?

A. Yes. There's a canard that's been around for a long time that goes something like this: "Writing is a lonely business." It's supposed to imply some wonderfully romantic things, chief among them being, of course, that writers have no help. Well, it's partly true, and that's why it's been around for so long. But no book is ever brought before the public on a writer's work alone. In my case all of the following are involved: an agent and her staff, the publisher, editorial director, book editor, managing editor, marketing manager, copy editor, proofreader, typesetters, production manager, compositors, pressmen, binders, warehousemen, truckers, salesmen, sales clerks, publicists, reviewers, and all those secretaries and switchboard operators. I've probably left some important people out, but you get the idea. The words in the book are ultimately the storyteller's responsibility, but without the efforts of all those other people, none of those words would ever have gotten beyond the diligent folks in the Postal Service.

Q. Anything else?

A. Yes. Robert V. Williams teaches in the California State College system. Most of what I know about reading I learned from him. And about writing stories he was adamant: writing simple, solid prose is not enough; you must know how to make a box to put it in.

Q. You ever going to stop?

A. One last thing. My wife has put up with a bunch of stuff because of me and from me. Being married to me is a slippery business, and I want it in writing that I love her. Trying to juggle a marriage, a family, a job now and then, and a guy carrying fiction around in his head takes some doing. It's less trying for everybody now that I've sold a few books and gotten generally good reviews, but before, it did get harrowing. In addition to all the daily things that can cause heat within a family, having one member of it traveling in a make-believe world for much of the time takes a toll on all the other members.

Then there is the inherent nuttiness of trying to make money by writing fiction. What you're doing, after all, is telling lies, the more believable the better, in order to make enough money so that you can quit your honest, respectable job and stay home to have more time to make up even more lies. It's a dubious ambition, suspicious if not sinister, and it gets even nuttier because, when you start to achieve some success at it, then, you see, strangers begin to compliment you in print for doing a thing which, if you did it in person every day, would eventually lead to a hearing in front of the commitment committee of the county board of mental health.

K. C. CONSTANTINE